Acclaim for Robert Galbraith's

The Cuckoo's Calling

"Robert Galbraith has written a highly entertaining book....Even better, he has introduced an appealing protagonist in Cormoran Strike, who's sure to be the star of many sequels to come....Its narrative moves forward with propulsive suspense. More important, Strike and his now-permanent assistant, Robin (playing Nora to his Nick, Salander to his Blomkvist), have become a team—a team whose further adventures the reader cannot help eagerly awaiting."
—Michiko Kakutani, *New York Times*

"One of the great pleasures of *The Cuckoo's Calling,* as with most detective stories, is observing the gumshoe's *Aha!* moments, without being told what they are.... *The Cuckoo's Calling* is *fun.*"
—Katy Waldman, *Slate*

"It's terrific....A brilliant achievement, mordantly funny, and monumentally absorbing.... A masterful novel, the kind of big, noisy, busy, beautiful book in which it is so easy and so pleasurable to become enmeshed."
—Julia Keller, *Chicago Tribune*

"Cormoran Strike is an amazing creation and I can't wait for his next outing. Strike is so instantly compelling that it's hard to believe this is a debut novel. I hope there are plenty more Cormoran Strike adventures to come. A beautifully written debut novel introducing one of the most unique and compelling detectives I've come across in years."
—Mark Billingham, author of *The Demands*

"A witty, twisty mystery.... *The Cuckoo's Calling* is masterfully plotted."
—Laura DeMarco, *Cleveland Plain Dealer*

"An expertly plotted contemporary detective novel, complete with a world-weary, rumpled, prosthetic-legged private eye."

—*O, The Oprah Magazine*

"*The Cuckoo's Calling* reminds me why I fell in love with crime fiction in the first place."

—Val McDermid, bestselling author of *The Vanishing Point*

"A page turner."

—Tom Chiarella, *Esquire*

"I couldn't stop myself from thoroughly enjoying *The Cuckoo's Calling*." —Carole E. Barrowman, *Milwaukee Journal Sentinel*

"Instantly absorbing, featuring a detective facing crumbling circumstances with resolve instead of clichéd self-destruction and a lovable sidekick with contagious enthusiasm for detection. Galbraith nimbly sidesteps celebrity superficiality, instead exploring the ugly truths in Lula Landry's six degrees of separation. Strike bears little resemblance to Jackson Brodie, but Kate Atkinson's fans will appreciate his reliance on deduction and observation along with Galbraith's skilled storytelling." —Christine Tran, *Booklist*

"A fascinating tale that explores the lifestyles of the rich and unhappy.... Laden with plenty of twists and distractions, this debut ensures that readers will be puzzled and totally engrossed for quite a spell. Galbraith's take on contemporary celebrity obsession makes for a grand beach read. It's like a mash-up of Charles Dickens and Penny Vincenzi." —*Library Journal*

"Not a word is wasted in this atmospheric novel. Despite Strike's shortcomings, the reader can't help but root for him as he navigates through the underbelly of London after dark and hobnobs with the rich and famous. Strike would be a perfect protagonist for a series of novels, and the reader can only hope that that is Galbraith's intention." —Hilary Daninhirsch, *Mystery Scene*

The Cuckoo's Calling

ALSO BY ROBERT GALBRAITH

The Silkworm

Career of Evil

The Cuckoo's Calling

Robert Galbraith

MULHOLLAND BOOKS

LITTLE, BROWN AND COMPANY

New York   Boston   London

To the real Deeby
with many thanks

———————————

Copyright © 2013 by Robert Galbraith Limited
Excerpt from *The Silkworm* copyright © 2014 by Robert Galbraith Limited

Mulholland Books / Little, Brown and Company
Hachette Book Group
1290 Avenue of the Americas, New York, NY 10104
mulhollandbooks.com

First published in hardcover in North America by Mulholland Books, April 2013
First Mulholland Books paperback edition, April 2014
First Mulholland Books media tie-in paperback edition, May 2018
Originally published in Great Britain by Sphere, April 2013

Mulholland Books is an imprint of Little, Brown and Company, a division of Hachette Book Group, Inc. The Mulholland Books name and logo are trademarks of Hachette Book Group, Inc.

The publisher is not responsible for websites (or their content) that are not owned by the publisher.

The Hachette Speakers Bureau provides a wide range of authors for speaking events. To find out more, go to hachettespeakersbureau.com or call (866) 376-6591.

ISBN 978-0-316-20684-6 (hc) / 978-0-316-33016-9 (large print) / 978-0-316-20685-3 (pb) / 978-0-316-48637-8 (media tie-in pb)
LCCN 2013933193

10 9 8 7 6 5 4 3 2 1

LSC-C

Printed in the United States of America

Why were you born when the snow was falling?
You should have come to the cuckoo's calling,
Or when grapes are green in the cluster,
Or, at least, when lithe swallows muster
    For their far off flying
    From summer dying.

Why did you die when the lambs were cropping?
You should have died at the apples' dropping,
When the grasshopper comes to trouble,
And the wheat-fields are sodden stubble,
    And all winds go sighing
    For sweet things dying.

Christina G. Rossetti, "A Dirge"

Prologue

Is demum miser est, cuius nobilitas miserias nobilitat.

Unhappy is he whose fame makes
his misfortunes famous.

Lucius Accius, *Telephus*

THE BUZZ IN THE STREET was like the humming of flies. Photographers stood massed behind barriers patrolled by police, their long-snouted cameras poised, their breath rising like steam. Snow fell steadily on to hats and shoulders; gloved fingers wiped lenses clear. From time to time there came outbreaks of desultory clicking, as the watchers filled the waiting time by snapping the white canvas tent in the middle of the road, the entrance to the tall red-brick apartment block behind it, and the balcony on the top floor from which the body had fallen.

Behind the tightly packed paparazzi stood white vans with enormous satellite dishes on the roofs, and journalists talking, some in foreign languages, while soundmen in headphones hovered. Between recordings, the reporters stamped their feet and warmed their hands on hot beakers of coffee from the teeming café a few streets away. To fill the time, the woolly-hatted cameramen filmed the backs of the photographers, the balcony, the tent concealing the body, then repositioned themselves for wide shots that encompassed the chaos that had exploded inside the sedate and snowy Mayfair street, with its lines of glossy black doors framed by white stone porticos and flanked by topiary shrubs. The entrance to number 18 was bounded with tape. Police officials, some of them white-clothed forensic experts, could be glimpsed in the hallway beyond.

The television stations had already had the news for several hours. Members of the public were crowding at either end of the road, held at bay by more police; some had come, on purpose, to look, others had paused on their way to work. Many held mobile telephones aloft to take pictures before moving on. One young man, not knowing which was the crucial balcony, photographed each of them in turn, even though the middle one was packed with a row of shrubs, three neat, leafy orbs, which barely left room for a human being.

A group of young girls had brought flowers, and were filmed handing them to the police, who as yet had not decided on a place for them, but laid them self-consciously in the back of the police van, aware of camera lenses following their every move.

The correspondents sent by twenty-four-hour news channels kept up a steady stream of comment and speculation around the few sensational facts they knew.

"...from her penthouse apartment at around two o'clock this morning. Police were alerted by the building's security guard..."

"...no sign yet that they are moving the body, which has led some to speculate..."

"...no word on whether she was alone when she fell..."

"...teams have entered the building and will be conducting a thorough search."

A chilly light filled the interior of the tent. Two men were crouching beside the body, ready to move it, at last, into a body bag. Her head had bled a little into the snow. The face was crushed and swollen, one eye reduced to a pucker, the other showing as a sliver of dull white between distended lids. When the sequined top she wore glittered in slight changes of light, it gave a disquieting impression of movement, as though she breathed again, or was tensing muscles, ready to rise. The snow fell with soft fingertip plunks on the canvas overhead.

"Where's the bloody ambulance?"

Detective Inspector Roy Carver's temper was mounting. A paunchy man with a face the color of corned beef, whose shirts were usually ringed with sweat around the armpits, his short supply of patience had been exhausted hours ago. He had been here nearly as long as the corpse; his feet were so cold that he could no longer feel them, and he was light-headed with hunger.

"Ambulance is two minutes away," said Detective Sergeant Eric Wardle, unintentionally answering his superior's question as he entered the tent with his mobile pressed to his ear. "Just been organizing a space for it."

Carver grunted. His bad temper was exacerbated by the conviction that Wardle was excited by the presence of the photographers. Boyishly good-looking, with thick, wavy brown hair now frosted with snow, Wardle had, in Carver's opinion, dawdled on their few forays outside the tent.

"At least that lot'll shift once the body's gone," said Wardle, still looking out at the photographers.

"They won't go while we're still treating the place like a fucking murder scene," snapped Carver.

Wardle did not answer the unspoken challenge. Carver exploded anyway.

"The poor cow jumped. There was no one else there. Your so-called witness was coked out of her—"

"It's coming," said Wardle, and to Carver's disgust, he slipped back out of the tent, to wait for the ambulance in full sight of the cameras.

The story forced news of politics, wars and disasters aside, and every version of it sparkled with pictures of the dead woman's flawless face, her lithe and sculpted body. Within hours, the few known facts had spread like a virus to millions: the public row with the famous boyfriend, the journey home alone, the overheard screaming and the final, fatal fall...

The boyfriend fled into a rehab facility, but the police remained inscrutable; those who had been with her on the evening before her death were hounded; thousands of columns of newsprint were filled, and hours of television news, and the woman who swore she had overheard a second argument moments before the body fell became briefly famous too, and was awarded smaller-sized photographs beside the images of the beautiful dead girl.

But then, to an almost audible groan of disappointment, the witness was proven to have lied, and *she* retreated into rehab, and the famous prime suspect emerged, as the man and the lady in a weatherhouse who can never be outside at the same time.

So it was suicide after all, and after a moment's stunned hiatus, the story gained a weak second wind. They wrote that she was unbalanced, unstable, unsuited to the superstardom her wildness and her beauty had snared; that she had moved among an immoral moneyed class that had corrupted her; that the decadence of her new life had unhinged an already fragile personality. She became a morality tale stiff with Schadenfreude, and so many columnists made allusion to Icarus that *Private Eye* ran a special column.

And then, at last, the frenzy wore itself into staleness, and even the journalists had nothing left to say, but that too much had been said already.

Three Months Later

Part One

Nam in omni adversitate fortunae infelicissimum est genus infortunii, fuisse felicem.

For in every ill-turn of fortune the most unhappy sort of unfortunate man is the one who has been happy.

Boethius, *De Consolatione Philosophiae*

1

Though Robin Ellacott's twenty-five years of life had seen their moments of drama and incident, she had never before woken up in the certain knowledge that she would remember the coming day for as long as she lived.

Shortly after midnight, her long-term boyfriend, Matthew, had proposed to her under the statue of Eros in the middle of Piccadilly Circus. In the giddy relief following her acceptance, he confessed that he had been planning to pop the question in the Thai restaurant where they just had eaten dinner, but that he had reckoned without the silent couple beside them, who had eavesdropped on their entire conversation. He had therefore suggested a walk through the darkening streets, in spite of Robin's protests that they both needed to be up early, and finally inspiration had seized him, and he had led her, bewildered, to the steps of the statue. There, flinging discretion to the chilly wind (in a most un-Matthew-like way), he had proposed, on one knee, in front of three down-and-outs huddled on the steps, sharing what looked like a bottle of meths.

It had been, in Robin's view, the most perfect proposal, ever, in the history of matrimony. He had even had a ring in his pocket, which she was now wearing; a sapphire with two diamonds, it fitted perfectly, and all the way into town she kept staring at it on her hand as it rested on her lap. She and Matthew had a story to tell now, a funny family story, the kind you told your children, in which his planning (she loved that he had planned it) went awry, and turned into something spontaneous. She loved the tramps, and the moon, and Matthew, panicky and flustered, on one knee; she loved Eros, and dirty old Piccadilly, and the black cab they had taken home to

Clapham. She was, in fact, not far off loving the whole of London, which she had not so far warmed to, during the month she had lived there. Even the pale and pugnacious commuters squashed into the Tube carriage around her were gilded by the radiance of the ring, and as she emerged into the chilly March daylight at Tottenham Court Road underground station, she stroked the underside of the platinum band with her thumb, and experienced an explosion of happiness at the thought that she might buy some bridal magazines at lunchtime.

Male eyes lingered on her as she picked her way through the roadworks at the top of Oxford Street, consulting a piece of paper in her right hand. Robin was, by any standards, a pretty girl; tall and curvaceous, with long strawberry-blonde hair that rippled as she strode briskly along, the chill air adding color to her pale cheeks. This was the first day of a week-long secretarial assignment. She had been temping ever since coming to live with Matthew in London, though not for much longer; she had what she termed "proper" interviews lined up now.

The most challenging part of these uninspiring piecemeal jobs was often finding the offices. London, after the small town in Yorkshire she had left, felt vast, complex and impenetrable. Matthew had told her not to walk around with her nose in an *A–Z*, which would make her look like a tourist and render her vulnerable; she therefore relied, as often as not, on poorly hand-drawn maps that somebody at the temping agency had made for her. She was not convinced that this made her look more like a native-born Londoner.

The metal barricades and the blue plastic Corimec walls surrounding the roadworks made it much harder to see where she ought to be going, because they obscured half the landmarks drawn on the paper in her hand. She crossed the torn-up road in front of a towering office block, labeled "Center Point" on her map, which resembled a gigantic concrete waffle with its dense grid of uniform square windows, and made her way in the rough direction of Denmark Street.

She found it almost accidentally, following a narrow alleyway called Denmark Place out into a short street full of colorful shop fronts: windows full of guitars, keyboards and every kind of musical ephemera. Red and white barricades surrounded another open hole in the road, and workmen in fluorescent jackets greeted her with early-morning wolf-whistles, which Robin pretended not to hear.

She consulted her watch. Having allowed her usual margin of time for getting lost, she was a quarter of an hour early. The nondescript black-painted doorway of the office she sought stood to the left of the 12 Bar Café; the name of the occupant of the office was written on a scrappy piece of lined paper taped beside the buzzer for the second floor. On an ordinary day, without the brand-new ring glittering upon her finger, she might have found this off-putting; today, however, the dirty paper and the peeling paint on the door were, like the tramps from last night, mere picturesque details on the backdrop of her grand romance. She checked her watch again (the sapphire glittered and her heart leapt; she would watch that stone glitter all the rest of her life), then decided, in a burst of euphoria, to go up early and show herself keen for a job that did not matter in the slightest.

She had just reached for the bell when the black door flew open from the inside, and a woman burst out on to the street. For one strangely static second the two of them looked directly into each other's eyes, as each braced to withstand a collision. Robin's senses were unusually receptive on this enchanted morning; the split-second view of that white face made such an impression on her that she thought, moments later, when they had managed to dodge each other, missing contact by a centimeter, after the dark woman had hurried off down the street, around the corner and out of sight, that she could have drawn her perfectly from memory. It was not merely the extraordinary beauty of the face that had impressed itself on her memory, but the other's expression: livid, yet strangely exhilarated.

Robin caught the door before it closed on the dingy stairwell. An old-fashioned metal staircase spiraled up around an equally antiquated birdcage lift. Concentrating on keeping her high heels from catching in the metalwork stairs, she proceeded to the first landing, passing a door carrying a laminated and framed poster saying *Crowdy Graphics,* and continued climbing. It was only when she reached the glass door on the floor above that Robin realized, for the first time, what kind of business she had been sent to assist. Nobody at the agency had said. The name on the paper beside the outside buzzer was engraved on the glass panel: *C. B. Strike,* and, underneath it, the words *Private Detective.*

Robin stood quite still, with her mouth slightly open, experiencing a moment of wonder that nobody who knew her could have understood. She had never confided in a solitary human being (even Matthew) her lifelong, secret, childish ambition. For this to happen today, of all days! It felt like a wink from God (and this too she somehow connected with the magic of the day; with Matthew, and the ring; even though, properly considered, they had no connection at all).

Savoring the moment, she approached the engraved door very slowly. She stretched out her left hand (sapphire dark, now, in this dim light) towards the handle; but before she had touched it, the glass door too flew open.

This time, there was no near-miss. Sixteen unseeing stone of disheveled male slammed into her; Robin was knocked off her feet and catapulted backwards, handbag flying, arms windmilling, towards the void beyond the lethal staircase.

2

STRIKE ABSORBED THE IMPACT, HEARD the high-pitched scream and reacted instinctively: throwing out a long arm, he seized a fistful of
cloth and flesh; a second shriek of pain echoed around the stone walls
and then, with a wrench and a tussle, he had succeeded in dragging
the girl back on to firm ground. Her shrieks were still echoing off the
walls, and he realized that he himself had bellowed, "Jesus Christ!"

The girl was doubled up in pain against the office door, whimper-
ing. Judging by the lopsided way she was hunched, with one hand
buried deep under the lapel of her coat, Strike deduced that he had
saved her by grabbing a substantial part of her left breast. A thick, wavy
curtain of bright blonde hair hid most of the girl's blushing face, but
Strike could see tears of pain leaking out of one uncovered eye.

"Fuck—sorry!" His loud voice reverberated around the stairwell.
"I didn't see you—didn't expect anyone to be there . . ."

From under their feet, the strange and solitary graphic designer
who inhabited the office below yelled, "What's happening up there?"
and a second later, a muffled complaint from above indicated that the
manager of the bar downstairs, who slept in an attic flat over Strike's
office, had also been disturbed—perhaps woken—by the noise.

"Come in here . . ."

Strike pushed open the door with his fingertips, so as to have no
accidental contact with her while she stood huddled against it, and
ushered her into the office.

"Is everything all right?" called the graphic designer querulously.

Strike slammed the office door behind him.

"I'm OK," lied Robin, in a quavering voice, still hunched over
with her hand on her chest, her back to him. After a second or two,

she straightened up and turned around, her face scarlet and her eyes still wet.

Her accidental assailant was massive; his height, his general hairiness, coupled with a gently expanding belly, suggested a grizzly bear. One of his eyes was puffy and bruised, the skin just below the eyebrow cut. Congealing blood sat in raised white-edged nail tracks on his left cheek and the right side of his thick neck, revealed by the crumpled open collar of his shirt.

"Are you M–Mr. Strike?"

"Yeah."

"I–I'm the temp."

"The what?"

"The temp. From Temporary Solutions?"

The name of the agency did not wipe the incredulous look from his battered face. They stared at each other, unnerved and antagonistic.

Just like Robin, Cormoran Strike knew that he would forever remember the last twelve hours as an epoch-changing night in his life. Now, it seemed, the Fates had sent an emissary in a neat beige trench coat, to taunt him with the fact that his life was bubbling towards catastrophe. There was not supposed to be a temp. He had intended his dismissal of Robin's predecessor to end his contract.

"How long have they sent you for?"

"A–a week to begin with," said Robin, who had never been greeted with such a lack of enthusiasm.

Strike made a rapid mental calculation. A week at the agency's exorbitant rate would drive his overdraft yet further into the region of irreparable; it might even be the final straw his main creditor kept implying he was waiting for.

" 'Scuse me a moment."

He left the room via the glass door, and turned immediately right, into a tiny dank toilet. Here he bolted the door, and stared into the cracked, spotted mirror over the sink.

The reflection staring back at him was not handsome. Strike had the high, bulging forehead, broad nose and thick brows of a young Beethoven who had taken to boxing, an impression only heightened by the swelling and blackening eye. His thick curly hair, springy as carpet, had ensured that his many youthful nicknames had included "Pubehead." He looked older than his thirty-five years.

Ramming the plug into the hole, he filled the cracked and grubby sink with cold water, took a deep breath and completely submerged his throbbing head. Displaced water slopped over his shoes, but he ignored it for the relief of ten seconds of icy, blind stillness.

Disparate images of the previous night flickered through his mind: emptying three drawers of possessions into a kitbag while Charlotte screamed at him; the ashtray catching him on the brow-bone as he looked back at her from the door; the journey on foot across the dark city to his office, where he had slept for an hour or two in his desk chair. Then the final, filthy scene, after Charlotte had tracked him down in the early hours, to plunge in those last few *banderillas* she had failed to implant before he had left her flat; his resolution to let her go when, after clawing his face, she had run out of the door; and then that moment of madness when he had plunged after her— a pursuit ended as quickly as it had begun, with the unwitting intervention of this heedless, superfluous girl, whom he had been forced to save, and then placate.

He emerged from the cold water with a gasp and a grunt, his face and head pleasantly numb and tingling. With the cardboard-textured towel that hung on the back of the door he rubbed himself dry and stared again at his grim reflection. The scratches, washed clean of blood, looked like nothing more than the impressions of a crumpled pillow. Charlotte would have reached the underground by now. One of the insane thoughts that had propelled him after her had been fear that she would throw herself on the tracks. Once, after a particularly vicious row in their mid-twenties, she had climbed on to a rooftop, where she had swayed drunkenly, vowing to jump. Perhaps he ought to be glad that the Temporary Solution had forced him to abandon the chase. There could be no going back from the scene in the early hours of this morning. This time, it had to be over.

Tugging his sodden collar away from his neck, Strike pulled back the rusty bolt and headed out of the toilet and back through the glass door.

A pneumatic drill had started up in the street outside. Robin was standing in front of the desk with her back to the door; she whipped her hand back out of the front of her coat as he re-entered the room, and he knew that she had been massaging her breast again.

"Is—are you all right?" Strike asked, carefully not looking at the site of the injury.

"I'm fine. Listen, if you don't need me, I'll go," said Robin with dignity.

"No—no, not at all," said a voice issuing from Strike's mouth, though he listened to it with disgust. "A week—yeah, that'll be fine. Er—the post's here..." He scooped it from the doormat as he spoke and scattered it on the bare desk in front of her, a propitiatory offering. "Yeah, if you could open that, answer the phone, generally sort of tidy up—computer password's Hatherill23, I'll write it down..." This he did, under her wary, doubtful gaze. "There you go—I'll be in here."

He strode into the inner office, closed the door carefully behind him and then stood quite still, gazing at the kitbag under the bare desk. It contained everything he owned, for he doubted that he would ever see again the nine tenths of his possessions he had left at Charlotte's. They would probably be gone by lunchtime; set on fire, dumped in the street, slashed and crushed, doused in bleach. The drill hammered relentlessly in the street below.

And now the impossibility of paying off his mountainous debts, the appalling consequences that would attend the imminent failure of this business, the looming, unknown but inevitably horrible sequel to his leaving Charlotte; in Strike's exhaustion, the misery of it all seemed to rear up in front of him in a kind of kaleidoscope of horror.

Hardly aware that he had moved, he found himself back in the chair in which he had spent the latter part of the night. From the other side of the insubstantial partition wall came muffled sounds of movement. The Temporary Solution was no doubt starting up the computer, and would shortly discover that he had not received a single work-related email in three weeks. Then, at his own request, she would start opening all his final demands. Exhausted, sore and hungry, Strike slid face down on to the desk again, muffling his eyes and ears in his encircling arms, so that he did not have to listen while his humiliation was laid bare next door by a stranger.

3

FIVE MINUTES LATER THERE WAS a knock on the door and Strike, who had been on the verge of sleep, jerked upright in his chair.

"Sorry?"

His subconscious had become entangled with Charlotte again; it was a surprise to see the strange girl enter the room. She had taken off her coat to reveal a snugly, even seductively fitting cream sweater. Strike addressed her hairline.

"Yeah?"

"There's a client here for you. Shall I show him in?"

"There's a what?"

"A client, Mr. Strike."

He looked at her for several seconds, trying to process the information.

"Right, OK—no, give me a couple of minutes, please, Sandra, and then show him in."

She withdrew without comment.

Strike wasted barely a second on asking himself why he had called her Sandra, before leaping to his feet and setting about looking and smelling less like a man who had slept in his clothes. Diving under his desk into his kitbag, he seized a tube of toothpaste, and squeezed three inches into his open mouth; then he noticed that his tie was soaked in water from the sink, and that his shirt front was spattered with flecks of blood, so he ripped both off, buttons pinging off the walls and filing cabinet, dragged a clean though heavily creased shirt out of the kitbag instead and pulled it on, thick fingers fumbling. After stuffing the kitbag out of sight behind his empty filing cabinet, he hastily reseated himself and checked the inner corners of his eyes for debris, all the while wondering whether this so-called client was the real thing, and whether he would be prepared to pay actual money for detective services. Strike had come to realize, over the course of an eighteen-month spiral into financial ruin, that neither of these things could be taken for granted. He was still chasing two clients for full payment of their bills; a third had refused to disburse a penny, because Strike's findings had not been to his taste, and given that he was sliding ever deeper into debt, and that a rent review of the area was threatening his tenancy of the central London office that he had been so pleased to secure, Strike was in no position to involve a lawyer. Rougher, cruder methods of debt collection had become a staple of his recent fantasies; it would have given him much pleasure to watch the smuggest of his defaulters cowering in the shadow of a baseball bat.

The door opened again; Strike hastily removed his index finger from his nostril and sat up straight, trying to look bright and alert in his chair.

"Mr. Strike, this is Mr. Bristow."

The prospective client followed Robin into the room. The immediate impression was favorable. The stranger might be distinctly rabbity in appearance, with a short upper lip that failed to conceal large front teeth; his coloring was sandy, and his eyes, judging by the thickness of his glasses, myopic; but his dark gray suit was beautifully tailored, and the shining ice-blue tie, the watch and the shoes all looked expensive.

The snowy smoothness of the stranger's shirt made Strike doubly conscious of the thousand or so creases in his own clothes. He stood up to give Bristow the full benefit of his six feet three inches, held out a hairy-backed hand and attempted to counter his visitor's sartorial superiority by projecting the air of a man too busy to worry about laundry.

"Cormoran Strike; how d'you do."

"John Bristow," said the other, shaking hands. His voice was pleasant, cultivated and uncertain. His gaze lingered on Strike's swollen eye.

"Could I offer you gentlemen some tea or coffee?" asked Robin.

Bristow asked for a small black coffee, but Strike did not answer;

he had just caught sight of a heavy-browed young woman in a frumpy tweed suit, who was sitting on the threadbare sofa beside the door of the outer office. It beggared belief that two potential clients could have arrived at the same moment. Surely he had not been sent a second temp?

"And you, Mr. Strike?" asked Robin.

"What? Oh—black coffee, two sugars, please, Sandra," he said, before he could stop himself. He saw her mouth twist as she closed the door behind her, and only then did he remember that he did not have any coffee, sugar or, indeed, cups.

Sitting down at Strike's invitation, Bristow looked round the tatty office in what Strike was afraid was disappointment. The prospective client seemed nervous in the guilty way that Strike had come to associate with suspicious husbands, yet a faint air of authority clung to him, conveyed mainly by the obvious expense of his suit. Strike wondered how Bristow had found him. It was hard to get word-of-mouth business when your only client (as she regularly sobbed down the telephone) had no friends.

"What can I do for you, Mr. Bristow?" he asked, back in his own chair.

"It's—um—actually, I wonder whether I could just check…I think we've met before."

"Really?"

"You wouldn't remember me, it was years and years ago…but I think you were friends with my brother Charlie. Charlie Bristow? He died—in an accident—when he was nine."

"Bloody hell," said Strike. "Charlie…yeah, I remember."

And, indeed, he remembered perfectly. Charlie Bristow had been one of many friends Strike had collected during a complicated, peripatetic childhood. A magnetic, wild and reckless boy, pack leader of the coolest gang at Strike's new school in London, Charlie had taken one look at the enormous new boy with the thick Cornish accent, and appointed him his best friend and lieutenant. Two giddy months of bosom friendship and bad behavior had followed. Strike, who had always been fascinated by the smooth workings of other children's homes, with their sane, well-ordered families, and the bedrooms they were allowed to keep for years and years, retained a vivid memory of Charlie's house, which had been large and luxurious. There had been a long sunlit lawn, a tree house, and iced lemon squash served by Charlie's mother.

And then had come the unprecedented horror of the first day back at school after Easter break, when their form teacher had told them that Charlie would never return, that he was dead, that he had ridden his bike over the edge of a quarry, while holidaying in Wales. She had been a mean old bitch, that teacher, and she had not been able to resist telling the class that Charlie, who as they would remember *often disobeyed grown-ups,* had been *expressly forbidden* to ride anywhere near the quarry, but that he had done so anyway, *perhaps showing off*—but she had been forced to stop there, because two little girls in the front row were sobbing.

From that day onwards, Strike had seen the face of a laughing blond boy fragmenting every time he looked at, or imagined, a quarry. He would not have been surprised if every member of Charlie Bristow's old class had been left with the same lingering fear of the great dark pit, the sheer drop and the unforgiving stone.

"Yeah, I remember Charlie," he said.

Bristow's Adam's apple bobbed a little.

"Yes. Well it's your name, you see. I remember so clearly Charlie talking about you, on holiday, in the days before he died; 'my friend Strike,' 'Cormoran Strike.' It's unusual, isn't it? Where does 'Strike' come from, do you know? I've never met it anywhere else."

Bristow was not the first person Strike had known who would snatch at any procrastinatory subject—the weather, the congestion charge, their preferences in hot drinks—to postpone discussion of what had brought them to his office.

"I've been told it's something to do with corn," he said, "measuring corn."

"Really, is it? Nothing to do with hitting, or walkouts, ha ha... no... Well you see, when I was looking for someone to help me with this business, and I saw your name in the book," Bristow's knee began jiggling up and down, "you can perhaps imagine how it—well, it felt like—like a sign. A sign from Charlie. Saying I was right."

His Adam's apple bobbed as he swallowed.

"OK," said Strike cautiously, hoping that he had not been mistaken for a medium.

"It's my sister, you see," said Bristow.

"Right. Is she in some kind of trouble?"

"She's dead."

Strike just stopped himself saying, "What, her too?"

"I'm sorry," he said carefully.

Bristow acknowledged the condolence with a jerky inclination of the head.

"I—this isn't easy. Firstly, you should know that my sister is—was—Lula Landry."

Hope, so briefly re-erected at the news that he might have a client, fell slowly forwards like a granite tombstone and landed with an agonizing blow in Strike's gut. The man sitting opposite him was delusional, if not actually unhinged. It was an impossibility akin to two identical snowflakes that this whey-faced, leporine man could have sprung from the same genetic pool as the bronze-skinned, colt-limbed, diamond-cut beauty that had been Lula Landry.

"My parents adopted her," said Bristow meekly, as though he knew what Strike was thinking. "We were all adopted."

"Uh huh," said Strike. He had an exceptionally accurate memory; thinking back to that huge, cool, well-ordered house, and the blazing acres of garden, he remembered a languid blonde mother presiding at the picnic table, the distant booming voice of an intimidating father; a surly older brother picking at the fruit cake, Charlie himself making his mother laugh as he clowned; but no little girl.

"You wouldn't have met Lula," Bristow went on, again as though Strike had spoken his thoughts aloud. "My parents didn't adopt her until after Charlie had died. She was four years old when she came to us; she'd been in care for a couple of years. I was nearly fifteen. I can still remember standing at the front door and watching my father carrying her up the drive. She was wearing a little red knitted hat. My mother's still got it."

And suddenly, shockingly, John Bristow burst into tears. He sobbed into his hands, hunch-shouldered, quaking, while tears and snot slid through the cracks in his fingers. Every time he seemed to have himself under some kind of control, more sobs burst forth.

"I'm sorry—sorry—Jesus..."

Panting and hiccoughing, he dabbed beneath his glasses with a wadded handkerchief, trying to regain control.

The office door opened and Robin backed in, carrying a tray. Bristow turned his face away, his shoulders heaving and shaking. Through the open door Strike caught another glimpse of the be-suited woman in the outer office; she was now scowling at him from over the top of a copy of the *Daily Express*.

Robin laid out two cups, a milk jug, a sugar bowl and a plate of chocolate biscuits, none of which Strike had ever seen before, smiled in perfunctory fashion at his thanks and made to leave.

"Hang on a moment, Sandra," said Strike. "Could you...?"

He took a piece of paper from his desk and slid it on to his knee. While Bristow made soft gulping noises, Strike wrote, very swiftly and as legibly as he could manage:

> Please google Lula Landry and find out whether she was adopted, and if so, by whom. Do not discuss what you are doing with the woman outside (what is she doing here?). Write down the answers to questions above and bring them to me here, without saying what you've found.

He handed the piece of paper to Robin, who took it wordlessly and left the room.

"Sorry—I'm so sorry," Bristow gasped, when the door had closed. "This is—I'm not usually—I've been back at work, seeing clients..." He took several deep breaths. With his pink eyes the resemblance to an albino rabbit was heightened. His right knee was still jiggling up and down.

"It's just been a dreadful time," he whispered, taking deep breaths. "Lula...and my mother's dying..."

Strike's mouth was watering at the sight of the chocolate biscuits, because he had eaten nothing for what felt like days; but he felt it would strike an unsympathetic note to start snacking while Bristow jiggled and sniffed and mopped his eyes. The pneumatic drill was still hammering like a machine gun down in the street.

"She's given up completely since Lula died. It's broken her. Her cancer was supposed to be in remission, but it's come back, and they say there's nothing more they can do. I mean, this is the second time. She had a sort of breakdown after Charlie. My father thought another child would make it better. They'd always wanted a girl. It wasn't easy for them to be approved, but Lula was mixed race, and harder to place, so," he finished, on a strangled sob, "they managed to get her.

"She was always b-beautiful. She was d-discovered in Oxford Street, out shopping with my mother. Taken on by Athena. It's one of the most prestigious agencies. She was modeling f-full time by seventeen. By the time she died, she was worth around ten million. I don't know why I'm telling you all this. You probably know it all. Everyone knew—thought they knew—all about Lula."

He picked up his cup clumsily; his hands were trembling so much that coffee slopped over the edge on to his sharply pressed suit trousers.

"What exactly is it that you would like me to do for you?" Strike asked.

Bristow replaced the cup shakily on the desk, then gripped his hands together tightly.

"They say my sister killed herself. I don't believe it."

Strike remembered the television pictures: the black body bag on a stretcher, flickering in a storm of camera flashes as it was loaded into an ambulance, the photographers clustering around as it started to move, holding up their cameras to the dark windows, white lights bouncing off the black glass. He knew more about the death of Lula Landry than he had ever meant or wanted to know; the same would be true of virtually any sentient being in Britain. Bombarded with the story, you grew interested against your will, and before you knew it, you were so well informed, so opinionated about the facts of the case, you would have been unfit to sit on a jury.

"There was an inquest, wasn't there?"

"Yes, but the detective in charge of the case was convinced from the outset that it was suicide, purely because Lula was on lithium. The things he overlooked—they've even spotted some of them on the internet."

Bristow jabbed a nonsensical finger at Strike's bare desktop, where a computer might have been expected to stand.

A perfunctory knock and the door opened; Robin strode in, handed Strike a folded note and withdrew.

"Sorry, d'you mind?" said Strike. "I've been waiting for this message."

He unfolded the note against his knee, so that Bristow could not see through the back, and read:

> Lula Landry was adopted by Sir Alec and Lady Yvette Bristow when she was four. She grew up as Lula Bristow but took her mother's maiden name when she started modeling. She has an older brother called John, who is a lawyer. The girl waiting outside is Mr. Bristow's girlfriend and a secretary at his firm. They work for Landry, May, Patterson, the firm started by Lula and John's maternal grandfather. The photograph of John Bristow on LMP's home page is identical to the man you're talking to.

Strike crumpled the note and dropped it into the waste-paper basket at his feet. He was staggered. John Bristow was not a fantasist; and he, Strike, appeared to have been sent a temp with more initiative, and better punctuation, than any he had ever met.

"Sorry, go on," he said to Bristow. "You were saying—about the inquest?"

"Yeah," said Bristow, dabbing the end of his nose with the wet handkerchief. "Well, I'm not denying that Lula had problems. She put Mum through hell, as a matter of fact. It started around the same time our father died—you probably know all this, God knows there was enough about it in the press . . . but she was expelled from school for dabbling in drugs; she ran off to London, Mum found her living rough with addicts; the drugs exacerbated the mental problems; she absconded from a treatment center—there were endless scenes and dramas. In the end, though, they realized she had bipolar disorder and put her on the right medication, and ever since then, as long as she was taking her tablets, she was fine; you'd never have known there was anything wrong with her. Even the coroner accepted that she *had* been taking her medication, the autopsy proved it.

"But the police and the coroner couldn't see past the girl who had a history of poor mental health. They insisted that she was depressed, but I can tell you myself that Lula wasn't depressed at all. I saw her on the morning before she died, and she was absolutely fine. Things were going very well for her, particularly career-wise. She'd just signed a contract that would have brought in five million over two years; she asked me to look over it for her, and it was a bloody good deal. The designer was a great friend of hers, Somé, I expect you've heard of him? And she was booked solid for months; there was a shoot in Morocco coming up, and she loved the traveling. So you see, there was no reason whatsoever for her to take her own life."

Strike nodded politely, inwardly unimpressed. Suicides, in his experience, were perfectly capable of feigning an interest in a future they had no intention of inhabiting. Landry's rosy, golden-hued morning mood might easily have turned dark and hopeless in the day and half a night that had preceded her death; he had known it happen. He remembered the lieutenant in the King's Royal Rifle Corps, who had risen in the night after his own birthday party, of which, by all accounts, he had been the life and soul. He had penned his family a note, telling them to call the police and not go into the garage. The body had been found hanging from the garage ceiling by his fifteen-year-old son, who had not noticed the note as he hurried through the kitchen on the way to fetch his bicycle.

"That's not all," said Bristow. "There's evidence, hard evidence. Tansy Bestigui's, for a start."

"She was the neighbor who said she heard an argument upstairs?"

"Exactly! She heard a man shouting up there, right before Lula went over the balcony! The police rubbished her evidence, purely because—well, she'd taken cocaine. But that doesn't mean she didn't know what she'd heard. Tansy maintains to this day that Lula was arguing with a man seconds before she fell. I know, because I've discussed it with her very recently. Our firm is handling her divorce. I'm sure I'd be able to persuade her to talk to you.

"And then," said Bristow, watching Strike anxiously, trying to gauge his reaction, "there was the CCTV footage. A man walking towards Kentigern Gardens about twenty minutes before Lula fell, and then footage of the same man running hell for leather away from Kentigern Gardens after she'd been killed. They never found out who he was; never managed to trace him."

With a kind of furtive eagerness, Bristow now drew from an inside pocket of his jacket a slightly crumpled clean envelope and held it out.

"I've written it all down. The timings and everything. It's all in here. You'll see how it fits together."

The appearance of the envelope did nothing to increase Strike's confidence in Bristow's judgment. He had been handed such things before: the scribbled fruits of lonely and misguided obsessions; one-track maunderings on pet theories; complex timetables twisted to fit fantastic contingencies. The lawyer's left eyelid was flickering, one of his knees was jerking up and down and the fingers proffering the envelope were trembling.

For a few seconds Strike weighed these signs of strain against Bristow's undoubtedly hand-made shoes, and the Vacheron Constantin watch revealed on his pale wrist when he gesticulated. This was a man who could and would pay; perhaps long enough to enable Strike to clear one installment of the loan that was the most pressing of his debts. With a sigh, and an inner scowl at his own conscience, Strike said:

"Mr. Bristow—"

"Call me John."

"John . . . I'm going to be honest with you. I don't think it would be right to take your money."

Red blotches blossomed on Bristow's pale neck, and on the undistinguished face, as he continued to hold out the envelope.

"What do you mean, it wouldn't be right?"

"Your sister's death was probably as thoroughly investigated as anything can be. Millions of people, and media from all over the world, were following the police's every move. They would have been twice as thorough as usual. Suicide is a difficult thing to have to accept—"

"I don't accept it. I'll never accept it. She didn't kill herself. Someone pushed her over that balcony."

The drill outside stopped suddenly, so that Bristow's voice rang loudly through the room; and his hair-trigger fury was that of a meek man pushed to his absolute limit.

"I see. I get it. You're another one, are you? Another fucking armchair psychologist? Charlie's dead, my father's dead, Lula's dead and my mother's dying—I've lost everyone, and I need a bereavement counselor, not a detective. D'you think I haven't heard it about a hundred fucking times before?"

Bristow stood up, impressive for all his rabbity teeth and blotchy skin.

"I'm a pretty rich man, Strike. Sorry to be crass about it, but there you are. My father left me a sizable trust fund. I've looked into the going rate for this kind of thing, and I would have been happy to pay you double."

A double fee. Strike's conscience, once firm and inelastic, had been weakened by repeated blows of fate; this was the knockout punch. His baser self was already gamboling off into the realms of happy speculation: a month's work would give him enough to pay off the temp and some of the rent arrears; two months, the more pressing debts... three months, a chunk of the overdraft gone... four months...

But John Bristow was speaking over his shoulder as he moved towards the door, clutching and crumpling the envelope that Strike had refused to take.

"I wanted it to be you because of Charlie, but I found out a bit about you, I'm not a complete bloody idiot. Special investigation branch, military police, wasn't it? Decorated as well. I can't say I was impressed by your offices," Bristow was almost shouting now, and Strike was aware that the muffled female voices in the outer office had fallen silent, "but apparently I was wrong, and you can afford to turn down work. Fine! Bloody forget it. I'm sure I'll find somebody else to do the job. Sorry to have troubled you!"

4

THE MEN'S CONVERSATION HAD BEEN carrying, with increasing clarity, through the flimsy dividing wall for a couple of minutes; now, in the sudden silence following the cessation of the drill, Bristow's words were plainly audible.

Purely for her own amusement, in the high spirits of this happy day, Robin had been trying to act convincingly the part of Strike's regular secretary, and not to give away to Bristow's girlfriend that she had only been working for a private detective for half an hour. She concealed as best she could any sign of surprise or excitement at the outbreak of shouting, but she was instinctively on Bristow's side, whatever the cause of the conflict. Strike's job and his black eye had a certain beaten-up glamour, but his attitude towards her was deplorable, and her left breast was still sore.

Bristow's girlfriend had been staring at the closed door ever since the men's voices had first become audible over the noise of the drill. Thick-set and very dark, with a limp bob and what might have been a monobrow if she had not plucked it, she looked naturally cross. Robin had often noticed how couples tended to be of roughly equivalent personal attractiveness, though of course factors such as money often seemed to secure a partner of significantly better looks than oneself. Robin found it endearing that Bristow, who on the evidence of his smart suit and his prestigious firm could have set his sights on somebody much prettier, had chosen this girl, who she assumed was warmer and kinder than her appearance suggested.

"Are you sure you wouldn't like a coffee, Alison?" she asked.

The girl looked around as though surprised at being spoken to, as though she had forgotten that Robin was there.

"No thanks," she said, in a deep voice that was surprisingly melodious. "I knew he'd get upset," she added, with an odd kind of satisfaction. "I've tried to talk him out of doing this, but he wouldn't listen. Sounds like this so-called detective is turning him down. Good for him."

Robin's surprise must have shown, because Alison went on, with a trace of impatience:

"It'd be better for John if he'd just accept the facts. She killed herself. The rest of the family have come to terms with it, I don't know why he can't."

There was no point pretending that she did not know what the woman was talking about. Everyone knew what had happened to Lula Landry. Robin could remember exactly where she had been when she had heard that the model had dived to her death on a sub-zero night in January: standing at the sink in the kitchen of her parents' house. The news had come over the radio, and she had emitted a little cry of surprise, and run out of the kitchen in her nightshirt to tell Matthew, who was staying for the weekend. How could the death of someone you had never met affect you so? Robin had greatly admired Lula Landry's looks. She did not much like her own milkmaid's coloring: the model had been dark, luminous, fine-boned and fierce.

"It hasn't been very long since she died."

"Three months," said Alison, shaking out her *Daily Express.* "Is he any good, this man?"

Robin had noticed Alison's contemptuous expression as she took in the dilapidated condition, and undeniable grubbiness, of the little waiting room, and she had just seen, online, the pristine, palatial office where the other woman worked. Her answer was therefore prompted by self-respect rather than any desire to protect Strike.

"Oh yes," she replied coolly. "He's one of the best."

She slit open a pink, kitten-embellished envelope with the air of a woman who daily dealt with exigencies much more complex and intriguing than Alison could possibly imagine.

Meanwhile, Strike and Bristow were facing each other across the inner room, the one furious, the other trying to find a way to reverse his position without jettisoning his self-respect.

"All I want, Strike," said Bristow hoarsely, the color high in his thin face, "is *justice.*"

He might have struck a divine tuning fork; the word rang through the shabby office, calling forth an inaudible but plangent note in Strike's breast. Bristow had located the pilot light Strike shielded when everything else had been blown to ashes. He stood in desperate need of money, but Bristow had given him another, better reason to jettison his scruples.

"OK. I understand. I mean it, John; I understand. Come back and sit down. If you still want my help, I'd like to give it."

Bristow glared at him. There was no noise in the office but the distant shouts of the workmen below.

"Would you like your—er, wife, is she?—to come in?"

"No," said Bristow, still tense, with his hand on the doorknob. "Alison doesn't think I ought to be doing this. I don't know why she wanted to come along, actually. Probably hoping you'd turn me down."

"Please—sit down. Let's go over this properly."

Bristow hesitated, then moved back towards his abandoned chair.

His self-restraint crumbling at last, Strike took a chocolate biscuit and crammed it, whole, into his mouth; he took an unused notepad from his desk drawer, flicked it open, reached for a pen and managed to swallow the biscuit in the time it took Bristow to resume his seat.

"Shall I take that?" he suggested, pointing to the envelope Bristow was still clutching.

The lawyer handed it over as though unsure he could trust Strike with it. Strike, who did not wish to peruse the contents in front of Bristow, put it aside with a small pat, which was intended to show that it was now a valued component of the investigation, and readied his pen.

"John, if you could give me a brief outline of what happened on the day your sister died, it would be very helpful."

By nature methodical and thorough, Strike had been trained to investigate to a high and rigorous standard. First, allow the witness to tell their story in their own way: the untrammeled flow often revealed details, apparent inconsequentialities, that would later prove invaluable nuggets of evidence. Once the first gush of impression and recollection had been harvested, then it was time to solicit and arrange facts rigorously and precisely: *people, places, property . . .*

"Oh," said Bristow, who seemed, after all his vehemence, unsure where to start, "I don't really . . . let's see . . ."

"When was the last time you saw her?" Strike prompted.

"That would have been—yes, the morning before she died. We . . . we had an argument, as a matter of fact, though thank God we made it up."

"What time was this?"

"It was early. Before nine, I was on my way in to the office. Perhaps a quarter to nine?"

"And what did you argue about?"

"Oh, about her boyfriend, Evan Duffield. They'd just got back together again. The family had thought it was over and we'd been so pleased. He's a horrible person, an addict and a chronic self-publicist; about the worst influence on Lula you could imagine.

"I might have been a bit heavy-handed, I—I see that now. I was eleven years older than Lula. I felt protective of her, you know. Perhaps I was bossy at times. She was always telling me that I didn't understand."

"Understand what?"

"Well . . . anything. She had lots of issues. Issues with being adopted. Issues with being black in a white family. She used to say I had it easy . . . I don't know. Perhaps she was right."

He blinked rapidly behind his glasses. "The row was really the continuation of a row we'd had on the telephone the night before. I just couldn't believe she'd been so stupid as to go back to Duffield. The relief we all felt when they split up . . . I mean, given her own history with drugs, hooking up with an addict . . ." He drew breath. "She didn't want to hear it. She never did. She was furious with me. She'd actually given instructions to the security man at the flats not to let me past the front desk next morning, but—well, Wilson waved me through anyway."

Humiliating, thought Strike, to have to rely on the pity of doormen.

"I wouldn't have gone up," said Bristow miserably, blotches of color dappling his thin neck again, "but I had the contract with Somé to give back to her; she'd asked me to look over it and she needed to sign it . . . She could be quite blasé about things like that. Anyway, she wasn't too happy that they'd let me upstairs, and we rowed again, but it burned itself out quite quickly. She calmed down.

"So then I told her that Mum would appreciate a visit. Mum had just got out of hospital, you see. She'd had a hysterectomy. Lula said she might pop in and see her later, at her flat, but that she couldn't be sure. She had things on."

Bristow took a deep breath; his right knee started jiggling up and down again and his knobble-knuckled hands washed each other in dumb show.

"I don't want you to think badly of her. People thought her selfish, but she'd been the youngest in the family and rather indulged, and then she was ill and, naturally, the center of attention, and then she was plunged into this extraordinary life where things, people, revolved around her, and she was pursued everywhere by the paparazzi. It wasn't a normal existence."

"No," said Strike.

"So, anyway, I told Lula how groggy and sore Mum was feeling, and she said she might look in on her later. I left; I nipped into my office to get some files from Alison, because I wanted to work from Mum's flat that day and keep her company. I next saw Lula at Mum's, mid-morning. She sat with Mum for a while in the bedroom until my uncle arrived to visit, and then nipped into the study where I was working, to say goodbye. She hugged me before she . . ."

Bristow's voice cracked, and he stared down into his lap.

"More coffee?" Strike suggested. Bristow shook his bowed head. To give him a moment to pull himself together, Strike picked up the tray and headed for the outer office.

Bristow's girlfriend looked up from her newspaper, scowling, when Strike appeared. "Aren't you finished?" she asked.

"Evidently not," said Strike, with no attempt at a smile. She glared at him while he addressed Robin.

"Could I get another cup of coffee, er . . . ?"

Robin stood up and took the tray from him in silence.

"John needs to be back in the office at half past ten," Alison informed Strike, in a slightly louder voice. "We'll need to be off in ten minutes at the most."

"I'll bear that in mind," Strike assured her blandly, before returning to the inner office, where Bristow was sitting as though in prayer, his head bowed over his clasped hands.

"I'm sorry," he muttered, as Strike sat back down. "It's still difficult talking about it."

"No problem," said Strike, picking up his notebook again. "So Lula came to see your mother? What time was that?"

"Elevenish. It all came out at the inquest, what she did after that. She got her driver to take her to some boutique that she liked, and then she went back to her flat. She had an appointment at home with a makeup artist she knew, and her friend Ciara Porter joined her there. You'll have seen Ciara Porter, she's a model. Very blonde. They were photographed together as angels, you probably saw it: naked except for handbags and wings. Somé used the picture in his advertising campaign after Lula died. People said it was tasteless.

"So Lula and Ciara spent the afternoon together at Lula's flat, and then they left to go out to dinner, where they met up with Duffield and some other people. The whole group went on to Uzi, the nightclub, and they were there until past midnight.

"Then Duffield and Lula argued. Lots of people saw it happen. He manhandled her a bit, tried to make her stay, but she left the club alone. Everyone thought he'd done it, afterwards, but he turned out to have a cast-iron alibi."

"Cleared on the evidence of his drug dealer, wasn't he?" asked Strike, still writing.

"Yes, exactly. So—so Lula arrived back at her flat around twenty past one. She was photographed going inside. You probably remember that picture. It was everywhere afterwards."

Strike remembered: one of the world's most photographed women, head bowed, shoulders hunched, eyes heavy and arms folded tightly around her torso, twisting her face away from the photographers. Once the verdict of suicide had been clearly established, it had taken on a macabre aspect: the rich and beautiful young woman, less than an hour from her death, attempting to conceal her wretchedness from the lenses she had courted, and which had so adored her.

"Were there usually photographers outside her door?"

"Yes, especially if they knew she was with Duffield, or they wanted to get a shot of her coming home drunk. But they weren't only there for her that night. An American rapper was supposed to be arriving to stay in the same building that evening; Deeby Macc's his name. His record company had rented the apartment beneath hers. In the event he never stayed there, because with the police all over the building it was easier for him to go to a hotel. But the photographers who had chased Lula's car when she left Uzi joined the ones who were waiting for Macc outside the flats, so that made quite a crowd of them around the entrance of the building, though they all drifted away not long after she'd gone inside. Somehow they got a tip-off that Macc wouldn't be there for hours.

"It was a bitterly cold night. Snowing. Below freezing. So the street was empty when she fell."

Bristow blinked and took another sip of cold coffee, and Strike thought about the paparazzi who had left before Lula Landry fell from her balcony. Imagine, he thought, what a shot of Landry diving to her death would have gone for; enough to retire on, perhaps.

"John, your girlfriend says you need to be somewhere at half past ten."

"What?"

Bristow seemed to return to himself. He checked the expensive watch and gasped.

"Good God, I had no idea I'd been here so long. What—what happens now?" he asked, looking slightly bewildered. "You'll read my notes?"

"Yeah, of course," Strike assured him, "and I'll call you in a couple of days when I've done some preliminary work. I expect I'll have a lot more questions then."

"All right," said Bristow, getting dazedly to his feet. "Here—take my card. And how would you like me to pay?"

"A month's fee in advance will be great," said Strike. Quashing feeble stirrings of shame, and remembering that Bristow himself had offered a double fee, he named an exorbitant amount, and to his delight Bristow did not quibble, nor ask whether he accepted credit cards nor even promise to drop the money in later, but drew out a real check-book and a pen.

"If, say, a quarter of it could be in cash," Strike added, chancing his luck; and was staggered for the second time that morning when Bristow said, "I did wonder whether you'd prefer..." and counted out a pile of fifties in addition to the check.

They emerged into the outer office at the very moment that Robin was about to enter with Strike's fresh coffee. Bristow's girlfriend stood up when the door opened, and folded her newspaper with the air of one who had been kept waiting too long. She was almost as tall as Bristow, large-framed, with a surly expression and big, mannish hands.

"So you've agreed to do it, have you?" she asked Strike. He had the impression that she thought he was taking advantage of her rich boyfriend. Very possibly she was right.

"Yes, John's hired me," he replied.

"Oh well," she said, ungraciously. "You're pleased, I expect, John."

The lawyer smiled at her, and she sighed and patted his arm, like a tolerant but slightly exasperated mother to a child. John Bristow raised his hand in a salute, then followed his girlfriend out of the room, and their footsteps clanged away down the metal stairs.

5

STRIKE TURNED TO ROBIN, WHO had sat back down at the computer. His coffee was sitting beside the piles of neatly sorted mail lined up on the desk beside her.

"Thanks," he said, taking a sip, "and for the note. Why are you a temp?"

"What d'you mean?" she asked, looking suspicious.

"You can spell and punctuate. You catch on quick. You show initiative—where did the cups and the tray come from? The coffee and biscuits?"

"I borrowed them all from Mr. Crowdy. I told him we'd return them by lunchtime."

"Mr. who?"

Mr. Crowdy, the man downstairs. The graphic designer."

"And he just let you have them?"

"Yes," she said, a little defensively. "I thought, having offered the client coffee, we ought to provide it."

Her use of the plural pronoun was like a gentle pat to his morale.

"Well, that was efficiency way beyond anything Temporary Solutions has sent here before, take it from me. Sorry I kept calling you Sandra; she was the last girl. What's your real name?"

"Robin."

"Robin," he repeated. "That'll be easy to remember."

He had some notion of making a jocular allusion to Batman and his dependable sidekick, but the feeble jest died on his lips as her face turned brilliantly pink. Too late, he realized that the most unfortunate construction could be put on his innocent words. Robin swung the swivel chair back towards the computer monitor, so that all Strike could see was an edge of a flaming cheek. In one frozen moment of mutual mortification, the room seemed to have shrunk to the size of a telephone kiosk.

"I'm going to nip out for a bit," said Strike, putting down his virtually untouched coffee and moving crabwise towards the door, taking down the overcoat hanging beside it. "If anyone calls . . ."

"Mr. Strike—before you go, I think you ought to see this."

Still flushed, Robin took, from on top of the pile of opened letters beside her computer, a sheet of bright pink writing paper and a matching envelope, both of which she had put into a clear plastic pocket. Strike noticed her engagement ring as she held the things up.

"It's a death threat," she said.

"Oh yeah," said Strike. "Nothing to worry about. They come in about once a week."

"But—"

"It's a disgruntled ex-client. Bit unhinged. He thinks he's throwing me off the scent by using that paper."

"Surely, though—shouldn't the police see it?"

"Give them a laugh, you mean?"

"It isn't funny, it's a death threat!" she said, and Strike realized why she had placed it, with its envelope, in the plastic pocket. He was mildly touched.

"Just file it with the others," he said, pointing towards the filing cabinets in the corner. "If he was going to kill me he'd have made his move before now. You'll find six months' worth of letters in there somewhere. Will you be all right to hold the fort for a bit while I'm out?"

"I'll cope," she said, and he was amused by the sour note in her voice, and her obvious disappointment that nobody was going to fingerprint the be-kittened death threat.

"If you need me, my mobile number's on the cards in the top drawer."

"Fine," she said, looking at neither the drawer nor him.

"If you want to go out for lunch, feel free. There's a spare key in the desk somewhere."

"OK."

"See you later, then."

He paused just outside the glass door, on the threshold of the tiny dank bathroom. The pressure in his guts was becoming painful, but he felt that her efficiency, and her impersonal concern for his safety, entitled her to some consideration. Resolving to wait until he reached the pub, Strike headed down the stairs.

Out in the street, he lit a cigarette, turned left and proceeded past the closed 12 Bar Café, up the narrow walkway of Denmark Place past a window full of multicolored guitars, and walls covered in fluttering fliers, away from the relentless pounding of the pneumatic drill. Skirting the rubble and wreckage of the street at the foot of Center Point, he marched past a gigantic gold statue of Freddie Mercury that stood over the entrance of the Dominion Theatre across the road, head bowed, one fist raised in the air, like some pagan god of chaos.

The ornate Victorian face of the Tottenham pub rose up behind the rubble and roadworks, and Strike, pleasurably aware of the large amount of cash in his pocket, pushed his way through its doors, into a serene Victorian atmosphere of gleaming scrolled dark wood and brass fittings. Its frosted glass half-partitions, its aged leather banquettes, its bar mirrors covered in gilt, cherubs and horns of plenty spoke of a confident and ordered world that was in satisfying contrast to the ruined street. Strike ordered a pint of Doom Bar and took it to the back of the almost deserted pub, where he placed his glass on a high circular table, under the garish glass cupola in the ceiling, and headed straight into the Gents, which smelled strongly of piss.

Ten minutes later, and feeling considerably more comfortable, Strike was a third of the way into his pint, which was deepening the anesthetic effect of his exhaustion. The Cornish beer tasted of home, peace and long-gone security. There was a large and blurry painting of a Victorian maiden, dancing with roses in her hands, directly opposite him. Frolicking coyly as she gazed at him through a shower of petals, her enormous breasts draped in white, she was as unlike a real woman as the table on which his pint rested, or the obese man with the ponytail who was working the pumps at the bar.

And now Strike's thoughts swarmed back to Charlotte, who was indubitably real; beautiful, dangerous as a cornered vixen, clever, sometimes funny, and, in the words of Strike's very oldest friend, "fucked to the core." Was it over, really over, this time? Cocooned in his tiredness, Strike recalled the scenes of last night and this morning. Finally she had done something he could not forgive, and the pain would, no doubt be excruciating once the anesthetic wore off: but in the meantime, there were certain practicalities to be faced. It had been Charlotte's flat that they had been living in; her stylish, expensive maisonette in Holland Park Avenue, which meant that he was, as of two o'clock that morning, voluntarily homeless.

("Bluey, just move in with me. For God's sake, you know it makes sense. You can save money while you're building up the business, and I can look after you. You shouldn't be on your own while you're recuperating. Bluey, don't be silly . . .

Nobody would ever call him Bluey again. Bluey was dead.)

It was the first time in their long and turbulent relationship that he had walked out. Three times previously it had been Charlotte who had called a halt. There had been an unspoken awareness between them, always, that if ever he left, if ever he decided he had had enough, the parting would be of an entirely different order to all those she had instigated, none of which, painful and messy though they had been, had ever felt definitive.

Charlotte would not rest until she had hurt him as badly as she could in retaliation. This morning's scene, when she had tracked him to his office, had doubtless been a mere foretaste of what would unfold in the months, even years, to come. He had never known anyone with such an appetite for revenge.

Strike limped to the bar, secured a second pint and returned to the table for further gloomy reflection. Walking out on Charlotte had left him on the brink of true destitution. He was so deeply in debt that all that stood between him and a sleeping bag in a doorway was John Bristow. Indeed, if Gillespie called in the loan that had formed the down payment on Strike's office, Strike would have no alternative but to sleep rough.

("I'm just calling to check how things are going, Mr. Strike, because this month's installment still hasn't arrived . . . Can we expect it within the next few days?")

And finally (since he had started looking at the inadequacies of his life, why not make a comprehensive survey?) there was his recent weight gain; a full stone and a half, so that he not only felt fat and unfit, but was putting unnecessary additional strain on the prosthetic lower leg he was now resting on the brass bar beneath the table. Strike was developing the shadow of a limp purely because the additional load was causing some chafing. The long walk across London in the small hours, kitbag over his shoulder, had not helped. Knowing that he was heading into penury, he had been determined to travel there in the cheapest fashion.

He returned to the bar to buy a third pint. Back at his table beneath the cupola, he drew out his mobile phone and called a friend in the Metropolitan Police whose friendship, though of only a few years' duration, had been forged under exceptional conditions.

Just as Charlotte was the only person to call him "Bluey," so Detective Inspector Richard Anstis was the only person to call Strike "Mystic Bob," which name he bellowed at the sound of his friend's voice.

"Looking for a favor," Strike told Anstis.

"Name it."

"Who handled the Lula Landry case?"

While Anstis searched out their numbers, he asked after Strike's business, right leg and fiancée. Strike lied about the status of all three.

"Glad to hear it," said Anstis cheerfully. "OK, here's Wardle's number. He's all right; loves himself, but you'll be better off with him than Carver; he's a cunt. I can put in a word with Wardle. I'll ring him right now for you, if you like."

Strike tweaked a tourist leaflet from a wooden display on the wall, and copied down Wardle's number in the space beside a picture of the Horse Guards.

"When're you coming over?" Anstis asked. "Bring Charlotte one night."

"Yeah, that'd be great. I'll give you a ring; got a lot on just now."

After hanging up, Strike sat in deep thought for a while, then called an acquaintance much older than Anstis, whose life path had run in a roughly opposite direction.

"Calling in a favor, mate," said Strike. "Need some information."

"On what?"

"You tell me. I need something I can use for leverage with a copper."

The conversation ran to twenty-five minutes, and involved many pauses, which grew longer and more pregnant until finally Strike was given an approximate address and two names, which he also copied down beside the Horse Guards, and a warning, which he did not write down, but took in the spirit in which he knew it was intended. The conversation ended on a friendly note, and Strike, now yawning widely, dialed Wardle's number, which was answered almost immediately by a loud, curt voice.

"Wardle."

"Yeah, hello. My name's Cormoran Strike, and—"

"You're what?"

"Cormoran Strike," said Strike, "is my name."

"Oh yeah," said Wardle. "Anstis just rang. You're the private dick? Anstis said you were interested in talking about Lula Landry?"

"Yeah, I am," said Strike again, suppressing another yawn as he examined the painted panels on the ceiling; bacchanalian revels that became, as he looked, a feast of fairies: *Midsummer Night's Dream,* a man with a donkey's head. "But what I'd really like is the file."

Wardle laughed.

"You didn't save *my* fucking life, mate."

"Got some information you might be interested in. Thought we could do an exchange."

There was a short pause.

"I take it you don't want to do this exchange over the phone?"

"That's right," said Strike. "Is there anywhere you like to have a pint after a hard day's work?"

Having jotted down the name of a pub near Scotland Yard, and agreed that a week today (failing any nearer date) would suit him too, Strike rang off.

It had not always been thus. A couple of years ago, he had been able to command the compliance of witnesses and suspects; he had been like Wardle, a man whose time had more value than most of those with whom he consorted, and who could choose when, where and how long interviews would be. Like Wardle, he had needed no uniform; he had been constantly cloaked in officialdom and prestige. Now, he was a limping man in a creased shirt, trading on old acquaintances, trying to do deals with policemen who would once have been glad to take his calls.

"Arsehole," said Strike aloud, into his echoing glass. The third pint had slid down so easily that there was barely an inch left.

His mobile rang; glancing at the screen, he saw his office number. No doubt Robin was trying to tell him that Peter Gillespie was after money. He let her go straight to voicemail, drained his glass and left.

The street was bright and cold, the pavement damp, and the puddles intermittently silver as clouds scudded across the sun. Strike lit another cigarette outside the front door, and stood smoking it in the doorway of the Tottenham, watching the workmen as they moved around the pit in the road. Cigarette finished, he ambled off down Oxford Street to kill time until the Temporary Solution had left, and he could sleep in peace.

6

ROBIN HAD WAITED TEN MINUTES, to make sure that Strike was not about to come back, before making several delightful telephone calls from her mobile phone. The news of her engagement was received by her friends with either squeals of excitement or envious comments, which gave Robin equal pleasure. At lunchtime, she awarded herself an hour off, bought three bridal magazines and a packet of replacement biscuits (which put the petty cash box, a labeled shortbread tin, into her debt to the tune of forty-two pence), and returned to the empty office, where she spent a happy forty minutes examining bouquets and bridal gowns, and tingling all over with excitement.

When her self-appointed lunch hour was over, Robin washed and returned Mr. Crowdy's cups and tray, and his biscuits. Noting how eagerly he attempted to detain her in conversation on her second appearance, his eyes wandering distractedly from her mouth to her breasts, she resolved to avoid him for the rest of the week.

Still Strike did not return. For want of anything else to do, Robin neatened the contents of her desk drawers, disposing of what she recognized as the accumulated waste of other temporaries: two squares of dusty milk chocolate, a bald emery board and many pieces of paper carrying anonymous telephone numbers and doodles. There was a box of old-fashioned metal acro clips, which she had never come across before, and a considerable number of small, blank blue notebooks, which, though unmarked, had an air of officialdom. Robin, experienced in the world of offices, had the feeling that they might have been pinched from an institutional store cupboard.

The office telephone rang occasionally. Her new boss seemed to be a person of many names. One man asked for "Oggy"; another for

"Monkey Boy," while a dry, clipped voice asked that "Mr. Strike" return Mr. Peter Gillespie's call as soon as possible. On each occasion, Robin contacted Strike's mobile phone, and reached only his voicemail. She therefore left verbal messages, wrote down each caller's name and number on a Post-it note, took it into Strike's office and stuck it neatly on his desk.

The pneumatic drill rumbled on and on outside. Around two o'clock, the ceiling began to creak as the occupant of the flat overhead became more active; otherwise, Robin might have been alone in the whole building. Gradually solitude, coupled with the feeling of pure delight that threatened to burst her ribcage every time her eyes fell on the ring on her left hand, emboldened her. She began to clean and tidy the tiny room under her interim control.

In spite of its general shabbiness, and an overlying grubbiness, Robin soon discovered a firm organizational structure that pleased her own neat and orderly nature. The brown card folders (oddly old-fashioned, in these days of neon plastic) lined up on the shelves behind her desk were arranged in date order, each with a handwritten serial number on the spine. She opened one of them, and saw that the acro clips had been used to secure loose leaves of paper into each file. Much of the material inside was in a deceptive, difficult-to-read hand. Perhaps this was how the police worked; perhaps Strike was an ex-policeman.

Robin discovered the stack of pink death threats to which Strike had alluded in the middle drawer of the filing cabinet, beside a slim sheaf of confidentiality agreements. She took one of these out and read it: a simple form, requesting that the signatory refrain from discussing, outside hours, any of the names or information they might be privy to during their working day. Robin pondered for a moment, then carefully signed and dated one of the documents, carried it through to Strike's inner office, and placed it on his desk, so that he might add his name on the dotted line supplied. Taking this one-sided vow of secrecy gave back to her some of the mystique, even glamour, that she had imagined lay beyond the engraved glass door, before it had flown open and Strike had nearly bowled her down the stairwell.

It was after placing the form on Strike's desk that she spotted the kitbag stuffed away in a corner behind the filing cabinet. The edge of his dirty shirt, an alarm clock and a soap bag peeked from between the open teeth of the bag's zip. Robin closed the door between inner and outer offices as though she had accidentally witnessed something embarrassing and private. She added together the dark-haired beauty fleeing the building that morning, Strike's various injuries and what seemed, in retrospect, to have been a slightly delayed, but determined, pursuit. In her new and joyful condition of betrothal, Robin was disposed to feel desperately sorry for anyone with a less fortunate love life than her own—if desperate pity could describe the exquisite pleasure she actually felt at the thought of her own comparative paradise.

At five o'clock, and in the continuing absence of her temporary boss, Robin decided that she was free to go home. She hummed to herself as she filled in her own time sheet, bursting into song as she buttoned up her trench coat; then she locked the office door, slid the spare key back through the letter box and proceeded, with some caution, back down the metal stairs, towards Matthew and home.

7

STRIKE HAD SPENT THE EARLY afternoon at the University of London Union building, where, by dint of walking determinedly past reception with a slight scowl on his face, he had gained the showers without being challenged or asked for his student card. He had then eaten a stale ham roll and a bar of chocolate in the café. After that he had wandered, blank-eyed in his tiredness, smoking between the cheap shops he visited to buy, with Bristow's cash, the few necessities he needed now that bed and board were gone. Early evening found him holed up in an Italian restaurant, several large boxes propped up at the back, beside the bar, and spinning out his beer until he had half forgotten why he was killing time.

It was nearly eight before he returned to the office. This was the hour when he found London most lovable; the working day over, her pub windows were warm and jewel-like, her streets thrummed with life, and the indefatigable permanence of her aged buildings, softened by the street lights, became strangely reassuring. We have seen plenty like you, they seemed to murmur soothingly, as he limped along Oxford Street carrying a boxed-up camp bed. Seven and a half million hearts were beating in close proximity in this heaving old city, and many, after all, would be aching far worse than his. Walking wearily past closing shops, while the heavens turned indigo above him, Strike found solace in vastness and anonymity.

It was some feat to force the camp bed up the metal stairwell to the second floor, and by the time he reached the entrance bearing his name the pain in the end of his right leg was excruciating. He leaned for a moment, bearing all his weight on his left foot, panting against the glass door, watching it mist.

"You fat cunt," he said aloud. "You knackered old dinosaur."

Wiping the sweat off his forehead, he unlocked the door, and heaved his various purchases over the threshold. In the inner office he pushed his desk aside and set up the bed, unrolled the sleeping bag, and filled his cheap kettle at the sink outside the glass door.

His dinner was still in a Pot Noodle, which he had chosen because it reminded him of the fare he used to carry in his ration pack: some deep-rooted association between quickly heated and rehydrated food and makeshift dwelling places had made him reach automatically for the thing. When the kettle had boiled, he added the water to the tub, and ate the rehydrated pasta with a plastic fork he had taken from the ULU café, sitting in his office chair, looking down into the almost deserted street, the traffic rumbling past in the twilight at the end of the road, and listening to the determined thud of a bass from two floors below, in the 12 Bar Café.

He had slept in worse places. There had been the stone floor of a multistory car park in Angola, and the bombed-out metal factory where they had erected tents, and woken coughing up black soot in the mornings; and, worst of all, the dank dormitory of the commune in Norfolk to which his mother had dragged him and one of his half-sisters when they were eight and six respectively. He remembered the comfortless ease of hospital beds in which he had lain for months, and various squats (also with his mother), and the freezing woods in which he had camped on army exercises. However basic and uninviting the camp bed looked lying under the one naked light bulb, it was luxurious compared with all of them.

The act of shopping for what he needed, and of setting up the bare necessities for himself, had lulled Strike back into the familiar soldierly state of doing what needed to be done, without question or complaint. He disposed of the Pot Noodle tub, turned on the lamp and sat himself down at the desk where Robin had spent most of the day.

As he assembled the raw components of a new file—the hardback folder, the blank paper and an acro clip; the notebook in which he had recorded Bristow's interview; the pamphlet from the Tottenham; Bristow's card—he noticed the new tidiness of the drawers, the lack of dust on the computer monitor, the absence of empty cups and debris, and a faint smell of Pledge. Mildly intrigued, he opened the petty cash tin, and saw there, in Robin's neat, rounded writing, the note that he owed her forty-two pence for chocolate biscuits. Strike pulled forty of the pounds Bristow had given him from his wallet and deposited them in the tin; then, as an afterthought, counted out forty-two pence in coins and laid it on top.

Next, with one of the pens Robin had assembled neatly in the top drawer, Strike began to write, fluently and rapidly, beginning with the date. The notes of Bristow's interview he tore out and attached separately to the file; the actions he had taken thus far, including calls to Anstis and to Wardle, were noted, their numbers preserved (but the details of his other friend, the provider of useful names and addresses, were not put on file).

Finally Strike gave his new case a serial number, which he wrote, along with the legend **Sudden Death, Lula Landry,** on the spine, before stowing the file in its place at the far right of the shelf.

Now, at last, he opened the envelope which, according to Bristow, contained those vital clues that police had missed. The lawyer's handwriting, neat and fluid, sloped backwards in densely written lines. As Bristow had promised, the contents dealt mostly with the actions of a man whom he called "the Runner."

The Runner was a tall black man, whose face was concealed by a scarf and who appeared on the footage of a camera on a late-night bus which ran from Islington towards the West End. He had boarded this bus around fifty minutes before Lula Landry died. He was next seen on CCTV footage taken in Mayfair, walking in the direction of Landry's house, at 1:39 a.m. He had paused on camera and appeared to consult a piece of paper (**poss an address or directions?** Bristow had added helpfully in his notes) before walking out of sight.

Footage taken from the same CCTV camera shortly after showed the Runner sprinting back past the camera at 2:12 and out of sight. **Second black man also running — poss lookout? Disturbed in car theft? Car alarm went off around the corner at this time,** Bristow had written.

Finally there was CCTV footage of **a black man closely resembling the Runner** walking along a road close to Gray's Inn Square, several miles away, later in the morning of Landry's death. **Face still concealed,** Bristow had written.

Strike paused to rub his eyes, wincing because he had forgotten that one of them was bruised. He was now in that light-headed, twitchy state that signified true exhaustion. With a long, grunting sigh he considered Bristow's notes, with one hairy fist holding a pen ready to make his own annotations.

Bristow might interpret the law with dispassion and objectivity in the office that had provided him with his smart engraved business card, but the contents of this envelope merely confirmed Strike's view that his client's personal life was dominated by an unjustifiable obsession. Whatever the origin of Bristow's preoccupation with the Runner—whether because he nursed a secret fear of that urban bogeyman, the criminal black male, or for some other, deeper, more personal reason—it was unthinkable that the police had not investigated the Runner, and his (possibly lookout, possibly car thief) companion, and certain that they had had good reason for excluding him from suspicion.

Yawning widely, Strike turned to the second page of Bristow's notes.

At 1:45, Derrick Wilson, the security guard on duty at the desk overnight, felt unwell and went into the back bathroom, where he remained for approximately a quarter of an hour. For fifteen minutes prior to Lula's death, therefore, the lobby of her building was deserted and anybody could have entered and exited without being seen. Wilson only came out of the bathroom after Lula fell, when he heard Tansy Bestigui screaming.

This window of opportunity tallies exactly with the time the Runner would have reached 18 Kentigern Gardens if he passed the security camera on the junction of Alderbrook and Bellamy Roads at 1:39.

"And how," murmured Strike, massaging his forehead, "did he see through the front door, to know the guard was in the bog?"

I have spoken to Derrick Wilson, who is happy to be inter-viewed.

And I bet you've paid him to do it, Strike thought, noting the security guard's telephone number beneath these concluding words.

He laid down the pen with which he had been intending to add his own notes, and clipped Bristow's jottings into the file. Then he turned off the desk lamp and limped out to pee in the toilet on the landing. After brushing his teeth over the cracked basin, he locked the glass door, set his alarm clock and undressed.

By the neon glow of the street lamp outside, Strike undid the straps of his prosthetic, easing it from the aching stump, removing the gel liner that had become an inadequate cushion against pain. He laid the false leg beside his recharging mobile phone, maneuvered himself into his sleeping bag and lay with his hands behind his head, staring up at the ceiling. Now, as he had feared, the leaden fatigue of the body was not enough to still the misfiring mind. The old infection was active again; tormenting him, dragging at him.

What would she be doing now?

Yesterday evening, in a parallel universe, he had lived in a beautiful apartment in a most desirable part of London, with a woman who made every man who laid eyes on her treat Strike with a kind of incredulous envy.

"Why don't you just move in with me? Oh, for God's sake, Bluey, doesn't it make sense? Why not?"

He had known, from the very first, that it was a mistake. They had tried it before, and each time it had been more calamitous than the last.

"We're engaged, for God's sake, why won't you live with me?"

She had said things that were supposed to be proofs that, in the process of almost losing him forever, she had been as irrevocably changed as he had, with his one and a half legs.

"I don't need a ring. Don't be ridiculous, Bluey. You need all your money for the new business."

He closed his eyes. There could be no going back from this morning. She had lied once too often, about something too serious. But he went over it all again, like a sum he had long since solved, afraid he had made some elementary mistake. Painstakingly he added together the constantly shifting dates, the refusal to check with chemist or doctor, the fury with which she had countered any request for clarification, and then the sudden announcement that it was over, with never a shred of proof that it had been real. Along with every other suspicious circumstance, there was his hard-won knowledge of her mythomania, her need to provoke, to taunt, to test.

"Don't you dare fucking *investigate* me. Don't you dare treat me like some drugged-up *squaddie*. I am not a fucking case to be solved; you're supposed to love me and you won't take my word even on *this*..."

But the lies she told were woven into the fabric of her being, her life; so that to live with her and love her was to become slowly enmeshed by them, to wrestle her for the truth, to struggle to maintain a foothold on reality. How could it have happened, that he, who from his most extreme youth had needed to investigate, to know for sure, to winkle the truth out of the smallest conundrums, could have fallen in love so hard, and for so long, with a girl who spun lies as easily as other women breathed?

"It's over," he told himself. "It had to happen."

But he had not wanted to tell Anstis, and he could not face telling anyone else, not yet. There were friends all over London who would welcome him eagerly to their homes, who would throw open their guest rooms and their fridges, eager to condole and to help. The price of all of those comfortable beds and home-cooked meals, however, would be to sit at kitchen tables, once the clean-pajamaed children were in bed, and relive the filthy final battle with Charlotte, submitting to the outraged sympathy and pity of his friends' girlfriends and wives. To this he preferred grim solitude, a Pot Noodle and a sleeping bag.

He could still feel the missing foot, ripped from his leg two and a half years before. It was there, under the sleeping bag; he could flex the vanished toes if he wanted to. Exhausted as Strike was, it took a while for him to fall asleep, and when he did, Charlotte wove in and out of every dream, gorgeous, vituperative and haunted.

Part Two

Non ignara mali miseris succurrere disco.

No stranger to trouble myself, I am learning to care for the unhappy.

Virgil, *Aeneid*, Book 1

1

" 'With all the gallons of newsprint and hours of televised talk that have been poured forth on the subject of Lula Landry's death, rarely has the question been asked: *why do we care?*

" 'She was beautiful, of course, and beautiful girls have been helping to shift newspapers ever since Dana Gibson cross-hatched lazy-lidded sirens for the *New Yorker*.

" 'She was black, too, or rather, a delicious shade of *café au lait,* and this, we were constantly told, represented progression within an industry concerned merely with surfaces. (I am dubious: could it not be that, this season, *café au lait* was the "in" shade? Have we seen a sudden influx of black women into the industry in Landry's wake? Have our notions of female beauty been revolutionized by her success? Are black Barbies now outselling white?)

" 'The family and friends of the flesh-and-blood Landry will be distraught, of course, and have my profound sympathy. We, however, the reading, watching public, have no personal grief to justify our excesses. Young women die, every day, in "tragic" (which is to say, unnatural) circumstances: in car crashes, from overdoses, and, occasionally, because they attempted to starve themselves into conformity with the body shape sported by Landry and her ilk. Do we spare any of these dead girls more than a passing thought, as we turn the page, and obscure their ordinary faces?' "

Robin paused to take a sip of coffee and clear her throat.

"So far, so sanctimonious," muttered Strike.

He was sitting at the end of Robin's desk, pasting photographs into an open folder, numbering each one, and writing a description of the subject of each in an index at the back. Robin continued where she had left off, reading from her computer monitor.

" 'Our disproportionate interest, even grief, bears examination. Right up until the moment that Landry took her fatal dive, it is a fair bet that tens of thousands of women would have changed places with her. Sobbing young girls laid flowers beneath the balcony of Landry's £4.5 million penthouse flat after her crushed body was cleared away. Has even one aspiring model been deterred in her pursuit of tabloid fame by the rise and brutal fall of Lula Landry?' "

"Get on with it," said Strike. "Her, not you," he added hastily. "It's a woman writing, right?"

"Yes, a Melanie Telford," said Robin, scrolling back to the top of the screen to reveal the head shot of a jowly middle-aged blonde. "Do you want me to skip the rest?"

"No, no, keep going."

Robin cleared her throat once more and continued.

" 'The answer, surely, is no.' That's the bit about aspiring models being deterred."

"Yeah, got that."

"Right, well...'A hundred years after Emmeline Pankhurst, a generation of pubescent females seeks nothing better than to be reduced to the status of a cut-out paper doll, a flat avatar whose fictionalized adventures mask such disturbance and distress that she threw herself from a third-story window. Appearance is all: the designer Guy Somé was quick to inform the press that she jumped wearing one of his dresses, which sold out in the twenty-four hours after her death. What better advert could there be than that Lula Landry chose to meet her maker in Somé?

" 'No, it is not the young woman whose loss we bemoan, for she was no more real to most of us than the Gibson girls who dripped from Dana's pen. What we mourn is the physical image flickering across a multitude of red-tops and celeb mags; an image that sold us clothes and handbags and a notion of celebrity that, in her demise, proved to be empty and transient as a soap bubble. What we actually miss, were we honest enough to admit it, are the entertaining antics of that paper-thin good-time girl, whose strip-cartoon existence of drug abuse, riotous living, fancy clothes and dangerous on-off boyfriend we can no longer enjoy.

" 'Landry's funeral was covered as lavishly as any celebrity wedding in the tawdry magazines who feed on the famous, and whose publishers will surely mourn her demise longer than most. We were permitted glimpses of various celebrities in tears, but her family were given the tiniest picture of all; they were a surprisingly unphotogenic lot, you see.

" 'Yet the account of one mourner genuinely touched me. In response to the inquiry of a man who she may not have realized was a reporter, she revealed that she had met Landry at a treatment facility, and that they had become friends. She had taken her place in a rear pew to say farewell, and slipped as quietly away again. She has not sold her story, unlike so many others who consorted with Landry in life. It may tell us something touching about the real Lula Landry, that she inspired genuine affection in an ordinary girl. As for the rest of us—' "

"Doesn't she give this ordinary girl from the treatment facility a name?" interrupted Strike.

Robin scanned the story silently.

"No."

Strike scratched his imperfectly shaven chin.

"Bristow didn't mention any friend from a treatment facility."

"D'you think she could be important?" asked Robin eagerly, turning in her swivel chair to look at him.

"It could be interesting to talk to someone who knew Landry from therapy, instead of nightclubs."

Strike had only asked Robin to look up Landry's connections on the internet because he had nothing else for her to do. She had already telephoned Derrick Wilson, the security guard, and arranged a meeting with Strike on Friday morning at the Phoenix Café in Brixton. The day's post had comprised two circulars and a final demand; there had been no calls, and she had already organized everything in the office that could be alphabetized, stacked or arranged according to type and color.

Inspired by her Google proficiency of the previous day, therefore, he had set her this fairly pointless task. For the past hour or so she had been reading out odd snippets and articles about Landry and her associates, while Strike put into order a stack of receipts, telephone bills and photographs relating to his only other current case.

"Shall I see whether I can find out more about that girl, then?" asked Robin.

"Yeah," said Strike absently, examining a photograph of a stocky, balding man in a suit and a very ripe-looking redhead in tight jeans. The besuited man was Mr. Geoffrey Hook; the redhead, however, bore no resemblance to Mrs. Hook, who, prior to Bristow's arrival in his office, had been Strike's only client. Strike stuck the photograph into Mrs. Hook's file and labeled it No. 12, while Robin turned back to the computer.

For a few moments there was silence, except for the flick of photographs and the tapping of Robin's short nails against the keys. The door into the inner office behind Strike was closed to conceal the camp bed and other signs of habitation, and the air was heavy with the scent of artificial limes, due to Strike's liberal use of cheap air-freshener before Robin had arrived. Lest she perceive any tinge of sexual interest in his decision to sit at the other end of her desk, he had pretended to notice her engagement ring for the first time before sitting down, then made polite, studiously impersonal conversation about her fiancé for five minutes. He learned that he was a newly qualified accountant called Matthew; that it was to live with Matthew that Robin had moved to London from Yorkshire the previous month, and that the temping was a stopgap measure before finding a permanent job.

"D'you think she could be in one of these pictures?" Robin asked, after a while. "The girl from the treatment center?"

She had brought up a screen full of identically sized photographs, each showing one or more people dressed in dark clothes, all heading from left to right, making for the funeral. Crash barriers and the blurred faces of a crowd formed the backdrop to each picture.

Most striking of all was the picture of a very tall, pale girl with golden hair drawn back into a ponytail, on whose head was perched a confection of black net and feathers. Strike recognized her, because everyone knew who she was: Ciara Porter, the model with whom Lula had spent much of her last day on earth; the friend with whom

Landry had been photographed for one of the most famous shots of her career. Porter looked beautiful and somber as she walked towards Lula's funeral service. She seemed to have attended alone, because there was no disembodied hand supporting her thin arm or resting on her long back.

Next to Porter's picture was that of a couple captioned *Film producer Freddie Bestigui and wife Tansy.* Bestigui was built like a bull, with short legs, a broad barrel chest and a thick neck. His hair was gray and brush-cut; his face a crumpled mass of folds, bags and moles, out of which his fleshy nose protruded like a tumor. Nevertheless, he cut an imposing figure in his expensive black overcoat, with his skeletal young wife on his arm. Almost nothing could be discerned of Tansy's true appearance, behind the upturned fur of her coat collar and the enormous round sunglasses.

Last in this top row of photographs was *Guy Somé, fashion designer.* He was a thin black man who was wearing a midnight-blue frock coat of exaggerated cut. His face was bowed and his expression indiscernible, due to the way the light fell on his dark head, though three large diamond earrings in the lobe facing the camera had caught the flashes and glittered like stars. Like Porter, he appeared to have arrived unaccompanied, although a small group of mourners, unworthy of their own legends, had been captured within the frame of his picture.

Strike drew his chair nearer to the screen, though still keeping more than an arm's length between himself and Robin. One of the unidentified faces, half severed by the edge of the picture, was John Bristow, recognizable by the short upper lip and the hamsterish teeth. He had his arm around a stricken-looking older woman with white hair; her face was gaunt and ghastly, the nakedness of her grief touching. Behind this pair was a tall, haughty-looking man who gave the impression of deploring the surroundings in which he found himself.

"I can't see anyone who might be this ordinary girl," said Robin, moving the screen down to scrutinize more pictures of famous and beautiful people looking sad and serious. "Oh, look . . . Evan Duffield."

He was dressed in a black T-shirt, black jeans and a military-style black overcoat. His hair, too, was black; his face all sharp planes and hollows; icy blue eyes stared directly into the camera lens. Though taller than both of them, he looked fragile compared to the companions flanking him: a large man in a suit and an anxious-looking older woman, whose mouth was open and who was making a gesture as though to clear a path ahead of them. The threesome reminded Strike of parents steering a sick child away from a party. Strike noticed that, in spite of Duffield's air of disorientation and distress, he had made a good job of applying his eyeliner.

"Look at those flowers!"

Duffield slid up into the top of the screen and vanished: Robin had paused on the photograph of an enormous wreath in the shape of what Strike took, initially, to be a heart, before realizing it represented two curved angel wings, composed of white roses. An inset photograph showed a close-up of the attached card.

" 'Rest in peace, Angel Lula. Deeby Macc,' " Robin read aloud.

"Deeby Macc? The rapper? So they knew each other, did they?"

"No, I don't think so; but there was that whole thing about him renting a flat in her building; she'd been mentioned in a couple of his songs, hadn't she? The press were all excited about him staying there . . ."

"You're well informed on the subject."

"Oh, you know, just magazines," said Robin vaguely, scrolling back through the funeral photographs.

"What kind of name is 'Deeby'?" Strike wondered aloud.

"It comes from his initials. It's 'D. B.' really," she enunciated clearly. "His real name's Daryl Brandon Macdonald."

"A rap fan, are you?"

"No," said Robin, still intent on the screen. "I just remember things like that."

She clicked off the images she was perusing and began tapping away on the keyboard again. Strike returned to his photographs. The next showed Mr. Geoffrey Hook kissing his ginger-haired companion, hand palpating one large, canvas-covered buttock, outside Ealing Broadway Tube station.

"Here's a bit of film on YouTube, look," said Robin. "Deeby Macc talking about Lula after she died."

"Let's see it," said Strike, rolling his chair forwards a couple of feet and then, on second thought, back one.

The grainy little video, three inches by four, jerked into life. A large black man wearing some kind of hooded top with a fist picked out in studs on the chest sat in a black leather chair, facing an unseen interviewer. His hair was closely shaven and he wore sunglasses.

"...Lula Landry's suicide?" said the interviewer, who was English.

"That was fucked-up, man, that was fucked-up," replied Deeby, running his hand over his smooth head. His voice was soft, deep and hoarse, with the very faintest trace of a lisp. "That's what they do to success: they hunt you down, they tear you down. That's what envy does, my friend. The motherfuckin' press chased her out that window. Let her rest in peace, I say. She's getting peace right now."

"Pretty shocking welcome to London for you," said the interviewer, "with her, y'know, like, falling past your window?"

Deeby Macc did not answer at once. He sat very still, staring at the interviewer through his opaque lenses. Then he said:

"I wasn't there, or you got someone who says I was?"

The interviewer's yelp of nervous, hastily stifled laughter jarred.

"God, no, not at all—not..."

Deeby turned his head and addressed someone standing off-camera.

"Think I oughta've brought my lawyers?"

The interviewer brayed with sycophantic laughter. Deeby looked back at him, still unsmiling.

"Deeby Macc," said the breathless interviewer, "thank you very much for your time."

An outstretched white hand slid forwards on to the screen; Deeby raised his own in a fist. The white hand reconstituted itself, and they bumped knuckles. Somebody off-screen laughed derisively. The video ended.

" 'The motherfuckin' press chased her out that window,' " Strike repeated, rolling his chair back to its original position. "Interesting point of view."

He felt his mobile phone vibrate in his trouser pocket, and drew it out. The sight of Charlotte's name attached to a new text caused a surge of adrenaline through his body, as though he had just sighted a crouching beast of prey.

I will be out on Friday morning between 9 and 12 if you want to collect your things.

"What?" He had the impression that Robin had just spoken.

"I said, there's a horrible piece here about her birth mother."

"OK. Read it out."

He slid his mobile back into his pocket. As he bent his large head again over Mrs. Hook's file, his thoughts seemed to reverberate as though a gong had been struck inside his skull.

Charlotte was behaving with sinister reasonableness; feigning adult calm. She had taken their endlessly elaborate duel to a new level, never before reached or tested: "Now let's do it like grown-ups." Perhaps a knife would plunge between his shoulder blades as he walked through the front door of her flat; perhaps he would walk into the bedroom to discover her corpse, wrists slit, lying in a puddle of congealing blood in front of the fireplace.

Robin's voice was like the background drone of a vacuum cleaner. With an effort, he refocused his attention.

" '... sold the romantic story of her liaison with a young black man to as many tabloid journalists as were prepared to pay. There is nothing romantic, however, about Marlene Higson's story as it is remembered by her old neighbors.

" ' "She was turning tricks," says Vivian Cranfield, who lived in the flat above Higson's at the time she fell pregnant with Landry. "There were men coming in and out of her place every hour of the day and night. She never knew who that baby's father was, it could have been any of them. She never wanted the baby. I can still remember her out in the hall, crying, on her own, while her mum was busy with a punter. Tiny little thing in her nappy, hardly walking... someone must have called Social Services, and not before time. Best thing that ever happened to that girl, getting adopted."

" 'The truth will, no doubt, shock Landry, who has talked at length in the press about her reunion with her long-lost birth mother...' — this was written," explained Robin, "before Lula died."

"Yeah," said Strike, closing the folder abruptly. "D' you fancy a walk?"

2

THE CAMERAS LOOKED LIKE MALEVOLENT shoeboxes atop their pole, each with a single blank, black eye. They pointed in opposite directions, staring the length of Alderbrook Road, which bustled with pedestrians and traffic. Both pavements were crammed with shops, bars and cafés. Double-deckers rumbled up and down bus lanes.

"This is where Bristow's Runner was caught on film," observed Strike, turning his back on Alderbrook Road to look up the much quieter Bellamy Road, which led, lined with tall and palatial houses, into the residential heart of Mayfair. "He passed here twelve minutes after she fell . . . this'd be the quickest route from Kentigern Gardens. Night buses run here. Best bet to pick up a taxi. Not that that'd be a smart move if you'd just murdered a woman."

He buried himself again in an extremely battered *A–Z*. Strike did not seem worried that anyone might mistake him for a tourist. No doubt, thought Robin, it would not matter if they did, given his size.

Robin had been asked to do several things, in the course of her brief temping career, that were outside the terms of a secretarial contract, and had therefore been a little unnerved by Strike's suggestion of a walk. She was pleased, however, to acquit Strike of any flirtatious intent. The long walk to this spot had been conducted in almost total silence, Strike apparently deep in thought, and occasionally consulting his map.

Upon their arrival in Alderbrook Road, however, he had said:

"If you spot anything, or you think of anything I haven't, tell me, won't you?"

This was rather thrilling: Robin prided herself on her observational powers; they were one reason she had secretly cherished the childhood ambition that the large man beside her was living. She looked intelligently up and down the street, and tried to visualize what someone might have been up to, on a snowy night, in sub-zero temperatures, at two in the morning.

"This way," said Strike, however, before any insights could occur to her, and they walked off, side by side, along Bellamy Road. It curved gently to the left and continued for some sixty houses, which were almost identical, with their glossy black doors, their short railings either side of clean white steps and their topiary-filled tubs. Here and there were marble lions and brass plaques, giving names and professional credentials; chandeliers glinted from upper windows, and one door stood open to reveal a checkerboard floor, oil paintings in gold frames and a Georgian staircase.

As he walked, Strike pondered some of the information that Robin had managed to find on the internet that morning. As Strike had suspected, Bristow had not been honest when he asserted that the police had made no effort to trace the Runner and his sidekick. Buried in voluminous and rabid press coverage that survived online were appeals for the men to come forward, but they seemed to have yielded no results.

Unlike Bristow, Strike did not find any of this suggestive of police incompetence, or of a plausible murder suspect left uninvestigated. The sudden sounding of a car alarm around the time that the two men had fled the area suggested a good reason for their reluctance to talk to the police. Moreover, Strike did not know whether Bristow was familiar with the varying quality of CCTV footage, but he himself had extensive experience of frustrating blurry black-and-white images from which it was impossible to glean a true likeness.

Strike had also noticed that Bristow had said not a word in person, or in his notes, about the DNA evidence gathered from inside his sister's flat. He strongly suspected, from the fact that the police had been happy to exclude the Runner and his friend from further inquiries, that no trace of foreign DNA had been found there. However, Strike knew that the truly deluded would happily discount such trivialities as DNA evidence, citing contamination, or conspiracy. They saw what they wanted to see, blind to inconvenient, implacable truth.

But the Google searches of the morning had suggested a possible explanation for Bristow's fixation on the Runner. His sister had been researching her biological roots, and had managed to trace her birth mother, who sounded, even when allowance was made for press sensationalism, an unsavory character. Doubtless revelations such as those that Robin had found online would have been unpleasant not just for Landry, but for her whole adoptive family. Was it part of Bristow's instability (for Strike could not pretend to himself that his client gave the impression of a well-balanced man) that he believed Lula, so fortunate in some ways, had tempted fate? That she had stirred up trouble in trying to plumb the secrets of her origins; that she had woken a demon that had reached out of the distant past, and killed her? Was that why a black man in her vicinity so disturbed him?

Deeper and deeper into the enclave of the wealthy Strike and Robin walked, until they arrived at the corner of Kentigern Gardens. Like Bellamy Road, it projected an aura of intimidating, self-contained prosperity. The houses here were high Victorian, red brick with stone dressings and heavy pedimented windows on four floors, with their own small stone balconies. White marble porticos framed each entrance, and three white steps led from the pavement to more glossy black front doors. Everything was expensively well maintained, clean and regimented. There were only a few cars parked here; a small sign declared that permits were needed for the privilege.

No longer set apart by police tape and massing journalists, number 18 had faded back into graceful conformity with its neighbors.

"The balcony she fell from was on the top floor," said Strike, "about forty feet up, I'd say."

He contemplated the handsome frontage. The balconies on the top three floors, Robin saw, were shallow, with barely standing room between the balustrade and the long windows.

"The thing is," Strike told Robin, while he squinted at the balcony high above them, "pushing someone from that height wouldn't guarantee death."

"Oh—but surely?" protested Robin, contemplating the awful drop between top balcony and hard road.

"You'd be surprised. I spent a month in a bed next to a Welsh bloke who got blown off a building about that height. Smashed his legs and pelvis, lot of internal bleeding, but he's still with us."

Robin glanced at Strike, wondering why he had been in bed for a month; but the detective was oblivious, now scowling at the front door.

"Keypad," he muttered, noting the metal square inset with buttons, "and a camera over the door. Bristow didn't mention a camera. Could be new."

He stood for a few minutes testing theories against the intimidating red-brick face of these fantastically expensive fortresses. Why had Lula Landry chosen to live here in the first place? Sedate, traditional, stuffy, Kentigern Gardens was surely the natural domain of a different kind of rich: Russian and Arab oligarchs; corporate giants splitting their time between town and their country estates; wealthy spinsters, slowly decaying amidst their art collections. He found it a strange choice of abode for a girl of twenty-three, who ran, according to every story Robin had read out that morning, with a hip, creative crowd, whose celebrated sense of style owed more to the street than the salon.

"It looks very well protected, doesn't it?" said Robin.

"Yeah, it does. And that's without the crowd of paparazzi who were standing guard over it that night."

Strike leaned back against the black railings of number 23, staring at number 18. The windows of Landry's former residence were taller than those on the lower floors, and its balcony, unlike the other two, had not been decorated with topiary shrubs. Strike slipped a packet of cigarettes out of his pocket and offered Robin one; she shook her head, surprised, because she had not seen him smoke in the office. Having lit up and inhaled deeply, he said, with his eyes on the front door:

"Bristow thinks someone got in and out that night, undetected."

Robin, who had already decided that the building was impenetrable, thought that Strike was about to pour scorn on the theory, but she was wrong.

"If they did," said Strike, eyes still on the door, "it was planned, and planned well. Nobody could've got past photographers, a keypad, a security guard and a closed inner door, and out again, on luck alone. Thing is," he scratched his chin, "that degree of premeditation doesn't fit with such a slapdash murder."

Robin found the choice of adjective callous.

"Pushing someone over a balcony's a spur-of-the-moment thing," said Strike, as though he had felt her inner wince. "Hot blood. Blind temper."

He found Robin's company satisfactory and restful, not only because she was hanging off his every word, and had not troubled to break his silences, but because that little sapphire ring on her third finger was like a neat full stop: this far, and no further. It suited him perfectly. He was free to show off, in a very mild way, which was one of the few pleasures remaining to him.

"But what if the killer was already inside?"

"That's a lot more plausible," said Strike, and Robin felt very pleased with herself. "And if a killer was already in there, we've got the choice between the security guard himself, one or both of the Bestiguis, or some unknown person who was hiding in the building without anyone's knowledge. If it was either of the Bestiguis, or Wilson, there's no getting-in-and-out problem; all they had to do was return to the places they were supposed to be. There was still the risk she could have survived, injured, to tell the tale, but a hot-blooded, unpremeditated crime makes a lot more sense if one of them did it. A row and a blind shove."

Strike smoked his cigarette and continued to scrutinize the front of the building, in particular the gap between the windows on the first floor and those on the third. He was thinking primarily about Freddie Bestigui, the film producer. According to what Robin had found on the internet, Bestigui had been in bed asleep when Lula Landry toppled over the balcony two floors above. The fact that it was Bestigui's own wife who had sounded the alarm, and insisted that the killer was still upstairs while her husband stood beside her, implied that she, at least, did not think him guilty. Nevertheless, Freddie Bestigui had been the man in closest proximity to the dead girl at the time of her death. Laymen, in Strike's experience, were obsessed with motive: opportunity topped the professional's list.

Unwittingly confirming her civilian status, Robin said:

"But why would someone pick the middle of the night to have an argument with her? Nothing ever came out about her not getting on with her neighbors, did it? And Tansy Bestigui definitely couldn't have done it, could she? Why would she run downstairs and tell the security guard if she'd just pushed Lula over the balcony?"

Strike did not answer directly; he seemed to be following his own train of thought, and after a moment or two replied:

"Bristow's fixated on the quarter of an hour after his sister went inside, after the photographers had left and the security guard had abandoned the desk because he was ill. That meant the lobby became briefly navigable—but how was anyone outside the building supposed to know that Wilson had left his post? The front door's not made of glass."

"Plus," interjected Robin intelligently, "they'd have needed to know the key code to open the front door."

"People get slack. Unless the security people change it regularly, loads of undesirables could have known that code. Let's have a look down here."

They walked in silence right to the end of Kentigern Gardens, where they found a narrow alleyway which ran, at a slightly oblique angle, along the rear of Landry's block of houses. Strike was amused to note that the alley was called Serf's Way. Wide enough to allow a single car to pass, it had plentiful lighting and was devoid of hiding places, with long, high, smooth walls on either side of the cobbled passageway. They came in due course to a pair of large, electrically operated garage doors, with an enormous *PRIVATE* sign affixed to the wall beside them, which guarded the entrance to the underground cache of parking spaces for the Kentigern Gardeners.

When he judged that they were roughly level with the back of number 18, Strike made a leap, caught hold of the top of the wall and heaved himself up to look into a long row of small, carefully manicured gardens. Between each patch of smooth and well-tended lawn and the house to which it belonged was a shadowy stairwell to basement level. Anyone wishing to climb the rear of the house would, in

Strike's opinion, require ladders, or a partner to belay him, and some sturdy ropes.

He let himself slide back down the wall, emitting a stifled grunt of pain as he landed on the prosthetic leg.

"It's nothing," he said, when Robin made a concerned noise; she had noticed the vestige of a limp, and wondered whether he had sprained an ankle.

The chafing on the end of the stump was not helped by hobbling off over the cobbles. It was much harder, given the rigid construction of his false ankle, to navigate uneven surfaces. Strike asked himself ruefully whether he had really needed to hoist himself up on the wall at all. Robin might be a pretty girl, but she could not hold a candle to the woman he had just left.

3

"AND YOU'RE *SURE* HE'S A detective, are you? Because anyone can do that. Anyone can google people."

Matthew was irritable after a long day, a disgruntled client and an unsatisfactory encounter with his new boss. He did not appreciate what struck him as naive and misplaced admiration for another man on the part of his fiancée.

"*He* wasn't googling people," said Robin. "*I* was the one doing the googling, while he was working on another case."

"Well I don't like the sound of the set-up. He's sleeping in his office, Robin; don't you think there's something a bit fishy there?"

"I told you, I think he's just split up with his partner."

"Yeah, I'll bet he has," said Matthew.

Robin dropped his plate down on top of her own and stalked off into the kitchen. She was angry at Matthew, and vaguely annoyed with Strike, too. She had enjoyed tracking Lula Landry's acquaintance across cyberspace that day; but seeing it retrospectively through Matthew's eyes, it seemed to her that Strike had given her a pointless, time-filling job.

"Look, I'm not *saying* anything," Matthew said, from the kitchen doorway. "I just think he sounds weird. And what's with the little afternoon walks?"

"It wasn't a *little afternoon walk,* Matt. We went to see the scene of the—we went to see the place where the client thinks something happened."

"Robin, there's no need to make such a bloody mystery about it," Matthew laughed.

"I've signed a confidentiality agreement," she snapped over her shoulder. "I can't tell you about the case."

"The case."

He gave another short, scoffing laugh.

Robin strode around the tiny kitchen, putting away ingredients, slamming cupboard doors. After a while, watching her figure as she moved around, Matthew came to feel that he might have been unreasonable. He came up behind her as she was scraping the leftovers into the bin, put his arms around her, buried his face in her neck and cupped and stroked the breast that bore the bruises Strike had accidentally inflicted, and which had irrevocably colored Matthew's view of the man. He murmured conciliatory phrases into Robin's honey-colored hair; but she pulled away from him to put the plates into the sink.

Robin felt as though her own worth had been impugned. Strike had seemed interested in the things she had found online. Strike expressed gratitude for her efficiency and initiative.

"How many proper interviews have you got next week?" Matthew asked, as she turned on the cold tap.

"Three," she shouted over the noise of the gushing water, scrubbing the top plate aggressively.

She waited until he had walked away into the sitting room before turning off the tap. There was, she noticed, a fragment of frozen pea caught in the setting of her engagement ring.

4

STRIKE ARRIVED AT CHARLOTTE'S FLAT at half past nine on Friday morning. This gave her, he reasoned, half an hour to be well clear of the place before he entered it, assuming that she really was intending to leave, rather than lie in wait for him. The grand and gracious white buildings that lined the wide street; the plane trees; the butcher's shop that might have been stuck in the 1950s; the cafés bustling with the upper middle classes; the sleek restaurants; they had always felt slightly unreal and stagey to Strike. Perhaps he had always known, deep down, that he would not stay, that he did not belong.

Until the moment he unlocked the front door, he expected her to be there; yet as soon as he stepped over the threshold, he knew that the place was empty. The silence had that slack quality that speaks only of the indifference of uninhabited rooms, and his footsteps sounded alien and overloud as he made his way down the hall.

Four cardboard boxes stood in the middle of the sitting room, open for him to inspect. Here were his cheap and serviceable belongings, heaped together, like jumble-sale objects. He lifted a few things up to check the deeper levels, but nothing seemed to have been smashed, ripped or covered in paint. Other people his age had houses and washing machines, cars and television sets, furniture and gardens and mountain bikes and lawn mowers: he had four boxes of crap, and a set of matchless memories.

The silent room in which he stood spoke of a confident good taste, with its antique rug and its pale flesh-pink walls; its fine dark-wood furniture and its overflowing bookcases. The only change he spotted since Sunday night stood on the glass end table beside the sofa. On Sunday night there had been a picture of himself and Charlotte, laughing on the beach at St. Mawes. Now a black-and-white studio portrait of Charlotte's dead father smiled benignly at Strike from the same silver picture frame.

Over the mantelpiece hung a portrait of an eighteen-year-old Charlotte, in oils. It showed the face of a Florentine angel in a cloud of long dark hair. Hers was the kind of family that commissioned painters to immortalize its young: a background utterly alien to Strike, and one he had come to know like a dangerous foreign country. From Charlotte he had learned that the kind of money he had never known could coexist with unhappiness and savagery. Her family, for all their gracious manners, their suavity and flair, their erudition and occasional flamboyance, was even madder and stranger than his own. That had been a powerful link between them, when first he and Charlotte had come together.

A strange stray thought came to him now, as he looked up at that portrait: that this was the reason it had been painted, so that one day, its large hazel-green eyes would watch him leave. Had Charlotte known what it would feel like, to prowl the empty flat under the eyes of her stunning eighteen-year-old self? Had she realized that the painting would do her work better than her physical presence?

He turned away, striding through the other rooms, but she had left nothing for him to do. Every trace of him, from his tooth floss to his army boots, had been taken and deposited in the boxes. He studied the bedroom with particular attention, and the room looked back at him, with its dark floorboards, white curtains and delicate dressing table, calm and composed. The bed, like the portrait, seemed a living, breathing presence. *Remember what happened here, and what can never happen again.*

He carried the four boxes one by one out on to the doorstep, on the last trip coming face to face with the smirking next-door neighbor, who was locking his own front door. He wore rugby shirts with the collars turned up, and always brayed with panting laughter at Charlotte's lightest witticisms.

"Having a clear-out?" he asked.

Strike shut Charlotte's door firmly on him.

He slid the door keys off his key ring in front of the hall mirror, and laid them carefully on the half-moon table, next to the bowl of potpourri. Strike's face in the glass was creviced and dirty-looking; his right eye still puffy; yellow and mauve. A voice from seventeen years before came to him in the silence: "How the fuck did a pube-headed trog like you ever pull *that,* Strike?" And it seemed incredible that he ever had, as he stood there in the hall he would never see again.

One last moment of madness, the space between heartbeats, like the one that had sent him hurtling after her five days previously: he would stay here, after all, waiting for her to return; then cupping her perfect face in his hands and saying "Let's try again."

But they had already tried, again and again and again, and always, when the first crashing wave of mutual longing subsided, the ugly wreck of the past lay revealed again, its shadow lying darkly over everything they tried to rebuild.

He closed the front door behind him for the last time. The braying neighbor had vanished. Strike lifted the four boxes down the steps on to the pavement, and waited to hail a black cab.

5

STRIKE HAD TOLD ROBIN THAT he would be late into the office on her last morning. He had given her the spare key, and told her to let herself in.

She had been very slightly hurt by his casual use of the word "last." It told her that however well they had got along, albeit in a guarded and professional way; however much more organized his office was, and how much cleaner the horrible washroom outside the glass door; however much better the bell downstairs looked, without that scrappy piece of paper taped beneath it, but a neatly typed name in the clear plastic holder (it had taken her half an hour, and cost her two broken nails, to prize the cover off); however efficient she had been at taking messages, however intelligently she had discussed the almost certainly nonexistent killer of Lula Landry, Strike had been counting down the days until he could get rid of her.

That he could not afford a temporary secretary was perfectly obvious. He had only two clients; he seemed (as Matthew kept mentioning, as though sleeping in an office was a mark of terrible depravity) to be homeless; Robin saw, of course, that from Strike's point of view it made no sense to keep her on. But she was not looking forward to Monday. There would be a strange new office (Temporary Solutions had already telephoned through the address); a neat, bright, bustling place, no doubt, full of gossipy women as most of these offices were, all engaged in activities that meant less than nothing to her. Robin might not believe in a murderer; she knew that Strike did not believe either; but the process of proving one nonexistent fascinated her.

Robin had found the whole week more exciting than she would

ever have confessed to Matthew. All of it, even calling Freddie Bestigui's production company, BestFilms, twice a day, and receiving
repeated refusals to her requests to be put through to the film
producer, had given her a sense of importance she had rarely experienced during her working life. Robin was fascinated by the interior
workings of other people's minds: she had been halfway through a
psychology degree when an unforeseen incident had finished her
university career.

Half past ten, and Strike had still not returned to the office, but
a large woman wearing a nervous smile, an orange coat and a purple knitted beret *had* arrived. This was Mrs. Hook, a name familiar
to Robin because it was that of Strike's only other client. Robin
installed Mrs. Hook on the sagging sofa beside her own desk, and
fetched her a cup of tea. (Acting on Robin's awkward description of
the lascivious Mr. Crowdy downstairs, Strike had bought cheap cups
and a box of their own tea bags.)

"I know I'm early," said Mrs. Hook, for the third time, taking in-
effectual little sips of boiling tea. "I haven't seen you before, are you
new?"

"I'm temporary," said Robin.

"As I expect you've guessed, it's my husband," said Mrs. Hook,
not listening. "I suppose you see women like me all the time, don't
you? Wanting to know the worst. I dithered for ages and ages. But
it's best to know, isn't it? Best to know. I thought Cormoran would
be here. Is he out on another case?"

"That's right," said Robin, who suspected that Strike was actually
doing something related to his mysterious personal life; there had
been a caginess about him as he had told her he would be late.

"Do you know who his father is?" asked Mrs. Hook.

"No, I don't," said Robin, thinking that they were talking about
the poor woman's husband.

"Jonny Rokeby," said Mrs. Hook, with a kind of dramatic relish.

"Jonny Roke—"

Robin caught her breath, realizing simultaneously that Mrs. Hook
meant Strike, and that Strike's massive frame was looming up outside
the glass door. She could see that he was carrying something very large.

"Just one moment, Mrs. Hook," she said.

"What?" asked Strike, peering around the edge of the cardboard box, as Robin darted out of the glass door and closed it behind her.

"Mrs. Hook's here," she whispered.

"Oh, for fuck's sake. She's an hour early."

"I know. I thought you might want to, um, organize your office a bit before you take her in there."

Strike eased the cardboard box on to the metal floor.

"I've got to bring these in off the street," he said.

"I'll help," offered Robin.

"No, you go and make polite conversation. She's taking a pottery class and she thinks her husband's sleeping with his accountant."

Strike limped off down the stairs, leaving the box beside the glass door.

Jonny Rokeby; could it be true?

"He's on his way, just coming," Robin told Mrs. Hook brightly, resettling herself at her desk. "Mr. Strike told me you do pottery. I've always wanted to try..."

For five minutes, Robin barely listened to the exploits of the pottery class, and the sweetly understanding young man who taught them. Then the glass door opened and Strike entered, unencumbered by boxes and smiling politely at Mrs. Hook, who jumped up to greet him.

"Oh, Cormoran, your eye!" she said. "Has somebody punched you?"

"No," said Strike. "If you'll give me a moment, Mrs. Hook, I'll get out your file."

"I know I'm early, Cormoran, and I'm awfully sorry...I couldn't sleep at all last night..."

"Let me take your cup, Mrs. Hook," said Robin, and she successfully distracted the client from glimpsing, in the seconds it took Strike to slip through the inner door, the camp bed, the sleeping bag and the kettle.

A few minutes later, Strike re-emerged on a waft of artificial limes, and Mrs. Hook vanished, with a terrified look at Robin, into his office. The door closed behind them.

Robin sat down at her desk again. She had already opened the morning's post. She swung side to side on her swivel chair; then she moved to the computer and casually brought up Wikipedia. Then, with a disengaged air, as though she was unaware of what her fingers were up to, she typed in the two names: *Rokeby Strike.*

The entry appeared at once, headed by a black-and-white photograph of an instantly recognizable man, famous for four decades. He had a narrow Harlequin's face and wild eyes, which were easy to caricature, the left one slightly off-kilter due to a weak divergent squint; his mouth was wide open, sweat pouring down his face, hair flying as he bellowed into a microphone.

> Jonathan Leonard "Jonny" Rokeby, b. August 1st 1948, is the lead singer of 70s rock band <u>The Deadbeats,</u> member of the <u>Rock and Roll Hall of Fame,</u> multi–<u>Grammy Award</u> winner…

Strike looked nothing like him; the only slight resemblance was in the inequality of the eyes, which in Strike was, after all, a transient condition.

Down the entry Robin scrolled:

> …<u>multi-platinum</u> album <u>Hold It Back</u> in 1975. A record-breaking tour of America was interrupted by a drugs bust in LA and the arrest of new <u>guitarist David Carr,</u> with whom…

until she reached Personal Life:

> Rokeby has been married three times: to art-school girlfriend Shirley Mullens (1969–1973), with whom he has one daughter, Maimie; to model, actress and human rights activist <u>Carla Astolfi</u> (1975–1979), with whom he has two daughters, <u>television presenter Gabriella Rokeby</u> and jewelry designer <u>Daniella Rokeby,</u> and (1981–present) to film producer <u>Jenny Graham,</u> with whom he has two sons, Edward and Al. Rokeby also has a daughter, <u>Prudence Donleavy,</u> from his relationship with the actress <u>Lindsey Fanthrope,</u> and a son, Cormoran, with 1970s <u>supergroupie Leda Strike.</u>

A piercing scream rose in the inner office behind Robin. She jumped to her feet, her chair skittering away from her on its wheels. The scream became louder and shriller. Robin ran across the office to pull open the inner door.

Mrs. Hook, divested of orange coat and purple beret, and wearing what looked like a flowery pottery smock over jeans, had thrown herself on Strike's chest and was punching it, all the while making a noise like a boiling kettle. On and on the one-note scream went, until it seemed that she must draw breath or suffocate.

"Mrs. Hook!" cried Robin, and she seized the woman's flabby upper arms from behind, attempting to relieve Strike of the responsibility of fending her off. Mrs. Hook, however, was much more powerful than she looked; though she paused to breathe, she continued to punch Strike until, having no choice, he caught both her wrists and held them in midair.

At this, Mrs. Hook twisted free of his loose grip and flung herself on Robin instead, howling like a dog.

Patting the sobbing woman on the back, Robin maneuvered her, by minuscule increments, back into the outer office.

"It's all right, Mrs. Hook, it's all right," she said soothingly, lowering her into the sofa. "Let me get you a cup of tea. It's all right."

"I'm very sorry, Mrs. Hook," said Strike formally, from the doorway into his office. "It's never easy to get news like this."

"I th-thought it was Valerie," whimpered Mrs. Hook, her disheveled head in her hands, rocking backwards and forwards on the groaning sofa. "I th-thought it was Valerie, n-not my own—n-not my own *sister.*"

"I'll get tea!" whispered Robin, appalled.

She was almost out of the door with the kettle when she remembered that she had left Jonny Rokeby's life story up on the computer monitor. It would look too odd to dart back to switch it off in the middle of this crisis, so she hurried out of the room, hoping that Strike would be too busy with Mrs. Hook to notice.

It took a further forty minutes for Mrs. Hook to drink her second cup of tea and sob her way through half the toilet roll Robin had liberated from the bathroom on the landing. At last she left, clutching the folder full of incriminating photographs, and the index detailing the time and place of their creation, her breast heaving, still mopping her eyes.

Strike waited until she was clear of the end of the street, then went out, humming cheerfully, to buy sandwiches for himself and Robin, which they enjoyed together at her desk. It was the friendliest gesture that he had made during their week together, and Robin was sure that this was because he knew that he would soon be free of her.

"You know I'm going out this afternoon to interview Derrick Wilson?" he asked.

"The security guard who had diarrhea," said Robin. "Yes."

"You'll be gone when I get back, so I'll sign your time sheet before I go. And listen, thanks for..."

Strike nodded at the now empty sofa.

"Oh, no problem. Poor woman."

"Yeah. She's got the goods on him anyway. And," he continued, "thanks for everything you've done this week."

"It's my job," said Robin lightly.

"If I could afford a secretary...but I expect you'll end up pulling down a serious salary as some fat cat's PA."

Robin felt obscurely offended.

"That's not the kind of job I want," she said.

There was a slightly strained silence.

Strike was undergoing a small internal struggle. The prospect of Robin's desk being empty next week was a gloomy one; he found her company pleasantly undemanding, and her efficiency refreshing; but it would surely be pathetic, not to mention profligate, to pay for companionship, as though he were some rich, sickly Victorian magnate? Temporary Solutions were rapacious in their demand for commission; Robin was a luxury he could not afford. The fact that she had not questioned him about his father (for Strike had noticed Jonny Rokeby's Wikipedia entry on the computer monitor) had impressed him further in her favor, for this showed unusual restraint, and was a standard by which he often judged new acquaintances. But it could make no difference to the cold practicalities of the situation: she had to go.

And yet he was close to feeling about her as he had felt towards a grass snake that he had succeeded in trapping in Trevaylor Woods when he was eleven, and about which he had had a long, pleading argument with his Auntie Joan: "*Please* let me keep it . . . *please* . . ."

"I'd better get going," he said, after he had signed her time sheet, and thrown his sandwich wrappers and his empty water bottle into the bin underneath her desk. "Thanks for everything, Robin. Good luck with the job hunt."

He took down his overcoat, and left through the glass door.

At the top of the stairs, on the precise spot where he had both nearly killed and then saved her, he came to a halt. Instinct was clawing at him like an importuning dog.

The glass door banged open behind him and he turned. Robin was pink in the face.

"Look," she said. "We could come to a private arrangement. We could cut out Temporary Solutions, and you could pay me directly."

He hesitated.

"They don't like that, temping agencies. You'll be drummed out of the service."

"It doesn't matter. I've got three interviews for permanent jobs next week. If you'd be OK about me taking time off to go to them—"

"Yeah, no problem," he said, before he could stop himself.

"Well then, I could stay for another week or two."

A pause. Sense entered into a short, violent skirmish with instinct and inclination, and was overwhelmed.

"Yeah . . . all right. Well, in that case, will you try Freddie Bestigui again?"

"Yes, of course," said Robin, masking her glee under a show of calm efficiency.

"I'll see you Monday afternoon, then."

It was the first grin he had ever dared give her. He supposed he ought to be annoyed with himself, and yet Strike stepped out into the cool early afternoon with no feeling of regret, but rather a curious sense of renewed optimism.

6

STRIKE HAD ONCE TRIED TO count the number of schools he had attended in his youth, and had reached the figure of seventeen with the
suspicion that he had forgotten a couple. He did not include the brief
period of supposed home schooling which had taken place during
the two months he had lived with his mother and half-sister in a squat
in Atlantic Road in Brixton. His mother's then boyfriend, a white
Rastafarian musician who had rechristened himself Shumba, felt that
the school system reinforced patriarchal and materialistic values with
which his common-law stepchildren ought not to be tainted. The
principal lesson that Strike had learned during his two months of
home-based education was that cannabis, even if administered spiri-
tually, could render the taker both dull and paranoid.

He took an unnecessary detour through Brixton Market on the
way to the café where he was meeting Derrick Wilson. The fishy
smell of the covered arcades; the colorful open faces of the supermar-
kets, teeming with unfamiliar fruit and vegetables from Africa and
the West Indies; the halal butchers and the hairdressers, with large
pictures of ornate braids and curls, and rows and rows of white polystyrene heads bearing wigs in the windows: all of it took Strike back
twenty-six years, to the months he had spent wandering the Brixton
streets with Lucy, his young half-sister, while his mother and Shumba
lay dozily on dirty cushions back at the squat, vaguely discussing the
important spiritual concepts in which the children ought to be instructed.

Seven-year-old Lucy had yearned for hair like the West Indian
girls. On the long drive back to St. Mawes that had terminated
their Brixton life, she had expressed a fervent desire for beaded

braids from the back seat of Uncle Ted and Aunt Joan's Morris Minor. Strike remembered Aunt Joan's calm agreement that the style was very pretty, a frown line between her eyebrows reflected in the rearview mirror. Joan had tried, with diminishing success through the years, not to disparage their mother in front of the children. Strike had never discovered how Uncle Ted had found out where they were living; all he knew was that he and Lucy had let themselves into the squat one afternoon to find their mother's enormous brother standing in the middle of the room, threatening Shumba with a bloody nose. Within two days, he and Lucy were back in St. Mawes, at the primary school they attended intermittently for years, taking up with old friends as though they had not left, and swiftly losing the accents they had adopted for camouflage, wherever Leda had last taken them.

He had not needed the directions Derrick Wilson had given Robin, because he knew the Phoenix Café on Coldharbour Lane of old. Occasionally Shumba and his mother had taken them there: a tiny, brown-painted, shed-like place where you could (if not a vegetarian, like Shumba and his mother) eat large and delicious cooked breakfasts, with eggs and bacon piled high, and mugs of tea the color of teak. It was almost exactly as he remembered: cozy, snug and dingy, its mirrored walls reflecting tables of mock-wood Formica, stained floor tiles of dark red and white, and a tapioca-colored ceiling covered in molded wallpaper. The squat middle-aged waitress had short straightened hair and dangling orange plastic earrings; she moved aside to let Strike past the counter.

A heavily built West Indian man was sitting alone at one table, reading a copy of the *Sun,* under a plastic clock that bore the legend *Pukka Pies.*

"Derrick?"

"Yeah . . . you Strike?"

Strike shook Wilson's big, dry hand, and sat down. He estimated Wilson to be almost as tall as himself when standing. Muscle as well as fat swelled the sleeves of the security guard's sweatshirt; his hair was close-cropped and he was clean-shaven, with fine almond-shaped eyes. Strike ordered pie and mash off the scrawled menu board on the back wall, pleased to reflect that he could charge the £4.75 to expenses.

"Yeah, the pie 'n' mash is good here," said Wilson.

A faint Caribbean lilt lifted his London accent. His voice was deep, calm and measured. Strike thought that he would be a reassuring presence in a security guard's uniform.

"Thanks for meeting me, I appreciate it. John Bristow's not happy with the results of the inquest on his sister. He's hired me to take another look at the evidence."

"Yeah," said Wilson, "I know."

"How much did he give you to talk to me?" Strike asked casually.

Wilson blinked, then gave a slightly guilty, deep-throated chuckle.

"Pony," he said. "But if it makes the man feel better, yuh know? It won't change nuthin'. She killed huhself. But ask your questions. I don't mind."

He closed the *Sun*. The front page bore a picture of Gordon Brown looking baggy-eyed and exhausted.

"You'll have gone over everything with the police," said Strike, opening his notebook and setting it down beside his plate, "but it would be good to hear, first hand, what happened that night."

"Yeah, no problem. An' Kieran Kolovas-Jones might be comin'," Wilson added.

He seemed to expect Strike to know who this was.

"Who?" asked Strike.

"Kieran Kolovas-Jones. He was Lula's regular driver. He wants to talk to you too."

"OK, great," said Strike. "When will he be here?"

"I dunno. He's on a job. He'll come if he can."

The waitress put a mug of tea in front of Strike, who thanked her and clicked out the nib of his pen. Before he could ask anything, Wilson said:

"You're ex-milit'ry, Mister Bristow said."

"Yeah," said Strike.

"Mi nephew's in Afghanistan," said Wilson, sipping his tea. "Helmand Province."

"What regiment?"

"Signals," said Wilson.

"How long's he been out there?"

"Four month. His mother's not sleeping," said Wilson. "How come you left?"

"Got my leg blown off," said Strike, with an honesty that was not habitual.

It was only part of the truth, but the easiest part to communicate to a stranger. He could have stayed; they had been keen to keep him; but the loss of his calf and foot had merely precipitated a decision he had felt stealing towards him in the past couple of years. He knew that his personal tipping point was drawing nearer; that moment by which, unless he left, he would find it too onerous to go, to readjust to civilian life. The army shaped you, almost imperceptibly, with the years; wore you into a surface conformity that made it easier to be swept along by the tidal force of military life. Strike had never become entirely submerged, and had chosen to go before that happened. Even so, he remembered the SIB with a fondness that was unaffected by the loss of half a limb. He would have been glad to remember Charlotte with the same uncomplicated affection.

Wilson acknowledged Strike's explanation with a slow nod of the head.

"Tough," he said, in his deep voice.

"I got off light compared with some."

"Yeah. Guy in mi nephew's platoon got blown up two weeks ago."

Wilson sipped his tea.

"How did you get on with Lula Landry?" Strike asked, pen poised. "Did you see a lot of her?"

"Just in and out past the desk. She always said hullo and please and thank you, which is more'n a whole lotta these rich fuckers manage," said Wilson laconically. "Longest chat we ever had was about Jamaica. She was thinking of doing a job over there; asking me where tuh stay, what's it like. And I got her autograph for mi nephew, Jason, for his birthday. Got her to sign a card, sent it outta Afghanistan. Just three weeks before she died. She asked after Jason by name every time I saw her after that, and I liked the girl for that, y'know? I been knocking around the security game forra long time. There's people who'd expect you to take a bullet for them and they don't bother re-memb'ring yuh name. Yeah, she was all right."

Strike's pie and mash arrived, steaming hot. The two men ac-corded it a moment's respectful silence as they contemplated the heaped plate. Mouth watering, Strike picked up his knife and fork and said:

"Can you talk me through what happened the night Lula died? She went out, what time?"

The security guard scratched his forearm thoughtfully, pushing up the sleeve of his sweatshirt; Strike saw tattoos there, crosses and initials.

"Musta bin just gone seven that evening. She was with her friend Ciara Porter. I remember, as they were going out the door, Mr. Bes-tigui come in. I remember that, because he said something to Lula. I didn't hear what it was. She didn't like it, though. I could tell by the look on her face."

"What kind of look?"

"Offended," said Wilson, the answer ready. "So then I seen the two of them on the monitor, Lula and Porter, getting in their car. We gotta camera over the door, see. It's linked to a monitor on the desk, so we can see who's buzzing to get in."

"Does it record footage? Can I see a tape?"

Wilson shook his head.

"Mr. Bestigui didn't want nothing like that on the door. No recording devices. He was the first to buy a flat, before they were all finished, so he had input into the arrangements."

"The camera's just a high-tech peephole, then?"

Wilson nodded. There was a fine scar running from just beneath his left eye to the middle of his cheekbone.

"Yeah. So I seen the girls get into their car. Kieran, guy who's coming to meet us here, wasn't driving her that night. He was sup-posedta be picking up Deeby Macc."

"Who was her chauffeur that night?"

"Guy called Mick, from Execars. She'd had him before. I seen all the photographers crowdin' round the car as it pulled away. They'd been sniffin' around all week, because they knew she was back with Evan Duffield."

"What did Bestigui do, once Lula and Ciara had left?"

"He collected his post from me and went up the stairs to his flat."

Strike was putting down his fork with every mouthful, to make notes.

"Anyone go in or out after that?"

"Yeah, the caterers—they'd been up at the Bestiguis' because they were having guests that night. An American couple arrived just after eight and went up to Flat One, and nobody come in or out till they left again, near midnight. Didn't see no one else till Lula come home, round half past one.

"I heard the paps shouting her name outside. Big crowd by that time. A bunch of them had followed her from the nightclub, and there was a load waiting there already, looking out for Deeby Macc. He was supposedta be getting there round half twelve. Lula pressed the bell and I buzzed her in."

"She didn't punch the code into the keypad?"

"Not with them all around her; she wanted to get in quick. They were yelling, pressing in on her."

"Couldn't she have gone in through the underground car park and avoided them?"

"Yeah, she did that sometimes when Kieran was with her, 'cause she'd given him a control for the electric doors to the garage. But Mick didn't have one, so it had to be the front.

"I said good morning, and I asked about the snow, 'cause she had some in her hair; she was shivering, wearin' a skimpy little dress. She said it was way below freezing, something like that. Then she said, 'I wish they'd fuck off. Are they gonna stay there all night?' 'Bout the paps. I told her they were still waiting for Deeby Macc; he was late. She looked pissed off. Then she got in the lift and went up to her flat."

"She looked pissed off?"

"Yeah, really pissed off."

"Suicidal pissed off?"

"No," said Wilson. "Angry pissed off."

"Then what happened?"

"Then," said Wilson, "I had to go into the back room. My guts were starting to feel really bad. I needed the bathroom. Urgent, yuh know. I'd caught what Robson had. He was off sick with his belly. I was away maybe fifteen minutes. No choice. Never had the shits like it.

"I was still in the can when the bawling started. No," he corrected himself, "first thing I heard was a bang. Big bang in the distance. I realized later, that must've been the body—Lula, I mean—falling.

"*Then* the bawlin' started, getting louder, coming down the stairs. So I pull up my pants and go running out into the lobby, and there's Mrs. Bestigui, shaking and screaming and acting like one mad bitch in her underwear. She says Lula's dead, that she's been pushed off her balcony by a man in her flat.

"I tell her to stay where she is and I run out the front door. And there she was. Lyin' in the middle of the road, face down in the snow."

Wilson swigged his tea, and continued to cradle the mug in his large hand as he said:

"Half her head was caved in. Blood in the snow. I could tell her neck was broken. And there was—yeah."

The sweet and unmistakable smell of human brains seemed to fill Strike's nostrils. He had smelled it many times. You never forgot.

"I ran back inside," resumed Wilson. "Both the Bestiguis were in the lobby; he was tryin' to get her back upstairs, inna some clothes, and she was still bawling. I told them to call the police and to keep an eye on the lift, in case he tried to come down that way.

"I grabbed the master key out the back room and I ran upstairs. No one on the stairwell. I unlocked the door of Lula's flat—"

"Didn't you think of taking anything with you, to defend yourself?" Strike interrupted. "If you thought there was someone in there? Someone who'd just killed a woman?"

There was a long pause, the longest so far.

"Didn't think I'd need nothing," said Wilson. "Thought I could take him, no problem."

"Take who?"

"Duffield," said Wilson quietly. "I thought Duffield was up there."

"Why?"

"I thought he musta come in while I was in the bathroom. He knew the key code. I thought he musta gone upstairs and she'd let him in. I'd heard them rowing before. I'd heard him angry. Yeah. I thought he'd pushed her.

"But when I got up to the flat, it was empty. I looked in every room and there was no one there. I opened the wardrobes, even, but nothing.

"The windows in the lounge was wide open. It was below freezing that night. I didn't close them, I didn't touch nothing. I come out and pressed the button on the lift. The doors opened straight away; it was still at her floor. It was empty.

"I ran back downstairs. The Bestiguis were in their flat when I passed their door; I could hear them; she was still bawling and he was still shouting at her. I didn't know whether they'd called the police yet. I grabbed my mobile off the security desk and I went back out the front door, back to Lula, because—well, I didn't like to leave her lying there alone. I was gonna call the police from the street, make sure they were coming. But I heard the siren before I'd even pressed nine. They were there quick."

"One of the Bestiguis had called them, had they?"

"Yeah. He had. Two uniformed coppers in a panda car."

"OK," said Strike. "I want to be clear on this one point: you believed Mrs. Bestigui when she said she'd heard a man up in the top flat?"

"Oh yeah," said Wilson.

"Why?"

Wilson frowned slightly, thinking, his eyes on the street over Strike's right shoulder.

"She hadn't given you any details at this point, had she?" Strike asked. "Nothing about what she'd been doing when she heard this man? Nothing to explain why she was awake at two in the morning?"

"No," said Wilson. "She never gave me no explanation like that. It was the way she was acting, y'know. Hysterical. Shaking like a wet dog. She kept saying 'There's a man up there, he threw her over.' She was proper scared.

"But there was nobody there; I can swear that to you on the lives of mi kids. The flat was empty, the lift was empty, the stairwell was empty. If he was there, where did he go?"

"The police came," Strike said, returning mentally to the dark, snowy street, and the broken corpse. "What happened then?"

"When Mrs. Bestigui saw the police car out her window, she came straight back down in her dressing gown, with her husband running after her; she come out into the street, into the snow, and starts bawling at them that there's a murderer in the building.

"Lights are going on all over the place now. Faces at windows. Half the street's woken up. People coming out on to the pavements.

"One of the coppers stayed with the body, calling for back-up on his radio, while the other one went with us—me and the Bestiguis—back inside. He told them to go back in their flat and wait, and then he got me to show him the building. We went up to the top floor again; I opened up Lula's door, showed him the flat, the open window. He checked the place over. I showed him the lift, still on her floor. We went back down the stairs. He asked about the middle flat, so I opened it up with the master key.

"It was dark, and the alarm went off when we went in. Before I could find the light switch or get to the alarm pad, the copper walked straight into the table in the middle of the hall and knocked over this massive vase of roses. Smashed and went everywhere, glass an' water an' flowers all over the floor. That caused a loada trouble, later...

"We checked the place. Empty, all the cupboards, every room. The windows were closed and bolted. We went back to the lobby.

"Plainclothes police had arrived by this time. They wanted keys to the basement gym, the pool and the car park. One of 'em went off to take a statement from Mrs. Bestigui, another one was out front, calling for more back-up, because there are more neighbors coming out in the street now, and half of them are talking on the phone while they're standing there, and some of them are taking pictures. The uniformed coppers are trying to make them go back into their houses. It's snowing, really heavy snow...

"They got a tent up over the body when forensics arrived. The press arrived round the same time. The police taped off half the street, blocked it off with their cars."

Strike had cleaned his plate. He shoved it aside, ordered fresh mugs of tea for both of them and took up his pen again.

"How many people work at number eighteen?"

"There's three guards—me, Colin McLeod an' Ian Robson. We work in shifts, someone always on duty, round the clock. I shoulda been off that night, but Robson called me roundabout four in the afternoon, said he had this stomach bug, felt really bad with it. So I said I'd stay on, work through the next shift. He'd swapped with me the previous month so I could sort out a bit of fambly business. I owed him.

"So it shouldn'ta been me there," said Wilson, and for a moment he sat in silence, contemplating the way things should have been.

"The other guards got on OK with Lula, did they?"

"Yeah, they'd tell yuh same as me. Nice girl."

"Anyone else work there?"

"We gotta couple of Polish cleaners. They both got bad English. You won't get much outta them."

Wilson's testimony, Strike thought, as he scribbled into one of the SIB notebooks he had filched on one of his last visits to Aldershot, was of an unusually high quality: concise, precise and observant. Very few people answered the question they had been posed; even fewer knew how to organize their thoughts so that no follow-up questions were needed to prize information out of them. Strike was used to playing archaeologist among the ruins of people's traumatized memories; he had made himself the confidant of thugs; he had bullied the terrified, baited the dangerous and laid traps for the cunning. None of these skills were required with Wilson, who seemed almost wasted on a pointless trawl through John Bristow's paranoia.

Nevertheless, Strike had an incurable habit of thoroughness. It would no more have occurred to him to skimp on the interview than to spend the day lying in his underpants on his camp bed, smoking. Both by inclination and by training, because he owed himself respect quite as much as the client, he proceeded with the meticulousness for which, in the army, he had been both feted and detested.

"Can we back up briefly and go through the day preceding her death? What time did you arrive for work?"

"Nine, same as always. Took over from Colin."

"Do you keep a log of who goes in and out of the building?"

"Yeah, we sign everyone in and out, 'cept residents. There's a book at the desk."

"Can you remember who went in and out that day?"

Wilson hesitated.

"John Bristow came to see his sister early that morning, didn't he?" prompted Strike. "But she'd told you not to let him up?"

"He's told you that, has he?" asked Wilson, looking faintly relieved. "Yeah, she did. But I felt sorry for the man, y'know? He had a contrac' to give back to her; he was worried about it, so I let him go up."

"Had anyone else come into the building that you know of?"

"Yeah, Lechsinka was already there. She's one of the cleaners. She always arrives at seven; she was mopping the stairwell when I got in. Nobody else came until the guy from the security comp'ny, to service the alarms. We get it done every six months. He musta come around nine forty; something like that."

"Was this someone you knew, the man from the security firm?"

"No, he was a new guy. Very young. They always send someone diff'rent. Missus Bestigui and Lula were still at home, so I let him into the middle flat, and showed him where the control panel was an' got him started. Lula went out while I was still in there, showin' the guy the fuse box an' the panic buttons."

"You saw her go out, did you?"

"Yeah, she passed the open door."

"Did she say hello?"

"No."

"You said she usually did?"

"I don't think she noticed me. She looked like she was in a hurry. She was going to see her sick mother."

"How d'you know, if she didn't speak to you?"

"Inquest," said Wilson succinctly. "After I'd shown the security guy where everything was, I went back downstairs, an' after Missus Bestigui went out, I let him into their flat to check that system too. He didn't need me tuh stay with him there; the positions of the fuse boxes and panic buttons are the same in all the flats."

"Where was Mr. Bestigui?"

"He'd already left for work. Eight he leaves, every day."

Three men in hard hats and fluorescent yellow jackets entered the café and sat at a neighboring table, newspapers under their arms, work boots clogged with filth.

"How long would you say you were away from the desk each time you were with the security guy?"

"Mebbe five minutes in the middle flat," said Wilson. "A minute each for the others."

"When did the security guy leave?"

"Late morning. I can't remember exactly."

"But you're sure he left?"

"Oh yeah."

"Anyone else visit?"

"There was a few deliveries, but it was quiet compared to how the rest of the week had been."

"Earlier in the week had been busy, had it?"

"Yeah, we'd had a lot of coming and going, because of Deeby Macc arriving from LA. People from the production company were in and out of Flat Two, checking the place was set up for him, filling up the fridge and that."

"Can you remember what deliveries there were that day?"

"Packages for Macc an' Lula. An' roses—I helped the guy up with them, because they come in a massive," Wilson placed his large hands apart to show the size, "a huh-*uge* vase, and we set 'em up on a table in the hallway of Flat Two. That's the roses that got smashed."

"You said that caused trouble; what did you mean?"

"Mister Bestigui had sent them to Deeby Macc an' when he heard they'd been ruined he was pissed off. Shoutin' like a maniac."

"When was this?"

"While the police were there. When they were trying to interview his wife."

"A woman had just fallen to her death past his front windows, and he was upset that someone had wrecked his flowers?"

"Yeah," said Wilson, with a slight shrug. "He's like that."

"Does he know Deeby Macc?"

Wilson shrugged again.

"Did this rapper ever come to the flat?"

Wilson shook his head.

"After we had all this trouble, he went to a hotel."

"How long were you away from the desk when you helped put the roses in Flat Two?"

"Mebbe five minutes; ten at most. After that, I was on the desk all day."

"You mentioned packages for Macc and Lula."

"Yeah, from some designer, but I gave them to Lechsinka to put in the flats. It was clothes for him an' handbags for her."

"And as far as you're aware, everyone who went in that day went out again?"

"Oh yeah," said Wilson. "All logged in the book at the front desk."

"How often is the code on the external keypad changed?"

"It's been changed since she died, because half the Met knew it by the time they were finished," said Wilson. "But it din change the three months Lula lived there."

"D'you mind telling me what it was?"

"Nineteen sixty-six," said Wilson.

" 'They think it's all over'?"

"Yeah," said Wilson. "McLeod was always bellyaching about it. Wanted it changed."

"How many people d'you think knew the door code before Lula died?"

"Not that many."

"Delivery men? Postmen? Bloke who reads the gas meter?"

"People like that are always buzzed in by us, from the desk. The residents don't normally use the keypad, because we can see them on camera, so we open the door for them. The keypad's only there in case there's no one on the desk; sometimes we'd be in the back room, or helping with something upstairs."

"And the flats all have individual keys?"

"Yeah, and individual alarm systems."

"Was Lula's set?"

"No."

"What about the pool and the gym? Are they alarmed?"

"Jus' keys. Everyone who lives in the building gets a set of pool and gym keys along with their flat keys. And one key to the door leading to the underground car park. That door's got an alarm on it."

"Was it set?"

"Dunno, I wasn't there when they checked that one. It shoulda been. The guy from the security firm had checked all the alarms that morning."

"Were all these doors locked that night?"

Wilson hesitated.

"Not all of them. The door to the pool was open."

"Had anyone used it that day, do you know?"

"I can't remember anyone using it."

"So how long had it been open?"

"I dunno. Colin was on the previous night. He shoulda checked it."

"OK," said Strike. "You said you thought the man Mrs. Bestigui had heard was Duffield, because you'd heard them arguing previously. When was that?"

"Not long before they split, 'bout two months before she died. She'd thrown him out of her flat and he was hammerin' on the door and kicking it, trying to break it down, calling her filthy names. I went upstairs to get him out."

"Did you use force?"

"Didn't need to. When he saw me coming he picked up his stuff—she'd thrown his jacket and his shoes out after him—and just walked out past me. He was stoned," said Wilson. "Glassy eyes, y'know. Sweating. Filthy T-shirt with crap all down it. I never knew what the fuck she saw in him.

"And here's Kieran," he added, his tone lightening. "Lula's driver."

7

A MAN IN HIS MID-TWENTIES was edging his way into the tiny café. He was short, slight and extravagantly good-looking.

"Hey, Derrick," he said, and the driver and security guard exchanged a dap greeting, gripping each other's hands and bumping knuckles, before Kolovas-Jones took his seat beside Wilson.

A masterpiece produced by an indecipherable cocktail of races, Kolovas-Jones's skin was an olive-bronze, his cheekbones chiseled, his nose slightly aquiline, his black-lashed eyes a dark hazel, his straight hair slicked back off his face. His startling looks were thrown into relief by the conservative shirt and tie he wore, and his smile was consciously modest, as though he sought to disarm other men, and preempt their resentment.

"Where'sa car?" asked Derrick.

"Electric Lane." Kolovas-Jones pointed with his thumb over his shoulder. "I got maybe twenty minutes. Gotta be back at the West End by four. Howya doing?" he added, holding out his hand to Strike, who shook it. "Kieran Kolovas-Jones. You're . . . ?"

"Cormoran Strike. Derrick says you've got—"

"Yeah, yeah," said Kolovas-Jones. "I dunno whether it matters, probably not, but the police didn't give a shit. I just wanna know I've told someone, right? I'm not saying it wasn't suicide, you understand," he added. "I'm just saying I'd like this thing cleared up. Coffee, please, love," he added to the middle-aged waitress, who remained impassive, impervious to his charm.

"What's worrying you?" Strike asked.

"I always drove her, right?" said Kolovas-Jones, launching into his story in a way that told Strike he had rehearsed it. "She always asked for me."

"Did she have a contract with your company?"

"Yeah. Well . . ."

"It's run through the front desk," said Derrick. "One of the services provided. If anyone wants a car, we call Execars, Kieran's company."

"Yeah, but she always asked for me," Kolovas-Jones reiterated firmly.

"You got on with her, did you?"

"Yeah, we got on good," said Kolovas-Jones. "We'd got—you know—I'm not saying close—well, close, yeah, kinda. We were friendly; the relationship had gone beyond driver and client, right?"

"Yeah? How far beyond?"

"Nah, nothing like that," said Kolovas-Jones, with a grin. "Nothing like that."

But Strike saw that the driver was not at all displeased that the idea had been mooted, that it had been thought plausible.

"I'd been driving her for a year. We talked a lot, y'know. Had a lot in common. Similar backgrounds, y'know?"

"In what way?"

"Mixed race," said Kolovas-Jones. "And things were a bit dysfunctional in my family, right, so I knew where she was coming from. She didn't know that many people like her, not once she got famous. Not to talk to properly."

"Being mixed race was an issue for her, was it?"

"Growing up black in a white family, what d'you think?"

"And you had a similar childhood?"

"Me father's half West Indian, half Welsh; me mother's half Scouse, half Greek. Lula usedta say she envied me," he said, sitting up a little straighter. "She said, 'You know where you come from, even if it is bloody everywhere.' And on my birthday, right," he added, as though he had not yet sufficiently impressed upon Strike something which he felt was important, "she give me this Guy Somé jacket that was worth, like, nine hundred quid."

Evidently expected to show a reaction, Strike nodded, wondering whether Kolovas-Jones had come along simply to tell somebody how close he had been to Lula Landry. Satisfied, the driver went on:

"So, right, the day she died—day before, I should say—I drove her to her mum's in the morning, right? And she was not happy. She never liked going to see her mother."

"Why not?"

"Because that woman's fucking weird," said Kolovas-Jones. "I drove them both out for a day, once, I think it was the mother's birthday. She's fucking creepy, Lady Yvette. *Darling, my darling* to Lula, every other word. She used to hang off her. Just fucking strange and possessive and over the top, right?

"Anyway, that day, right, her mum had just got out of hospital, so that wasn't gonna be fun, was it? Lula wasn't looking forward to seeing her. She was uptight like I hadn't seen her before.

"And then I told her I couldn't drive her that night, because I was booked for Deeby Macc, and she wasn't happy about that, neither."

"Why not?"

" 'Cause she liked me driving her, didn't she?" said Kolovas-Jones, as though Strike was being obtuse. "I used to help her out with the paps and stuff, do a bit of bodyguard stuff to get her in and out of places."

By the merest flicker of his facial muscles, Wilson managed to convey what he thought of the suggestion that Kolovas-Jones was bodyguard material.

"Couldn't you have swapped with another driver, and driven her instead of Macc?"

"I coulda, but I didn't want to," Kolovas-Jones confessed. "I'm a big Deeby fan. Wanted to meet him. That's what Lula was pissed off about. Anyway," he hurried on, "I took her to her mum's, and waited, and then, this is the bit I wanted to tell you about, right?

"She come out of her mother's place and she was strange. Not like I'd ever seen her, right? Quiet, really quiet. Like she was in shock or something. Then she asked me for a pen, and she started scribbling something on a bit of blue paper. Wasn't talking to me. Wasn't saying anything. Just writing.

"So, I drove her to Vashti, 'cause she was supposedta be meeting her friend there for lunch, right—"

"What's Vashti? What friend?"

"Vashti—it's this shop—boutique, they call it. There's a café in it. Trendy place. And the friend was..." Kolovas-Jones clicked his fingers repeatedly, frowning. "She was that friend she'd made when she was in hospital for her mental problems. What was her fucking name? I used to drive the two of them around. Christ...Ruby? Roxy? Raquelle? Something like that. She was living at the St. Elmo hostel in Hammersmith. She was homeless.

"Anyway, Lula goes into the shop, right, and she'd told me on the way to her mother's she was gonna have lunch there, right, but she's only in there a quarter of an hour or something, then she comes out alone and tells me to drive her home. So that was a bit fucking strange, right? And Raquelle, or whatever her name is—it'll come back to me—wasn't with her. We usedta give Raquelle a lift home normally, when they'd been out together. And the blue piece of paper was gone. And Lula never said a word to me all the way back home."

"Did you mention this blue paper to the police?"

"Yeah. They didn't think it was worth shit," said Kolovas-Jones. "Said it was probably a shopping list."

"Can you remember what it looked like?"

"It was just blue. Like airmail paper."

He looked down at his watch.

"I gotta go in ten."

"So that was the last time you ever saw Lula?"

"Yeah, it was."

He picked at the corner of a fingernail.

"What was your first thought, when you heard she was dead?"

"I dunno," said Kolovas-Jones, chewing at the hangnail he had been picking. "I was fucking shocked. You don't expect that, do you? Not when you've just seen someone hours before. The press were all saying it was Duffield, because they'd had a row in that nightclub and stuff. I thought it might've been him, to tell you the truth. Bastard."

"You knew him, did you?"

"I drove them a coupla times," said Kolovas-Jones. A flaring of his nostrils, a tightness around the lines of his mouth, together suggested a bad smell.

"What did you think of him?"

"I thought he was a talentless tosser." With unexpected virtuosity, he suddenly adopted a flat, drawling voice: *"Are we gonna need him later, Lules? He'd better wait, yeah?"* said Kolovas-Jones, crackling with temper. "Never once spoke to me directly. Ignorant, sponging piece of shit."

Derrick said, sotto voce, "Kieran's an actor."

"Just bit parts," said Kolovas-Jones. "So far."

And he digressed into a brief exposition of the television dramas in which he had appeared, exhibiting, in Strike's estimation, a marked desire to be considered more than he felt himself to be; to become endowed, in fact, with that unpredictable, dangerous and transformative quality: fame. To have had it so often in the back of his car and not yet to have caught it from his passengers must (thought Strike) have been tantalizing and, perhaps, infuriating.

"Kieran auditioned for Freddie Bestigui," said Wilson. "Didn't you?"

"Yeah," said Kolovas-Jones, with a lack of enthusiasm that told the outcome plainly.

"How did that come about?" asked Strike.

"Usual way," said Kolovas-Jones, with a hint of hauteur. "Through my agent."

"Nothing came of it?"

"They decided to go in another direction," said Kolovas-Jones. "They wrote out the part."

"OK, so you picked up Deeby Macc from, where—Heathrow?—that night?"

"Terminal Five, yeah," said Kolovas-Jones, apparently brought back to a sense of mundane reality, and glancing at his watch. "Listen, I'd better get going."

"All right if I walk you back to the car?" asked Strike.

Wilson showed himself happy to go along too; Strike paid the bill for all three of them and they left. Out on the pavement, Strike offered both his companions cigarettes; Wilson declined, Kolovas-Jones accepted.

A silver Mercedes was parked a short distance away, around the corner in Electric Lane.

"Where did you take Deeby when he arrived?" Strike asked Kolovas-Jones, as they approached the car.

"He wanted a club, so I took him to Barrack."

"What time did you get him there?"

"I dunno...half eleven? Quarter to twelve? He was wired. Didn't want to sleep, he said."

"Why Barrack?"

"Friday night at Barrack's best hip-hop night in London," said Kolovas-Jones, on a slight laugh, as though this was common knowledge. "And he musta liked it, 'cause it was gone three by the time he came out again."

"So did you drive him to Kentigern Gardens and find the police there, or...?"

"I'd already heard on the car radio what had happened," said Kolovas-Jones. "I told Deeby when he got back to the car. His entourage all started making phone calls, waking up people at the record company, trying to make other arrangements. They got him a suite at Claridge's; I drove him there. I didn't get home till gone five. Switched on the news and watched it all on Sky. Fucking unbelievable."

"I've been wondering who let the paparazzi staking out number eighteen know that Deeby wasn't going to be there for hours. Someone tipped them off; that's why they'd left the street before Lula fell."

"Yeah? I dunno," said Kolovas-Jones.

He increased his pace very slightly, reaching the car ahead of the other two and unlocking it.

"Didn't Macc have a load of luggage with him? Was it in the car with you?"

"Nah, it'd all been sent ahead by the record company days before. He got off the plane with just a carry-on bag—and about ten security people."

"So you weren't the only car sent for him?"

"There were four cars—but Deeby himself was with me."

"Where did you wait for him, while he was in the nightclub?"

"I just parked the car and waited," said Kolovas-Jones. "Just off Glasshouse Street."

"With the other three cars? Were you all together?"

"You don't find four parking spaces side by side in the middle of London, mate," said Kolovas-Jones. "I dunno where the others were parked."

Still holding the driver's door open, he glanced at Wilson, then back at Strike.

"How's any of this matter?" he demanded.

"I'm just interested," said Strike, "in how it works, when you're with a client."

"It's fucking tedious," said Kolovas-Jones, with a sudden flash of irritation, "that's what it is. Driving's mostly waiting around."

"Have you still got the control for the doors to the underground garage that Lula gave you?" Strike asked.

"What?" said Kolovas-Jones, although Strike would have taken an oath that the driver had heard him. The flicker of animosity was undisguised now, and it seemed to extend not only to Strike, but also to Wilson, who had listened without comment since noting aloud that Kolovas-Jones was an actor.

"Have you still got—"

"Yeah, I've still got it. I still drive Mr. Bestigui, don't I?" said Kolovas-Jones. "Right, I gotta go. See ya, Derrick."

He threw his half-smoked cigarette into the road and got into the car.

"If you remember anything else," said Strike, "like the name of the friend Lula was meeting in Vashti, will you give me a call?"

He handed Kolovas-Jones a card. The driver, already pulling on his seat belt, took it without looking at it.

"I'm gonna be late."

Wilson raised his hand in farewell. Kolovas-Jones slammed the car door, revved the engine and reversed out of the parking space, scowling.

"He's a bit of a star-fucker," said Wilson, as the car pulled away. It was a kind of apology for the younger man. "He loved drivin' her. He tries to drive all the famous ones. He's been hoping Bestigui'll cast him in something for two years. He was well pissed off when he didn't get that part."

"What was it?"

"Drug dealer. Some film."

They walked off together in the direction of Brixton underground station, past a gaggle of black schoolgirls in uniforms with blue plaid skirts. One girl's long beaded hair made Strike think, again, of his sister, Lucy.

"Bestigui's still living at number eighteen, is he?" asked Strike.

"Oh yeah," said Wilson.

"What about the other two flats?"

"There's a Ukrainian commodities broker and his wife renting Flat Two now. Got a Russian interested in Three, but he hasn't made an offer yet."

"Is there any chance," asked Strike, as they were momentarily impeded by a tiny hooded, bearded man like an Old Testament prophet, who stopped in front of them and slowly stuck out his tongue, "that I could come and have a look inside sometime?"

"Yeah, all right," said Wilson after a pause in which his gaze slid furtively over Strike's lower legs. "Buzz mi. But it'll have to be when Bestigui's out, y'understand. He's one quarrelsome man, and I need my job."

8

THE KNOWLEDGE THAT HE WOULD be sharing his office again on Monday added piquancy to Strike's weekend solitude, rendering it less irksome, more valuable. The camp bed could stay out; the door between inner and outer offices could remain open; he was able to attend to bodily functions without fear of causing offense. Sick of the smell of artificial limes, he managed to force open the painted-shut window behind his desk, which allowed a cold, clean breeze to wipe the fusty corners of the two small rooms. Avoiding every CD, every track, that transported him back to those excruciating, exhilarating periods he had shared with Charlotte, he selected Tom Waits to play loudly on the small CD player he had thought he would never see again, and which he had found at the bottom of one of the boxes he had brought from Charlotte's. He busied himself setting up his portable television, with its paltry indoor aerial; he loaded his worn clothes into a black bin bag and walked to a launderette half a mile away; back at the office, he hung up his shirts and underwear on a rope he slung across one side of the inner office, then watched the three o'clock match between Arsenal and Spurs.

Through all these mundane acts, he felt as though he was accompanied by the specter that had haunted him during his months in hospital. It lurked in the corners of his shabby office; he could hear it whispering to him whenever his attention on the task in hand grew slack. It urged him to consider how far he had fallen; his age; his penury; his shattered love life; his homelessness. *Thirty-five,* it whispered, *and nothing to show for all your years of graft except a few cardboard boxes and a massive debt.* The specter directed his eyes to cans of beer in the supermarket, where he bought more Pot Noodles; it mocked him as he ironed shirts on the floor. As the day wore on, it jeered at him for his self-imposed habit of smoking outside in the street, as though he were still in the army, as though this petty self-discipline could impose form and order on the amorphous, disastrous present. He began to smoke at his desk, with the butts mounting in a cheap tin ashtray he had swiped, long ago, from a bar in Germany.

But he had a job, he kept reminding himself; a paid job. Arsenal beat Spurs, and Strike was cheered; he turned off the television and, defying the specter, moved straight to his desk and resumed work.

At liberty, now, to collect and collate evidence in whatever way he chose, Strike continued to conform to the protocols of the Criminal Procedure and Investigation Act. The fact that he believed himself to be hunting a figment of John Bristow's disturbed imagination made no difference to the thoroughness and accuracy with which he now wrote up the notes he had made during his interviews with Bristow, Wilson and Kolovas-Jones.

Lucy telephoned him at six in the evening, while he was hard at work. Though his sister was younger than Strike by two years, she seemed to feel herself older. Weighed down, young, by a mortgage, a stolid husband, three children and an onerous job, Lucy seemed to crave responsibility, as though she could never have enough anchors. Strike had always suspected that she wanted to prove to herself and the world that she was nothing like their fly-by-night mother, who had dragged the two of them all over the country, from school to school, house to squat to camp, in pursuit of the next enthusiasm or man. Lucy was the only one of his eight half-siblings with whom Strike had shared a childhood; he was fonder of her than of almost anyone else in his life, and yet their interactions were often unsatisfactory, laden with familiar anxieties and arguments. Lucy could not disguise the fact that her brother worried and disappointed her. In consequence, Strike was less inclined to be honest with her about his present situation than he would have been with many a friend.

"Yeah, it's going great," he told her, smoking at the open window, watching people drift in and out of the shops below. "Business has doubled lately."

"Where are you? I can hear traffic."

"At the office. I've got paperwork to do."

"On Saturday? How does Charlotte feel about that?"

"She's away; she's gone to visit her mother."

"How are things going between you?"

"Great," he said.

"Are you sure?"

"Yeah, I'm sure. How's Greg?"

She gave him a brief precis of her husband's workload, then returned to the attack.

"Is Gillespie still on your back for repayment?"

"No."

"Because you know what, Stick"—the childhood nickname boded ill: she was trying to soften him up—"I've been looking into this, and you could apply to the British Legion for—"

"Fucking hell, Lucy," he said, before he could stop himself.

"What?"

The hurt and indignation in her voice were only too familiar: he closed his eyes.

"I don't need help from the British Legion, Luce, all right?"

"There's no need to be so *proud* . . ."

"How are the boys?"

"They're fine. Look, Stick, I just think it's outrageous that Rokeby's getting his lawyer to hassle you, when he's never given you a penny in his life. He ought to have made it a gift, seeing what you've been through and how much he's—"

"Business is good. I'm going to pay off the loan," said Strike. A teenaged couple on the corner of the street were having an argument.

"Are you *sure* everything's all right between you and Charlotte? Why's she visiting her mother? I thought they hated each other?"

"They're getting on better these days," he said, as the teenage girl gesticulated wildly, stamped her foot and walked away.

"Have you bought her a ring yet?" asked Lucy.

"I thought you wanted me to get Gillespie off my back?"

"Is she all right about not having a ring?"

"She's been great about it," said Strike. "She says she doesn't want one; she wants me to put all my money into the business."

"Really?" said Lucy. She always seemed to think that she made a good job of dissimulating her deep dislike of Charlotte. "Are you going to come to Jack's birthday party?"

"When is it?"

"I sent you an invitation over a week ago, Stick!"

He wondered whether Charlotte had slipped it into one of the boxes he had left unpacked on the landing, not having room for all his possessions in the office.

"Yeah, I'll be there," he said; there was little he wanted to do less.

The call terminated, he returned to his computer and continued work. His notes from the Wilson and Kolovas-Jones interviews were soon completed, but a sense of frustration persisted. This was the first case that he had taken since leaving the army that required more than surveillance work, and it might have been designed to remind him daily that he had been stripped of all power and authority. Film producer Freddie Bestigui, the man who had been in closest proximity to Lula Landry at the time of her death, remained unreachable behind his faceless minions, and, in spite of John Bristow's confident assertion that he would be able to persuade her to talk to Strike, there was not yet a secured interview with Tansy Bestigui.

With a faint sense of impotence, and with almost as much contempt for the occupation as Robin's fiancé felt for it, Strike fought off his lowering sense of gloom by resorting to more internet searches connected with the case. He found Kieran Kolovas-Jones online: the driver had been telling the truth about the episode of *The Bill* in which he had had two lines (Gang Member Two . . . Kieran Kolovas-Jones). He had a theatrical agent, too, whose website featured a small photograph of Kieran, and a short list of credits including walk-on parts in *East Enders* and *Casualty*. Kieran's photograph on the Execars home page was much larger. Here, he stood alone in a peaked hat and uniform, looking like a film star, evidently the handsomest driver on their books.

Evening shaded into night beyond the windows; while Tom Waits growled and moaned from the portable CD player in the corner,

Strike chased the shadow of Lula Landry across cyberspace, occa-sionally adding to the notes he had already taken while speaking to Bristow, Wilson and Kolovas-Jones.

He could find no Facebook page for Landry, nor did she ever seem to have joined Twitter. Her refusal to feed her fans' ravenous appetite for personal information seemed to have inspired others to fill the void. There were countless websites dedicated to the repro-duction of her pictures, and to obsessive commentary on her life. If half of the information here was factual, Bristow had given Strike but a partial and sanitized version of his sister's drive towards self-destruction, a tendency which seemed to have revealed itself first in early adolescence, when her adoptive father, Sir Alec Bristow, a genial-looking bearded man who had founded his own electron-ics company, Albris, had dropped dead of a heart attack. Lula had subsequently run away from two schools, and been expelled from a third, all of them expensive private establishments. She had slit her own wrist and been found in a pool of blood by a dormitory friend; she had lived rough, and been tracked to a squat by the police. A fan site called LulaMyInspirationForeva.com, run by a person of un-known sex, asserted that the model had briefly supported herself, during this time, as a prostitute.

Then had come sectioning under the Mental Health Act, the se-cure ward for young people with severe illnesses, and a diagnosis of bipolar disorder. Barely a year later, while shopping in a clothing store on Oxford Street with her mother, there had come the fairy-tale approach from a scout for a modeling agency.

Landry's early photographs showed a sixteen-year-old with the face of Nefertiti, who managed to project to the lens an extraor-dinary combination of worldliness and vulnerability, with long thin legs like a giraffe's and a jagged scar running down the inside of her left arm that fashion editors seemed to have found an interesting adjunct to her spectacular face, for it was sometimes given promi-nence in photographs. Lula's extreme beauty was on the very edge of absurdity, and the charm for which she was celebrated (in both news-paper obituaries and hysterical blogs) sat alongside a reputation for sudden outbursts of temper and a dangerously short fuse. Press and public seemed to have both loved her, and loved loathing her. One female journalist found her "strangely sweet, possessed of an unexpected naiveté"; another, "at bottom, a calculating little diva, shrewd and tough."

At nine o'clock Strike walked to Chinatown and bought himself a meal; then he returned to the office, swapped Tom Waits for Elbow, and searched out online accounts of Evan Duffield, the man who, by common consent, even that of Bristow, had not killed his girlfriend.

Until Kieran Kolovas-Jones had displayed professional jealousy, Strike could not have said why Duffield was famous. He now discovered that Duffield had been elevated from obscurity by his participation in a critically acclaimed independent film, in which he had played a character indistinguishable from himself: a heroin-addicted musician stealing to support his habit.

Duffield's band had released a well-reviewed album on the back of their lead singer's newfound fame, and split up in considerable acrimony around the time that he had met Lula. Like his girlfriend, Duffield was extraordinarily photogenic, even in the unretouched long-lens photographs of him sloping along a street in filthy clothes, even in those shots (and there were several) where he was lunging in fury at photographers. The conjunction of these two damaged and beautiful people seemed to have supercharged the fascination with both; each reflecting more interest on to the other, which rebounded on themselves; it was a kind of perpetual motion.

The death of his girlfriend had fixed Duffield more securely than ever in that firmament of the idolized, the vilified, the deified. A certain darkness, a fatalism, hung around him; both his most fervent admirers and his detractors seemed to take pleasure in the idea that he had one booted foot in the afterworld already; that there was an inevitability about his descent into despair and oblivion. He seemed to make a veritable parade of his frailties, and Strike lingered for some minutes over another of those tiny, jerky YouTube videos, in which Duffield, patently stoned, talked on and on, in the voice Kolovas-Jones had so accurately parodied, about dying being no more than checking out of the party, and making a confused case for there being little need to cry if you had to leave early.

On the night that Lula had died, according to a multitude of sources, Duffield had left the nightclub shortly after his girlfriend, wearing—and Strike found it hard to see this as anything other than deliberate showmanship—a wolf's mask. His account of what he had got up to for the rest of the night might not have satisfied online conspiracy theorists, but the police seemed to have been convinced that he had had nothing to do with subsequent events at Kentigern Gardens.

Strike followed the speculative train of his own thoughts over the rough terrain of news sites and blogs. Here and there he stumbled upon pockets of feverish speculation, of theories about Landry's death that mentioned clues the police had failed to follow up, and which seemed to have fed Bristow's own conviction that there had been a murderer. LulaMyInspirationForeva had a long list of Unanswered Questions, which included, at number five, *"Who called off the paps before she fell?"*; at number nine, *"Why did the men with the covered faces runnin away from her flat at 2 a.m. never come forward? Where are they and who wer they?"*; and at number thirteen, *"Why was luLa wearing a different outfit to the one she came home in when she fell off the balcony?"*

Midnight found Strike drinking a can of lager and reading about the posthumous controversy that Bristow had mentioned, of which he had been vaguely aware while it unfolded, without being very interested. A furor had sprung up, a week after the inquest had returned a verdict of suicide, around the advertising shot for the wares of designer Guy Somé. It featured two models posing in a dirty alleyway, naked except for strategically placed handbags, scarves and jewels. Landry was perched on a dustbin, Ciara Porter sprawled on the ground. Both wore huge curving angel's wings: Porter's a swan-like white; Landry's a greenish black fading to glossy bronze.

Strike stared at the picture for minutes, trying to analyze precisely why the dead girl's face drew the eye so irresistibly, how she managed to dominate the picture. Somehow she made the incongruity, the staginess of it, believable; she really did look as though she had been slung from heaven because she was too venal, because she so coveted the accessories she was clutching to herself. Ciara Porter, in all her alabaster beauty, became nothing but a counterpoint; in her pallor and her passivity, she looked like a statue.

The designer, Guy Somé, had drawn much criticism upon himself, some of it vicious, for choosing to use the picture. Many people felt that he was capitalizing on Landry's recent death, and sneered at the professions of deep affection for Landry that Somé's spokesman made on his behalf. LulaMyInspirationForeva, however, asserted that Lula would have wanted the picture to be used; that she and Guy Somé had been bosom friends: *Lula loved guy like a brother and would want him to pay this final tribute to her work and her beauty. This is an iconic shot that will live forever and will continue to keep Lula alive in the memories of we who loved her.*

Strike drank the last of his lager and contemplated the final four words of this sentence. He had never been able to understand the assumption of intimacy fans felt with those they had never met. People had sometimes referred to his father as "Old Jonny" in his presence, beaming, as if they were talking about a mutual friend, repeating well-worn press stories and anecdotes as though they had been personally involved. A man in a pub in Trescothick had once said to Strike: "Fuck, I know your old man better than you do!" because he was able to name the session musician who had played on the Deadbeats' biggest album, and whose tooth Rokeby had famously broken when he slapped the end of his saxophone in anger.

It was one in the morning. Strike had become almost deaf to the constant muffled thuds of the bass guitar from two floors below, and to the occasional creaks and hisses from the attic flat above, where the bar manager enjoyed luxuries like showers and home-cooked food. Tired, but not yet ready to climb into his sleeping bag, he managed to discover Guy Somé's approximate address by further perusal of the internet, and noted the close proximity of Charles Street to Kentigern Gardens. Then he typed in the web address www.arrse.co.uk, like a man turning automatically into his local after a long shift at work.

He had not visited the Army Rumor Service site since Charlotte had found him, months previously, browsing it on his computer, and had reacted the way other women might had they found their partners viewing online porn. There had been a row, generated by what she took to be his hankering for his old life and his dissatisfaction with the new.

Here was the army mindset in its every particular, written in the language he too could speak fluently. Here were the acronyms he had known by heart; the jokes impenetrable to outsiders; every concern of service life, from the father whose son was being bullied at his school in Cyprus, to retrospective abuse of the Prime Minister's performance at the Chilcot Inquiry. Strike wandered from post to post, occasionally snorting in amusement, yet aware all the time that he was lowering his resistance to the specter he could feel, now, breathing on the back of his neck.

This had been his world and he had been happy there. For all the inconveniences and hardships of military life, for all that he had emerged from the army minus half his leg, he did not regret a day of the time he had spent serving. And yet, he had not been of these people, even while among them. He had been a monkey, and then a suit, feared and disliked about equally by the average squaddie.

If ever the SIB talk to you, you should say "No comment, I want a lawyer." Alternatively, a simple "Thank you for noticing me" will suffice.

Strike gave a final grunt of laughter, and then, abruptly, shut down the site and turned off the computer. He was so tired that the removal of his prosthesis took twice the time it usually did.

9

ON SUNDAY MORNING, WHICH WAS fine, Strike headed back to the ULU to shower. Once again, by consciously filling out his own bulk and allowing his features to slide, as they did naturally, into a scowl, he made himself sufficiently intimidating to repel challenges as he marched, eyes down, past the desk. He hung around the changing rooms, waiting for a quiet moment so that he would not have to shower in full view of any of the changing students, for the sight of his false leg was a distinguishing feature he did not want to impress on anybody's memory.

Clean and shaven, he caught the Tube to Hammersmith Broadway, enjoying the tentative sunshine gleaming through the glass-covered shopping precinct through which he emerged on to the street. The distant shops on King Street were heaving with people; it might have been a Saturday. This was a bustling and essentially soulless commercial center, and yet Strike knew it to be a bare ten minutes' walk to a sleepy, countrified stretch of the Thames embankment.

While he walked, traffic rumbling past him, he remembered Sundays in Cornwall in his childhood, when everything closed down except the church and the beach. Sunday had had a particular flavor in those days; an echoing, whispering quiet, the gentle chink of china and the smell of gravy, the TV as dull as the empty high street, and the relentless rush of the waves on the beach when he and Lucy had run down on to the shingle, forced back on to primitive resources.

His mother had once said to him: "If Joan's right, and I end up in hell, it'll be eternal Sunday in bloody St. Mawes."

Strike, who was heading away from the commercial center towards the Thames, phoned his client as he walked.

"John Bristow?"

"Yeah, sorry to disturb you at the weekend, John..."

"Cormoran?" said Bristow, immediately friendly. "Not a problem, not a problem at all! How did it go with Wilson?"

"Very good, very useful, thanks. I wanted to know whether you can help me find a friend of Lula's. It's a girl she met in therapy. Her Christian name begins with an R—something like Rachel or Raquelle—and she was living at the St. Elmo hostel in Hammersmith when Lula died. Does that ring any bells?"

There was a moment's silence. When Bristow spoke again, the disappointment in his voice verged on annoyance.

"What do you want to speak to *her* for? Tansy's quite clear that the voice she heard from upstairs was male."

"I'm not interested in this girl as a suspect, but as a witness. Lula had an appointment to meet her at a shop, Vashti, right after she saw you at your mother's flat."

"Yeah, I know; that came out at the inquest. I mean—well, of course, you know your job, but—I don't really see how she would know anything about what happened that night. Listen—wait a moment, Cormoran...I'm at my mother's and there are other people here...need to find a quieter spot..."

Strike heard the sounds of movement, a murmured "Excuse me," and Bristow came back on the line.

"Sorry, I didn't want to say all this in front of the nurse. Actually, I thought, when you rang, you might be someone else calling up to talk to me about Duffield. Everybody I know has rung to tell me."

"Tell you what?"

"You obviously don't read the *News of the World*. It's all there, complete with pictures: Duffield turned up to visit my mother yesterday, out of the blue. Photographers outside the house; it caused a lot of inconvenience and upset with the neighbors. I was out with Alison, or I'd never have let him in."

"What did he want?"

"Good question. Tony, my uncle, thinks it was money—but Tony usually thinks people are after money; anyway, I've got power of attorney, so there was nothing doing there. God knows why he came.

The one small mercy is that Mum doesn't seem to have realized who he is. She's on immensely strong painkillers."

"How did the press find out he was coming?"

"That," said Bristow, "is an excellent question. Tony thinks he phoned them himself."

"How is your mother?"

"Poorly, very poorly. They say she could hang on for weeks, or— or it could happen at any moment."

"I'm sorry to hear that," said Strike. He raised his voice as he passed underneath a flyover, across which traffic was moving noisily. "Well, if you do happen to remember the name of Lula's Vashti friend..."

"I'm afraid I still don't really understand why you're so interested in her."

"Lula made this girl travel all the way from Hammersmith to Notting Hill, spent fifteen minutes with her and then walked out. Why didn't she stay? Why meet for such a short space of time? Did they argue? Anything out of the ordinary that happens around a sudden death could be relevant."

"I see," said Bristow hesitantly. "But...well, that sort of behavior wasn't really out of the ordinary for Lula. I did tell you that she could be a bit...a bit selfish. It would be like her to think that a token appearance would keep the girl happy. She often had these brief enthusiasms for people, you know, and then dropped them."

His disappointment at Strike's chosen line of inquiry was so evident that the detective felt it might be politic to slip in a little covert justification of the immense fee his client was paying.

"The other reason I was calling was to let you know that tomorrow evening I'm meeting one of the CID officers who covered the case. Eric Wardle. I'm hoping to get hold of the police file."

"Fantastic!" Bristow sounded impressed. "That's quick work!"

"Yeah, well, I've got good contacts in the Met."

"Then you'll be able to get some answers about the Runner! You've read my notes?"

"Yeah, very useful," said Strike.

"And I'm trying to fix up a lunch with Tansy Bestigui this week, so you can meet her and hear her testimony first hand. I'll ring your secretary, shall I?"

"Great."

There was this to be said for having an underworked secretary he could not afford, Strike thought, once he had rung off: it gave a professional impression.

St. Elmo's Hostel for the Homeless turned out to be situated right behind the noisy concrete flyover. A plain, ill-proportioned and contemporaneous cousin of Lula's Mayfair house, red brick with humbler, grubby white facings; no stone steps, no garden, no elegant neighbors, but a chipped door opening directly on to the street, peeling paint on the window ledges and a forlorn air. The utilitarian modern world had encroached until it sat huddled and miserable, out of synch with its surroundings, the flyover a mere twenty yards away, so that the upper windows looked directly out upon the concrete barriers and the endlessly passing cars. An unmistakably institutional flavor was given by the large silver buzzer and speaker beside the door, and the unapologetically ugly black camera, with its dangling wires, that hung from the lintel in a wire cage.

An emaciated young girl with a sore at the corner of her mouth stood smoking outside the front door, wearing a dirty man's jumper that swamped her. She was leaning up against the wall, staring blankly towards the commercial center barely five minutes' walk away, and when Strike pressed the buzzer for admission to the hostel, she gave him a look of deep calculation, apparently assessing his potentialities.

A small, fusty, grimy-floored lobby with shabby wooden paneling lay just inside the door. Two locked glass-paneled doors stood to left and right, affording him glimpses of a bare hall and a depressed-looking side room with a table full of leaflets, an old dartboard and a wall liberally peppered with holes. Straight ahead was a kiosk-like front desk, protected by another metal grille.

A gum-chewing woman behind the desk was reading a newspaper. She seemed suspicious and ill-disposed when Strike asked whether he could speak to a girl whose name was something like Rachel, and who had been a friend of Lula Landry's.

"You a journalist?"

"No, I'm not; I'm a friend of a friend."

"Should know her name, then, shouldn't you?"

"Rachel? Raquelle? Something like that."

A balding man strode into the kiosk behind the suspicious woman.

"I'm a private detective," said Strike, raising his voice, and the bald man looked around, interested. "Here's my card. I've been hired by Lula Landry's brother, and I need to talk to—"

"Oh, you looking for Rochelle?" asked the bald man, approaching the grille. "She's not here, pal. She left."

His colleague, evincing some irritation at his willingness to talk to Strike, ceded her place at the counter and vanished from sight.

"When was this?"

"It'd be weeks now. Coupla months, even."

"Any idea where she went?"

"No idea, mate. Probably sleeping rough again. She's come and gone a good few times. She's a difficult character. Mental health problems. Carrianne might know something though, hang on. Carrianne! Hey! Carrianne!"

The bloodless young girl with the scabbed lip came in out of the sunshine, her eyes narrowed.

"Wha'?"

"Rochelle, have you seen her?"

"Why would I wanna see that fuckin' bitch?"

"So you haven't seen her?" asked the bald man.

"No. Gorra fag?"

Strike gave her one; she put it behind her ear.

"She's still round 'ere somewhere. Janine said she seen 'er," said Carrianne. "Rochelle reckoned she'd gorra flat or some't. Lying fuckin' bitch. An' Lula Landry left her ev'rything. *Not*. Whadd'ya want Rochelle for?" she asked Strike, and it was clear that she was wondering whether there was money in it, and whether she might do instead.

"Just to ask some questions."

"Warrabout?"

"Lula Landry."

"Oh," said Carrianne, and her card-counting eyes flickered. "They weren't such big fuckin' mates. You don't wanna believe everything Rochelle says, the lying bitch."

"What did she lie about?" asked Strike.

"Fuckin' everything. I reckon she stole half the stuff she pretended Landry bought 'er."

"Come on, Carrianne," said the bald man gently. "They *were* friends," he told Strike. "Landry used to come and pick her up in her car. It caused," he said, with a glance at Carrianne, "a bit of tension."

"Not from me it fuckin' didn't," snapped Carrianne. "I thought Landry was a fuckin' jumped-up bitch. She weren't even that good-lookin'."

"Rochelle told me she's got an aunt in Kilburn," said the bald man.

"She dun gerron with 'er, though," said the girl.

"Have you got a name or an address for the aunt?" asked Strike, but both shook their heads. "What's Rochelle's surname?"

"I don't know; do you, Carrianne? We often know people just by their Christian names," he told Strike.

There was little more to be gleaned from them. Rochelle had last stayed at the hostel more than two months previously. The bald man knew that she had attended an outpatients' clinic at St. Thomas's for a while, though he had no idea whether she still went.

"She's had psychotic episodes. She's on a lot of medication."

"She didn't give a shit when Lula died," said Carrianne, suddenly. "She didn't give a flying fuck."

Both men looked at her. She shrugged, as one who has simply expressed an unpalatable truth.

"Listen, if Rochelle turns up again, will you give her my details and ask her to call me?"

Strike gave both of them cards, which they examined with interest. While their attention was thus engaged, he deftly twitched the gum-chewing woman's *News of the World* out of the small opening at the bottom of the grille and stowed it under his arm. He then bade them both a cheerful goodbye, and left.

It was a warm spring afternoon. Strike strode on down towards Hammersmith Bridge, its pale sage-green paint and ornate gilding picturesque in the sun. A single swan bobbed along the Thames beside the far bank. The offices and shops seemed a hundred miles away. Turning right, he headed along the walkway beside the river wall and a line of low, riverside terraced buildings, some balconied or draped in wisteria.

Strike bought himself a pint in the Blue Anchor, and sat outside on a wooden bench with his face to the water and his back to the royal-blue and white frontage. Lighting a cigarette, he turned to page four of the paper, where a color photograph of Evan Duffield (head bowed, large bunch of white flowers in his hand, black coat flapping behind him) was surmounted by the headline: DUFFIELD'S DEATHBED VISIT TO LULA MOTHER.

The story was anodyne, really nothing more than an extended caption to the picture. The eyeliner and the flapping greatcoat, the slightly haunted, spaced-out expression, recalled Duffield's appearance as he had headed towards his late girlfriend's funeral. He was described, in the few lines of type below, as "troubled actor-musician Evan Duffield."

Strike's mobile vibrated in his pocket and he pulled it out. He had received a text message from an unfamiliar number.

News of the World page four Evan Duffield. Robin.

He grinned at the small screen before slipping the phone back in his pocket. The sun was warm on his head and shoulders. Seagulls cawed, wheeling overhead, and Strike, happily aware that he was due nowhere, and expected by no one, settled to read the paper from cover to cover on the sunny bench.

10

Robin stood swaying with the rest of the tightly packed commuters on a northbound Bakerloo Tube train, everyone wearing the tense and doleful expressions appropriate to a Monday morning. She felt the phone in her coat pocket buzz, and extricated it with difficulty, her elbow pressing unpleasantly into some unspecified flabby portion of a suited, bad-breathed man beside her. When she saw that the message was from Strike, she felt momentarily excited, nearly as excited as she had been to see Duffield in the paper yesterday. Then she scrolled down, and read:

Out. Key behind cistern of toilet. Strike.

She did not force the phone back into her pocket, but continued to clutch it as the train rattled on through dark tunnels, and she tried not to breathe in the flabby man's halitosis. She was disgruntled. The previous day, she and Matthew had eaten lunch, in company with two university friends of Matthew's, at his favorite gastropub, the Windmill on the Common. When Robin had spotted the picture of Evan Duffield in an open copy of the *News of the World* at a nearby table, she had made a breathless excuse, right in the middle of one of Matthew's stories, and hurried outside to text Strike.

Matthew had said, later, that she had shown bad manners, and even worse not to explain what she was up to, in favor of maintaining that ludicrous air of mystery.

Robin gripped the hand strap tightly, and as the train slowed, and her heavy neighbor leaned into her, she felt both a little foolish, and resentful towards the two men, most particularly the detective, who was evidently uninterested in the unusual movements of Lula Landry's ex-boyfriend.

By the time she had marched through the usual chaos and debris to Denmark Street, extracted the key from behind the cistern as instructed, and been snubbed yet again by a superior-sounding girl in Freddie Bestigui's office, Robin was in a thoroughly bad temper.

Though he did not know it, Strike was, at that very moment, passing the scene of the most romantic moments of Robin's life. The steps below the statue of Eros were swarming with Italian teenagers this morning, as Strike went by on the St. James's side, heading for Glasshouse Street.

The entrance to Barrack, the nightclub which had so pleased Deeby Macc that he had remained there for hours, fresh off the plane from Los Angeles, was only a short walk from Piccadilly Circus. The facade looked as if it was made out of industrial concrete, and the name was picked out in shining black letters, vertically placed. The club extended up over four floors. As Strike had expected, its doorway was surmounted by CCTV cameras, whose range, he thought, would cover most of the street. He walked around the building, noting the fire exits, and making for himself a rough sketch of the area.

After a second long internet session the previous evening, Strike felt that he had a thorough grasp of the subject of Deeby Macc's publicly declared interest in Lula Landry. The rapper had mentioned the model in the lyrics of three tracks, on two separate albums; he had also spoken about her in interviews as his ideal woman and soul mate. It was difficult to gauge how seriously Macc intended to be taken when he made these comments; allowance had to be made, in all the print interviews Strike had read, firstly for the rapper's sense of humor, which was both dry and sly, and secondly for the awe tinged with fear every interviewer seemed to feel when confronted with him.

An ex–gang member who had been imprisoned for gun and drug offenses in his native Los Angeles, Macc was now a multimillionaire, with a number of lucrative businesses aside from his recording career. There was no doubt that the press had become "excited," to use Robin's word, when news had leaked out that Macc's record company had rented him the apartment below Lula's. There had been much rabid speculation as to what might happen when Deeby Macc found himself a floor away from his supposed dream woman, and how this incendiary new element might affect the volatile relationship between Landry and Duffield. These non-stories had all been peppered with undoubtedly spurious comments from friends of both—"He's already called her and asked her to dinner," "She's preparing a small party for him in her flat when he hits London." Such speculation had almost eclipsed the flurry of outraged comment from sundry columnists that the twice-convicted Macc, whose music (they said) glorified his criminal past, was entering the country at all.

When he had decided that the streets surrounding Barrack had no more to tell him, Strike continued on foot, making notes of yellow lines in the vicinity, of Friday-night parking restrictions and of those establishments nearby that also had their own security cameras. His notes complete, he felt that he had earned a cup of tea and a bacon roll on expenses, both of which he enjoyed in a small café, while reading an abandoned copy of the *Daily Mail*.

His mobile rang as he was starting his second cup of tea, halfway through a gleeful account of the Prime Minister's gaffe in calling an elderly female voter "bigoted" without realizing that his microphone was still turned on.

A week ago, Strike had allowed his unwanted temp's calls to go to voicemail. Today, he picked up.

"Hi, Robin, how're you?"

"Fine. I'm just calling to give you your messages."

"Fire away," said Strike, as he drew out a pen.

"Alison Cresswell's just called—John Bristow's secretary—to say she's booked a table at Cipriani at one o'clock tomorrow, so that he can introduce you to Tansy Bestigui."

"Great."

"I've tried Freddie Bestigui's production company again. They're getting irritated. They say he's in LA. I've left another request for him to call you."

"Good."

"And Peter Gillespie's telephoned again."

"Uh huh," said Strike.

"He says it's urgent, and could you please get back to him as soon as possible."

Strike considered asking her to call Gillespie back and tell him to go and fuck himself.

"Yeah, will do. Listen, could you text me the address of the night-club Uzi?"

"Right."

"And try and find a number for a bloke called Guy Somé? He's a designer."

"It's pronounced 'ghee,' " said Robin.

"What?"

"His Christian name. It's pronounced the French way: 'Ghee.' "

"Oh, right. Well, could you try and find a contact number for him?"

"Fine," said Robin.

"Ask him if he'd be prepared to talk to me. Leave a message saying who I am, and who's hired me."

"Fine."

It was borne in on Strike that Robin's tone was frosty. After a second or two, he thought he might know why.

"By the way, thanks for that text you sent yesterday," he said. "Sorry I didn't get back to you; it would have looked strange if I'd started texting, where I was. But if you could call Nigel Clements, Duffield's agent, and ask for an appointment, that would be great too."

Her animosity fell away at once, as he had meant it to; her voice was many degrees warmer when she spoke again; verging, in fact, on excited.

"But Duffield can't have had anything to do with it, can he? He had a cast-iron alibi!"

"Yeah, well, we'll see about that," said Strike, deliberately ominous. "And listen, Robin, if another death threat comes in—they usually arrive on Mondays..."

"Yes?" she said eagerly.

"File it," said Strike.

He could not be sure—it seemed unlikely; she struck him as so prim—but he thought he heard her mutter, "Sod you, then," as she hung up.

Strike spent the rest of the day engaged in tedious but necessary spadework. When Robin had texted him the address, he visited his second nightclub of the day, this time in South Kensington. The contrast with Barrack was extreme; Uzi's discreet entrance might have been to a smart private house. There were security cameras over its doors, too. Strike then took a bus to Charles Street, where he was fairly sure Guy Somé lived, and walked what he guessed to be the most direct route between the designer's address and the house where Landry had died.

His leg was aching badly again by late afternoon, and he stopped for a rest and more sandwiches before setting out for the Feathers, near Scotland Yard, and his appointment with Eric Wardle.

It was another Victorian pub, this time with enormous windows reaching almost from floor to ceiling, looking out on to a great gray 1920s building decorated with statues by Jacob Epstein. The nearest of these sat over the doors, and stared down through the pub windows; a fierce seated deity was being embraced by his infant son, whose body was weirdly twisted back on itself, to show his genitalia. Time had eroded all shock value.

Inside the Feathers, machines were clinking and jingling and flashing primary-colored lights; the wall-mounted plasma TVs, surrounded with padded leather, were showing West Bromwich Albion versus Chelsea with the sound off, while Amy Winehouse throbbed and moaned from hidden speakers. The names of ales were painted on the cream wall above the long bar, which faced a wide dark-wood staircase with curving steps and shining brass handrails, leading up to the first floor.

Strike had to wait to be served, giving him time to look around. The place was full of men, most of whom had military-short hair; but a trio of girls with tangerine tans stood around a high table, throwing back their over-straightened peroxide hair, in their tiny, tight spangled dresses, shifting their weight unnecessarily on their teetering heels. They were pretending not to know that the only solitary drinker, a handsome, boyish man in a leather jacket, who was sitting on a high bar seat beside the nearby window, was examining them, point by point, with a practiced eye. Strike bought himself a pint of Doom Bar and approached their appraiser.

"Cormoran Strike," he said, reaching Wardle's table. Wardle had the kind of hair Strike envied in other men; nobody would ever have called Wardle "pubehead."

"Yeah, I thought it might be you," said the policeman, shaking hands. "Anstis said you were a big bloke."

Strike pulled up a bar stool, and Wardle said, without preamble:

"What've you got for me, then?"

"There was a fatal stabbing just off Ealing Broadway last month. Guy called Liam Yates? Police informant, wasn't he?"

"Yeah, he got a knife in the neck. But we know who did it," said Wardle, with a patronizing laugh. "Half the crooks in London know. If that's your information—"

"Don't know where he is, though, do you?"

With a quick glance at the determinedly unconscious girls, Wardle slid a notebook out of his pocket.

"Go on."

"There's a girl who works in Betbusters on the Hackney Road called Shona Holland. She lives in a rented flat two streets away from the bookie's. She's got an unwelcome house guest at the moment called Brett Fearney, who used to beat up her sister. Apparently he's not the sort of bloke you refuse a favor."

"Got the full address?" asked Wardle, who was scribbling hard.

"I've just given you the name of the tenant and half the postcode. How about trying a bit of detective work?"

"And where did you say you got this?" asked Wardle, still jotting rapidly with the notebook balanced under the table on his knee.

"I didn't," replied Strike equably, sipping his beer.

"Got some interesting friends, haven't you?"

"Very. Now, in a spirit of fair exchange . . ."

Wardle, replacing his notebook in his pocket, laughed.

"What you've just given me might be a crock of shit."

"It isn't. Play fair, Wardle."

The policeman eyed Strike for a moment, apparently torn between amusement and suspicion.

"What are you after, then?"

"I told you on the phone: bit of inside information on Lula Landry."

"Don't you read the papers?"

"Inside information, I said. My client thinks there was foul play."

Wardle's expression hardened.

"Hooked up with a tabloid, have we?"

"No," said Strike. "Her brother."

"John Bristow?"

Wardle took a long pull on his pint, his eyes on the upper thighs of the nearest girl, his wedding ring reflecting red lights from the pinball machine.

"Is he still fixated on the CCTV footage?"

"He mentioned it," admitted Strike.

"We tried to trace them," said Wardle, "those two black guys. We put out an appeal. Neither of them turned up. No big surprise—a car alarm went off just about the time they would have been passing it—or trying to get into it. Maserati. Very tasty."

"Reckon they were nicking cars, do you?"

"I don't say they went there specifically to nick cars; they might have spotted an opportunity, seeing it parked there—what kind of tosser leaves a Maserati parked on the street? But it was nearly two in the morning, the temperature was below zero, and I can't think of many innocent reasons why two men would choose to meet at that time, in a Mayfair street where neither of them, as far as we could find out, lived."

"No idea where they came from, or where they went afterwards?"

"We're pretty sure the one Bristow's obsessed with, the one who was walking towards her flat just before she fell, got off the number thirty-eight bus in Wilton Street at a quarter past eleven. There's no saying what he did before he passed the camera at the end of Bellamy Road an hour and a half later. He tanked back past it about ten minutes after Landry jumped, sprinted up Bellamy Road and most probably turned right down Weldon Street. There's some footage of a guy more or less

meeting his description—tall, black, hoodie, scarf round the face—
caught on Theobalds Road about twenty minutes later."

"He made good time if he got to Theobalds Road in twenty minutes," commented Strike. "That's out towards Clerkenwell, isn't it?
Must be two, two and a half miles. And the pavements were frozen."

"Yeah, well, it might not've been him. The footage was shit. Bristow thought it was very suspicious that he had his face covered, but
it was minus ten that night, and I was wearing a balaclava to work
myself. Anyway, whether he was in Theobalds Road or not, nobody
ever came forward to say they'd recognized him."

"And the other one?"

"Sprinted off down Halliwell Street, about two hundred yards
down; no idea where he went after that."

"Or when he entered the area?"

"Could've come from anywhere. We haven't got any other footage
of him."

"Aren't there supposed to be ten thousand CCTV cameras in London?"

"They aren't everywhere yet. Cameras aren't the answer to our
problems, unless they're maintained and monitored. The one in Gar-
riman Street was out, and there aren't any in Meadowfield Road or
Hartley Street. You're like everyone else, Strike; you want your civil
liberties when you've told the missus you're at the office and you're at
a lap-dancing club, but you want twenty-four-hour surveillance on
your house when someone's trying to force your bathroom window
open. Can't have it both ways."

"I'm not after it either way," said Strike. "I'm just asking what you
know about Runner Two."

"Muffled up to the eyeballs, like his mate; all you could see were his
hands. If I'd been him, and had a guilty conscience about the Maserati,
I'd have holed up in a bar and exited with a bunch of other people;
there's a place called Bojo's off Halliwell Street he could've gone and
mingled with the punters. We checked," Wardle said, forestalling
Strike's question. "Nobody recognized him from the footage."

They drank for a moment in silence.

"Even if we'd found them," said Wardle, setting down his glass, "the most we could've got from them is an eyewitness account of her jumping. There wasn't any unexplained DNA in her flat. Nobody had been in that place who shouldn't have been in there."

"It isn't just the CCTV footage that's giving Bristow ideas," said Strike. "He's been seeing a bit of Tansy Bestigui."

"Don't talk to me about Tansy fucking Bestigui," said Wardle irritably.

"I'm going to have to mention her, because my client reckons she's telling the truth."

"Still at it, is she? Still hasn't given it up? I'll tell you about Mrs. Bestigui, shall I?"

"Go on," said Strike, one hand wrapped around the beer at his chest.

"Carver and I got to the scene about twenty, twenty-five minutes after Landry hit the road. Uniformed police were already there. Tansy Bestigui was still going strong with the hysterics when we saw her, gibbering and shaking and screaming that there was a murderer in the building.

"Her story was that she got up out of bed around two and went for a pee in the bathroom; she heard shouting from two flats above and saw Landry's body fall past the window.

"Now, the windows in those flats are triple-glazed or something. They're designed to keep the heat and the air conditioning in, and the noise of the hoi polloi out. By the time we were interviewing her, the street below was full of panda cars and neighbors, but you'd never have known it from up there except for the flashing blue lights. We could've been inside a fucking pyramid for all the noise that got inside that place.

"So I said to her, 'Are you sure you heard shouting, Mrs. Bestigui? Because this flat seems to be pretty much soundproofed.'

"She wouldn't back down. Swore she'd heard every word. According to her, Landry screamed something like 'You're too late,' and a man's voice said, 'You're a fucking liar.' Auditory hallucinations, they call them," said Wardle. "You start hearing things when you snort so much coke your brains start dribbling out of your nose."

He took another long pull on his pint.

"Anyway, we proved beyond doubt she couldn't have heard it. The Bestiguis moved into a friend's house the next day to get away from the press, so we put a few blokes in their flat, and a guy up on Landry's balcony, shouting his head off. The lot on the first floor couldn't hear a word he was saying, and they were stone-cold sober, and making an effort.

"But while we were proving she was talking shit, Mrs. Bestigui was phoning half of London to tell them she was the sole witness to the murder of Lula Landry. The press were already on to it, because some of the neighbors had heard her screaming about an intruder. Papers had tried and convicted Evan Duffield before we even got back to Mrs. Bestigui.

"We put it to her that we'd now proven she couldn't have heard what she said she'd heard. Well, she wasn't ready to admit it had all been in her own head. She'd got a lot riding on it now, with the press swarming outside her front door like she was Lula Landry reborn. So she came back with 'Oh, didn't I say? I opened them. Yeah, I opened the windows for a breath of fresh air.' "

Wardle gave a scathing laugh.

"Sub-zero outside, and snowing."

"And she was in her underwear, right?"

"Looking like a rake with two plastic tangerines tied to it," said Wardle, and the simile came out so easily that Strike was sure he was far from the first to have heard it. "We went ahead and double-checked the new story; we dusted for prints, and right enough, she hadn't opened the windows. No prints on the latches or anywhere else; the cleaner had done them the morning before Landry died, and hadn't been in since. As the windows were locked and bolted when we arrived, there's only one conclusion to be drawn, isn't there? Mrs. Tansy Bestigui is a fucking liar."

Wardle drained his glass.

"Have another one," said Strike, and he headed for the bar without waiting for an answer.

He noticed Wardle's curious gaze roaming over his lower legs as he returned to the table. Under different circumstances, he might have banged the prosthesis hard against the table leg, and said "It's this one." Instead, he set down two fresh pints and some pork scratch-ings, which to his irritation were served in a small white ramekin, and continued where they had left off.

"Tansy Bestigui definitely witnessed Landry falling past the win-dow, though, didn't she? Because Wilson reckons he heard the body fall right before Mrs. Bestigui started screaming."

"Maybe she saw it, but she wasn't having a pee. She was doing a couple of lines of charlie in the bathroom. We found it there, cut and ready for her."

"Left some, had she?"

"Yeah. Presumably the body falling past the window put her off."

"The window's visible from the bathroom?"

"Yeah. Well, just."

"You got there pretty quickly, didn't you?"

"Uniformed lot were there in about eight minutes, and Carver and I were there in about twenty." Wardle lifted his glass, as though to toast the force's efficiency.

"I've spoken to Wilson, the security guard," said Strike.

"Yeah? He didn't do bad," said Wardle, with a trace of conde-scension. "It wasn't his fault he had the runs. But he didn't touch anything, and he did a proper search right after she'd jumped. Yeah, he did all right."

"He and his colleagues were a bit lazy on the door codes."

"People always are. Too many pin numbers and passwords to re-member. Know the feeling."

"Bristow's interested in the possibilities of the quarter of an hour when Wilson was in the bog."

"We were, too, for about five minutes, before we'd satisfied our-selves that Mrs. Bestigui was a publicity-mad cokehead."

"Wilson mentioned that the pool was unlocked."

"Can he explain how a murderer got into the pool area, or back to it, without walking right past him? A fucking *pool,*" said Wardle, "nearly as big as the one I've got at my gym, and all for the use of three fucking people. A *gym* on the ground floor behind the security desk. Underground fucking parking. Flats done up with marble and shit like . . . like a fucking five-star hotel."

The policeman sat shaking his head very slowly over the unequal distribution of wealth.

"Different world," he said.

"I'm interested in the middle flat," said Strike.

"Deeby Macc's?" said Wardle, and Strike was surprised to see a grin of genuine warmth spread across the policeman's face. "What about it?"

"Did you go in there?"

"I had a look, but Bryant had already searched it. Empty. Windows bolted, alarm set and working properly."

"Is Bryant the one who knocked into the table and smashed a big floral arrangement?"

Wardle snorted.

"Heard about that, did you? Mr. Bestigui wasn't too chuffed about it. Oh yeah. Two hundred white roses in a crystal vase the size of a dustbin. Apparently he'd read that Macc asks for white roses in his rider. His *rider*," Wardle said, as though Strike's silence implied an ignorance of what the term meant. "Stuff they ask for in their dressing rooms. I'd've thought *you'd* know about this stuff."

Strike ignored the insinuation. He had hoped for better from Anstis.

"Ever find out why Bestigui wanted Macc to have roses?"

"Just schmoozing, isn't it? Probably wanted to put Macc in a film. He was fucked off to the back teeth when he heard Bryant had ruined them. Yelling the place down when he found out."

"Anyone find it strange that he was upset about a bunch of flowers, when his neighbor's lying in the street with her head smashed in?"

"He's one obnoxious fucker, Bestigui," said Wardle, with feeling. "Used to people jumping to attention when he speaks. He tried treating all of us like staff, till he realized that wasn't clever."

"But the shouting wasn't really about the flowers. He was trying to drown out his wife, give her a chance to pull herself together. He kept forcing his way in between her and anyone who wanted to question her. Big guy as well, old Freddie."

"What was he worried about?"

"That the longer she bawled and shook like a frozen whippet, the more bloody obvious it became that she'd been doing coke. He must've known it was lying around somewhere in the flat. He can't have been delighted to have the Met come bursting in. So he tried to distract everyone with a tantrum about his five-hundred-quid floral arrangement.

"I read somewhere that he's divorcing her. I'm not surprised. He's used to the press tiptoeing around him, because he's such a litigious bastard; he can't have enjoyed all the attention he got after Tansy shot her mouth off. The press made hay while they could. Rehashed old stories about him throwing plates at underlings. Punches in meetings. They say he paid his last wife a massive lump sum to stop her talking about his sex life in court. He's pretty well known as a prize shit."

"You didn't fancy him as a suspect?"

"Oh, we fancied him a lot; he was on the spot and he's got a rep for violence. It never looked likely, though. If his wife knew that he'd done it, or that he'd been out of the flat at the moment Landry fell, I'm betting she'd have told us so: she was out of control when we got there. But she said he'd been in bed, and the bedclothes were disarranged and looked slept in.

"Plus, if he'd managed to sneak out of the flat without her realizing it, and gone up to Landry's place, we're left with the problem of how he got past Wilson. He can't have taken the lift, so he'd have passed Wilson in the stairwell, coming down."

"So the timings rule him out?"

Wardle hesitated.

"Well, it's just possible. *Just,* assuming Bestigui can move a damn sight faster than most men of his age and weight, and that he started running the moment he pushed her over. But there's still the fact that we didn't find his DNA anywhere in the flat, the question of how he got out of the flat without his wife knowing he'd gone, and the small matter of why Landry would have let him in. All her friends agreed she didn't like him. Anyway," Wardle finished the dregs of his pint, "Bestigui's the kind of man who'd hire a killer if he wanted someone taken care of. He wouldn't sully his own hands."

"Another one?"

Wardle checked his watch.

"My shout," he said, and he ambled up to the bar. The three young women standing around the high table fell silent, watching him greedily. Wardle threw them a smirk as he walked back past with his drinks, and they glanced over at him as he resumed the bar stool beside Strike.

"How d'you think Wilson shapes up as a possible killer?" Strike asked the policeman.

"Badly," said Wardle. "He couldn't have got up and down quickly enough to meet Tansy Bestigui on the ground floor. Mind you, his CV's a crock of shit. He was employed on the basis of being ex-police, and he was never in the force."

"Interesting. Where was he?"

"He's been knocking around the security world for years. He admitted he'd lied to get his first job, about ten years ago, and he'd just kept it on his CV."

"He seems to have liked Landry."

"Yeah. He's older than he looks," said Wardle, inconsequentially. "He's a grandfather. They don't show age like us, do they, Afro-Caribbeans? I wouldn't've put him as any older than you." Strike wondered idly how old Wardle thought he was.

"You got forensics to check out her flat?"

"Oh yeah," said Wardle, "but that was purely because the higher-ups wanted to put the thing beyond reasonable doubt. We knew within the first twenty-four hours it had to be suicide. We went the extra mile, though, with the whole fucking world watching."

He spoke with poorly disguised pride.

"The cleaner had been through the whole place that morning—sexy Polish girl, crap English, but bloody thorough with a duster—so the day's prints stood out good and clear. Nothing unusual."

"Wilson's prints were in there, presumably, because he searched the place after she fell?"

"Yeah, but nowhere suspicious."

"So as far as you're concerned, there were only three people in the whole building when she fell. Deeby Macc should have been there, but..."

"...he went straight from the airport to a nightclub, yeah," said Wardle. Again, a broad and apparently involuntary grin illuminated his face. "I interviewed Deeby at Claridges the day after she died. Massive bloke. Like you," he said, with a glance at Strike's bulky torso, "only fit." Strike took the hit without demur. "Proper ex-gangster. He's been in and out of the nick in LA. He nearly didn't get a visa to get into the UK.

"He had an entourage with him," said Wardle. "All hanging around the room, rings on every finger, tattoos on their necks. He was the biggest, though. One scary fucker Deeby'd be, if you met him down an alleyway. Politer than Bestigui by ten fucking miles. Asked me how the hell I could do my job without a gun."

The policeman was beaming. Strike could not help drawing the conclusion that Eric Wardle, CID, was, in this case, as starstruck as Kieran Kolovas-Jones.

"Wasn't a long interview, seeing as he'd only just got off a plane and never set foot inside Kentigern Gardens. Routine. I got him to sign his latest CD for me at the end," Wardle added, as though he could not help himself. "That brought the house down, he loved it. The missus wanted to put it on eBay, but I'm keeping..."

Wardle stopped talking with an air of having given away a little more than he had intended. Amused, Strike helped himself to a handful of pork scratchings.

"What about Evan Duffield?"

"Him," said Wardle. The stardust that had sparkled over the policeman's account of Deeby Macc was gone; the policeman was scowling. "Little junkie shit. He pissed us around from start to finish. He went straight into rehab the day after she died."

"I saw. Where?"

"Priory, where else? Fucking rest cure."

"So when did you interview him?"

"Next day, but we had to find him first; his people were being as obstructive as possible. Same story as Bestigui, wasn't it? They didn't want us to know what he'd really been doing. My missus," said Wardle, scowling even harder, "thinks he's sexy. You married?"

"No," said Strike.

"Anstis told me you left the army to get married to some woman who looks like a supermodel."

"What was Duffield's story, once you got to him?"

"They'd had a big bust-up in the club, Uzi. Plenty of witnesses to that. She left, and his story was that he followed her, about five minutes later, wearing this fucking wolf mask. It covers the whole head. Lifelike, hairy thing. He told us he'd got it from a fashion shoot."

Wardle's expression was eloquent of contempt.

"He liked putting this thing on to get in and out of places, to piss off the paparazzi. So, after Landry left Uzi, he got in his car—he had a driver outside, waiting for him—and went to Kentigern Gardens. Driver confirmed all that. Yeah, all right," Wardle corrected himself impatiently, "he confirmed that he drove a man in a wolf's head, who he assumed was Duffield as he was of Duffield's height and build, and wearing what looked like Duffield's clothes, and speaking in Duffield's voice, to Kentigern Gardens."

"But he didn't take the wolf head off on the journey?"

"It's only about fifteen minutes to her flat from Uzi. No, he didn't take it off. He's a childish little prick.

"So then, by Duffield's own account, he saw the paps outside her flat and decided not to go in after all. He told the driver to take him off to Soho, where he let him out. Duffield walked round the corner to his dealer's flat in d'Arblay Street, where he shot up."

"Still wearing the wolf's head?"

"No, he took it off there," said Wardle. "The dealer, name of Whycliff, is an ex–public schoolboy with a habit way worse than Duffield's. He gave a full statement agreeing that Duffield had come round at about half past two. It was only the pair of them there, and yeah, I'd take long odds that Whycliff would lie for Duffield, but a woman on the ground floor heard the doorbell ring and says she saw Duffield on the stair.

"Anyway, Duffield left Whycliff's around four, with the bloody wolf's head back on, and rambled off towards the place where he thought his car and driver were waiting; except that the driver was gone. The driver claimed a misunderstanding. He thought Duffield was an arsehole; he made that clear when we took his statement. Duffield wasn't paying him; the car was on Landry's account.

"So then Duffield, who's got no money on him, walks all the way to Ciara Porter's place in Notting Hill. We found a few people who'd seen a man wearing a wolf's head strolling along relevant streets, and there's footage of him cadging a free box of matches from a woman in an all-night garage."

"Can you make out his face?"

"No, because he only shoved the wolf head up to speak to her, and all you can see is its snout. She said it was Duffield, though.

"He got to Porter's around half four. She let him sleep on the sofa, and about an hour later she got the news about Landry being dead, and woke him up to tell him. Cue histrionics and rehab."

"You checked for a suicide note?" asked Strike.

"Yeah. There was nothing in the flat, nothing on her laptop, but that wasn't a surprise. She did it on the spur of the moment, didn't she? She was bipolar, she'd just argued with that little tosser and it pushed her over—well, you know what I mean."

Wardle checked his watch, and drained the last of his pint.

"I'm gonna have to go. The wife'll be pissed off, I told her I'd only be half an hour."

The over-tanned girls had left without either man noticing. Out on the pavement, both lit up cigarettes.

"I hate this fucking smoking ban," said Wardle, zipping his leather jacket up to the neck.

"Have we got a deal, then?" asked Strike.

Cigarette between his lips, Wardle pulled on a pair of gloves.

"I dunno about that."

"C'mon, Wardle," said Strike, handing the policeman a card, which Wardle accepted as though it were a joke item. "I've given you Brett Fearney."

Wardle laughed outright.

"Not yet you haven't."

He slipped Strike's card into a pocket, inhaled, blew smoke skywards, then shot the larger man a look compounded of curiosity and appraisal.

"Yeah, all right. If we get Fearney, you can have the file."

11

"Evan Duffield's agent says his client isn't taking any further calls or giving any interviews about Lula Landry," said Robin next morning. "I did make it clear that you're not a journalist, but he was adamant. And the people in Guy Somé's office are ruder than Freddie Bestigui's. You'd think I was trying to get an audience with the Pope."

"OK," said Strike. "I'll see whether I can get at him through Bristow."

It was the first time that Robin had seen Strike in a suit. He looked, she thought, like a rugby player en route to an international: large, conventionally smart in his dark jacket and subdued tie. He was on his knees, searching through one of the cardboard boxes he had brought from Charlotte's flat. Robin was averting her gaze from his boxed-up possessions. They were still avoiding any mention of the fact that Strike was living in his office.

"Aha," he said, finally locating, from amid a pile of his mail, a bright blue envelope: the invitation to his nephew's party. "Bollocks," he added, on opening it.

"What's the matter?"

"It doesn't say how old he is," said Strike. "My nephew."

Robin was curious about Strike's relations with his family. As she had never been officially informed, however, that Strike had numerous half-brothers and -sisters, a famous father and a mildly infamous mother, she bit back all questions and continued to open the day's paltry mail.

Strike got up off the floor, replaced the cardboard box in a corner of the inner office and returned to Robin.

"What's that?" he asked, seeing a sheet of photocopied newsprint on the desk.

"I kept it for you," she said diffidently. "You said you were glad you'd seen that story about Evan Duffield...I thought you might be interested in this, if you haven't already seen it."

It was a neatly clipped article about film producer Freddie Bestigui, taken from the previous day's *Evening Standard*.

"Excellent; I'll read that on the way to lunch with his wife."

"Soon to be ex," said Robin. "It's all in that article. He's not very lucky in love, Mr. Bestigui."

"From what Wardle told me, he's not a very lovable man," said Strike.

"How did you get that policeman to talk to you?" Robin said, unable to hold back her curiosity on this point. She was desperate to learn more about the process and progress of the investigation.

"We've got a mutual friend," said Strike. "Bloke I knew in Afghanistan; Met officer in the TA."

"You were in Afghanistan?"

"Yeah." Strike was pulling on his overcoat, the folded article on Freddie Bestigui and the invitation to Jack's party between his teeth.

"What were you doing in Afghanistan?"

"Investigating a Killed In Action," said Strike. "Military police."

"Oh," said Robin.

Military police did not tally with Matthew's impression of a charlatan, or a waster.

"Why did you leave?"

"Injured," said Strike.

He had described that injury to Wilson in the starkest of terms, but he was wary of being equally frank with Robin. He could imagine her shocked expression, and he stood in no need of her sympathy.

"Don't forget to call Peter Gillespie," Robin reminded him, as he headed out of the door.

Strike read the photocopied article as he rode the Tube to Bond Street. Freddie Bestigui had inherited his first fortune from a father who had made a great deal of money in haulage; he had made his second by producing highly commercial films that serious critics treated with derision. The producer was currently going to court to refute claims, by two newspapers, that he had behaved with gross impropriety towards a young female employee, whose silence he had subsequently bought. The accusations, carefully hedged around with many "alleged"s and "reported"s, included aggressive sexual advances and a degree of physical bullying. They had been made "by a source close to the alleged victim," the girl herself having refused either to press charges or to speak to the press. The fact that Freddie was currently divorcing his latest wife, Tansy, was mentioned in the concluding paragraph, which ended with a reminder that the unhappy couple had been in the building on the night that Lula Landry took her own life. The reader was left with the odd impression that the Bestiguis' mutual unhappiness might have influenced Landry in her decision to jump.

Strike had never moved in the kinds of circles that dined at Cipriani. It was only as he walked up Davies Street, the sun warm on his back and imparting a ruddy glow to the red-brick building ahead, that he thought how odd it would be, yet not unlikely, if he ran into one of his half-siblings there. Restaurants like Cipriani were part of the regular lives of Strike's father's legitimate children. He had last heard from three of them while in Selly Oak Hospital, undergoing physiotherapy. Gabi and Danni had jointly sent flowers; Al had visited once, laughing too loudly and scared of looking at the lower end of the bed. Afterwards, Charlotte had imitated Al braying and wincing. She was a good mimic. Nobody ever expected a girl that beautiful to be funny, yet she was.

The interior of the restaurant had an art deco feeling, the bar and chairs of mellow polished wood, with pale yellow tablecloths on the circular tables and white-jacketed, bow-tied waiters and waitresses. Strike spotted his client immediately among the clattering, jabbering diners, sitting at a table set for four and talking, to Strike's surprise, to two women instead of one, both with long, glossy brown hair. Bristow's rabbity face was full of the desire to please, or perhaps placate.

The lawyer jumped up to greet Strike when he saw him, and introduced Tansy Bestigui, who held out a thin, cool hand, but did not smile, and her sister, Ursula May, who did not hold out a hand at all. While the preliminaries of ordering drinks and handing around menus were navigated, Bristow nervous and over-talkative throughout, the sisters subjected Strike to the kind of brazenly critical stares that only people of a certain class feel entitled to give.

They were both as pristine and polished as life-size dolls recently removed from their cellophane boxes; rich-girl thin, almost hipless in their tight jeans, with tanned faces that had a waxy sheen especially noticeable on their foreheads, their long, gleaming dark manes with center partings, the ends trimmed with spirit-level exactitude.

When Strike finally chose to look up from his menu, Tansy said, without preamble:

"Are you really" (she pronounced it "rarely") "Jonny Rokeby's son?"

"So the DNA test said," he replied.

She seemed uncertain whether he was being funny or rude. Her dark eyes were fractionally too close together, and the Botox and fillers could not smooth away the petulance in her expression.

"Listen, I've just been telling John," she said curtly. "I'm not going public again, OK? I'm perfectly happy to tell you what I heard, because I'd love you to prove I was right, but you mustn't tell anyone I've talked to you."

The unbuttoned neck of her thin silk shirt revealed an expanse of butterscotch skin stretched over her bony sternum, giving an unattractively knobbly effect; yet two full, firm breasts jutted from her narrow ribcage, as though they had been borrowed for the day from a fuller-figured friend. "We could have met somewhere more discreet," commented Strike.

"No, it's fine, because nobody here will know who you are. You don't look anything like your father, do you? I met him at Elton's last summer. Freddie knows him. D'you see much of Jonny?"

"I've met him twice," said Strike.

"Oh," said Tansy.

The monosyllable contained equal parts of surprise and disdain.

Charlotte had had friends like this; sleek-haired, expensively educated and clothed, all of them appalled by her strange yen for the enormous, battered-looking Strike. He had come up against them for years, by phone and in person, with their clipped vowels and their stockbroker husbands, and the brittle toughness Charlotte had never been able to fake.

"I don't think she should be talking to you at all," said Ursula abruptly. Her tone and expression would have been appropriate had Strike been a waiter who had just thrown aside his apron and joined them, uninvited, at the table. "I think you're making a big mistake, Tanz."

Bristow said: "Ursula, Tansy simply—"

"It's up to me what I do," Tansy snapped at her sister, as though Bristow had not spoken, as though his chair was empty. "I'm only going to say what I heard, that's all. It's all off the record; John's agreed to that."

Evidently she too viewed Strike as domestic class. He was irked not only by their tone, but also by the fact that Bristow was giving witnesses assurances without his say-so. How could Tansy's evidence, which could have come from nobody but her, be kept off the record?

For a few moments all four of them ran their eyes over the culinary options in silence. Ursula was the first to put down her menu. She had already finished a glass of wine. She helped herself to another, and glanced restlessly around the restaurant, her eyes lingering for a second on a blonde minor royal, before passing on.

"This place used to be full of the most fabulous people, even at lunchtime. Cyprian only ever wants to go to bloody Wiltons, with all the other stiffs in suits..."

"Is Cyprian your husband, Mrs. May?" asked Strike.

He guessed that it would needle her if he crossed what she evidently saw as an invisible line between them; she did not think that sitting at a table with her gave him a right to her conversation. She scowled, and Bristow rushed to fill the uncomfortable pause.

"Yes, Ursula's married to Cyprian May, one of our senior partners."

"So I'm getting the family discount on my divorce," said Tansy, with a slightly bitter smile.

"And her ex will go absolutely ballistic if she starts dragging the press back into their lives," Ursula said, her dark eyes boring into

Strike's. "They're trying to thrash out a settlement. It could seriously prejudice her alimony if that all kicks off again. So you'd better be discreet."

With a bland smile, Strike turned to Tansy:

"You had a connection with Lula Landry, then, Mrs. Bestigui? Your brother-in-law works with John?"

"It never came up," she said, looking bored.

The waiter returned to take their orders. When he had left, Strike took out his notebook and pen.

"What are you doing with those?" demanded Tansy, in a sudden panic. "I don't want anything written down! John?" she appealed to Bristow, who turned to Strike with a flustered and apologetic expression.

"D'you think you could just listen, Cormoran, and, ah, skip the note-taking?"

"No problem," said Strike easily, removing his mobile phone from his pocket and replacing the notebook and pen. "Mrs. Bestigui—"

"You can call me Tansy," she said, as though this concession made up for her objections to the notebook.

"Thanks very much," said Strike, with the merest trace of irony. "How well did you know Lula?"

"Oh, hardly at all. She was only there for three months. It was just 'Hi' and 'Nice day.' She wasn't interested in us, we weren't nearly hip enough for her. It was a bore, to be honest, having her there. Paps outside the front door all the time. I had to put on makeup even to go to the gym."

"Isn't there a gym in the building?" asked Strike.

"I do Pilates with Lindsey Parr," said Tansy, irritably. "You sound like Freddie; he was always complaining that I didn't use the facilities at the flat."

"And how well did Freddie know Lula?"

"Hardly at all, but that wasn't for lack of trying. He had some idea about luring her into acting; he kept trying to invite her downstairs. She never came, though. And he followed her to Dickie Carbury's house, the weekend before she died, while I was away with Ursula."

"I didn't know that," said Bristow, looking startled.

Strike noticed Ursula's quick smirk at her sister. He had the impression that she had been looking for an exchange of complicit glances, but Tansy did not oblige.

"I didn't know until later," Tansy told Bristow. "Yah, Freddie cadged an invitation from Dickie; there was a whole group of them there: Lula, Evan Duffield, Ciara Porter, all that tabloidy, druggie, trendy gang. Freddie must have stuck out like a sore thumb. I know he's not much older than Dickie, but he looks ancient," she added spitefully.

"What did your husband tell you about the weekend?"

"Nothing. I only found out he'd been there weeks later, because Dickie let it slip. I'm sure Freddie went to try and make up to Lula, though."

"Do you mean," asked Strike, "that he was interested in Lula sexually, or . . . ?"

"Oh yah, I'm sure he was; he's always liked dark girls better than blondes. What he really loves, though, is getting a bit of celebrity meat into his films. He drives directors mad, trying to crowbar in celebrities, to get a bit of extra press. I'll bet he was hoping to get her signed up for a film, and I wouldn't be at all surprised," Tansy added, with unexpected shrewdness, "if he had something planned around her and Deeby Macc. Imagine the press, with the fuss there was already about the two of them. Freddie's got a genius for that stuff. He loves publicity for his films as much as he hates it for himself."

"Does he know Deeby Macc?"

"Not unless they've met since we separated. He hadn't met Macc before Lula died. God, he was thrilled that Macc was coming to stay in the building; he started talking about casting him the moment he heard."

"Casting him as what?"

"I don't know," she said irritably. "Anything. Macc's got a huge following; Freddie wasn't going to pass that chance up. He'd probably have had a part written specially for him if he'd been interested. Oh, he would have been all over him. Telling him all about his pretend black grandmother." Tansy's voice was contemptuous. "That's what he always does when he meets famous black people: tells them he's a quarter Malay. Yeah, *whatever,* Freddie."

"Isn't he a quarter Malay?" asked Strike.

She gave a snide little laugh.

"I don't know; I never met any of Freddie's grandparents, did I? He's about a hundred years old. I know he'll say anything if he thinks there's money in it."

"Did anything ever come of these plans to get Lula and Macc into his films, as far as you're aware?"

"Well, I'm sure Lula was flattered to be asked; most of these model girls are dying to prove they can do something other than stare into a camera, but she never signed up to anything, did she, John?"

"Not as far as I know," said Bristow. "Although . . . but that was something different," he mumbled, turning blotchily pink again. He hesitated, then, responding to Strike's interrogative gaze, he said:

"Mr. Bestigui visited my mother a couple of weeks ago, out of the blue. She's exceptionally poorly, and . . . well, I wouldn't want to . . ."

His glance at Tansy was uncomfortable.

"Say what you like, I don't care," she said, with what seemed like genuine indifference.

Bristow made the strange jutting and sucking movement that temporarily hid the hamsterish teeth.

"Well, he wanted to talk to my mother about a film of Lula's life. He, ah, framed his visit as something considerate and sensitive. Asking for her family's blessing, official sanction, you know. Lula dead barely three months . . . Mum was distressed beyond measure. Unfortunately, I was not there when he called," said Bristow, and his tone implied that he was generally to be found standing guard over his mother. "I wish, in a way, I had been. I wish I'd heard him out. I mean, if he's got researchers working on Lula's life story, much as I deplore the idea, he might know something, mightn't he?"

"What kind of thing?" asked Strike.

"I don't know. Something about her early life, perhaps? Before she came to us?"

The waiter arrived to place starters in front of them all. Strike waited until he had gone, and then asked Bristow:

"Have you tried to speak to Mr. Bestigui yourself, and find out whether he knew anything about Lula that the family didn't?"

"That's just what's so difficult," said Bristow. "When Tony—my uncle—heard what had happened, he contacted Mr. Bestigui to protest about him badgering my mother, and from what I've heard, there was a very heated argument. I don't think Mr. Bestigui would welcome further contact from the family. Of course, the situation's further complicated by the fact that Tansy is using our firm for the divorce. I mean, there's nothing in that—we're one of the top family law firms, and with Ursula being married to Cyprian, naturally she would come to us ... But I'm sure it won't have made Mr. Bestigui feel any more kindly towards us."

Though he had kept his gaze on the lawyer all the time that Bristow was talking, Strike's peripheral vision was excellent. Ursula had thrown another tiny smirk in her sister's direction. He wondered what was amusing her. Doubtless her improved mood was not hindered by the fact that she was now on her fourth glass of wine.

Strike finished his starter and turned to Tansy, who was pushing her virtually untouched food around her plate.

"How long had you and your husband been at number eighteen before Lula moved in?"

"About a year."

"Was there anyone in the middle flat when she arrived?"

"Yah," said Tansy. "There was an American couple there with their little boy for six months, but they went back to the States not long after she arrived. After that, the property company couldn't get anyone interested at all. The recession, you know? They cost an arm and a leg, those flats. So it was empty until the record company rented it for Deeby Macc."

Both she and Ursula were distracted by the sight of a woman passing the table in what, to Strike, appeared to be a crocheted coat of lurid design.

"That's a Daumier-Cross coat," said Ursula, her eyes slightly narrowed over her wineglass. "There's a waiting list of, like, six months ..."

"It's Pansy Marks-Dillon," said Tansy. "Easy to be on the best-dressed list if your husband's got fifty mill. Freddie's the cheapest rich man in the world; I had to hide new stuff from him, or pretend it was fake. He could be such a bore sometimes."

"You always look wonderful," said Bristow, pink in the face.

"You're sweet," said Tansy Bestigui in a bored voice.

The waiter arrived to clear away their plates.

"What were you saying?" she asked Strike. "Oh, yah, the flats. Deeby Macc coming…except he didn't. Freddie was furious he never got there, because he'd put roses in his flat. Freddie is such a cheap bastard."

"How well do you know Derrick Wilson?" Strike asked.

She blinked.

"Well—he's the security guard; I don't know him, do I? He seemed all right. Freddie always said he was the best of the bunch."

"Really? Why was that?"

She shrugged.

"I don't know, you'd have to ask Freddie. And good luck with that," she added, with a little laugh. "Freddie'll talk to you when hell freezes over."

"Tansy," said Bristow, leaning in a little, "why don't you just tell Cormoran what you actually heard that night?"

Strike would have preferred Bristow not to intervene.

"Well," said Tansy. "It was getting on for two in the morning, and I wanted a drink of water."

Her tone was flat and expressionless. Strike noticed that, even in this small beginning, she had altered the story she had told the police.

"So I went to the bathroom to get one, and as I was heading back across the sitting room, towards the bedroom, I heard shouting. She—Lula—was saying, 'It's too late, I've already done it,' and then a man said, 'You're a lying fucking bitch,' and then—and then he threw her over. I actually saw her fall."

And Tansy made a tiny jerky movement with her hands that Strike understood to indicate flailing.

Bristow set down his glass, looking nauseated. Their main courses arrived. Ursula drank more wine. Neither Tansy nor Bristow touched their food. Strike picked up his fork and began to eat, trying not to look as though he was enjoying his *puntarelle* with anchovies.

"I screamed," whispered Tansy. "I couldn't stop screaming. I ran out of the flat, past Freddie, and downstairs. I just wanted to tell security that there was a man up there, so they could get him.

"Wilson came dashing out of the room behind the desk. I told him what had happened and he went straight out on to the street to see her, instead of running upstairs. Bloody fool. If only he'd gone upstairs first, he might have caught him! Then Freddie came down after me, and started trying to make me go back to our flat, because I wasn't dressed.

"Then Wilson came back, and told us she was dead, and told Freddie to call the police. Freddie virtually dragged me back upstairs—I was completely hysterical—and he dialed 999 from our sitting room. And then the police came. And nobody believed a single word I said."

She sipped her wine again, set down the glass and said quietly:

"If Freddie knew I was talking to you, he'd go ape."

"But you're quite sure, aren't you, Tansy," Bristow interjected, "that you heard a man up there?"

"Yah, of course I am," said Tansy. "I've just said, haven't I? There was definitely someone there."

Bristow's mobile rang.

"Excuse me," he muttered. "Alison . . . yes?" he said, picking up.

Strike could hear the secretary's deep voice, without being able to make out the words.

"Excuse me just a moment," Bristow said, looking harried, and he left the table.

A look of malicious amusement appeared on both sisters' smooth, polished faces. They glanced at each other again; then, somewhat to his surprise, Ursula asked Strike:

"Have you met Alison?"

"Briefly."

"You know they're together?"

"Yes."

"It's a bit pathetic, actually," said Tansy. "She's with John, but she's actually obsessed with Tony. Have you met Tony?"

"No," said Strike.

"He's one of the senior partners. John's uncle, you know?"

"Yes."

"Very attractive. He wouldn't go for Alison in a million years. I suppose she's settled for John as consolation prize."

The thought of Alison's doomed infatuation seemed to afford the sisters great satisfaction.

"This is all common gossip at the office, is it?" asked Strike.

"Oh, yah," said Ursula, with relish. "Cyprian says she's absolutely embarrassing. Like a puppy dog around Tony."

Her antipathy towards Strike seemed to have evaporated. He was not surprised; he had met the phenomenon many times. People liked to talk; there were very few exceptions; the question was how you made them do it. Some, and Ursula was evidently one of them, were amenable to alcohol; others liked a spotlight; and then there were those who merely needed proximity to another conscious human being. A subsection of humanity would become loquacious only on one favorite subject: it might be their own innocence, or somebody else's guilt; it might be their collection of pre-war biscuit tins; or it might, as in the case of Ursula May, be the hopeless passion of a plain secretary.

Ursula was watching Bristow through the window; he was standing on the pavement, talking hard into his mobile as he paced up and down. Her tongue properly loosened now, she said:

"I bet I know what that's about. Conway Oates's executors are making a fuss about how the firm handled his affairs. He was the American financier, you know? Cyprian and Tony are in a real bait about it, making John fly around trying to smooth things over. John always gets the shitty end of the stick."

Her tone was more scathing than sympathetic.

Bristow returned to the table, looking flustered.

"Sorry, sorry, Alison just wanted to give me some messages," he said.

The waiter came to collect their plates. Strike was the only one who had cleared his. When the waiter was out of earshot, Strike said:

"Tansy, the police disregarded your evidence because they didn't think you could have heard what you claimed to have heard."

"Well they were wrong, weren't they?" she snapped, her good humor gone in a trice. "I did hear it."

"Through a closed window?"

"It was open," she said, meeting none of her companions' eyes. "It was stuffy, I opened one of the windows on the way to get water."

Strike was sure that pressing her on the point would only lead to her refusing to answer any other questions.

"They also allege that you'd taken cocaine."

Tansy made a little noise of impatience, a soft "cuh."

"Look," she said, "I had some earlier, during dinner, OK, and they found it in the bathroom when they looked around the flat. The fucking *boredom* of the Dunnes. Anyone would have done a couple of lines to get through Benjy Dunne's bloody anecdotes. But I didn't imagine that voice upstairs. A man was there, and he killed her. *He killed her,*" repeated Tansy, glaring at Strike.

"And where do you think he went afterwards?"

"I don't know, do I? That's what John's paying you to find out. He sneaked out somehow. Maybe he climbed out the back window. Maybe he hid in the lift. Maybe he went out through the car park downstairs. I don't bloody know how he got out, I just know he was there."

"We believe you," interjected Bristow anxiously. "We believe you, Tansy. Cormoran needs to ask these questions to—to get a clear picture of how it all happened."

"The police did everything they could to discredit me," said Tansy, disregarding Bristow and addressing Strike. "They got there too late, and he'd already gone, so of course they covered it up. No one who hasn't been through what I went through with the press can understand what it was like. It was absolute bloody hell. I went into the clinic just to get away from it all. I can't believe it's legal, what the press are allowed to do in this country; and all for telling the truth, that's the bloody joke. I should've kept my mouth shut, shouldn't I? I would have, if I'd known what was coming."

She twisted her loose diamond ring around her finger.

"Freddie was asleep in bed when Lula fell, wasn't he?" Strike asked Tansy.

"Yah, that's right," she said.

Her hand slid up to her face and she smoothed nonexistent strands of hair off her forehead. The waiter returned with menus again, and Strike was forced to hold back his questions until they had ordered. He was the only one to ask for pudding; all the rest had coffee.

"When did Freddie get out of bed?" he asked Tansy, when the waiter had left.

"What do you mean?"

"You say he was in bed when Lula fell; when did he get up?"

"When he heard me screaming," she said, as though this was obvious. "I woke him up, didn't I?"

"He must have moved quickly."

"Why?"

"You said: 'I ran out of the flat, past Freddie, and downstairs.' So he was already in the room before you ran out to tell Derrick what had happened?"

A missed beat.

"That's right," she said, smoothing her immaculate hair again, shielding her face.

"So he went from fast asleep in bed, to awake and in the sitting room, within seconds? Because you started screaming and running pretty much instantaneously, from what you said?"

Another infinitesimal pause.

"Yah," she said. "Well—I don't know. I think I screamed—I screamed while I was frozen on the spot—for a moment, maybe— I was just so shocked—and Freddie came running out of the bedroom, and then I ran past him."

"Did you stop to tell him what you'd seen?"

"I can't remember."

Bristow looked as though he was about to stage one of his untimely interventions again. Strike held up a hand to forestall him; but Tansy plunged off on another tack, eager, he guessed, to leave the subject of her husband.

"I've thought and thought about how the killer got in, and I'm sure he must have followed her inside when she came in that morning, because of Derrick Wilson leaving his desk and being in the bathroom. I thought Wilson ought to have been bloody sacked for it, actually. If you ask me, he was having a sneaky sleep in the back room. I don't know how the killer would have known the key code, but I'm sure that's when he must have got in."

"Do you think you'd be able to recognize the man's voice again? The one you heard shouting?"

"I doubt it," she said. "It was just a man's voice. It could have been anyone. There was nothing unusual about it. I mean, afterwards I thought, *Was it Duffield?*" she said, gazing at him intently, "because I'd heard Duffield shouting upstairs, once before, from the top landing. Wilson had to throw him out; Duffield was trying to kick in Lula's door. I never understood what a girl with her looks was doing with someone like Duffield," she added in parenthesis.

"Some women say he's sexy," agreed Ursula, emptying the wine bottle into her glass, "but I can't see the appeal. He's just skanky and horrible."

"It's not even," said Tansy, twisting the loose diamond ring again, "as though he's got money."

"But you don't think it was his voice you heard that night?"

"Well, like I say, it could have been," she said impatiently, with a small shrug of her thin shoulders. "He's got an alibi, though, hasn't he? Loads of people said he was nowhere near Kentigern Gardens the night Lula was killed. He spent part of it at Ciara Porter's, didn't he? Bitch," Tansy added, with a small, tight smile. "Sleeping with her best friend's boyfriend."

"Were they sleeping together?" asked Strike.

"Oh, what do *you* think?" laughed Ursula, as though the question was too naive for words. "I know Ciara Porter, she modeled in this charity fashion show I was involved in setting up. She's such an airhead and such a slut."

The coffees had arrived, along with Strike's sticky toffee pudding.

"I'm sorry, John, but Lula didn't have very good taste in friends," said Tansy, sipping her espresso. "There was Ciara, and then there was that Bryony Radford. Not that she was a friend, exactly, but I wouldn't trust her as far as I could throw her."

"Who's Bryony?" asked Strike disingenuously, for he remembered who she was.

"Makeup artist. Charges a fortune, and such a bloody bitch," said

Ursula. "I used her once, before one of the Gorbachev Foundation balls, and afterwards she told ev—"

Ursula stopped abruptly, lowered her glass and picked up her coffee instead. Strike, who despite its undoubted irrelevance to the matter in hand was quite interested to know what Bryony had told everyone, began to speak, but Tansy talked loudly over him.

"Oh, and there was that ghastly girl Lula used to bring around to the flat, too, John, remember?"

She appealed to Bristow again, but he looked blank.

"You know, that ghastly—that rarely awful-colored girl she sometimes dragged back. A kind of hobo person. I mean . . . she literally smelled. When she'd been in the lift . . . you could smell it. And she took her into the pool, too. I didn't think blacks could swim."

Bristow was blinking rapidly, pink in the face.

"God knows what Lula was doing with her," said Tansy. "Oh, you must remember, John. She was fat. Scruffy. Looked a bit subnormal."

"I don't . . ." mumbled Bristow.

"Are you talking about Rochelle?" asked Strike.

"Oh, yah, I think that was her name. She was at the funeral, anyway," said Tansy. "I noticed her. She was sitting right at the back.

"Now, you will remember, won't you," she turned the full force of her dark eyes upon Strike, "that this is all entirely off the record. I mean, I cannot afford for Freddie to find out I'm talking to you. I'm not going to go through all that shit with the press again. Bill, please," she barked at the waiter.

When it arrived, she passed it without comment to Bristow.

As the sisters were preparing to leave, shaking their glossy brown hair back over their shoulders and pulling on expensive jackets, the door of the restaurant opened and a tall, thin, besuited man of around sixty entered, looked around and headed straight for their table. Silver-haired and distinguished-looking, impeccably dressed, there was a certain chilliness about his pale blue eyes. His walk was brisk and purposeful.

"This is a surprise," he said smoothly, stopping in the space between the two women's chairs. None of the other three had seen the man coming, and all bar Strike displayed equal parts of shock and something more than displeasure at the sight of him. For a fraction of a second, Tansy and Ursula froze, Ursula in the act of pulling sunglasses out of her bag.

Tansy recovered first.

"Cyprian," she said, offering her face for his kiss. "Yes, what a lovely surprise!"

"I thought you were going shopping, Ursula dear?" he said, his eyes on his wife as he gave Tansy a conventional peck on each cheek.

"We stopped for lunch, Cyps," she replied, but her color was heightened, and Strike sensed an ill-defined nastiness in the air.

The older man's pale eyes moved deliberately over Strike and came to rest on Bristow.

"I thought Tony was handling your divorce, Tansy?" he asked.

"He is," said Tansy. "This isn't a business lunch, Cyps. Purely social."

He gave a wintry smile.

"Let me escort you out, then, m'dears," he said.

With a cursory farewell to Bristow, and no word whatsoever for Strike, the two sisters permitted themselves to be shepherded out of the restaurant by Ursula's husband. When the door had swung shut behind the threesome, Strike asked Bristow:

"What was that about?"

"That was Cyprian," said Bristow. He seemed agitated as he fumbled with his credit card and the bill. "Cyprian May. Ursula's husband. Senior partner at the firm. He won't like Tansy talking to you. I wonder how he knew where we were. Probably got it out of Alison."

"Why won't he like her talking to me?"

"Tansy's his sister-in-law," said Bristow, putting on his overcoat. "He won't want her to make a fool of herself—as he'll see it—all over again. I'll probably get a real bollocking for persuading her to meet you. I expect he's phoning my uncle right now, to complain about me."

Bristow's hands, Strike noticed, were trembling.

The lawyer left in a taxi ordered by the maître d'. Strike headed away from Cipriani on foot, loosening his tie as he walked, and lost so deeply in thought that he was only jerked out of his reverie by a loud horn blast from a car he had not seen speeding towards him as he crossed Grosvenor Street.

With this salutary reminder that his safety would otherwise be in jeopardy, Strike headed for a patch of pale wall belonging to the Elizabeth Arden Red Door Spa, leaned up against it out of the pedestrian flow, lit up and pulled out his mobile phone. After some listening and fast-forwarding, he managed to locate that part of Tansy's recorded testimony that dealt with those moments immediately preceding Lula Landry's fall past her window.

. . . towards the bedroom, I heard shouting. She—Lula—was saying, "It's too late, I've already done it," and then a man said, "You're a lying fucking bitch," and then—and then he threw her over. I actually saw her fall.

He could just make out the tiny chink of Bristow's glass hitting the table top. Strike rewound again and listened.

. . . saying, "It's too late, I've already done it," and then a man said, "You're a lying fucking bitch," and then—and then he threw her over. I actually saw her fall.

He recalled Tansy's imitation of Landry's flailing arms, and the horror on her frozen face as she did it. Slipping his mobile back into his pocket, he took out his notebook and began to make notes for himself.

Strike had met countless liars; he could smell them; and he knew perfectly well that Tansy was of their number. She could not have heard what she claimed to have heard from her flat; the police had therefore deduced that she could not have heard it at all. Against Strike's expectation, however, in spite of the fact that every piece of evidence he had heard until this moment suggested that Lula Landry had committed suicide, he found himself convinced that Tansy Bestigui really believed that she had overheard an argument before Landry fell. That was the only part of her story that rang with authenticity, an authenticity that shone a garish light on the fakery with which she garnished it.

Strike pushed himself off the wall and began to walk east along Grosvenor Street, paying slightly more attention to traffic, but inwardly recalling Tansy's expression, her tone, her mannerisms, as she spoke of Lula Landry's final moments.

Why would she tell the truth on the essential point, but surround it with easily disproven falsehoods? Why would she lie about what she had been doing when she heard shouting from Landry's flat? Strike remembered Adler: "A lie would have no sense unless the truth were felt as dangerous." Tansy had come along today to make a last attempt to find someone who would believe her, and yet swallow the lies in which she insisted on swaddling her evidence.

He walked fast, barely conscious of the twinges from his right knee. At last he realized that he had walked all along Maddox Street and emerged on Regent Street. The red awnings of Hamleys Toy Shop fluttered a little in the distance, and Strike remembered that he had intended to buy a birthday present for his nephew's forthcoming birthday on the way back to the office.

The multicolored, squeaking, flashing maelstrom into which he walked registered on him only vaguely. Blindly he moved from floor to floor, untroubled by the shrieks, the whirring of airborne toy helicopters, the oinks of mechanical pigs moving across his distracted path. Finally, after twenty minutes or so, he came to rest near the HM Forces dolls. Here he stood, quite still, gazing at the ranks of miniature marines and paratroopers but barely seeing them; deaf to the whispers of parents trying to maneuver their sons around him, too intimidated to ask the strange, huge, staring man to move.

Part Three

Forsan et haec olim meminisse iuvabit.

Maybe one day it will be cheering even to remember these things.

Virgil, *Aeneid,* Book 1

1

It started to rain on Wednesday. London weather; dank and gray, through which the old city presented a stolid front: pale faces under black umbrellas, the eternal smell of damp clothing, the steady pattering on Strike's office window in the night.

The rain in Cornwall had a different quality, when it came: Strike remembered how it had lashed like whips against the panes of Aunt Joan and Uncle Ted's spare room, during those months in the neat little house that smelled of flowers and baking, while he had attended the village school in St. Mawes. Such memories swam to the forefront of his mind whenever he was about to see Lucy.

Raindrops were still dancing exuberantly on the windowsills on Friday afternoon, while at opposite ends of her desk, Robin wrapped Jack's new paratrooper doll, and Strike wrote her a check to the amount of a week's work, minus the commission of Temporary Solutions. Robin was about to attend the third of that week's "proper" interviews, and was looking neat and groomed in her black suit, with her bright gold hair pinned back in a chignon.

"There you are," they both said simultaneously, as Robin pushed across the desk a perfect parcel patterned with small spaceships, and Strike held out the check.

"Cheers," said Strike, taking the present. "I can't wrap."

"I hope he likes it," she replied, tucking the check away in her black handbag.

"Yeah. And good luck with the interview. D'you want the job?"

"Well, it's quite a good one. Human resources in a media consultancy in the West End," she said, sounding unenthusiastic. "Enjoy the party. I'll see you Monday."

The self-imposed penance of walking down into Denmark Street to smoke became even more irksome in the ceaseless rain. Strike stood, minimally shielded beneath the overhang of his office entrance, and asked himself when he was going to kick the habit and set to work to restore the fitness that had slipped away along with his solvency and his domestic comfort. His mobile rang while he stood there.

"Thought you might like to know your tip-off's paid dividends," said Eric Wardle, who sounded triumphant. Strike could hear engine noise and the sound of men talking in the background.

"Quick work," commented Strike.

"Yeah, well, we don't hang around."

"Does this mean I'm going to get what I was after?"

"That's what I'm calling about. It's a bit late today, but I'll bike it over Monday."

"Sooner rather than later suits me. I can hang on here at the office."

Wardle laughed a little offensively.

"You get paid by the hour, don't you? I'd've thought it suited you to string it out a bit."

"Tonight would be better. If you can get it here this evening, I'll make sure you're the first to know if my old mate drops any more tip-offs."

In the slight pause that followed, Strike heard one of the men in the car with Wardle say:

"... *Fearney's fucking face* ..."

"Yeah, all right," said Wardle. "I'll get it over later. Might not be till seven. Will you still be there?"

"I'll make sure I am," Strike replied.

The file arrived three hours later, while he was eating fish and chips out of a small polystyrene tray in his lap and watching the London evening news on his portable television. The courier buzzed the outer door and Strike signed for a bulky package sent from Scotland Yard. Once unwrapped, a thick gray folder full of photocopied material was disclosed. Strike took it back to Robin's desk, and began the lengthy process of digesting the contents.

Here were statements from those who had seen Lula Landry during the final evening of her life; a report on the DNA evidence lifted from her flat; photocopied pages of the visitors' book compiled by security at number 18, Kentigern Gardens; details of the medication Lula had been prescribed to control bipolar disorder; the autopsy report; medical records for the previous year; mobile phone and landline records; and a precis of the findings on the model's laptop. There was also a DVD, on which Wardle had scribbled CCTV 2 Runners.

The DVD drive on Strike's secondhand computer had not worked since he acquired it; he therefore slipped the disc into the pocket of the overcoat hanging by the glass door, and resumed his contemplation of the printed material contained within the ring-binder, his notebook open beside him.

Night descended outside the office, and a pool of golden light fell from the desk lamp on to each page as Strike methodically read the documents that had added up to a conclusion of suicide. Here, amid the statements shorn of superfluity, minutely detailed timings, the copied labels from the bottles of drugs found in Landry's bathroom cabinet, Strike tracked the truth he had sensed behind Tansy Bestigui's lies.

The autopsy indicated that Lula had been killed on impact with the road, and that she had died from a broken neck and internal bleeding. There was a certain amount of bruising to the upper arms. She had fallen wearing only one shoe. The photographs of the corpse confirmed LulaMyInspirationForeva's assertion that Landry had changed her clothes on coming home from the nightclub. Instead of the dress in which she had been photographed entering her building, the corpse wore a sequined top and trousers.

Strike turned to the shifting statements that Tansy had given to the police; the first simply claiming a trip to the bathroom from the bedroom; the second adding the opening of her sitting-room window. Freddie, she said, had been in bed throughout. The police had found half a line of cocaine on the flat marble rim of the bath, and a small plastic bag of the drug hidden inside a box of Tampax in the cabinet above the sink.

Freddie's statement confirmed that he had been asleep when Landry fell, and that he had been woken by his wife's screams; he said that he had hurried into the sitting room in time to see Tansy run past him in her underwear. The vase of roses he had sent to Macc, and which a clumsy policeman had smashed, were intended, he admitted, as a gesture of welcome and introduction; yes, he would have been glad to strike up an acquaintance with the rapper, and yes, it had crossed his mind that Macc might be perfect in a thriller now in development. His shock at Landry's death had undoubtedly made him overreact to the ruin of his floral gift. He had initially believed his wife when she said she had overheard the argument upstairs; he had subsequently come, reluctantly, to accept the police view that Tansy's account was indicative of cocaine consumption. Her drug habit had placed great strain on the marriage, and he had admitted to the police that he was aware that his wife habitually used the stimulant, though he had not known that she had a supply in the flat that night.

Bestigui further stated that he and Landry had never visited each other's flats, and that their simultaneous stay at Dickie Carbury's (which the police appeared to have heard about on a subsequent occasion, for Freddie had been reinterviewed after the initial statement) had barely advanced their acquaintance. "She associated mainly with the younger guests, while I spent most of the weekend with Dickie, who is a contemporary of mine." Bestigui's statement presented the unassailable front of a rock face without crampons.

After reading the police account of events inside the Bestiguis' flat, Strike added several sentences to his own notes. He was interested in the half a line of cocaine on the side of the bath, and even more interested in the few seconds after Tansy had seen the flailing figure of Lula Landry fall past the window. Much would depend, of course, on the layout of the Bestiguis' apartment (there was no map or diagram of it in the folder), but Strike was bothered by one consistent aspect of Tansy's shifting stories: she insisted throughout that her husband had been in bed, asleep, when Landry fell. He remembered the way she had shielded her face, by pretending to push back her hair, as he pressed her on the point. All in all, and notwithstanding the police view, Strike considered the precise location of both Bestiguis at the moment Lula Landry fell off her balcony to be far from proven.

He resumed his systematic perusal of the file. Evan Duffield's statement conformed in most respects to Wardle's secondhand tale. He admitted to having attempted to prevent his girlfriend leaving Uzi by seizing her by the upper arms. She had broken free and left; he had followed her shortly afterwards. There was a one-sentence mention of the wolf mask, couched in the unemotional language of the policeman who had interviewed him: "I am accustomed to wearing a wolf's-head mask when I wish to avoid the attentions of photographers." A brief statement from the driver who had taken Duffield from Uzi confirmed Duffield's account of visiting Kentigern Gardens and moving on to d'Arblay Street, where he had dropped his passenger and left. The antipathy Wardle claimed the driver had felt towards Duffield was not conveyed in the bald factual account prepared for his signature by the police.

There were a couple of other statements supporting Duffield's: one from a woman who claimed to have seen him climbing the stairs to his dealer's, one from the dealer, Whycliff, himself. Strike recalled Wardle's expressed opinion that Whycliff would lie for Duffield. The woman downstairs could have been cut in on any payment. The rest of the witnesses who claimed to have seen Duffield roaming the streets of London could only honestly say that they had seen a man in a wolf mask.

Strike lit a cigarette and read through Duffield's statement again. He was a man with a violent temper, who had admitted to attempting to force Lula to remain in the club. The bruising to the upper arms of the body was almost certainly his work. If, however, he had taken heroin with Whycliff, Strike knew that the odds of him being in a fit state to infiltrate number 18, Kentigern Gardens, or to work himself into a murderous rage, were negligible. Strike was familiar with the behavior of heroin addicts; he had met plenty at the last squat his mother had lived in. The drug rendered its slaves passive and docile; the absolute antithesis of shouting, violent alcoholics, or twitchy, paranoid coke-users. Strike had known every kind of substance-abuser, both inside the army and out. The glorification of

Duffield's habit by the media disgusted him. There was no glamour in heroin. Strike's mother had died on a filthy mattress in the corner of the room, and nobody had realized she was dead for six hours.

He got up, crossed the room and wrenched open the dark, rain-spattered window, so that the thud of the bass from the 12 Bar Café became louder than ever. Still smoking, he looked out at Charing Cross Road, glittering with car lights and puddles, where Friday-night revelers were striding and lurching past the end of Denmark Street, umbrellas wobbling, laughter ringing above the traffic. When, Strike wondered, would he next enjoy a pint on a Friday with friends? The notion seemed to belong to a different universe, a life left behind. The strange limbo in which he was living, with Robin his only real human contact, could not last, but he was still not ready to resume a proper social life. He had lost the army, and Charlotte and half a leg; he felt a need to become thoroughly accustomed to the man he had become, before he felt ready to expose himself to other people's surprise and pity. The bright orange cigarette stub flew down into the dark street and was extinguished in the watery gutter; Strike pushed down the window, returned to his desk and pulled the file firmly back towards him.

Derrick Wilson's statement told him nothing he did not already know. There was no mention in the file of Kieran Kolovas-Jones, or of his mysterious blue piece of paper. Strike turned next, with some interest, to the statements of the two women with whom Lula had spent her final afternoon, Ciara Porter and Bryony Radford.

The makeup artist remembered Lula as cheerful and excited about Deeby Macc's imminent arrival. Porter, however, stated that Landry "had not been herself," that she had seemed "low and anxious," and had refused to discuss what was upsetting her. Porter's statement added an intriguing detail that nobody had yet told Strike. The model asserted that Landry had made specific mention, that after-noon, of an intention to leave "everything" to her brother. No context was given; but the impression left was of a girl in a clearly morbid frame of mind.

Strike wondered why his client had not mentioned that his sister had declared her intention of leaving him everything. Of course,

Bristow already had a trust fund. Perhaps the possible acquisition of further vast sums of money did not seem as noteworthy to him as it would to Strike, who had never inherited a penny.

Yawning, Strike lit another cigarette to keep himself awake, and began to read the statement of Lula's mother. By Lady Yvette Bristow's own account, she had been drowsy and unwell in the aftermath of her operation; but she insisted that her daughter had been "perfectly happy" when she came to visit that morning, and had evinced nothing but concern for her mother's condition and prospects of recovery. Perhaps the blunt, unnuanced prose of the recording officer was to blame, but Strike took from Lady Bristow's recollections the impression of a determined denial. She alone suggested that Lula's death had been an accident, that she had somehow slipped over the balcony without meaning to; it had been, said Lady Bristow, an icy night.

Strike skim-read Bristow's statement, which tallied in all respects with the account he had given Strike in person, and proceeded to that of Tony Landry, John and Lula's uncle. He had visited Yvette Bristow at the same time as Lula on the day before the latter's death, and asserted that his niece had seemed "normal." Landry had then driven to Oxford, where he had attended a conference on international developments in family law, staying overnight in the Malmaison Hotel. His account of his whereabouts was followed by some incomprehensible comments about telephone calls. Strike turned, for elucidation, to the annotated copies of phone records.

Lula had barely used her landline in the week prior to her death, and not at all on the day before she died. From her mobile, however, she had made no fewer than sixty-six calls on her last day of life. The first, at 9:15 in the morning, had been to Evan Duffield; the second, at 9:35, to Ciara Porter. There followed a gap of hours, in which she had spoken to nobody on the mobile, and then, at 1:21, she had begun a positive frenzy of telephoning two numbers, almost alternately. One of these was Duffield's; the other belonged, according to the crabbed scribble beside the number's first appearance, to Tony Landry. Again and again she had telephoned these two men. Here and there were gaps of twenty minutes or so, during which she made no calls; then she would begin telephoning again, doubtless hitting "redial." All of this frenetic calling, Strike deduced, must have taken place once she was back in her flat with Bryony Radford and Ciara Porter, though neither of the two women's statements made mention of repeated telephoning.

Strike turned back to Tony Landry's statement, which cast no light on the reason his niece had been so anxious to contact him. He had turned off the sound on his mobile while at the conference, he said, and had not realized until much later that his niece had called him repeatedly that afternoon. He had no idea why she had done so and had not called her back, giving as his reason that by the time he realized that she had been trying to reach him, she had stopped calling, and he had guessed, correctly as it turned out, that she would be in a nightclub somewhere.

Strike was now yawning every few minutes; he considered making himself coffee, but could not muster the energy. Wanting his bed, but driven on by habit to complete the job in hand, he turned to the copies of security logbook pages showing the entrances and exits of visitors to number 18 on the day preceding Lula Landry's death. A careful perusal of signatures and initials revealed that Wilson had not been as meticulous in his record-keeping as his employers might have hoped. As Wilson had already told Strike, the movements of the building's residents were not recorded in the book; so the comings and goings of Landry and the Bestiguis were missing. The first entry Wilson had made was for the postman, at 9:10; next, at 9:22, came Florist delivery Flat 2; finally, at 9:50, Securibell. No time of departure was marked for the alarm checker.

Otherwise it had been (as Wilson had said) a quiet day. Ciara Porter had arrived at 12:50; Bryony Radford at 1:20. While Radford's departure was recorded with her own signature at 4:40, Wilson had added the entrance of caterers to the Bestiguis' flat at 7, Ciara's exit with Lula at 7:15 and the departure of the caterers at 9:15.

It frustrated Strike that the only page that the police had photocopied was the day before Landry's death, because he had hoped that he might find the surname of the elusive Rochelle somewhere in the entrance log's pages.

It was nearly midnight when Strike turned his attention to the police report on the contents of Landry's laptop. They appeared to have been searching, principally, for emails indicating suicidal mood or intent, and in this respect they had been unsuccessful. Strike scanned the emails Landry had sent and received in the last two weeks of her life.

It was strange, but nevertheless true, that the countless photographs of her otherworldly beauty had made it harder rather than easier for Strike to believe that Landry had ever really existed. The ubiquity of her features had made them seem abstract, generic, even if the face itself had been uniquely beautiful.

Now, however, out of these dry black marks on paper, out of erratically spelled messages littered with in-jokes and nicknames, the wraith of the dead girl rose before him in the dark office. Her emails gave him what the multitude of photographs had not: a realization in the gut, rather than the brain, that a real, living, laughing and crying human being had been smashed to death on that snowy London street. He had hoped to spot the flickering shadow of a murderer as he turned the file's pages, but instead it was the ghost of Lula herself who emerged, gazing up at him, as victims of violent crimes sometimes did, through the detritus of their interrupted lives.

He saw, now, why John Bristow insisted that his sister had had no thought of death. The girl who had typed out these words emerged as a warmhearted friend, sociable, impulsive, busy and glad to be so; enthusiastic about her job, excited, as Bristow had said, about the prospect of a trip to Morocco.

Most of the emails had been sent to the designer Guy Somé. They held nothing of interest except a tone of cheery confidentiality, and, once, a mention of her most incongruous friendship:

> Geegee, will you pleeeeeze make Rochelle something for her birthday, please please? I'll pay. Something nice (don't be horrible). For Feb 21st? Pleezy please. Love ya. Cuckoo.

Strike remembered the assertion of LulaMyInspirationForeva that Lula had loved Guy Somé "like a brother." His statement to the police was the shortest in the file. He had been in Japan for a week and had arrived home on the night of her death. Strike knew that Somé lived within easy walking distance of Kentigern Gardens, but the police appeared to have been satisfied with his assertion that, once home, he had simply gone to bed. Strike had already noted the fact that anyone walking from Charles Street would have approached Kentigern Gardens from the opposite direction to the CCTV camera on Alderbrook Road.

Strike closed the file at last. As he moved laboriously through his office, undressing, removing the prosthesis and unfolding the camp bed, he thought of nothing but his own exhaustion. He fell asleep quickly, lulled by the sounds of humming traffic, the pattering rain and the deathless breath of the city.

2

A LARGE MAGNOLIA TREE STOOD in the front garden of Lucy's house in Bromley. Later in the spring it would cover the front lawn in what looked like crumpled tissues; now, in April, it was a frothy cloud of white, its petals waxy as coconut shavings. Strike had only visited this house a few times, because he preferred to meet Lucy away from her home, where she always seemed most harried, and to avoid encounters with his brother-in-law, for whom his feelings were on the cooler side of tepid.

Helium-filled balloons, tied to the gate, bobbled in the light breeze. As Strike walked down the steeply sloping front path to the door, the package Robin had wrapped under his arm, he told himself that it would soon be over.

"Where's Charlotte?" demanded Lucy, short, blonde and round-faced, immediately upon opening the front door.

More big golden foil balloons, this time in the shape of the number seven, filled the hall behind her. Screams that might have denoted excitement or pain were issuing from some unseen region of the house, disturbing the suburban peace.

"She had to go back to Ayr for the weekend," lied Strike.

"Why?" asked Lucy, standing back to let him in.

"Another crisis with her sister. Where's Jack?"

"They're all through here. Thank God it's stopped raining, or we'd have had to have them in the house," said Lucy, leading him out into the back garden.

They found his three nephews tearing around the large back lawn with twenty assorted boys and girls in party clothes, who were shrieking their way through some game that involved running to various cricket stumps on which pictures of pieces of fruit had been taped. Parent helpers stood around in the weak sunlight, drinking wine out of plastic cups, while Lucy's husband, Greg, manned an iPod standing in a dock on a trestle table. Lucy handed Strike a lager, then dashed away from him almost immediately, to pick up the youngest of her three sons, who had fallen hard and was bawling with gusto.

Strike had never wanted children; it was one of the things on which he and Charlotte had always agreed, and it had been one of the reasons other relationships over the years had foundered. Lucy deplored his attitude, and the reasons he gave for it; she was always miffed when he stated life aims that differed from hers, as though he were attacking her decisions and choices.

"All right, there, Corm?" said Greg, who had handed over the control of the music to another father. Strike's brother-in-law was a quantity surveyor, who never seemed quite sure what tone to take with Strike, and usually settled for a combination of chippiness and aggression that Strike found irksome. "Where's that gorgeous Charlotte? Not split up again, have you? Ha ha ha. I can't keep track."

One of the little girls had been pushed over: Greg hurried off to help one of the other mothers deal with more tears and grass stains. The game roared on in chaos. At last, a winner was declared; there were more tears from the runner-up, who had to be placated with a consolation prize from the black bin bag sitting beside the hydrangeas. A second round of the same game was then announced.

"Hi there!" said a middle-aged matron, sidling up to Strike. "You must be Lucy's brother!"

"Yeah," he said.

"We heard all about your poor leg," she said, staring down at his shoes. "Lucy kept us all posted. Gosh, you wouldn't even know, would you? I couldn't even see you limping when you arrived. Isn't it amazing what they can do these days? I expect you can run faster now than you could before!"

Perhaps she imagined that he had a single carbon-fiber prosthetic blade under his trousers, like a Paralympian. He sipped his lager, and forced a humorless smile.

"Is it true?" she asked, ogling him, her face suddenly full of naked curiosity. "Are you really Jonny Rokeby's son?"

Some thread of patience, which Strike had not realized was strained to breaking point, snapped.

"Fucked if I know," he said. "Why don't you call him and ask?"

She looked stunned. After a few seconds, she walked away from him in silence. He saw her talking to another woman, who glanced towards Strike. Another child fell over, crashing its head on to the cricket stump decorated with a giant strawberry, and emitting an ear-splitting shriek. With all attention focused on the fresh casualty, Strike slipped back inside the house.

The front room was blandly comfortable, with a beige three-piece suite, an Impressionist print over the mantelpiece and framed photographs of his three nephews in their bottle-green school uniform displayed on shelves. Strike closed the door carefully on the noise from the garden, took from his pocket the DVD Wardle had sent, inserted it into the player and turned on the TV.

There was a photograph on top of the set, taken at Lucy's thirtieth birthday party. Lucy's father, Rick, was there with his second wife. Strike stood at the back, where he had been placed in every group photograph since he was five years old. He had been in possession of two legs then. Tracey, fellow SIB officer and the girl whom Lucy had hoped her brother would marry, was standing next to him. Tracey had subsequently married one of their mutual friends, and had recently given birth to a daughter. Strike had meant to send flowers, but had never got round to it.

He dropped his gaze to the screen, and pressed "play."

The grainy black-and-white footage began immediately. A white street, thick blobs of snow drifting past the eye of the camera. The 180° view showed the intersection of Bellamy and Alderbrook Roads.

A man walked, alone, into view, from the right side of the screen; tall, his hands deep in his pockets, swathed in layers, a hood over his head. His face looked strange in the black-and-white footage; it tricked the eye; Strike thought that he was looking at a stark white lower face and a dark blindfold, before reason told him that he was in fact looking at a dark upper face, and a white scarf tied over the nose, mouth and chin. There was some kind of mark, perhaps a blurry logo, on his jacket; otherwise his clothing was unidentifiable.

As the walker approached the camera, he bowed his head and appeared to consult something he drew out of his pocket. Seconds later, he turned up Bellamy Road and disappeared out of range of the camera. The digital clock in the lower right-hand portion of the screen registered 01:39.

The film jumped. Here again was the blurred view of the same intersection, apparently deserted, the same heavy flakes of snow obscuring the view, but now the clock in the lower corner read 02:12.

The two runners burst into view. The one in front was recognizable as the man who had walked out of range with his white scarf over his mouth; long-legged and powerful, he ran, his arms pumping, straight back down Alderbrook Road. The second man was smaller, slighter, hooded and hatted; Strike noticed the dark fists, clenched as he pelted along behind the first, losing ground to the taller man all the way. Under a street lamp, a design on the back of his sweatshirt was briefly illuminated; halfway along Alderbrook Road he veered suddenly left and up a side street.

Strike replayed the few seconds' footage again, and then again. He saw no sign of communication between the two runners; no sign that they had called to each other, or even looked for each other, as they sprinted away from the camera. It seemed to have been every man for himself.

He replayed the footage for a fourth time, and froze it, after several attempts, at the second when the design on the back of the slower man's sweatshirt had been illuminated. Squinting at the screen, he edged closer to the blurry picture. After a minute's prolonged staring, he was almost sure that the first word ended in "ck," but the second, which he thought began with a "J," was indecipherable.

He pressed "play" and let the film run on, trying to make out which street the second man had taken. Three times Strike watched him split away from his companion, and although its name was unreadable onscreen, he knew, from what Wardle had said, that it must be Halliwell Street.

The police had thought that the fact that the first man had picked up a friend off-camera diminished his plausibility as a killer. This was assuming that the two were, indeed, friends. Strike had to concede that the fact that they had been caught on film together, in such weather, and at such an hour, acting in an almost identical fashion, suggested complicity.

Allowing the footage to run on, he watched as it cut, in almost startling fashion, to the interior of a bus. A girl got on; filmed from a position above the driver, her face was foreshortened and heavily shadowed, though her blonde ponytail was distinctive. The man who followed her on to the bus bore, as far as it was possible to see, a strong resemblance to the one who had later walked up Bellamy Road towards Kentigern Gardens. He was tall and hooded, with a white scarf over his face, the upper part lost in shadow. All that was clear was the logo on his chest, a stylized GS.

The film jerked to show Theobalds Road. If the individual walking fast along it was the same person who had got on the bus, he had removed his white scarf, although his build and walk were strongly reminiscent. This time, Strike thought that the man was making a conscious effort to keep his head bowed.

The film ended in a blank black screen. Strike sat looking at it, deep in thought. When he recalled himself to his surroundings, it was a slight surprise to find them multicolored and sunlit.

He took his mobile out of his pocket and called John Bristow, but reached only voicemail. He left a message telling Bristow that he had now viewed the CCTV footage and read the police file; that there were a few more things he would like to ask, and would it be possible to meet Bristow sometime during the following week.

He then called Derrick Wilson, whose telephone likewise went to voicemail, to which he reiterated his request to come and view the interior of 18 Kentigern Gardens.

Strike had just hung up when the sitting-room door opened, and his middle nephew, Jack, sidled in. He looked flushed and overwrought.

"I heard you talking," Jack said. He closed the door just as carefully as his uncle had done.

"Aren't you supposed to be in the garden, Jack?"

"I've been for a pee," said his nephew. "Uncle Cormoran, did you bring me a present?"

Strike, who had not relinquished the wrapped parcel since arriving, handed it over and watched as Robin's careful handiwork was destroyed by small, eager fingers.

"*Cool,*" said Jack happily. "A *soldier.*"

"That's right," said Strike.

"He's got a gun an' *dev'rything.*"

"Yeah, he has."

"Did you have a gun when you were a soldier?" asked Jack, turning over the box to look at the picture of its contents.

"I had two," said Strike.

"Have you still got them?"

"No, I had to give them back."

"Shame," said Jack, matter-of-factly.

"Aren't you supposed to be playing?" asked Strike, as renewed shrieks erupted from the garden.

"I don't wanna," said Jack. "Can I take him out?"

"Yeah, all right," said Strike.

While Jack ripped feverishly at the box, Strike slipped Wardle's DVD out of the player and pocketed it. Then he helped Jack to free the plastic paratrooper from the restraints holding him to the cardboard insert, and to fix his gun into his hand.

Lucy found them both sitting there ten minutes later. Jack was making his soldier fire around the back of the sofa and Strike was pretending to have taken a bullet to the stomach.

"For God's sake, Corm, it's his party, he's supposed to be playing with the others! Jack, I *told* you you weren't allowed to open any presents yet—pick it up—no, it'll have to stay in here—*no,* Jack, you can play with it later—it's nearly time for tea anyway..."

Flustered and irritable, Lucy ushered her reluctant son back out of the room with a dark backwards look at her brother. When Lucy's lips were pursed she bore a strong resemblance to their Aunt Joan, who was no blood relation to either of them.

The fleeting similarity engendered in Strike an uncharacteristic spirit of cooperation. He behaved, in Lucy's terms, well throughout the rest of the party, devoting himself in the main to defusing brewing arguments between various overexcited children, then barricading himself behind a trestle table covered in jelly and ice cream, thus avoiding the intrusive interest of the prowling mothers.

3

STRIKE WAS WOKEN EARLY ON Sunday morning by the ringing of his mobile, which was recharging on the floor beside his camp bed. The caller was Bristow. He sounded strained.

"I got your message yesterday, but Mum's in a bad way and we haven't got a nurse for this afternoon. Alison's going to come over and keep me company. I could meet you tomorrow, in my lunch hour, if you're free? Have there been any developments?" he added hopefully.

"Some," said Strike cautiously. "Listen, where's your sister's laptop?"

"It's here in Mum's flat. Why?"

"How would you feel about me having a look at it?"

"Fine," said Bristow. "I'll bring it along tomorrow, shall I?"

Strike agreed that this would be a good idea. When Bristow had given him the name and address of his favorite place to eat near his office, and hung up, Strike reached for his cigarettes, and lay for a while smoking and contemplating the pattern made on the ceiling by the sun through the blind slats, savoring the silence and the solitude, the absence of children screaming, of Lucy's attempts to question him over the raucous yells of her youngest. Feeling almost kindly towards his peaceful office, he stubbed out the cigarette, got up and prepared to take his usual shower at ULU.

He finally reached Derrick Wilson, after several more attempts, late on Sunday evening.

"You can't come this week," said Wilson. "Mister Bestigui's round a lot at the moment. I gotta think about mi job, you understand me. I'll call you if there's a good time, all right?"

Strike heard a distant buzzer.

"Are you at work now?" called Strike, before Wilson could hang up.

He heard the security guard say, away from the receiver:

"(Just sign the book, mate.) What?" he added loudly, to Strike.

"If you're there now, could you check the logbook for the name of a friend who used to visit Lula sometimes?"

"What friend?" asked Wilson. "(Yeah, see yuh.)"

"The girl Kieran talked about; the friend from rehab. Rochelle. I want her surname."

"Oh, her, yeah," said Wilson. "Yeah, I'll take a look an' I'll buzz y—"

"Could you have a quick look now?"

He heard Wilson sigh.

"Yeah, all right. Wait there."

Indistinct sounds of movement, clunks and scrapings, then the flick of turning pages. While Strike waited, he contemplated various items of clothing designed by Guy Somé, which were arrayed on his computer screen.

"Yeah, she's here," said Wilson's voice in his ear. "Her name's Rochelle . . . I can' read . . . looks like Onifade."

"Can you spell it?"

Wilson did so, and Strike wrote it down.

"When's the last time she was there, Derrick?"

"Back in early November," said Wilson. "(Yeah, good evenin'.) I gotta go now."

He put the receiver down on Strike's thanks, and the detective returned to his can of Tennent's and his contemplation of modern day-wear, as envisaged by Guy Somé, in particular a hooded zip-up jacket with a stylized GS in gold on the upper left-hand side. The logo was much in evidence on all the ready-to-wear clothing in the menswear section of the designer's website. Strike was not entirely clear on the definition of "ready-to-wear"; it seemed a statement of the obvious, though whatever else the phrase might connote, it meant "cheaper." The second section of the site, named simply "Guy Somé," contained clothing that routinely ran into thousands of pounds. Despite Robin's best endeavors, the designer of these maroon suits, these narrow knitted ties, these minidresses embroidered with mirror fragments, these leather fedoras, was continuing to turn a corporate deaf ear to all requests for an interview concerning the death of his favorite model.

4

You think i wont fucking hurt you but your wrong you
cunt I am comming for you I fucking trusted you and you
did this to me. I am going to pull your fucking dick off
and stuff it down you throat They will find you chock-
ing on your own dick when ive finish with you your own
mother wont no you i am going to fucking kill you Strike
you peice of shit

"It's a nice day out there."

"Will you please read this? Please?"

It was Monday morning, and Strike had just returned from a smoke in the sunny street and a chat with the girl from the record shop opposite. Robin's hair was loose again; she obviously had no more interviews today. This deduction, and the effects of sunlight after rain, combined to lift Strike's spirits. Robin, however, looked strained, standing behind her desk and holding out a pink piece of paper embellished with the usual kittens.

"Still at it, is he?"

Strike took the letter and read it through, grinning.

"I don't understand why you aren't going to the police," said Robin. "The things he's saying he wants to do to you..."

"Just file it," said Strike dismissively, tossing the letter down and rifling through the rest of the paltry pile of mail.

"Yes, well, that's not all," said Robin, clearly annoyed by his attitude. "Temporary Solutions have just called."

"Yeah? What did they want?"

"They asked for me," said Robin. "They obviously suspect I'm still here."

"And what did you say?"

"I pretended to be somebody else."

"Quick thinking. Who?"

"I said my name was Annabel."

"When asked to come up with a fake name on the spot, people usually choose one beginning with 'A,' did you know that?"

"But what if they send somebody to check?"

"Well?"

"It's you they'll try and get money from, not me! They'll try and make you pay a recruitment fee!"

He smiled at her genuine anxiety that he would have to pay money he could not afford. He had been intending to ask her to telephone the office of Freddie Bestigui again, and to begin a search through online telephone directories for Rochelle Onifade's Kilburn-based aunt. Instead he said:

"OK, we'll vacate the premises. I was going to check out a place called Vashti this morning, before I meet Bristow. Maybe it'd look more natural if we both went."

"Vashti? The boutique?" said Robin, at once.

"Yeah. You know it, do you?"

It was Robin's turn to smile. She had read about it in magazines: it epitomized London glamour to her; a place where fashion editors found items of fabulous clothing to show their readers, pieces that would have cost Robin six months' salary.

"I know of it," she said.

He took down her trench coat and handed it to her.

"We'll pretend you're my sister, Annabel. You can be helping me pick out a present for my wife."

"What's the death-threat man's problem?" asked Robin, as they sat side by side on the Tube. "Who is he?"

She had suppressed her curiosity about Jonny Rokeby, and about the dark beauty who had fled Strike's building on her first day at work, and the camp bed they never mentioned; but she was surely entitled to ask questions about the death threats. It was she, after all, who had so far slit open three pink envelopes, and read the unpleasant and violent outpourings scrawled between gamboling kittens. Strike never even looked at them.

"He's called Brian Mathers," said Strike. "He came to see me last June because he thought his wife was sleeping around. He wanted her followed, so I put her under surveillance for a month. Very ordinary woman: plain, frumpy, bad perm; worked in the accounts department of a big carpet warehouse. Spent her weekdays in a poky little office with three female colleagues, went to bingo every Thursday, did the weekly shop on Fridays at Tesco, and on Saturdays went to the local Rotary Club with her husband."

"When did he think she was sleeping around?" asked Robin.

Their pale reflections were swaying in the opaque black window; drained of color in the harsh overhead light, Robin looked older, yet ethereal, and Strike craggier, uglier.

"Thursday nights."

"And was she?"

"No, she really was going to bingo with her friend Maggie, but all four Thursdays that I watched her, she made herself deliberately late home. She drove around a little bit after she'd left Maggie. One night she went into a pub and had a tomato juice on her own, sitting in a corner looking timid. Another night she waited in her car at the end of their street for forty-five minutes before driving around the corner."

"Why?" asked Robin, as the train rattled loudly through a lengthy tunnel.

"Well that's the question, isn't it? Proving something? Trying to get him worked up? Taunting him? Punishing him? Trying to inject a bit of excitement into their dull marriage? Every Thursday, just a bit of unexplained time.

"He's a twitchy bugger, and he'd swallowed the bait all right. It was driving him mad. He was sure she was meeting a lover once a week, that her friend Maggie was covering for her. He'd tried following her himself, but he was convinced that she went to bingo on those occasions because she knew he was watching."

"So you told him the truth?"

"Yeah, I did. He didn't believe me. He got very worked up and started shouting and screaming about everyone being in a conspiracy against him. Refused to pay my bill.

"I was worried he was going to end up doing her an injury, which was where I made my big mistake. I phoned her and told her he'd paid me to watch her, that I knew what she was doing, and that her husband was heading for breaking point. For her own sake, she ought to be careful how far she pushed him. She didn't say a word, just hung up on me.

"Well, he was checking her mobile regularly. He saw my number, and drew the obvious conclusion."

"That you'd told her he was having her watched?"

"No, that I had been seduced by her charms and was her new lover."

Robin clapped her hands over her mouth. Strike laughed.

"Are your clients usually a bit mad?" asked Robin, when she had freed her mouth again.

"He is, but they're usually just stressed."

"I was thinking about John Bristow," Robin said hesitantly. "His girlfriend thinks he's deluded. And you thought he might be a bit . . . you know . . . didn't you?" she asked. "We heard," she added, a little shamefacedly, "through the door. The bit about 'armchair psychologists.' "

"Right," said Strike. "Well . . . I might have changed my mind."

"What do you mean?" asked Robin, her clear gray-blue eyes wide. The train was jolting to a halt; figures were flashing past the windows, becoming less blurred with every second. "Do you—are you saying he's not—that he might be right—that there really was a . . . ?"

"This is our stop."

The white-painted boutique they sought stood on some of the most expensive acreage in London, in Conduit Street, close to the junction with New Bond Street. To Strike, its colorful windows displayed a multitudinous mess of life's unnecessities. Here were beaded cushions and scented candles in silver pots; slivers of artistically draped chiffon; gaudy kaftans worn by faceless mannequins; bulky handbags of an ostentatious ugliness; all spread against a pop-art backdrop, in a gaudy celebration of consumerism he found irritating to retina and spirit. He could imagine Tansy Bestigui and Ursula May in here, examining price tags with expert eyes, selecting four-figure bags of alligator skin with a pleasureless determination to get their money's worth out of their loveless marriages.

Beside him, Robin too was staring at the window display, but only dimly registering what she was looking at. A job offer had been made to her that morning, by telephone, while Strike was smoking downstairs, just before Temporary Solutions had called. Every time she contemplated the offer, which she would have to accept or decline within the next two days, she felt a jab of some intense emotion to the stomach that she was trying to persuade herself was pleasure, but increasingly suspected was dread.

She ought to take it. There was much in its favor. It paid exactly what she and Matthew had agreed she ought to aim for. The offices were smart and well placed for the West End. She and Matthew would be able to lunch together. The employment market was sluggish. She should be delighted.

"How did the interview go on Friday?" asked Strike, squinting at a sequined coat he found obscenely unattractive.

"Quite well, I think," said Robin vaguely.

She recalled the excitement she had felt mere moments ago when Strike had hinted that there might, after all, have been a killer. Was he serious? Robin noted that he was now staring hard at this massive assemblage of fripperies as though they might be able to tell him something important, and this was surely (for a moment she saw with Matthew's eyes, and thought in Matthew's voice) a pose adopted for effect, or show. Matthew kept hinting that Strike was somehow a fake. He seemed to feel that being a private detective was a far-fetched job, like astronaut or lion tamer; that real people did not do such things.

Robin reflected that if she took the human resources job, she might never know (unless she saw it, one day, on the news) how this investigation turned out. To prove, to solve, to catch, to protect: these were things worth doing; important and fascinating. Robin knew that Matthew thought her somehow childish and naive for feeling this way, but she could not help herself.

Strike had turned his back on Vashti, and was looking at something in New Bond Street. His gaze, Robin saw, was fixed on the red letter box standing outside Russell and Bromley, its dark rectangular mouth leering at them across the road.

"OK, let's go," said Strike, turning back to her. "Don't forget, you're my sister and we're shopping for my wife."

"But what are we trying to find out?"

"What Lula Landry and her friend Rochelle Onifade got up to in there, on the day before Landry died. They met here, for fifteen minutes, then parted. I'm not hopeful; it's three months ago, and they might not have noticed anything. Worth a try, though."

The ground floor of Vashti was devoted to clothing; a sign pointing up the wooden stairs indicated that a café and "lifestyle" were housed above. A few women were browsing the shining steel clothes racks; all of them thin and tanned, with long, clean, freshly blow-dried hair. The assistants were an eclectic bunch; their clothing eccentric, their hairstyles outré. One of them was wearing a tutu and fishnets; she was arranging a display of hats.

To Strike's surprise, Robin marched boldly over to this girl.

"Hi," she said brightly. "There's a fabulous sequined coat in your middle window. I wonder whether I could try it on?"

The assistant had a mass of fluffy white hair the texture of candy floss, gaudily painted eyes and no eyebrows.

"Yeah, no probs," she said.

As it turned out, however, she had lied: retrieving the coat from the window was distinctly problematic. It needed to be taken off the mannequin that was wearing it, and disentangled from its electronic tag; ten minutes later, the coat had still not emerged, and the original assistant had called two of her colleagues into the window display to help her. Robin, meanwhile, was drifting around without talking to Strike, picking out an assortment of dresses and belts. By the time the sequined coat was carried out from the window, all three assistants involved in its retrieval seemed somehow invested in its future, and all accompanied Robin towards the changing room, one volunteering to help her carry the pile of extras she had chosen, the other two bearing the coat.

The curtained changing rooms consisted of ironwork frames draped with thick cream silk, like tents. As he positioned himself close enough to listen to what went on inside, Strike felt that he was only now starting to appreciate the full range of his temporary secretary's talents.

Robin had taken over ten thousand pounds' worth of goods into the changing room with her, of which the sequined coat cost half. She would never have had the nerve to do this under normal circumstances, but something had got into her this morning: recklessness and bravado; she was proving something to herself, to Matthew, and even to Strike. The three assistants fussed around her, hanging up dresses and smoothing out the heavy folds of the coat, and Robin felt no shame that she could not have afforded even the cheapest of the belts now draped over the arm of the redhead with tattoos up both arms, and that none of the girls would ever receive the commission for which they were, undoubtedly, vying. She even allowed the assistant with pink hair to go and find a gold jacket she assured Robin would suit her admirably, and go wonderfully well with the green dress she had picked out.

Robin was taller than any of the shop girls, and when she had swapped her trench coat for the sequined one, they cooed and gasped.

"I must show my brother," she told them, after surveying her reflection with a critical eye. "It isn't for me, you see, it's for his wife."

And she strode back out through the changing-room curtains with the three assistants hovering behind her. The rich girls over by the clothing rack all turned to stare at Robin through narrow eyes as she asked boldly:

"What do you think?"

Strike had to admit that the coat he had thought so vile looked better on Robin than on the mannequin. She twirled on the spot for him, and the thing glittered like a lizard's skin.

"It's all right," he said, masculinely cautious, and the assistants smiled indulgently. "Yeah, it's quite nice. How much is it?"

"Not that much, by your standards," said Robin, with an arch look at her handmaidens. "Sandra would love this, though," she said firmly to Strike, who, caught off guard, grinned. "And it *is* her fortieth."

"She could wear it with anything," the candy floss girl assured Strike eagerly. "So versatile."

"OK, I'll try that Cavalli dress," said Robin blithely, turning back to the changing room.

"Sandra told me to come with him," she told the three assistants, as they helped her out of the coat, and unzipped the dress to which she had pointed. "To make sure he doesn't make another stupid mistake. He bought her the world's ugliest earrings for her thirtieth; they cost an arm and a leg and she's never had them out of the safe."

Robin did not know where the invention was coming from; she felt inspired. Stepping out of her jumper and skirt, she began to wriggle into a clinging poison-green dress. Sandra was becoming real to her as she talked: a little spoiled, somewhat bored, confiding in her sister-in-law over wine that her brother (a banker, Robin thought, though Strike did not really look like her idea of a banker) had no taste at all.

"So she said to me, take him to Vashti and get him to crack open his wallet. Oh yes, this is nice."

It was more than nice. Robin stared at her own reflection; she had never worn anything so beautiful in her life. The green dress was magically constructed to shrink her waist to nothingness, to carve her figure into flowing curves, to elongate her pale neck. She was a serpentine goddess in glittering viridian, and the assistants were all murmuring and gasping their appreciation.

"How much?" Robin asked the redhead.

"Two thousand eight hundred and ninety-nine," said the girl.

"Nothing to him," said Robin airily, striding out through the curtains to show Strike, whom they found examining a pile of gloves on a circular table.

His only comment on the green dress was "Yeah." He had barely looked at her.

"Well, maybe it's not Sandra's color," said Robin, with a sudden feeling of embarrassment; Strike was not, after all, her brother or her boyfriend; she had perhaps taken invention too far, parading in front of him in a skintight dress. She retreated into the changing room.

Stripped again to bra and pants she said:

"The last time Sandra was here, Lula Landry was in your café. Sandra said she was gorgeous in the flesh. Even better than in pictures."

"Oh yeah, she was," agreed the pink-haired girl, who was clutching to her chest the gold jacket she had fetched. "She used to be in here all the time, we used to see her every week. Do you want to try this?"

"She was in here the day before she died," said the candy floss–haired girl, helping Robin to wriggle into the gold jacket. "In this changing room, actually in this one."

"Really?" said Robin.

"It's not going to close over the bust, but it looks great open," said the redhead.

"No, that's no good, Sandra's a bit bigger than me, if anything," said Robin, ruthlessly sacrificing her fictional sister-in-law's figure. "I'll try that black dress. Did you say Lula Landry was here actually the day before she died?"

"Oh yeah," said the girl with pink hair. "We had trouble with her and one of our girls. Mel gave her the sack for it, didn't you, Mel? I can't remember her name now ... she was Australian ..."

"And she had it coming," said the tattooed redhead, who was holding up a black dress with lace inserts. "She was always pestering the famous customers. She barged in here on Lula without so much as a by-your-leave. I heard her do it, I was in the cubicle next door."

"She—followed—Lula—in here?" gasped Robin as she was inched into the black dress by the combined efforts of the three assistants. "When she was changing?"

"Well—Lula was on the phone—but that's hardly the point, is it?" asked red-haired Mel. "She marched in here with a random outfit Lula hadn't even asked for, just so she could ask Lula if she could get her a job as a makeup artist."

Robin twitched the tight black dress straight and braced herself for the raising of the zip. It was oppressive enough to be crammed in here with three girls eager for commission. Now she wondered what it would feel like to be pestered for a job while she stood semi-dressed behind a flimsy curtain.

"She was on the phone when the girl interrupted her, did you say?"

"Yeah," said Mel and then, with a certain defensiveness, "I couldn't help overhearing, I was in the next booth collecting stuff another client had left. They're only silk, these curtains."

"I'll bet she wasn't too pleased being interrupted if she was talking on the—"

" 'Course she wasn't," said Mel, and she imitated the model's outraged voice: " 'I didn't ask for that, what are you doing in here?' "

The pink-haired girl heaved the zip skywards and Robin's ribcage was slowly compressed by a hidden boned corset. Strike, who had moved as close as he dared to the silk curtains in the hope that the contents of one of Lula's telephone calls were about to be revealed, was disconcerted to hear Robin's next question emerge as a groan.

"What happened then?"

"Talk about brazen!" said Mel indignantly, and in an Australian accent quite as bad as Robin's she said: " 'Oh, I just thought you'd look so lovely in this, Lula, and by the way, I'm trying to break into the makeup game, can I give you my details?' Blah, blah, blah."

"What a cheek!" gasped Robin, now acutely uncomfortable in a lace and leather straitjacket. Two thirds of her breasts were squashed flat by the straining material, while the upper slopes overflowed the neckline. "No, I—I definitely don't think Sandra would like this . . . I might try the coat again . . . I bet Lula told the girl where to get off, did she?"

"Well, no, actually, because—Lula was in a bit of a state when she—no, she took her details just to get rid of her. I do *love* that coat on you, I really do," said Mel, reverting suddenly to a more professional, less gossipy tone.

Robin suspected that Mel saw her own shameless eavesdropping as justified if it had exposed the unprofessionalism of a colleague. To relate the contents of Lula's telephone conversation prior to the interruption might paint her as no less intrusive and rather more underhanded than her brazen subordinate.

Robin wriggled out of the black dress, trying to think of a way to melt Mel's new reserve. The girl with the candy floss hair came unexpectedly to her aid.

"I always said you should've gone to the police, Mel."

"I didn't hear anything that mattered," said Mel quickly. "I couldn't help overhearing her," she told Robin, helping her back into the sequined coat. "She wasn't exactly keeping her voice down—"

"And these curtains aren't thick," agreed Robin sycophantically. "You'd think she'd have more sense."

"Exactly, with the press all over her all the time—and anyway, it wouldn't have made any difference. He wasn't there, was he? That was proven."

Robin turned slowly this way and that, watching the play of light on the exorbitantly priced coat.

"You mean Evan Duffield?" she asked absently.

"I still think Mel should've gone to the police," said the candy floss–haired girl. "I said that at the time."

"He never went to her flat!" said Mel. The desire to justify herself had loosened her tongue. "No, all it was—he must've been saying he had something on and he didn't want to see her, because she was going, 'Come after, then, I'll wait up, it don't matter. I probably won't be home till one anyway. Please come, please.' Like, begging him. Anyway, she had her friend in the cubicle with her. Her friend heard everything, so she would've told the police, wouldn't she?"

Absently smoothing the iridescent surface of the coat she could never afford, Robin asked almost as an afterthought:

"And it was definitely Evan Duffield she was talking to, was it?"

"Of course it was," said Mel, as though Robin had insulted her intelligence. "Who else would she've been asking round to her place in the early hours? She sounded desperate to see him."

"God, his eyes," said the girl with the candy floss hair. "He is so gorgeous. And massive charisma in person. He came in here with her once. God, he's sexy."

Five minutes later, having agreed with Strike in front of the assistants that the sequined coat was the best of the bunch, Robin decided (with the assistants' agreement) that she ought to bring Sandra in to have a look at it the following day before they committed themselves. Strike reserved the five-thousand-pound coat under the name of Andrew Atkinson, gave an invented mobile phone number and left the boutique with Robin in a shower of friendly good wishes, as though they had already spent the money.

They walked fifty yards in silence, and Strike had lit up a cigarette before he said:

"Very, very impressive."

Robin glowed with pride.

5

STRIKE AND ROBIN PARTED AT Bond Street station. Robin took the underground back to the office to call BestFilms, look through on-line telephone directories for Rochelle Onifade's aunt, and evade Temporary Solutions ("Keep the door locked" was Strike's advice).

Strike bought himself a newspaper and caught the underground to Knightsbridge, then walked, having plenty of time to spare, to the Serpentine Bar and Kitchen, which Bristow had chosen for their lunch appointment.

The trip took him across Hyde Park, down leafy walkways and across the sandy bridle path of Rotten Row. He had jotted down the bare bones of the girl called Mel's evidence on the Tube, and now, in the sun-dappled greenery, his mind drifted, lingering on the memory of Robin as she had looked in the clinging green dress.

He had disconcerted her by his reaction, he knew that; but there had been a weird intimacy about the moment, and intimacy was precisely what he wanted least at the moment, most especially with Robin, bright, professional and considerate as she was. He enjoyed her company and he appreciated the way that she respected his privacy, keeping her curiosity in check. God knew, thought Strike, moving over to avoid a cyclist, he had come across that particular quality rarely enough in life, particularly from women. Yet the fact that he would, quite soon, be free of Robin was an inextricable part of his enjoyment of her presence; the fact that she was going to move on imposed, like her engagement ring, a happy boundary. He liked Robin; he was grateful to her; he was even (after this morning) impressed by her; but, having normal sight and an unimpaired libido, he was also reminded every day she bent over the computer monitor that she was a very sexy girl. Not beautiful; nothing like Charlotte; but attractive, nonetheless. That fact had never been so crudely presented to him as when she walked out of the changing room in the clinging green dress, and in consequence he had literally averted his eyes. He acquitted her of any deliberate provocation, but he was realistic, all the same, about the precarious balance that must be maintained for his own sanity. She was the only human with whom he was in regular contact, and he did not underestimate his current susceptibility; he had also gathered, from certain evasions and hesitations, that her fiancé disliked the fact that she had left the temping agency for this ad hoc agreement. It was safest all round not to let the burgeoning friendship become too warm; best not to admire openly the sight of her figure draped in jersey.

Strike had never been to the Serpentine Bar and Kitchen. It was set on the boating lake, a striking building that was more like a futuristic pagoda than anything he had ever seen. The thick white roof, looking like a giant book that had been placed down on its open pages, was supported by concertinaed glass. A huge weeping willow caressed the side of the restaurant and brushed the water's surface.

Though it was a cool, breezy day, the view over the lake was splendid in the sunlight. Strike chose an outdoor table right beside the water, ordered a pint of Doom Bar and read his paper.

Bristow was already ten minutes late when a tall, well-made, expensively suited man with foxy coloring stopped beside Strike's table.

"Mr. Strike?"

In his late fifties, with a full head of hair, a firm jaw and pronounced cheekbones, he looked like an almost-famous actor hired to play a rich businessman in a miniseries. Strike, whose visual memory was highly trained, recognized him immediately from the photographs that Robin had found online as the tall man who had looked as though he deplored his surroundings at Lula Landry's funeral.

"Tony Landry. John and Lula's uncle. May I sit down?"

His smile was perhaps the most perfect example of an insincere social grimace that Strike had ever witnessed; a mere baring of even white teeth. Landry eased himself out of his overcoat, draped it over the back of the seat opposite Strike and sat.

"John's delayed at the office," he said. The breeze ruffled his hair, showing how it had receded at the temples. "He asked Alison to call you and let you know. I happened to be passing her desk at the time, so I thought I'd come and deliver the message in person. It gives me an opportunity to have a private word with you. I've been expecting you to contact me; I know you're working your way slowly through all my niece's contacts."

He slid a pair of steel-rimmed glasses out of his top pocket, put them on and took a moment to consult the menu. Strike drank some beer and waited.

"I hear you've been speaking to Mrs. Bestigui?" said Landry, setting down the menu, taking off his glasses again and reinserting them into his suit pocket.

"That's right," said Strike.

"Yes. Well, Tansy is undoubtedly well intentioned, but she is doing herself no favors at all by repeating a story the police have proven, conclusively, could not have been true. No favors at all," repeated Landry portentously. "And so I have told John. His first duty ought to be to the firm's client, and what is in her best interests.

"I will have the ham hock terrine," he added to a passing waitress, "and a still water. Bottled. Well," he continued, "it's probably best to be direct, Mr. Strike.

"For many reasons, all of them good ones, I am not in favor of raking over the circumstances of Lula's death. I don't expect you to agree with me. You make money by digging through the seamy circumstances of family tragedies."

He flashed his aggressive, humorless smile again.

"I'm not entirely unsympathetic. We all have our livings to make, and no doubt there are plenty of people who would say my profession is just as parasitic as yours. It might be helpful to both of us, though, if I lay certain facts in front of you, facts I doubt John has chosen to disclose."

"Before we get into that," said Strike, "what exactly is keeping John at the office? If he isn't going to make it, I'll arrange an alternative appointment with him; I've got other people to see this afternoon. Is he still trying to sort out this Conway Oates business?"

He knew only what Ursula had told him, that Conway Oates had been an American financier, but this mention of the firm's dead client had the desired effect. Landry's pomposity, his desire to control the encounter, his comfortable air of superiority, vanished entirely, leaving him clothed in nothing but temper and shock.

"John hasn't—can he really have been so . . . ? That is strictly confidential business of the firm!"

"It wasn't John," said Strike. "Mrs. Ursula May mentioned that there's been a bit of trouble around Mr. Oates's estate."

Clearly thrown, Landry spluttered, "I am very surprised—I wouldn't have expected Ursula—Mrs. May . . ."

"So will John be along at all? Or have you given him something that will keep him busy all through lunch?"

He enjoyed watching Landry wrestle his own temper, trying to regain control of himself and the encounter.

"John will be here shortly," he said finally. "I hoped, as I said, to be able to lay certain facts in front of you, in private."

"Right, well, in that case, I'll need these," said Strike, removing a notebook and pen from his pocket.

Landry looked quite as put out by the sight of these objects as Tansy had.

"There's no need to take notes," he said. "What I'm about to say has no bearing—or at least, no direct bearing—on Lula's death. That is," he added pedantically, "it will add nothing to any theory other than that of suicide."

"All the same," said Strike, "I like to have my aide-memoire."

Landry looked as though he would like to protest, but thought better of it.

"Very well, then. Firstly, you should know that my nephew John was deeply affected by his adopted sister's death."

"Understandable," commented Strike, tilting the notebook so that the lawyer could not read it, and writing the words deeply affected, purely to annoy Landry.

"Yes, naturally. And while I would never go so far as to suggest that a private detective refuse a client on the basis that they are under strain, or depressed—as I said, we all have our livings to make—in this case . . ."

"You think it's all in his head?"

"That's not how I'd have phrased it, but bluntly, yes. John has already suffered more sudden bereavements than many people experience in a lifetime. You probably weren't aware that he's already lost a brother..."

"Yeah, I knew. Charlie was an old schoolmate of mine. That's why John hired me."

Landry contemplated Strike with what seemed to be surprise and disfavor.

"You were at Blakeyfield Prep?"

"Briefly. Before my mother realized she couldn't afford the fees."

"I see. I did not know that. Even so, perhaps you're not fully aware...John has always been—let's use my sister's expression for it—highly strung. His parents had to bring in psychologists after Charlie died, you know. I don't claim to be a mental health expert, but it seems to me that Lula's passing has, finally, tipped him over the..."

"Unfortunate choice of phrase, but I see what you mean," said Strike, writing Bristow off rocker. "How exactly has John been tipped over the edge?"

"Well, many would say that instigating this reinvestigation is irrational and pointless," said Landry.

Strike kept his pen poised over the notepad. For a moment, Landry's jaws moved as though he was chewing; then he said forcefully:

"Lula was a manic depressive who jumped out of the window after a row with her junkie boyfriend. There is no mystery. It was goddamn awful for all of us, especially her poor bloody mother, but those are the unsavory facts. I'm forced to the conclusion that John is having some kind of breakdown, and, if you don't mind me speaking frankly..."

"Feel free."

"...your collusion is perpetuating his unhealthy refusal to accept the truth."

"Which is that Lula killed herself?"

"A view that is shared by the police, the pathologist and the coroner. John, for reasons that are obscure to me, is determined to prove murder. How he thinks that will make any of us feel any better, I could not tell you."

"Well," said Strike, "people close to suicides often feel guilty. They think, however unreasonably, that they might have done more to help. A murder verdict would exonerate the family of any blame, wouldn't it?"

"None of us has anything to feel guilty about," said Landry, his tone steely. "Lula received the very best medical care from her early teens, and every material advantage her adoptive family could give her. 'Spoiled rotten' might be the phrase best suited to describe my adopted niece, Mr. Strike. Her mother would have literally died for her, and scant repayment she ever received."

"You thought Lula ungrateful, did you?"

"There's no need to bloody write that down. Or are those notes destined for some tawdry rag?"

Strike was interested in how completely Landry had jettisoned the suavity he had brought to the table. The waitress arrived with Landry's food. He did not thank her, but glared at Strike until she had passed on. Then he said:

"You're poking around where you can only do harm. I was stunned, frankly, when I found out what John was up to. Stunned."

"Hadn't he expressed doubts about the suicide theory to you?"

"He'd expressed shock, naturally, like all of us, but I certainly don't recall any suggestion of murder."

"Are you close to your nephew, Mr. Landry?"

"What has that got to do with anything?"

"It might explain why he didn't tell you what he was thinking."

"John and I have a perfectly amicable working relationship."

" 'Working relationship'?"

"Yes, Mr. Strike: we work together. Do we live in each other's pockets outside the office? No. But we are both involved in caring for my sister—Lady Bristow, John's mother, who is now a terminal case. Our out-of-hours conversations usually concern Yvette."

"John strikes me as a dutiful son."

"Yvette's all he has left now, and the fact that she's dying isn't helping his mental condition either."

"She's hardly all he's got left. There's Alison, isn't there?"

"I am not aware that that is a very serious relationship."

"Perhaps one of John's motives, in employing me, is a desire to give his mother the truth before she dies?"

"The truth won't help Yvette. Nobody enjoys accepting that they have reaped what they have sown."

Strike said nothing. As he had expected, the lawyer could not resist the temptation to clarify, and after a moment he continued:

"Yvette has always been morbidly maternal. She adores babies." He spoke as though this was faintly disgusting, a kind of perversion. "She would have been one of those embarrassing women who have twenty children if she could have found a man of sufficient virility. Thank God Alec was sterile—or hasn't John mentioned that?"

"He told me Sir Alec Bristow wasn't his natural father, if that's what you mean."

If Landry was disappointed not to be first with the information, he rallied at once.

"Yvette and Alec adopted the two boys, but she had no idea how to manage them. She is, quite simply, an atrocious mother. No control, no discipline; complete overindulgence and a point-blank refusal to see what is under her nose. I don't say it was all down to her parenting—who knows what the genetic influences were—but John was whiny, histrionic and clingy and Charlie was completely delinquent, with the result—"

Landry stopped talking abruptly, patches of color high in his cheeks.

"With the result that he rode over the edge of a quarry?" Strike suggested.

He had said it to watch Landry's reaction, and was not disappointed. He had the impression of a tunnel contracting, a distant door closing: a shutting down.

"Not to put too fine a point on it, yes. And it was a bit late, then, for Yvette to start screaming and clawing at Alec, and passing out cold on the floor. If she'd had an iota of control, the boy wouldn't have set out expressly to defy her. I was there," said Landry, stonily. "On a weekend visit. Easter Sunday. I had been for a walk down to the village, and I came back to find them all looking for him. I headed straight for the quarry. I knew, you see. It was the place he'd been forbidden to go — so there he was."

"You found the body, did you?"

"Yes, I did."

"That must have been highly distressing."

"Yes," said Landry, his lips barely moving. "It was."

"And it was after Charlie died, wasn't it, that your sister and Sir Alec adopted Lula?"

"Which was probably the single most stupid thing Alec Bristow ever agreed to," said Landry. "Yvette had already proven herself a disastrous mother; was she likely to be any more successful while in a state of abandoned grief? Of course, she'd always wanted a daughter, a baby to dress in pink, and Alec thought it would make her happy. He always gave Yvette anything she wanted. He was besotted with her from the moment she joined his typing pool, and he was an unvarnished East Ender. Yvette has always had a predilection for a bit of rough."

Strike wondered what the real source of Landry's anger could be.

"You don't get along with your sister, Mr. Landry?" asked Strike.

"We get along perfectly well; it is simply that I am not blind to what Yvette is, Mr. Strike, nor how much of her misfortune is her own damn fault."

"Was it difficult for them to get approved for another adoption after Charlie died?" asked Strike.

"I daresay it would have been, if Alec hadn't been a multimillionaire," snorted Landry. "I know the authorities were concerned about Yvette's mental health, and they were both a bit long in the tooth by then. It's a great pity that they weren't turned down. But Alec was a man of infinite resourcefulness and he had all sorts of strange contacts from his barrow-boy days. I don't know the details, but I'd be prepared to bet money changed hands somewhere. Even so, he couldn't manage a Caucasian. He brought another child of completely unknown provenance into the family, to be raised by a depressed and hysterical woman of no judgment. It was hardly a surprise to me that the result was catastrophic. Lula was as unstable as John and as wild as Charlie, and Yvette had just as little idea how to manage her."

Scribbling away for Landry's benefit, Strike wondered whether his belief in genetic predetermination accounted for some of Bristow's preoccupation with Lula's black relatives. Doubtless Bristow had been privy to his uncle's views through the years; children absorbed the views of their relatives at some deep, visceral level. He, Strike, had known in his bones, long before the words had ever been said in front of him, that his mother was not like other mothers, that there was (if he believed in the unspoken code that bound the rest of the adults around him) something shameful about her.

"You saw Lula the day she died, I think?" Strike said.

Landry's eyelashes were so fair they looked silver.

"Excuse me?"

"Yeah..." Strike flicked back through his notebook ostentatiously, coming to a halt at an entirely blank page. "...you met her at your sister's flat, didn't you? When Lula called in to see Lady Bristow?"

"Who told you that? John?"

"It's all in the police file. Isn't it true?"

"Yes, it's perfectly true, but I can't see how it's relevant to anything we've been discussing."

"I'm sorry; when you arrived, you said you'd been expecting to hear from me. I got the impression you were happy to answer questions."

Landry had the air of a man who has found himself unexpectedly snookered.

"I have nothing to add to the statement I gave to the police," he said at last.

"Which is," said Strike, leafing backwards through blank pages, "that you dropped in to visit your sister that morning, where you met your niece, and that you then drove to Oxford to attend a conference on international developments in family law?"

Landry was chewing on air again.

"That's correct," he said.

"What time would you say you arrived at your sister's flat?"

"It must have been about ten," said Landry, after a short pause.

"And you stayed how long?"

"Half an hour, perhaps. Maybe longer. I really can't remember."

"And you drove directly from there to the conference in Oxford?"

Over Landry's shoulder, Strike saw John Bristow questioning a waitress; he appeared out of breath and a little disheveled, as though he had been running. A rectangular leather case dangled from his hand. He glanced around, panting slightly, and when he spotted the back of Landry's head, Strike thought that he looked frightened.

6

"JOHN," SAID STRIKE, AS HIS client approached them.

"Hi, Cormoran."

Landry did not look at his nephew, but picked up his knife and fork and took a first bite of his terrine. Strike moved around the table to make room for Bristow to sit down opposite his uncle.

"Have you spoken to Reuben?" Landry asked Bristow coldly, once he had finished his mouthful of terrine.

"Yes. I've said I'll go over this afternoon and take him through all the deposits and drawings."

"I've just been asking your uncle about the morning before Lula died, John. About when he visited your mother's flat," said Strike.

Bristow glanced at Landry.

"I'm interested in what was said and done there," Strike continued, "because, according to the chauffeur who drove her back from her mother's flat, Lula seemed distressed."

"Of course she was distressed," snapped Landry. "Her mother had cancer."

"The operation she'd just had was supposed to have cured her, wasn't it?"

"Yvette had just had a hysterectomy. She was in pain. I don't doubt Lula was disturbed at seeing her mother in that condition."

"Did you talk much to Lula, when you saw her?"

A minuscule hesitation.

"Just chit-chat."

"And you two, did you speak to each other?"

Bristow and Landry did not look at each other. A longer pause, of a few seconds, before Bristow said:

"I was working in the home office. I heard Tony come in, heard him speaking to Mum and Lula."

"You didn't look in to say hello?" Strike asked Landry.

Landry considered him through slightly boiled-looking eyes, pale between the light lashes.

"You know, nobody here is obliged to answer your questions, Mr. Strike," said Landry.

"Of course not," agreed Strike, and he made a small and incomprehensible note in his pad. Bristow was looking at his uncle. Landry seemed to reconsider.

"I could see through the open door of the home study that John was hard at work, and I didn't want to disturb him. I sat with Yvette in her room for a while, but she was groggy from the painkillers, so I left her with Lula. I knew," said Landry, with the faintest undertone of spite, "that there was nobody Yvette would prefer to Lula."

"Lula's telephone records show that she called your mobile phone repeatedly after she left Lady Bristow's flat, Mr. Landry."

Landry flushed.

"Did you speak to her on the phone?"

"No. I had my mobile switched to silent; I was late for the conference."

"They vibrate, though, don't they?"

He wondered what it would take to make Landry leave. He was sure that the lawyer was close.

"I glanced at my phone, saw it was Lula and decided it could wait," he said shortly.

"You didn't call her back?"

"No."

"Didn't she leave any kind of message, to tell you what she wanted to talk about?"

"No."

"That seems odd, doesn't it? You'd just seen her at her mother's, and you say nothing very important passed between you; yet she spent much of the rest of the afternoon trying to contact you. Doesn't that seem as though she might have had something urgent to say to you? Or that she wanted to continue a conversation you'd been having at the flat?"

"Lula was the kind of girl who would call somebody thirty times in a row, on the flimsiest pretext. She was spoiled. She expected people to jump to attention at the sight of her name."

Strike glanced at Bristow.

"She was—sometimes—a bit like that," her brother muttered.

"Do you think your sister was upset purely because your mother was weak from her operation, John?" Strike asked Bristow. "Her driver, Kieran Kolovas-Jones, is emphatic that she came away from the flat in a dramatically altered mood."

Before Bristow could answer, Landry, abandoning his food, stood up and began to put on his overcoat.

"Is Kolovas-Jones that strange-looking colored boy?" he asked, looking down at Strike and Bristow. "The one who wanted Lula to get him modeling and acting work?"

"He's an actor, yeah," said Strike.

"Yes. On Yvette's birthday, the last before she became ill, I had a problem with my car. Lula and that man called by to give me a lift to the birthday dinner. Kolovas-Jones spent most of the journey badgering Lula to use her influence with Freddie Bestigui to get him an audition. Quite an *encroaching* young man. Very familiar in his manner. Of course," he added, "the less I knew about my adopted niece's love life, the better, as far as I was concerned."

Landry threw a ten-pound note down on the table.

"I'll expect you back at the office soon, John."

He stood in clear expectation of a response, but Bristow was not paying attention. He was staring, wide-eyed, at the picture on the news story that Strike had been reading when Landry arrived; it showed a young black soldier in the uniform of the 2nd Battalion The Royal Regiment of Fusiliers.

"What? Yes. I'll be straight back," he told his uncle distractedly, who was looking at him coldly. "Sorry," Bristow added to Strike, as Landry walked away. "It's just that Wilson—Derrick Wilson, you know, the security guard—he's got a nephew out in Afghanistan. For a moment, God forbid...but it's not him.

Wrong name. Dreadful, this war, isn't it? And is it worth this loss of life?"

Strike shifted the weight off his prosthesis—the trudge across the park had not helped the soreness in his leg—and made a noncommittal noise.

"Let's walk back," said Bristow, when they had finished eating. "I fancy some fresh air."

Bristow chose the most direct route, which involved navigating stretches of lawn that Strike would not have chosen to walk, on his own, because it demanded much more energy than tarmac. As they passed the memorial fountain to Diana, Princess of Wales, whispering, tinkling and gushing along its long channel of Cornish granite, Bristow suddenly announced, as though Strike had asked:

"Tony's never liked me much. He preferred Charlie. People said that Charlie looked like Tony did, when he was a boy."

"I can't say he spoke about Charlie with much fondness before you arrived, and he doesn't seem to have had much time for Lula, either."

"Didn't he give you his views on heredity?"

"By implication."

"No, well, he's not usually shy about them. It made an extra bond between Lula and me, the fact that Uncle Tony considered us a pair of sow's ears. It was worse for Lula; at least my biological parents must have been white. Tony's not what you'd call unprejudiced. We had a Pakistani trainee last year; she was one of the best we've ever had, but Tony drove her out."

"What made you go and work with him?"

"They made me a good offer. It's the family firm; my grandfather started it, not that that was an inducement. No one wants to be accused of nepotism. But it's one of the top family law firms in London, and it made my mother happy to think I was following in her father's footsteps. Did he have a go at my father?"

"Not really. He hinted that Sir Alec might have greased some palms to get Lula."

"Really?" Bristow sounded surprised. "I don't think that's true. Lula was in care. I'm sure the usual procedures were followed."

There was a short silence, after which Bristow said, a little timidly: "You, ah, don't look very much like *your* father."

It was the first time that he had acknowledged openly that he might have been sidetracked on to Wikipedia while researching private detectives.

"No," agreed Strike. "I'm the spitting image of my Uncle Ted."

"I gather that you and your father aren't—ah—I mean, you don't use his name?"

Strike did not resent the curiosity from a man whose family background was almost as unconventional and casualty-strewn as his own.

"I've never used it," he said. "I'm the extramarital accident that cost Jonny a wife and several million pounds in alimony. We're not close."

"I admire you," said Bristow, "for making your own way. For not relying on him." And when Strike did not answer, he added anxiously, "I hope you didn't mind me telling Tansy who your father is? It—it helped get her to talk to you. She's impressed by famous people."

"All's fair in securing a witness statement," said Strike. "You say that Lula didn't like Tony, and yet she took his name professionally?"

"Oh no, she chose Landry because it was Mum's maiden name; nothing to do with Tony. Mum was thrilled. I think there was another model called Bristow. Lula liked to stand out."

They wove their way through passing cyclists, bench-picnickers, dog walkers and roller skaters, Strike trying to disguise the increasing unevenness in his step.

"I don't think Tony's ever really loved anyone in his life, you know," said Bristow suddenly, as they stood aside to allow a helmeted child, wobbling along on a skateboard, to pass. "Whereas my mother's a very loving person. She loved all three of her children very much, and I sometimes think Tony didn't like it. I don't know why. It's something in his nature.

"There was a breach between him and my parents after Charlie died. I wasn't supposed to know what was said, but I heard enough. He as good as told Mum that Charlie's accident was her fault, that Charlie had been out of control. My father threw Tony out of the house. Mum and Tony were only really reconciled after Dad died."

To Strike's relief, they had reached Exhibition Road, and his limp became less perceptible.

"Do you think there was ever anything between Lula and Kieran Kolovas-Jones?" he asked, as they crossed the street.

"No, that's just Tony leaping to the most unsavory conclusion he can think of. He always thought the worst when it came to Lula. Oh, I'm sure Kieran would have been only too eager, but Lula was smitten by Duffield—more's the pity."

They walked on down Kensington Road, with the leafy park to their left, and then into the white-stuccoed territory of ambassadors' houses and royal colleges.

"Why do you think your uncle didn't come and say hello to you, when he called at your mother's the day she got out of hospital?"

Bristow looked intensely uncomfortable.

"Had there been a disagreement between you?"

"Not...not exactly," said Bristow. "We were in the middle of a very stressful time at work. I—ought not to say. Client confidentiality."

"Was this to do with the estate of Conway Oates?"

"How do you know that?" asked Bristow sharply. "Did Ursula tell you?"

"She mentioned something."

"Christ almighty. No discretion. *None.*"

"Your uncle found it hard to believe that Mrs. May could have been indiscreet."

"I'll bet he did," said Bristow, with a scornful laugh. "It's—well, I'm sure I can trust you. It's the kind of thing a firm like ours is touchy about, because with the kind of clients we attract—high net worth—any hint of financial impropriety is death. Conway Oates held a sizable client account with us. All the money's present and correct; but his heirs are a greedy bunch and they're claiming it was mismanaged. Considering how volatile the market's been, and how incoherent Conway's instructions became towards the end, they should be grateful there's anything left. Tony's irritable about the whole business and...well, he's a man who likes to spread the blame around. There have been scenes. I've copped my share of criticism. I usually do, with Tony."

Strike could tell, by the almost perceptible heaviness that seemed to be descending upon Bristow as he walked, that they were approaching his offices.

"I'm having difficulty contacting a couple of useful witnesses, John. Is there any chance you'd be able to put me in touch with Guy Somé? His people don't seem keen on letting anyone near him."

"I can try. I'll call him this afternoon. He adored Lula; he ought to want to help."

"And there's Lula's birth mother, too."

"Oh yes," sighed Bristow. "I've got her details somewhere. She's a dreadful woman."

"Have you met her?"

"No, I'm going on what Lula told me, and everything that was in the papers. Lula was determined to find out where she came from, and I think Duffield was encouraging her—I strongly suspect him of leaking the story to the press, though she always denied that . . . Anyway, she managed to track her down, this Higson woman, who told her that her father was an African student. I don't know whether that was true or not. It was certainly what Lula wanted to hear. Her imagination ran wild: I think she had visions of herself being the long-lost daughter of a high-ranking politician, or a tribal princess."

"But she never traced her father?"

"I don't know, but," said Bristow, displaying his usual enthusiasm for any line of inquiry that might explain the black man caught on film near her flat, "I'd have been the last person she'd have told if she did."

"Why?"

"Because we'd had some pretty nasty rows about the whole business. My mother had just been diagnosed with uterine cancer when Lula went searching for Marlene Higson. I told Lula that she could hardly have chosen a more insensitive moment to start tracing her roots, but she—well, frankly, she had tunnel vision where her own whims were concerned. We loved each other," said Bristow, running a weary hand over his face, "but the age difference got in the way. I'm sure she tried to look for her father, though, because that was what she wanted more than anything: to find her black roots, to find that sense of identity."

"Was she still in contact with Marlene Higson when she died?"

"Intermittently. I had the feeling that Lula was trying to cut the connection. Higson's a ghastly person; shamelessly mercenary. She sold her story to anyone who would pay, which, unfortunately, was a lot of people. My mother was devastated by the whole business."

"There are a couple of other things I wanted to ask you."

The lawyer slowed down willingly.

"When you visited Lula at her flat that morning, to return her contract with Somé, did you happen to see anyone who looked like they might have been from a security firm? There to check the alarms?"

"Like a repairman?"

"Or an electrician. Maybe in overalls?"

When Bristow screwed up his face in thought, his rabbity teeth protruded more than ever.

"I can't remember...let me think...As I passed the flat on the second floor, yes...there was a man in there fiddling with something on the wall...Would that have been him?"

"Probably. What did he look like?"

"Well, he had his back to me. I couldn't see."

"Was Wilson with him?"

Bristow came to a halt on the pavement, looking a little bewildered. Three suited men and women bustled past, some carrying files.

"I think," he said haltingly, "I think both of them were there, with their backs to me, when I walked back downstairs. Why do you ask? How can that matter?"

"It might not," said Strike. "But can you remember anything at all? Hair or skin color, maybe?"

Looking even more perplexed, Bristow said:

"I'm afraid I didn't really register. I suppose..." He screwed up his face again in concentration. "I remember he was wearing blue. I mean, if pressed, I'd say he was white. But I couldn't swear to it."

"I doubt you'll have to," said Strike, "but that's still a help."

He pulled out his notebook to remind himself of the questions he had wanted to put to Bristow.

"Oh, yeah. According to her witness statement to the police, Ciara Porter said that Lula had told her she wanted to leave everything to you."

"Oh," said Bristow unenthusiastically. "That."

He began to amble along again, and Strike moved with him.

"One of the detectives in charge of the case told me that Ciara had said that. A Detective Inspector Carver. He was convinced from the first that it was suicide and he appeared to think that this supposed talk with Ciara demonstrated Lula's intent to take her own life. It seemed a strange line of reasoning to me. Do suicides bother with wills?"

"You think Ciara Porter's inventing, then?"

"Not inventing," said Bristow. "Exaggerating, maybe. I think it's much more likely that Lula said something nice about me, because we'd just made up after our row, and Ciara, in hindsight, assuming that Lula was already contemplating suicide, turned whatever it was into a bequest. She's quite a—a fluffy sort of girl."

"A search was made for a will, wasn't it?"

"Oh yeah, the police looked very thoroughly. We—the family— didn't think Lula had ever made one; her lawyers didn't know of one, but naturally a search was made. Nothing was found, and they looked everywhere."

"Just supposing for a moment that Ciara Porter isn't misremembering what your sister said, though . . ."

"But Lula would never have left everything solely to me. Never."

"Why not?"

"Because that would have explicitly cut out our mother, which would have been immensely hurtful," said Bristow earnestly. "It isn't the money—Dad left Mum very well off—it's more the message that Lula would have been sending, cutting her out like that. Wills can cause all kinds of hurt. I've seen it happen countless times."

"Has your mother made a will?" Strike asked.

Bristow looked startled.

"I—yes, I believe so."

"May I ask who her legatees are?"

"I haven't seen it," said Bristow, a little stiffly. "How is this . . . ?"

"It's all relevant, John. Ten million quid is a hell of a lot of money."

Bristow seemed to be trying to decide whether or not Strike was being insensitive, or offensive. Finally he said:

"Given that there is no other family, I would imagine that Tony and I are the main beneficiaries. Possibly one or two charities will be remembered; my mother has always been generous to charities. However, as I'm sure you'll understand," pink blotches were rising again up Bristow's thin neck, "I am in no hurry to find out my mother's last wishes, given what must happen before they are acted upon."

"Of course not," said Strike.

They had reached Bristow's office, an austere eight-story building entered by a dark archway. Bristow stopped beside the entrance and faced Strike.

"Do you still think I'm deluded?" he asked, as a pair of dark-suited women swept up past them.

"No," said Strike, honestly enough. "No, I don't."

Bristow's undistinguished countenance brightened a little.

"I'll be in touch about Somé and Marlene Higson. Oh—and I nearly forgot. Lula's laptop. I've charged it for you, but it's password-protected. The police people found out the password, and they told my mother, but she can't remember what it was, and I never knew. Perhaps it was in the police file?" he added hopefully.

"Not as far as I can remember," said Strike, "but that shouldn't be too much of a problem. Where has this been since Lula died?"

"In police custody, and since then, at my mother's. Nearly all Lula's things are lying around at Mum's. She hasn't worked herself up to making decisions about them."

Bristow handed Strike the case and bid him farewell; then, with a small bracing movement of his shoulders, he headed up the steps and disappeared through the doors of the family firm.

7

THE FRICTION BETWEEN THE END of Strike's amputated leg and the prosthesis was becoming more painful with every step as he headed towards Kensington Gore. Sweating a little in his heavy overcoat, while a weak sun made the park shimmer in the distance, Strike asked himself whether the strange suspicion that had him in its grip was anything more than a shadow moving in the depths of a muddy pool: a trick of the light, an illusory effect of the wind-ruffled surface. Had these minute flurries of black silt been flicked up by a slimy tail, or were they nothing but meaningless gusts of algae-fed gas? Could there be something lurking, disguised, buried in the mud, for which other nets had trawled in vain?

Heading for Kensington Tube station, he passed the Queen's Gate into Hyde Park; ornate, rust-red and embellished with royal insignia. Incurably observant, he noted the sculpture of the doe and fawn on one pillar and the stag on the other. Humans often assumed symmetry and equality where none existed. The same, yet profoundly different...Lula Landry's laptop banged harder and harder into his leg as his limp worsened.

In his sore, stymied and frustrated state, there was a dull inevitability about Robin's announcement, when he finally reached the office at ten to five, that she was still unable to penetrate past the telephone receptionist of Freddie Bestigui's production company; and that she had had no success in finding anyone of the name Onifade with a British Telecom number in the Kilburn area.

"Of course, if she's Rochelle's aunt, she could have a different surname, couldn't she?" Robin pointed out, as she buttoned her coat and prepared to leave.

Strike agreed to it wearily. He had dropped on to the sagging sofa the moment he had come through the office door, something that Robin had never seen him do before. His face was pinched.

"Are you all right?"

"Fine. Any sign of Temporary Solutions this afternoon?"

"No," said Robin, pulling her belt tight. "Perhaps they believed me when I said I was Annabel? I did try and sound Australian."

He grinned. Robin closed the interim report she had been reading while she waited for Strike to return, set it neatly back on its shelf, bade Strike goodnight and left him sitting there, the laptop lying beside him on the threadbare cushions.

When the sound of Robin's footsteps was no longer audible, Strike stretched a long arm sideways to lock the glass door; then broke his own weekday ban on smoking in the office. Jamming the lit cigarette between his teeth, he pulled up his trouser leg and unlaced the strap holding the prosthesis to his thigh. Then he unrolled the gel liner from the stump of his leg and examined the end of his amputated tibia.

He was supposed to examine the skin surface for irritation every day. Now he saw that the scar tissue was inflamed and over-warm. There had been various creams and powders back in the bathroom cabinet at Charlotte's dedicated to the care of this patch of skin, subject as it was these days to forces for which it had not been designed. Perhaps she had thrown the corn powder and Oilatum into one of the still unpacked boxes? But he could not muster the energy to go and find out, nor did he want to refit the prosthesis just yet; and so he sat smoking on the sofa with the lower trouser leg hanging empty towards the floor, lost in thought.

His mind drifted. He thought about families, and names, and about the ways in which his and John Bristow's childhoods, outwardly so different, had been similar. There were ghostly figures in Strike's family history, too: his mother's first husband, for instance, of whom she had rarely spoken, except to say that she had hated being married from the first. Aunt Joan, whose memory had always been sharpest where Leda's had been most vague, said that the eighteen-year-old Leda had run out on her husband after only two weeks; that her sole motivation in marrying Strike Snr. (who, according to Aunt Joan, had arrived in St. Mawes with the fair) had been a new dress, and a change of name. Certainly, Leda had remained more faithful to her unusual married moniker than to any man. She had passed it to her son, who had never met its original owner, long gone before his unconnected birth.

Strike smoked, lost in thought, until the daylight in his office began to soften and dim. Then, at last, he struggled up on his one foot and, using the doorknob and the dado rail on the wall beyond the glass door to steady himself, hopped out to examine the boxes still stacked on the landing outside his office. At the bottom of one of them he found those dermatological products designed to assuage the burning and prickling in the end of his stump, and set to work to try and repair the damage first done by the long walk across London with his kitbag over his shoulder.

It was lighter now than it had been at eight o'clock two weeks ago; still daylight when Strike was seated, for the second time in ten days, in Wong Kei, the tall, white-fronted Chinese restaurant with a window view of an arcade center called Play to Win. It had been extremely painful to reattach the prosthetic leg, and still more to walk down Charing Cross Road on it, but he had disdained the use of the gray metal sticks he had also found in the box, relics of his release from Selly Oak Hospital.

While Strike ate Singapore noodles one-handed, he examined Lula Landry's laptop, which lay open on the table, beside his beer. The dark pink computer casing was patterned with cherry blossom. It did not occur to Strike that he presented an incongruous appearance to the world as he hunched, large and hairy, over the prettified, pink and palpably feminine device, but the sight had drawn smirks from two of the black-T-shirted waiters.

"How's tricks, Federico?" asked a pallid, straggly-haired young man at half past eight. The newcomer, who dropped into the seat opposite Strike, wore jeans, a psychedelic T-shirt, Converse sneakers, and a leather bag slung diagonally across his chest.

"Been worse," grunted Strike. "How're you? Want a drink?"

"Yeah, I'll have a lager."

Strike ordered the drink for his guest, whom he was accustomed, for long-forgotten reasons, to call Spanner. Spanner had a first-class degree in computer science, and was much better paid than his clothing suggested.

"I'm not that hungry, I had a burger after work," Spanner said, looking down the menu. "I could do a soup. Wonton soup, please," he added to the waiter. "Interesting choice of laptop, Fed."

"It's not mine," said Strike.

"It's the job, is it?"

"Yeah."

Strike slid the computer around to face Spanner, who surveyed the device with the mixture of interest and disparagement characteristic of those to whom technology is no necessary evil, but the stuff of life.

"Junk," said Spanner cheerfully. "Where've you been hiding yourself, Fed? People've been worried."

"Nice of them," said Strike, through a mouthful of noodles. "No need, though."

"I was round Nick and Ilsa's coupla nights ago and you were the only topic of conversation. They were saying you've gone underground. Oh, cheers," he said, as his soup arrived. "Yeah, they've been ringing your flat and they keep getting the answering machine. Ilsa reckons it's woman trouble."

It now occurred to Strike that the best way to inform his friends of his ruptured engagement might be through the medium of the unconcerned Spanner. The younger brother of one of Strike's old friends, Spanner was largely ignorant of, and indifferent to, the long and tortured history of Strike and Charlotte. Given that it was face-to-face sympathy and postmortems that Strike wanted to avoid, and that he had no intention of pretending forever that he and Charlotte had not split up, he agreed that Ilsa had correctly divined his main trouble, and that it would be better if his friends avoided calling Charlotte's flat henceforth.

"Bummer," said Spanner, and then, with the incuriosity towards human pain versus technological challenges that was characteristic of him, he pointed a spatulate fingertip at the Dell and asked: "What d'you want doing with this, then?"

"The police have already had a look at it," said Strike, lowering his voice even though he and Spanner were the only people nearby not speaking Cantonese, "but I want a second opinion."

"Police've got good techie people. I doubt I'm gonna find anything they haven't."

"They might not have been looking for the right stuff," said Strike, "and they might not've realized what it meant even if they found it. They seemed mostly interested in her recent emails, and I've already seen them."

"What am I looking for, then?"

"All activity on or leading up to the eighth of January. The most recent internet searches, stuff like that. I haven't got the password, and I'd rather not go back to the police and ask unless I have to."

"Shouldn't be a problem," said Spanner. He was not writing these instructions down, but typing them on to his mobile phone; Spanner was ten years younger than Strike, and he rarely wielded a pen by choice. "Who's it belong to, anyway?"

When Strike told him, Spanner said:

"The model? Whoa."

But Spanner's interest in human beings, even when dead or famous, was still secondary to his fondness for rare comics, technological innovation and bands of which Strike had never heard. After eating several spoonfuls of soup, Spanner broke the silence to inquire brightly how much Strike was planning to pay him for the work.

When Spanner had left with the pink laptop under his arm, Strike limped back to his office. He washed the end of his right leg carefully that night and then applied cream to the irritated and inflamed scar tissue. For the first time in many months, he took painkillers before easing himself into his sleeping bag. Lying there waiting for the raw ache to deaden, he wondered whether he ought to make an appointment to see the consultant in rehabilitation medicine under whose care he was supposed to fall. The symptoms of choke syndrome, the nemesis of amputees, had been described to him repeatedly: suppurating skin and swelling. He was wondering whether he might be showing the early signs, but he dreaded the prospect of returning to corridors stinking of disinfectant; of doctors with their detached interest in this one small mutilated portion of his body; of further minute adjustments to the prosthesis necessitating still more visits to that white-coated, confined world he had hoped he had left forever. He feared advice to rest the leg, to desist from normal ambulation; a forced return to crutches, the stares of passersby at his pinned-up trouser leg and the shrill inquiries of small children.

His mobile, charging as usual on the floor beside the camp bed, made the buzzing noise that announced the arrival of a text. Glad for any minor distraction from his throbbing leg, Strike groped in the dark and picked up the telephone from the floor.

Please could you give me a quick call when convenient? Charlotte

Strike did not believe in clairvoyance or psychic ability, yet his immediate irrational thought was that Charlotte had somehow sensed what he had just told Spanner; that he had twitched the taut, invisible rope still binding them, by placing their breakup on an official footing.

He stared at the message as though it was her face, as though he could read her expression on the tiny gray screen.

Please. (I know you don't have to: I'm asking you to, nicely.) *A quick call.* (I have a legitimate reason for desiring speech with you, so we can do it swiftly and easily; no rows.) *When convenient.* (I do you the courtesy of assuming that you have a busy life without me.)

Or, perhaps: *Please.* (To refuse is to be a bastard, Strike, and you've hurt me enough.) *A quick call.* (I know you're expecting a scene; well, don't worry, that last one, when you were such an unbelievable shit, has finished me with you forever.) *When convenient.* (Because, let's be honest, I always had to slot in around the army and every other damn thing that came first.)

Was it convenient now? he asked himself, lying in pain that the pills had yet to touch. He glanced at the time: ten past eleven. She was clearly still awake.

He put the mobile back on the floor beside him, where it lay silently charging, and raised a large hairy arm over his eyes, blotting out even the strips of light on the ceiling cast by the street lamps through the window slats. Against his will, he saw Charlotte the way that he had laid eyes on her for the first time in his life, as she sat alone on a windowsill at a student party in Oxford. He had never seen anything so beautiful in his life, and nor, judging by the sideways flickering of countless male eyes, the overloud laughter and voices, the angling of extravagant gestures towards her silent figure, had any of the rest of them.

Gazing across the room, the nineteen-year-old Strike had been visited by precisely the same urge that had come over him as a child whenever snow had fallen overnight in Aunt Joan and Uncle Ted's garden. He wanted his footsteps to be the first to make deep, dark holes in that tantalizingly smooth surface: he wanted to disturb and disrupt it.

"You're pissed," warned his friend, when Strike announced his intention to go and talk to her.

Strike agreed, downed the dregs of his seventh pint and strode purposefully over to the window ledge where she sat. He was vaguely aware of people nearby watching, primed, perhaps, for laughter, because he was massive, and looked like a boxing Beethoven, and had curry sauce all down his T-shirt.

She looked up at him when he reached her, with big eyes, and long dark hair, and soft, pale cleavage revealed by the gaping shirt.

Strike's strange, nomadic childhood, with its constant uprootings and graftings on to motley groups of children and teenagers, had forged in him an advanced set of social skills; he knew how to fit in, to make people laugh, to render himself acceptable to almost anyone. That night, his tongue had become numb and rubbery. He seemed to remember swaying slightly.

"Did you want something?" she asked.

"Yeah," he said. He pulled his T-shirt away from his torso and showed her the curry sauce. "What d'you reckon's the best way to get this out?"

Against her will (he saw her trying to fight it), she giggled.

Sometime later, an Adonis called the Honorable Jago Ross, known to Strike by sight and reputation, swung into the room with a posse of equally well-bred friends, and discovered Strike and Charlotte sitting side by side on the windowsill, deep in conversation.

"You're in the wrong fucking room, Char, darling," Ross had said, staking out his rights by the caressing arrogance of his tone. "Ritchie's party's upstairs."

"I'm not coming," she said, turning a smiling face upon him. "I've got to go and help Cormoran soak his T-shirt."

Thus had she publicly dumped her Old Harrovian boyfriend for Cormoran Strike. It had been the most glorious moment of Strike's nineteen years: he had publicly carried off Helen of Troy right under Menelaus's nose, and in his shock and delight he had not questioned the miracle, but simply accepted it.

Only later had he realized that what had seemed like chance, or fate, had been entirely engineered by her. She had admitted it to him months later: that she had, to punish Ross for some transgression, deliberately entered the wrong room, and waited for a man, any man, to approach her; that he, Strike, had been a mere instrument to torture Ross; that she had slept with him in the early hours of the following morning in a spirit of vengefulness and rage that he had mistaken for passion.

There, in that first night, had been everything that had subsequently broken them apart and pulled them back together: her self-destructiveness, her recklessness, her determination to hurt; her unwilling but genuine attraction to Strike, and her secure place of retreat in the cloistered world in which she had grown up, whose values she simultaneously despised and espoused. Thus had begun the relationship that had led to Strike lying here on his camp bed fifteen years later, racked with more than physical pain, and wishing that he could rid himself of her memory.

8

WHEN ROBIN ARRIVED NEXT MORNING, it was, for the second time, to a locked glass door. She let herself in with the spare key that Strike had now entrusted to her, approached the closed inner door and stood silent, listening. After a few seconds, she heard the faintly muffled but unmistakable sound of deep snoring.

This presented her with a delicate problem, because of their tacit agreement not to mention Strike's camp bed, or any of the other signs of habitation lying around the place. On the other hand, Robin had something of an urgent nature to communicate to her temporary boss. She hesitated, considering her options. The easiest route would be to try and wake Strike by clattering around the outer office, thereby giving him time to organize himself and the inner room, but that might take too long: her news would not keep. Robin therefore took a deep breath and rapped on the door.

Strike woke instantly. For one disoriented moment he lay there, registering the reproachful daylight pouring through the window. Then he remembered setting down the mobile phone after reading Charlotte's text, and knew that he had forgotten to set the alarm.

"Don't come in!" he bellowed.

"Would you like a cup of tea?" Robin called through the door.

"Yeah—yeah, that'd be great. I'll come out there for it," Strike added loudly, wishing, for the first time, that he had fitted a lock on the inner door. His false foot and calf was standing propped against the wall, and he was wearing nothing but boxer shorts.

Robin hurried away to fill the kettle, and Strike fought his way out of his sleeping bag. He dressed at speed, making a clumsy job of putting on the prosthesis, folding the camp bed into its corner, pushing the desk back into place. Ten minutes after she had knocked on the door, he limped into the outer office smelling strongly of deodorant, to find Robin at her desk, looking very excited about something.

"Your tea," she said, indicating a steaming mug.

"Great, thanks. Just give me a moment," he said, and he left to pee in the bathroom on the landing. As he zipped up his fly, he caught sight of himself in the mirror, crumpled-looking and unshaven. Not for the first time, he consoled himself that his hair looked the same whether brushed or unbrushed.

"I've got news," said Robin, when he had re-entered the office through the glass door and, with reiterated thanks, picked up his mug of tea.

"Yeah?"

"I've found Rochelle Onifade."

He lowered the mug.

"You're kidding. How the hell...?"

"I saw in the file that she was supposed to attend an outpatient clinic at St. Thomas's," said Robin excitedly, flushed and talking fast, "so I rang up the hospital yesterday evening, pretending to be her, and I said I'd forgotten the time of my appointment, and they told me it's at ten thirty on Thursday morning. You've got," she glanced at her computer monitor, "fifty-five minutes."

Why had he not thought to tell her to do this?

"You genius, you bloody genius..."

He had slopped hot tea over his hand, and put the mug down on her desk.

"D'you know exactly...?"

"It's in the psychiatric unit round the back of the main building," said Robin, exhilarated. "See, you go in off Grantley Road, there's a second car park..."

She had turned the monitor towards him to show him the map of St. Thomas's. He checked his wrist, but his watch was still in the inner room.

"You'll have time if you leave now," Robin urged him.

"Yeah—I'll get my stuff."

Strike hurried to fetch his watch, wallet, cigarettes and phone. He was almost through the glass door, cramming his wallet into his back pocket, when Robin said:

"Er—Cormoran..."

She had never called him by his first name before. Strike assumed that this accounted for her slight air of bashfulness; then he realized that she was pointing meaningfully at his navel. Looking down, he saw that he had done up the buttons on his shirt wrongly, and was exposing a patch of belly so hairy that it resembled black coconut matting.

"Oh—right—cheers..."

Robin turned her attention politely to her monitor while he undid and refastened the buttons.

"See you later."

"Yeah, 'bye," she said, smiling at him as he departed at speed; but within seconds he was back, panting slightly.

"Robin, I need you to check something."

She already had the pen in her hand, waiting.

"There was a legal conference in Oxford on the seventh of January. Lula Landry's uncle Tony attended it. International family law. Anything you can find out. Specifically about him being there."

"Right," said Robin, scribbling.

"Cheers. You're a genius."

And he was gone, with uneven steps, down the metal stairs.

Though she hummed to herself as she settled down at her desk, a little of Robin's cheerfulness drained away as she drank her tea. She had half hoped that Strike would invite her along to meet Rochelle Onifade, whose shadow she had hunted for two weeks.

Rush hour past, the crowds on the Tube had thinned. Strike was pleased, because the end of his stump was still smarting, to find a seat with ease. He had bought himself a pack of Extra Strong Mints at the station kiosk before boarding his train, and was now sucking four simultaneously, trying to conceal the fact that he had not had time to clean his teeth. His toothbrush and toothpaste were hidden inside his kitbag, even though it would have been much more convenient to leave them on the chipped sink in the bathroom. Catching sight of himself again, in the darkened train window, with his heavy stubble and his generally unkempt appearance, he asked himself why, when it was perfectly obvious that Robin knew he slept there, he maintained the fiction that he had some other home.

Strike's memory and map sense were more than adequate to the task of locating the entrance to the psychiatric unit at St. Thomas's, and he proceeded there without mishap, arriving at shortly after ten. He spent five minutes checking that the automatic double doors were the only entrance on Grantley Road, before positioning himself on a stone wall in the car park, some twenty yards away from the entrance, giving him a clear view of everyone entering and leaving.

Knowing only that the girl he sought was probably homeless, and certainly black, he had thought through his strategy for finding her on the Tube, and concluded that there was really only one option open to him. At twenty past ten, therefore, when he saw a tall, thin black girl walking briskly towards the entrance, he called out (even though she looked too well-groomed, too neatly dressed):

"Rochelle!"

She glanced up to see who had shouted, but kept walking without any sign that the name had a personal application, and disappeared into the building. Next came a couple, both white; then a group of people of assorted ages and races whom Strike guessed to be hospital workers; but on the mere off-chance he called again:

"Rochelle!"

Some of them glanced at him, but returned immediately to their conversations. Consoling himself that frequenters of this entrance were probably used to a degree of eccentricity in those they met in its vicinity, Strike lit a cigarette and waited.

Half past ten passed, and no black girl went through the doors. Either she had missed her appointment, or she had used a different entrance. A feather-light breeze tickled the back of his neck as he sat smoking, watching, waiting. The hospital building was enormous, a vast concrete box with rectangular windows; there were surely numerous entrances on every side.

Strike straightened his injured leg, which was still sore, and considered, again, the possibility that he would have to return to see his consultant. He found even this degree of proximity to a hospital slightly depressing. His stomach rumbled. He had passed a McDonald's on the way here. If he had not found her by midday, he would go and eat there.

Twice more he shouted "Rochelle!" at black women who entered and exited the building, and both times they glanced back, purely to see who had shouted, in one case giving him a look of disdain.

Then, just after eleven, a short, stocky black girl emerged from the hospital with a slightly awkward, rocking, side-to-side gait. He knew quite well that he had not missed her going in, not only because of her distinctive walk, but because she wore a very noticeable short coat of magenta-colored fake fur, which flattered neither her height nor her breadth.

"Rochelle!"

The girl stopped, turned and stared around, scowling, looking for the person who had called her name. Strike limped towards her, and she glared at him with an understandable mistrust.

"Rochelle? Rochelle Onifade? Hi. My name's Cormoran Strike. Can I have a word?"

"I always come in Redbourne Street entrance," she told him five minutes later, after he had given a garbled and fictitious account of the way he had found her. "I come out this way 'cause I was gonna go to McDonald's."

So that was where they went. Strike bought two coffees and two large cookies, and carried them to the window table where Rochelle was waiting, curious and suspicious.

She was uncompromisingly plain. Her greasy skin, which was the color of burned earth, was covered in acne pustules and pits; her small eyes were deep-set and her teeth were crooked and rather yellow. The chemically straightened hair showed four inches of black roots, then six inches of harsh, coppery wire-red. Her tight, too-short jeans, her shiny gray handbag and her bright white trainers looked cheap. However, the squashy fake-fur jacket, garish and unflattering though Strike found it, was of a different quality altogether: fully lined, as he saw when she took it off, with a patterned silk, and bearing the label not (as he had expected, remembering Lula Landry's email to the designer) of Guy Somé, but of an Italian of whom even Strike had heard.

"You sure you inna journalist?" she asked, in her low, husky voice.

Strike had already spent some time outside the hospital trying to establish his bona fides in this respect.

"No, I'm not a journalist. Like I said, I know Lula's brother."

"You a friend of his?"

"Yeah. Well, not exactly a friend. He's hired me. I'm a private detective."

She was instantly, openly scared.

"Whaddayuhwanna talk to me for?"

"There's nothing to worry about..."

"Whyd'yuhwanna talk to me, though?"

"It's nothing bad. John isn't sure that Lula committed suicide, that's all."

He guessed that the only thing keeping her in the seat was her terror of the construction he might put on instant flight. Her fear was out of all proportion to his manner or words.

"There's nothing to worry about," he assured her again. "John wants me to take another look at the circumstances, that's—"

"Does 'e say I've got something to do wiv 'er dying?"

"No, of course not. I'm just hoping you might be able to tell me about her state of mind, what she got up to in the lead-up to her death. You saw her regularly, didn't you? I thought you might be able to tell me what was going on in her life."

Rochelle made as though to speak, then changed her mind and attempted to drink her scalding coffee instead.

"So, what—'er brother's trying to make out she never killed 'erself? What, like she was pushed out the window?"

"He thinks it's possible."

She seemed to be trying to fathom something, to work it out in her head.

"I don't 'ave to talk to you. You ain't real police."

"Yeah, that's true. But wouldn't you like to help find out what—"

"She jumped," declared Rochelle Onifade firmly.

"What makes you so sure?" asked Strike.

"I jus' know."

"It seems to have come as a shock to nearly everyone else she knew."

"She wuz depressed. Yeah, she wuz on stuff for it. Like me. Sometimes it jus' takes you over. It's an illness," she said, although she made the words sound like "it's uh nillness."

Nillness, thought Strike, for a second distracted. He had slept badly. *Nillness,* that was where Lula Landry had gone, and where all of them, he and Rochelle included, were headed. Sometimes illness turned slowly to nillness, as was happening to Bristow's mother...sometimes nillness rose to meet you out of nowhere, like a concrete road slamming your skull apart.

He was sure that if he took out his notebook, she would clam up, or leave. He therefore continued to ask questions as casually as he could manage, asking her how she had come to attend the clinic, how she had first met Lula.

Still immensely suspicious, she gave monosyllabic answers at first, but slowly, gradually, she became more forthcoming. Her own history was pitiful. Early abuse, care, severe mental illness, foster homes and violent outbursts culminating, at sixteen, in homelessness. She had secured proper treatment as the indirect result of being hit by a car. Hospitalized when her bizarre behavior had made treating her physical wounds nearly impossible, a psychiatrist had at last been called in. She was on drugs now, which, when she took them, greatly eased her symptoms. Strike found it pathetic, and touching, that the outpatient clinic where she had met Lula Landry seemed to have become, for Rochelle, the highlight of her week. She spoke with some affection of the young psychiatrist who ran the group.

"So that's where you met Lula?"

"Di'n't her brother tell ya?"

"He was vague on the details."

"Yeah, she come to our group. She wuz referred."

"And you got talking?"

"Yeah."

"You became friends?"

"Yeah."

"You visited her at home? Swam in the pool?"

"Why shou'n't I?"

"No reason. I'm only asking."

She thawed very slightly.

"I don't like swimming. I don't like water over m'face. I went in the jacuzzi. And we went shoppin' an' stuff."

"Did she ever talk to you about her neighbors; the other people in her building?"

"Them Bestiguis? A bit. She din' like them. That woman's a bitch," said Rochelle, with sudden savagery.

"What makes you say that?"

"Have you met 'er? She look at me like I wuz dirt."

"What did Lula think of her?"

"She din' like 'er neither, nor her husband. He's a creep."

"In what way?"

"He jus' is," said Rochelle, impatiently; but then, when Strike did not speak, she went on. "He wuz always tryin' ter get her downstairs when his wife wuz out."

"Did Lula ever go?"

"No fuckin' chance," said Rochelle.

"You and Lula talked to each other a lot, I suppose, did you?"

"Yeah, we did, at f—Yeah, we did."

She looked out of the window. A sudden shower of rain had caught passersby unawares. Transparent ellipses peppered the glass beside them.

"At first?" said Strike. "Did you talk less as time went on?"

"I'm gonna have to go soon," said Rochelle, grandly. "I got things to do."

"People like Lula," said Strike, feeling his way, "can be spoiled. Treat people badly. They're used to getting their own—"

"I ain't no one's servant," said Rochelle fiercely.

"Maybe that's why she liked you? Maybe she saw you as someone more equal—not a hanger-on?"

"Yeah, igzactly," said Rochelle, mollified. "I weren't impressed by her."

"You can see why she'd want you as a friend, someone more down-to-earth..."

"Yeah."

"...and you had your illness in common, didn't you? So you understood her on a level most people wouldn't."

"And I'm black," said Rochelle, "and she wuz wanting to feel proper black."

"Did she talk to you about that?"

"Yeah, 'course," said Rochelle. "She wuz wanting to find out where she come from, where she belong."

"Did she talk to you about trying to find the black side of her family?"

"Yeah, of course. And she...yeah."

She had braked almost visibly.

"Did she ever find anyone? Her father?"

"No. She never found 'im. No fuckin' chance."

"Really?"

"Yeah, *really*."

She began eating fast. Strike was afraid that she would leave the moment she had finished.

"Was Lula depressed when you met her at Vashti, the day before she died?"

"Yeah, she wuz."

"Did she tell you why?"

"There don't 'ave to be a reason why. It's uh nillness."

"But she told you she was feeling bad, did she?"

"Yeah," she said, after a fractional hesitation.

"You were supposed to be having lunch together, weren't you?" he asked. "Kieran told me that he drove her to meet you. You know Kieran, right? Kieran Kolovas-Jones?"

Her expression softened; the corners of her mouth lifted.

"Yeah, I know Kieran. Yeah, she come to meet me at Vashti."

"But she didn't stop for lunch?"

"No. She wuz in a hurry," said Rochelle.

She bowed her head to drink more coffee, concealing her face.

"Why didn't she just ring you? You've got a phone, have you?"

"Yeah, I gotta phone," she snapped, bristling, and drew from the fur jacket a basic-looking Nokia, stuck all over with gaudy pink crystals.

"So why d'you think she didn't call to say she couldn't see you?"

Rochelle glowered at him.

"Because she didn't like using the phone, because of them listenin' in."

"Journalists?"

"Yeah."

She had almost finished her cookie.

"Journalists wouldn't have been very interested in her saying that she wasn't coming to Vashti, though, would they?"

"I dunno."

"Didn't you think it was odd, at the time, that she drove all the way to tell you she couldn't stay for lunch?"

"Yeah. No," said Rochelle. And then, with a sudden burst of fluency:

"When ya gotta driver it don't matter, does it? You jus' go wherever you want, don't cost you nothing extra, you just get them to take you, don't ya? She was passing, so she come in to tell me she wasn't gonna stop because she 'ad to get 'ome to see fucking Ciara Porter."

Rochelle looked as though she regretted the traitorous "fucking" as soon as it was out, and pursed her lips together as though to ensure no more swear words escaped her.

"And that was all she did, was it? She came into the shop, said 'I can't stop, I've got to get home and see Ciara' and left?"

"Yeah. More uh less," said Rochelle.

"Kieran says they usually gave you a lift home after you'd been out together."

"Yeah," she said. "Well. She wuz too busy that day, weren' she?"

Rochelle did a poor job of masking her resentment.

"Talk me through what happened in the shop. Did either of you try anything on?"

"Yeah," said Rochelle, after a pause. "She did." Another hesitation. "Long Alexander McQueen dress. He killed hiself and all," she added, in a distant voice.

"Did you go into the changing room with her?"

"Yeah."

"What happened in the changing room?" prompted Strike.

"Some silly Aussie cow come shoving in, askin' to do Lula's makeup or sumthin'," said Rochelle. "Stepped on my effing foot, never mind me."

Strike heard the bone-deep bitterness of the perennially over-looked, of the pushed aside.

"Yeah, I heard about that. The girl got sacked for it afterwards."

"Good," said Rochelle.

"Lula was pretty nice to her, though, wasn't she?" asked Strike. "Didn't she take her details?"

"That wasn't—" began Rochelle, but she stopped short. "It was only to get rid of her."

"What was Lula doing when the girl walked in?"

Her eyes reminded him of those of a bull he had once come face to face with as a small boy: deep set, deceptively stoic, unfathomable.

"Trying on the dress."

"I heard she was on the phone."

"Oh. Well, yeah. She mighta bin."

"Who was she on the phone to?"

"I dunno."

She drank, obscuring her face again with the paper cup.

"Was it Evan Duffield?"

"It mighta bin."

"Can you remember what she said?"

"No."

"One of the shop assistants overheard her, while she was on the phone. She seemed to be making an appointment to meet someone at her flat much later. In the early hours of the morning, the girl thought."

"Yeah?"

"So that doesn't seem like it could have been Duffield, does it, seeing as she already had an arrangement to meet him at Uzi?"

"Know a lot, don't you?" she said.

"Everyone knows they met at Uzi that night," said Strike. "It was in all the papers."

The dilating or contracting of Rochelle's pupils would be almost impossible to see, because of the virtually black irises surrounding them.

"Yeah, I s'pose," she conceded.

"Was it Deeby Macc?"

"No!" She yelped it on a laugh. "She din' know his number."

"Famous people can nearly always get each other's numbers," said Strike.

Rochelle's expression clouded. She glanced down at the blank screen on her gaudy pink mobile.

"I don' think she had his," she said.

"But you heard her trying to make an arrangement to meet someone in the small hours?"

"No," said Rochelle, avoiding his eyes, swilling the dregs of her coffee around the paper cup. "I can' remember nuthin' like that."

"You understand how important this could be?" said Strike, careful to keep his tone unthreatening. "If Lula made an arrangement to meet someone at the time she died? The police never knew about this, did they? You never told them?"

"I gotta go," she said, throwing down the last morsel of cookie, grabbing the strap of her cheap handbag and glaring at him.

Strike said:

"It's nearly lunchtime. Can I buy you anything else?"

"No."

But she did not move. He wondered how poor she was, whether she ate regularly or not. There was something about her, beneath the surliness, that he found touching: a fierce pride, a vulnerability.

"Yeah, all right then," she said, dropping her handbag and slumping back on to the hard chair. "I'll have a Big Mac."

He was afraid she might leave while he was at the counter, but when he returned with two trays, she was still there; she even thanked him grudgingly.

Strike tried a different tack.

"You know Kieran quite well, do you?" he asked, pursuing the glow that had illuminated her at the mention of his name.

"Yeah," she said, self-consciously. "I met him a lot with 'er. 'E wuz always driving 'er."

"He says that Lula was writing something in the back of the car, before she arrived at Vashti. Did she show you, or give you, anything she'd written?"

"No," she said. She crammed fries into her mouth and then said, "I ain't seen nuthin like that. Why, what was it?"

"I don't know."

"Maybe it were a shopping list or something?"

"Yeah, that's what the police thought. You're sure you didn't notice her carrying a bit of paper, a letter, an envelope?"

"Yeah, I'm sure."

"Where did she write down the Australian girl's details?"

"She didn't write 'em. The girl did. Back of a till thing."

"A receipt?"

"Yeah," said Rochelle. "Kieran know you're meeting me?"

"Yeah, I told him you were on my list. He told me you used to live at St. Elmo's."

This seemed to please her.

"Where are you living now?"

"What's it to you?" she demanded, suddenly fierce.

"It's nothing to me. I'm just making polite conversation."

This drew a small snort from Rochelle.

"I got my own place in Hammersmith now."

She chewed for a while and then, for the first time, proffered unsolicited information.

"We usedta listen to Deeby Macc in his car. Me, Kieran and Lula." And she began to rap:

> No hydroquinone, black to the backbone,
> Takin' Deeby lightly, better buy an early tombstone,
> I'm drivin' my Ferrari—fuck Johari—got my head on straight
> Nothin' talks like money talks—I'm shoutin' at ya, Mister Jake.

She looked proud, as though she had put him firmly in his place, with no retort possible.

"Tha's from 'Hydroquinone,' " she said. "On *Jake On My Jack.*"

"What's hydroquinone?" Strike asked.

"Skin light'ner. We usedta rap that with the car windows down," said Rochelle. A warm, reminiscent smile lit her face out of plainness.

"Lula was looking forward to meeting Deeby Macc, then, was she?"

"Yeah, she wuz," said Rochelle. "She knew 'e liked 'er, she wuz pleased with herself about that. Kieran wuz proper excited an' all, he kep' askin' Lula to introduce him. He wanted to meet Deeby."

Her smile faded; she picked morosely at her burger, then said:

"Is that all you wanna know, then? 'Cause I gotta go."

She began wolfing the remnants of her meal, cramming food into her mouth.

"Lula must have taken you to a lot of places, did she?"

"Yeah," said Rochelle, her mouth full of burger.

"Did you go to Uzi with her?"

"Yeah. Once."

She swallowed, and began to talk about the other places she had seen during the early phase of her friendship with Lula, which (in spite of Rochelle's determined attempts to repudiate any suggestion that she had been dazzled by the lifestyle of a multimillionairess) had all the romance of a fairy tale. Lula had snatched Rochelle away from the bleak world of her hostel and group therapy and swept her, once a week, into a whirl of expensive fun. Strike noted how very little Rochelle had told him about Lula the person, as opposed to Lula the holder of the magic plastic cards that bought handbags, jackets and jewelry, and the necessary means by which Kieran appeared regularly, like a genie, to whisk Rochelle away from her hostel. She described, in loving detail, the presents Lula had bought her, shops to which Lula had taken her, restaurants and bars to which they had gone together, places lined with celebrities. None of these, however, seemed to have impressed Rochelle in the slightest; for every name she mentioned there was a deprecating remark:

" 'E wuz a dick." "She's plastic all over." "They ain't nuthing special."

"Did you meet Evan Duffield?" Strike asked.

" 'Im." The monosyllable was heavy with contempt. " 'E's a twat."

"Is he?"

"Yeah, 'e is. Ask Kieran."

She gave the impression that she and Kieran stood together, sane, dispassionate observers of the idiots populating Lula's world.

"In what way was he a twat?"

" 'E treated 'er like shit."

"Like how?"

"Sold stories," said Rochelle, reaching for the last of her fries. "One time she tested ev'ryone. Told us all a diff'rent story to see which ones got in the papers. I wuz the only one who kep' their mouf shut, ev'ryone else blabbed."

"Who'd she test?"

"Ciara Porter. 'Im, Duffield. That Guy Summy," Rochelle pronounced his first name to rhyme with "die," "but then she reckoned it wasn't 'im. Made excuses for 'im. But 'e used 'er as much as anyone."

"In what way?"

"He di'n't want 'er to work for anyone else. Wanted 'er to do it all for 'is company, get 'im all the publicity."

"So, after she'd found out she could trust you . . ."

"Yeah, then she bought me the phone."

There was a missed beat.

"So she cud get in touch wiv me whenever she wanted."

She swept the sparkling pink Nokia suddenly off the table and stuffed it deep into the pocket of her squashy pink coat.

"I suppose you've had to take over the charges yourself now?" Strike asked.

He thought that she was going to tell him to mind his own business, but instead she said:

" 'Er family 'asn't noticed they're still payin' for it."

And this thought seemed to give her a slightly malicious pleasure.

"Did Lula buy you that jacket?" Strike asked.

"No," she snapped, furiously defensive. "I got this myself, I'm working now."

"Really? Where are you working?"

"Whut's it to you?" she demanded again.

"I'm showing polite interest."

A tiny, brief smile touched the wide mouth, and she relented again.

"I'm doing afternoons in a shop up the road from my new place."

"Are you in another hostel?"

"No," she said, and he sensed again the digging in, the refusal to go further that he would push at his peril. He changed tack.

"It must have been a shock to you when Lula died, was it?"

"Yeah. It wuz," she said, thoughtlessly; then, realizing what she had said, she backtracked. "I knew she wuz depressed, but you never 'spect people tuh do that."

"So you wouldn't say she was suicidal when you saw her that day?"

"I dunno. I never saw 'er for long enough, did I?"

"Where were you when you heard she'd died?"

"I wuz in the hostel. Loadsa people knew I knew her. Janine woke me up and told me."

"And your immediate thought was that it was suicide?"

"Yeah. An' I gotta go now. I gotta go."

She had made up her mind and he could see that he was not going to be able to stop her. After wriggling back into the ludicrous fur jacket, she hoisted her handbag on to her shoulder.

"Say hullo to Kieran for me."

"Yeah, I will."

"See yuh."

She waddled out of the restaurant without a backward glance.

Strike watched her walk past the window, her head down, her brows knitted, until she passed out of sight. It had stopped raining. Idly he pulled her tray towards him and finished her last few fries.

Then he stood up so abruptly that the baseball-capped girl who had been approaching his table to clear and wipe it jumped back a step with a little cry of surprise. Strike hurried out of the McDonald's and off up Grantley Road.

Rochelle was standing on the corner, clearly visible in her furry magenta coat, part of a knot of people waiting for the lights to

change at a pedestrian crossing. She was gabbling into the pink jew-
eled Nokia. Strike caught up with her, insinuating himself into the
group behind her, making of his bulk a weapon, so that people
moved aside to avoid him.

"...wanted to know who she was arrangin' to meet that
night...yeah, an'—"

Rochelle turned her head, watching traffic, and realized that Strike
was right behind her. Removing the mobile from her ear, she jabbed
at a button, cutting the call.

"What?" she asked him aggressively.

"Who were you calling then?"

"Mind yer own fuckin' business!" she said furiously. The waiting
pedestrians stared. "Are you followin' me?"

"Yeah," said Strike. "Listen."

The lights changed; they were the only two not to start off over
the road, and were jostled by the passing walkers.

"Will you give me your mobile number?"

The implacable bull's eyes looked back at him, unreadable, bland,
secretive.

"Wha' for?"

"Kieran asked me to get it," he lied. "I forgot. He thinks you left
a pair of sunglasses in his car."

He did not think she was convinced, but after a moment she dic-
tated a number, which he wrote down on the back of one of his own
cards.

"That all?" she asked aggressively, and she proceeded across the
road as far as an island, where the lights changed again. Strike limped
after her. She looked both angry and perturbed by his continuing
presence.

"*What?*"

"I think you know something you're not telling me, Rochelle."

She glared at him.

"Take this," said Strike, pulling a second card out of his overcoat
pocket. "If you think of anything you'd like to tell me, call, all right?
Call that mobile number."

She did not answer.

"If Lula was murdered," said Strike, while the cars whooshed by them, and rain glittered in the gutters at their feet, "and you know something, you could be in danger from the killer too."

This evoked a tiny, complacent, scathing smile. Rochelle did not think she was in danger. She thought she was safe.

The green man had appeared. Rochelle gave a toss of her dry, wiry hair and moved away across the road, ordinary, squat and plain, still clutching her mobile in one hand and Strike's card in the other. Strike stood alone on the island, watching her with a feeling of impotence and unease. She might never have sold her story to the newspapers, but he could not believe that she had bought that designer jacket, ugly though he found it, from the proceeds of a job in a shop.

9

THE JUNCTION OF TOTTENHAM COURT and Charing Cross Roads was still a scene of devastation, with wide gashes in the road, white hardboard tunnels and hard-hatted builders. Strike traversed the narrow walkways barricaded by metal fences, past the rumbling diggers full of rubble, bellowing workmen and more drills, smoking as he walked.

He felt weary and sore; very conscious of the pain in his leg, of his unwashed body, of the greasy food lying heavily in his stomach. On impulse, he took a detour right up Sutton Row, away from the clatter and grind of the roadworks, and called Rochelle. It went to voicemail, but it was her husky voice that answered: she had not given him a fake number. He left no message; he had already said everything he could think of saying; and yet he was worried. He half wished he had followed her, covertly, to find out where she was living.

Back on Charing Cross Road, limping on to the office through the temporary shadow of the pedestrian tunnel, he remembered the way that Robin had woken him up that morning: the tactful knock, the cup of tea, the studied avoidance of the subject of the camp bed. He ought not to have let it happen. There were other routes to intimacy than admiring a woman's figure in a tight dress. He did not want to explain why he was sleeping at work; he dreaded personal questions. And he had let a situation arise in which she had called him Cormoran and told him to do up his buttons. He ought never to have overslept.

As he climbed the metal stairs, past the closed door of Crowdy Graphics, Strike resolved to treat Robin with a slightly cooler edge of authority for the rest of the day, to counterbalance that glimpse of hairy belly.

The decision was no sooner made than he heard high-pitched laughter, and two female voices talking at the same time, issuing from his own office.

Strike froze, listening, panicking. He had not returned Charlotte's call. He tried to make out her tone and inflection; it would be like her to come in person and overwhelm his temp with charm, to make of his ally a friend, to saturate his own staff with Charlotte's version of the truth. The two voices melded in laughter again, and he could not tell whose they were.

"Hi, Stick," said a cheery voice as he pushed open the glass door.

His sister, Lucy, was sitting on the sagging sofa, with her hands around a mug of coffee, bags from Marks and Spencer and John Lewis heaped all around her.

Strike's first surge of relief that she was not Charlotte was nevertheless tainted with a lesser dread of what she and Robin had been talking about, and how much each of them now knew about his private life. As he returned Lucy's hug, he noticed that Robin had, again, closed the inner door on the camp bed and kitbag.

"Robin says you've been out detecting." Lucy seemed in high spirits, as she so often was when she was out alone, unencumbered by Greg and the boys.

"Yeah, we do that sometimes, detectives," said Strike. "Been shopping?"

"Yes, Sherlock, I have."

"D'you want to go out for a coffee?"

"I've already got one, Stick," she said, holding up the mug. "You're not very sharp today. Are you limping a bit?"

"Not that I've noticed."

"Have you seen Mr. Chakrabati recently?"

"Fairly recently," lied Strike.

"If it's all right," said Robin, who was putting on her trench coat, "I'll take lunch, Mr. Strike. I haven't had any yet."

The resolution of moments ago, to treat her with professional *froideur,* now seemed not only unnecessary but unkind. She had more tact than any woman he had ever met.

"That's fine, Robin, yeah," he said.

"Nice to meet you, Lucy," Robin said, and with a wave she disappeared, closing the glass door behind her.

"I really like her," said Lucy enthusiastically, as Robin's footsteps clanged away. "She's great. You should try and get her to stay on permanently."

"Yeah, she's good," said Strike. "What were you two having such a laugh about?"

"Oh, her fiancé—he sounds a bit like Greg. Robin says you've got an important case on. It's all right. She was very discreet. She says it's a suspicious suicide. That can't be very nice."

She gave him a meaningful look he chose not to understand.

"It's not the first time. I had a couple of those in the army, too."

But he doubted that Lucy was listening. She had taken a deep breath. He knew what was coming.

"Stick, have you and Charlotte split up?"

Better get it over with.

"Yeah, we have."

"Stick!"

"It's fine, Luce. I'm fine."

But her good humor had been obliterated in a great gush of fury and disappointment. Strike waited patiently, exhausted and sore, while she raged: she had known all along, known that Charlotte would do it all over again; she had lured him away from Tracey, and from his fantastic army career, rendered him as insecure as possible, persuaded him to move in, only to dump him—

"I ended it, Luce," he said, "and Tracey and I were over before..." but he might as well have commanded lava to flow backwards: why hadn't he realized that Charlotte would never change, that she had only returned to him for the drama of the situation, attracted by his injury and his medal? The bitch had played the ministering angel and then got bored; she was dangerous and wicked; measuring her own worth in the havoc she caused, glorying in the pain she inflicted...

"I left her, it was my choice..."

"Where have you been living? When did this happen? That absolute bloody *bitch*—no, I'm sorry, Stick, I'm not going to pretend anymore—all the years and years of *shit* she's put you through—oh God, Stick, why didn't you marry Tracey?"

"Luce, let's not do this, please."

He moved aside some of her John Lewis bags, full, he saw, of small pants and socks for her sons, and sat down heavily on the sofa. He knew he looked grubby and scruffy. Lucy seemed on the verge of tears; her day out in town was ruined.

"I suppose you haven't told me because you knew I'd do this?" she said at last, gulping.

"It might've been a consideration."

"All right, I'm sorry," she said furiously, her eyes shining with tears. "But that *bitch,* Stick. Oh God, tell me you're never going to go back to her. Please just tell me that."

"I'm not going back to her."

"Where are you staying—Nick and Ilsa's?"

"No. I've got a little place in Hammersmith" (the first place that occurred to him, associated, now, with homelessness). "Bedsit."

"Oh *Stick* ... come and stay with us!"

He had a fleeting vision of the all-blue spare room, and Greg's forced smile.

"Luce, I'm happy where I am. I just want to get on with work and be on my own for a bit."

It took him another half-hour to shift her out of his office. She felt guilty that she had lost her temper; apologized, then attempted to justify herself, which triggered another diatribe about Charlotte. When she finally decided to leave, he helped her downstairs with her bags, successfully distracting her from the boxes full of his possessions that still stood on the landing, and finally depositing her into a black cab at the end of Denmark Street.

Her round, mascara-streaked face looked back at him out of the rear window. He forced a grin and a wave before lighting another cigarette, and reflecting that Lucy's idea of sympathy compared unfavorably with some of the interrogation techniques they had used at Guantanamo.

10

ROBIN HAD FALLEN INTO THE habit of buying Strike a pack of sandwiches with her own, if he happened to be in the office over lunchtime, and reimbursing herself from petty cash.

Today, however, she did not hurry back. She had noticed, though Lucy had seemed oblivious, how unhappy Strike had been to find them in conversation. His expression, when he had entered the office, had been every bit as grim as the first time they had met.

Robin hoped that she had not said anything to Lucy that Strike would not like. Lucy had not exactly pried, but she had asked questions to which it was difficult to know the answer.

"Have you met Charlotte yet?"

Robin guessed that this was the stunning ex-wife or girlfriend whose exit she had witnessed on her first morning. Near-collision hardly constituted a meeting, however, so she answered:

"No, I haven't."

"Funny." Lucy had given a disingenuous little smile. "I'd have thought she'd have wanted to meet you."

For some reason, Robin had felt prompted to reply:

"I'm only temporary."

"Still," said Lucy, who seemed to understand the answer better than Robin did herself.

It was only now, wandering up and down the aisle of crisps without really concentrating on them, that the implications of what Lucy had said slid into place. Robin supposed that Lucy might have meant to flatter her, except that the mere possibility of Strike making any kind of pass was extremely distasteful to her.

("Matt, honestly, if you saw him ... he's enormous and he's got a face like some beaten-up boxer. He is not remotely attractive, I'm sure he's over forty, and..." she had cast around for more aspersions to cast upon Strike's appearance, "he's got that sort of pubey hair."

Matthew had only really become reconciled to her continuing employment with Strike now that Robin had accepted the media consultancy job.)

Robin selected two bags of salt and vinegar crisps at random, and headed towards the cash desk. She had not yet told Strike that she would be leaving in two and a half weeks' time.

Lucy had moved from the subject of Charlotte only to interrogate Robin on the amount of business coming through the shabby little office. Robin had been as vague as she dared, intuiting that if Lucy did not know how bad Strike's finances were, it was because he did not want her to know. Hoping that he would be pleased for his sister to think that business was good, she mentioned that his latest client was wealthy.

"Divorce case, is it?" asked Lucy.

"No," said Robin, "it's a... well, I've signed a confidentiality agreement... he's been asked to reinvestigate a suicide."

"Oh God, that won't be fun for Cormoran," said Lucy, with a strange note in her voice.

Robin looked confused.

"Hasn't he told you? Mind you, people usually know without telling. Our mother was a famous—groupie, they call it, don't they?" Lucy's smile was suddenly forced, and her tone, though she was striving for detachment and unconcern, had become brittle. "It's all on the internet. Everything is these days, isn't it? She died of an overdose and they said it was suicide, but Stick always thought her ex-husband did it. Nothing was ever proven. Stick was furious. It was all very sordid and horrible, anyway. Perhaps that's why the client chose Stick— I take it the suicide was an overdose?"

Robin did not reply, but it did not matter; Lucy went on without pausing for an answer:

"That's when Stick dropped out of university and joined the military police. The family was very disappointed. He's really bright, you know; nobody in our family had ever been to Oxford; but he just packed up and left and joined the army. And it seemed to suit him; he did really well there. I think it's a shame he left, to be honest. He could have stayed, even with, you know, his leg..."

Robin did not betray, by so much as a flicker of her eyelid, that she did not know.

Lucy sipped her tea.

"So whereabouts in Yorkshire are you from?"

The conversation had flowed pleasantly after that, right up until the moment that Strike had walked in on them laughing at Robin's description of Matthew's last excursion into DIY.

But Robin, heading back to the office with sandwiches and crisps, felt even sorrier for Strike than she had done before. His marriage— or, if they had not been married, his live-in relationship—had failed; he was sleeping in his office; he had been injured in the war, and now she discovered that his mother had died in dubious and squalid circumstances.

She did not pretend to herself that this compassion was untinged with curiosity. She already knew that she would certainly, at some point in the near future, try and find the online particulars of Leda Strike's death. At the same time, she felt guilty that she had been given another glimpse of a part of Strike she had not been meant to see, like that patch of virtually furry belly he had accidentally exposed that morning. She knew him to be a proud and self-sufficient man; these were the things she liked and admired about him, even if the way these qualities expressed themselves—the camp bed, the boxed possessions on the landing, the empty Pot Noodle tubs in the bin—aroused the derision of such as Matthew, who assumed that anyone living in un- comfortable circumstances must have been profligate or feckless.

Robin was not sure whether or not she imagined the slightly charged atmosphere in the office when she returned. Strike was sit- ting in front of her computer monitor, tapping away at the keyboard, and while he thanked her for the sandwiches, he did not (as was usual) turn away from work for ten minutes for a chat about the Landry case.

"I need this for a couple of minutes; will you be OK on the sofa?" he asked her, continuing to type.

Robin wondered whether Lucy had told Strike what they had discussed. She hoped not. Then she felt resentful for feeling guilty; after all, she had done nothing wrong. Her aggravation put a temporary stop on her great desire to know whether he had found Rochelle Onifade.

"Aha," said Strike.

He had found, on the Italian designer's website, the magenta fake-fur coat that Rochelle had been wearing that morning. It had become available for purchase only within the last two weeks, and it cost fifteen hundred pounds.

Robin waited for Strike to explain the exclamation, but he did not.

"Did you find her?" she asked, at last, when finally Strike turned from the computer to unwrap the sandwiches.

He told her about their encounter, but all the enthusiasm and gratitude of that morning, when he had called her "genius" over and again, was absent. Robin's tone, as she gave him the results of her own telephone inquiries, was, therefore, similarly cool.

"I called the Law Society about the conference in Oxford on January the seventh," she said. "Tony Landry attended. I pretended to be somebody he'd met there, who'd mislaid his card."

He did not seem particularly interested in the information he had requested, nor did he compliment her on her initiative. The conversation petered out in mutual dissatisfaction.

The confrontation with Lucy had exhausted Strike; he wanted to be alone. He also suspected that Lucy might have told Robin about Leda. His sister deplored the fact that their mother had lived and died in conditions of mild notoriety, yet in certain moods she seemed to be seized with a paradoxical desire to discuss it all, especially with strangers. Perhaps it was a kind of safety valve, because of the tight lid she kept on her past with her suburban friends, or perhaps she was trying to carry the fight into the enemy's territory, so anxious about what they might already know about her that she tried to forestall prurient interest before it could start. But he had never wanted Robin to know about his mother, or about his leg, or about Charlotte, or any of the other painful subjects which Lucy insisted on probing whenever she came close enough.

In his tiredness, and his bad mood, Strike extended to Robin, unfairly, his blanket irritation at women, who did not seem able just to leave a man in peace. He thought he might take his notes to the Tottenham this afternoon, where he would be able to sit and think without interruptions, and without being badgered for explanations.

Robin felt the atmospheric change keenly. Taking her cue from the silently munching Strike, she brushed herself free of crumbs, then gave him the morning's messages in a brisk and impersonal tone.

"John Bristow called with a mobile number for Marlene Higson. He's also got through to Guy Somé, who could meet you at ten o'clock on Thursday morning at his studio in Blunkett Street, if that suits. It's out in Chiswick, near Strand-on-the-Green."

"Great. Thanks."

They said very little else to each other that day. Strike spent the greater part of the afternoon at the pub, returning only at ten to five. The awkwardness between them persisted, and for the first time, he was quite pleased to see Robin leave.

Part Four

Optimumque est, ut volgo dixere, aliena insania frui.

And the best plan is, as the popular saying was, to profit by the folly of others.

Pliny the Elder, *Historia Naturalis*

1

STRIKE VISITED ULU EARLY TO shower, and dressed with unusual care, on the morning of his visit to the studio of Guy Somé. He knew, from his perusal of the designer's website, that Somé advocated the purchase and wear of such items as chaps in degraded leather, ties of metal mesh and black-brimmed headbands that seemed to have been made by cutting the tops out of old bowlers. With a faint feeling of defiance, Strike put on the conventional, comfortable dark blue suit he had worn to Cipriani.

The studio he sought had been a disused nineteenth-century warehouse, which stood on the north bank of the Thames. The glittering river dazzled his eyes as he tried to find the entrance, which was not clearly marked; nothing on the outside proclaimed the use to which the building was being put.

At last he discovered a discreet, unmarked bell, and the door was opened electronically from within. The stark but airy hallway was chilly with air-conditioning. A jingling and clacking noise preceded the entrance into the hall of a girl with tomato-red hair, dressed in head-to-toe black and wearing many silver bangles.

"Oh," she said, seeing Strike.

"I've got an appointment with Mr. Somé at ten," he told her. "Cormoran Strike."

"Oh," she said again. "OK."

She disappeared the same way she had come. Strike used the wait to call the mobile telephone number of Rochelle Onifade, as he had been doing ten times a day since he had met her. There was no response.

Another minute passed, and then a small black man was suddenly crossing the floor towards Strike, catlike and silent on rubber soles. He walked with an exaggerated swing of his hips, his upper body quite still except for a little counterbalancing sway of the shoulders, his arms almost rigid.

Guy Somé was nearly a foot shorter than Strike and had perhaps a hundredth of his body fat. The front of the designer's tight black T-shirt was decorated with hundreds of tiny silver studs which formed an apparently three-dimensional image of Elvis's face, as though his chest were a Pin Art toy. The eye was further confused by the fact that a well-defined six-pack moved underneath the tight Lycra. Somé's snug gray jeans bore a faint dark pinstripe, and his trainers seemed to be made out of black suede and patent leather.

His face contrasted strangely with his taut, lean body, for it abounded in exaggerated curves: the eyes exophthalmic so that they appeared fishlike, looking out of the sides of his head. The cheeks were round, shining apples and the full-lipped mouth was a wide oval: his small head was almost perfectly spherical. Somé looked as though he had been carved out of soft ebony by a master hand that had grown bored with its own expertise, and started to veer towards the grotesque.

He held out a hand with a slight crook of the wrist.

"Yeah, I can see a bit of Jonny," he said, looking up into Strike's face; his voice was camp and faintly cockney. "Much *butcher*, though."

Strike shook hands. There was surprising strength in the fingers. The red-haired girl came jingling back.

"I'll be busy for an hour, Trudie, no calls," Somé told her. "Bring us some tea and bicks, darling."

He executed a dancer's turn, beckoning to Strike to follow him.

Down a whitewashed corridor they passed an open door, and a flat-faced middle-aged oriental woman stared back at Strike through the gauzy film of gold stuff she was throwing over a dummy; the room around her was as brilliantly lit as a surgical theater, but full of workbenches, cramped and cluttered with bolts of fabric, the walls a collage of fluttering sketches, photographs and notes. A tiny blonde woman, dressed in what appeared to Strike to be a giant black tubular bandage, opened a door and crossed the corridor in front of them; she gave him precisely the same cold, blank stare as the red-haired Trudie. Strike felt abnormally huge and hairy; a woolly mammoth attempting to blend in among capuchin monkeys.

He followed the strutting designer to the end of the corridor and up a spiral staircase of steel and rubber, at the top of which was a large white rectangular office space. Floor-to-ceiling windows all along the right-hand side showed a stunning view of the Thames and the south bank. The rest of the whitewashed walls were hung with photographs. What arrested Strike's attention was an enormous twelve-foot-tall blowup of the infamous "Fallen Angels" on the wall opposite Somé's desk. On closer inspection, however, he realized that it was not the shot with which the world was familiar. In this version, Lula had thrown back her head in laughter: the strong column of her throat rose vertically out of the long hair, which had become disarranged in her amusement, so that a single dark nipple protruded. Ciara Porter was looking up at Lula, the beginnings of laughter on her own face, but slower to get the joke: the viewer's attention was drawn, as in the more famous version of the picture, immediately to Lula.

She was represented elsewhere; everywhere. There on the left, among a group of models all wearing transparent shifts in rainbow colors; further along, in profile, with gold leaf on her lips and eyelids. Had she learned how to compose her face into its most photogenic arrangement, to project emotion so beautifully? Or had she simply been a pellucid surface through which her feelings naturally shone?

"Park your arse anywhere," said Somé, dropping into a seat behind a dark wood and steel desk covered in sketches; Strike pulled up a chair composed of a single length of contorted perspex. There was a T-shirt lying on the desk, which carried a picture of Princess Diana as a garish Mexican Madonna, glittering with bits of glass and beads, and complete with a flaming scarlet heart of shining satin, on which an embroidered crown was perched lopsided.

"You like?" said Somé, noticing the direction of Strike's gaze.

"Oh yeah," lied Strike.

"Sold out nearly everywhere; bad-taste letters from Catholics; Joe

Mancura wore one on *Jools Holland*. I'm thinking of doing William as Christ on a long-sleeve for winter. Or Harry, do you think, with an AK47 to hide his cock?"

Strike smiled vaguely. Somé crossed his legs with a little more flourish than was strictly necessary and said, with startling bravado:

"So, the Accountant thinks Cuckoo might've been killed? I always called Lula 'Cuckoo,' " he added, unnecessarily.

"Yeah. John Bristow's a lawyer, though."

"I know he is, but Cuckoo and I always called him the Accountant. Well, I did, and Cuckoo sometimes joined in, if she was feeling wicked. He was forever nosing into her percentages and trying to wring every last cent out of everyone. I suppose he's paying you the detective equivalent of the minimum wage?"

"He's paying me a double wage, actually."

"Oh. Well he's probably a bit more generous now he's got Cuckoo's money to play with."

Somé chewed on a fingernail, and Strike was reminded of Kieran Kolovas-Jones; the designer and driver were similar in build, too, small but well proportioned.

"All right, I'm being a bitch," said Somé, taking his nail out of his mouth. "I never liked John Bristow. He was always on Cuckoo's case about something. Get a life. Get out of the *closet*. Have you heard him rhapsodizing about his mummy? Have you met his *girlfriend*? Talk about a beard: I think she's got one."

He rattled out the words in one nervy, spiteful stream, pausing to open a hidden drawer in the desk, from which he took out a packet of menthol cigarettes. Strike had already noticed that Somé's nails were bitten to their quicks.

"Her family was the whole reason she was so fucked up. I used to tell her, 'Drop them, sweetie, move on.' But she wouldn't. That was Cuckoo for you, always flogging a dead horse."

He offered Strike one of the pure white cigarettes, which the detective declined, before lighting one with an engraved Zippo. As he flipped the lid of the lighter shut, Somé said:

"I wish *I'd* thought of calling in a private detective. It never occurred to me. I'm glad someone's done it. I just cannot believe she committed suicide. My therapist says that's denial. I'm having therapy twice a week, not that it makes any fucking difference. I'd be snaffling Valium like Lady Bristow if I could still design when I'm on it, but I tried it the week after Cuckoo died and I was like a zombie. I suppose it got me through the funeral."

Jingling and rattling from the spiral staircase announced the reappearance of Trudie, who emerged through the floor in jerky stages. She laid upon the desk a black lacquered tray, on which stood two silver filigree Russian tea glasses, in each of which was a pale green steaming concoction with wilted leaves floating in it. There was also a plate of wafer-thin biscuits that looked as though they might be made of charcoal. Strike remembered his pie and mash and his mahogany-colored tea at the Phoenix with nostalgia.

"Thanks, Trudie. And get me an ashtray, darling."

The girl hesitated, clearly on the verge of protesting.

"Just *do* it," snarled Somé. "I'm the fucking boss, I'll burn the building down if I want to. Pull the fucking batteries out of the fire alarms. But get the ashtray *first*.

"The alarm went off last week, and set off all the sprinklers downstairs," Somé explained to Strike. "So now the backers don't want anyone smoking in the building. They can stick that one right up their tight little bumholes."

He inhaled deeply, then exhaled through his nostrils.

"Don't you ask questions? Or do you just sit there looking scary until someone blurts out a confession?"

"We can do questions," said Strike, pulling out his notebook and pen. "You were abroad when Lula died, weren't you?"

"I'd just got back, a couple of hours before." Somé's fingers twitched a little on the cigarette. "I'd been in Tokyo, hardly any sleep for eight days. Touched down at Heathrow at about ten thirty with *the* most fucking appalling jet lag. I can't sleep on planes. I wanna be awake if I'm going to crash."

"How did you get home from the airport?"

"Cab. Elsa had fucked up my car booking. There should've been a driver there to meet me."

"Who's Elsa?"

"The girl I sacked for fucking up my car booking. It was the last thing I fucking wanted, to have to find a cab at that time of night."

"Do you live alone?"

"No. By midnight I was tucked up in bed with Viktor and Rolf. My cats," he added with a flicker of a grin. "I took an Ambien, slept for a few hours, then woke up at five in the morning. I switched on Sky News from the bed, and there was a man in a horrible sheepskin hat, standing in the snow in Cuckoo's street, saying she was dead. The ticker-tape across the bottom of the screen was saying it too."

Somé inhaled heavily on the cigarette, and white smoke curled out of his mouth with his next words.

"I nearly fucking died. I thought I was still asleep, or that I'd woken up in the wrong fucking *dimension* or something...I started calling everyone...Ciara, Bryony...all their phones were engaged. And all the time I was watching the screen, thinking they'd flash up something saying there had been a mistake, that it wasn't her. I kept praying it was the bag lady. Rochelle."

He paused, as though he expected some comment from Strike. The latter, who had been making notes as Somé spoke, asked, still writing:

"You know Rochelle, do you?"

"Yeah. Cuckoo brought her in here once. In it for all she could get."

"What makes you say that?"

"She hated Cuckoo. Jealous as fuck; I could see it, even if Cuckoo couldn't. She was in it for the freebies, she didn't give a monkey's whether Cuckoo lived or died. Lucky for her, as it turned out...

"So, the longer I watched the news, I knew there wasn't a mistake. I fell a-fucking-part."

His fingers trembled a little on the snow-white stick he was sucking.

"They said that a neighbor had overheard an argument; so of course I thought it was Duffield. I thought Duffield had knocked her through the window. I was all set to tell the pigs what a cunt he is; I was ready to stand in the dock and testify to the fucker's character. And if this ash falls off my cigarette," he continued in precisely the same tone, "I will fire that little bitch."

As though she had heard him, Trudie's rapid footfalls grew louder and louder until she emerged again into the room, breathing heavily and clutching a heavy glass ashtray.

"*Thank* you," said Somé, with a pointed inflection, as she placed it in front of him and scurried back downstairs.

"Why did you think it was Duffield?" asked Strike, once he judged Trudie to be safely out of earshot.

"Who else would Cuckoo have let in at two in the morning?"

"How well do you know him?"

"Well enough, little piss ant that he is." Somé picked up his mint tea. "Why do women do it? Cuckoo, too...she wasn't stupid— actually, she was razor-sharp—so what did she see in Evan Duffield? I'll tell you," he said, without pausing for an answer. "It's that wounded-poet crap, that soul-pain shit, that too-much-of-a-tortured-genius-to-wash bollocks. Brush your teeth, you little bastard. You're not fucking Byron."

He slammed his glass down and cupped his right elbow in his left hand, steadying his forearm and continuing to draw heavily on the cigarette.

"No man would put up with the likes of Duffield. Only women. Maternal instinct gone warped, if you ask me."

"You think he had it in him to kill her, do you?"

"Of course I do," said Somé dismissively. "Of course he has. All of us have got it in us, somewhere, to kill, so why would Duffield be any exception? He's got the mentality of a vicious twelve-year-old. I can imagine him in one of his rages, having a tantrum and then just—"

With his cigarette-free hand he made a violent shoving movement.

"I saw him shouting at her once. At my after-show party, last year. I got in between them; I told him to have a go at me instead. I might be a little poof," Somé said, the round-cheeked face set, "but I'd back myself against that drugged-up fuck any day. He was a tit at the funeral, too."

"Really?"

"Yeah. Lurching around, off his face. No fucking respect. I was full of tranks myself or I'd've told him what I thought of him. Pretending to be devastated, hypocritical little shit."

"You never thought it was suicide?"

Somé's strange, bulging eyes bored into Strike.

"Never. Duffield says he was at his dealer's, disguised as a wolf. What kind of fucking alibi is that? I hope you're checking him out. I hope you're not dazzled by his fucking celebrity, like the police."

Strike remembered Wardle's comments on Duffield.

"I don't think they found Duffield dazzling."

"They've got more taste than I credited them with, then," said Somé.

"Why are you so sure it wasn't suicide? Lula had had mental health problems, hadn't she?"

"Yeah, but we had a pact, like Marilyn Monroe and Montgomery Clift. We'd sworn that if either of us was thinking seriously of killing themselves, we'd call the other. She would've called me."

"When did you last hear from her?"

"She phoned me on the Wednesday, while I was still in Tokyo," said Somé. "Silly cow always forgot it was eight hours ahead; I had my phone on mute at two in the morning, so I didn't pick up; but she left a message, and she was *not* suicidal. Listen to this."

He reached into his desk drawer again, pressed several buttons, then held the mobile out to Strike.

And Lula Landry spoke close and real, slightly raw and throaty, in Strike's ear, in deliberately affected mockney.

"Aw wight, darlin'? Got something to tell you, I'm not sure whether you're going to like it but it's a biggie, and I'm so fucking happy I've gotta tell someone, so ring me when you can, OK, can't wait, mwah mwah."

Strike handed back the phone.

"Did you call her back? Did you find out what the big news was?"

"No." Somé ground out his cigarette and reached immediately for another one. "The Japs had me in back-to-back meetings; every time I thought of calling her, the time difference was in the way. Anyway ... to tell you the truth, I thought I knew what she was going to say, and I wasn't any too fucking pleased about it. I thought she was pregnant."

Somé nodded several times with the fresh cigarette clutched between his teeth; then he removed it to say:

"Yeah, I thought she'd gone and got herself knocked up."

"By Duffield?"

"I hoped to fuck not. I didn't know at the time that they'd got back together. She wouldn't have dared hook up with him if I'd been in the country; no, she waited till I was in Japan, the sneaky little bitch. She knew I hated him, and she cared what I thought. We were like family, Cuckoo and me."

"Why did you think she might be pregnant?"

"It was the way she sounded. You've heard it—she was so excited...I had this feeling. It was the kind of thing Cuckoo would've done, and she'd have expected me to be as pleased as she was, and fuck her career, fuck *me,* counting on her to launch my brand-new accessories line..."

"Was this the five-million-pound contract her brother told me about?"

"Yeah, and I'll bet the Accountant pushed her to hold out for as much as she could get, too," said Somé, with another flash of temper. "It wasn't like Cuckoo to try and wring every last penny out of me. She knew it was going to be fabulous, and would take her to a whole new level if she fronted it. It shouldn't have been all about the money. Everyone associated her with my stuff; her big break came on a shoot for *Vogue* when she wore my Jagged dress. Cuckoo loved my clothes, she loved *me,* but people get to a certain level, and everyone's telling them they're worth more, and they forget who put them there, and suddenly it's all about the bottom line."

"You must've thought she was worth it, to commit to a five-million-pound contract?"

"Yeah, well, I'd pretty much designed the range *for* her, so having to shoot around a fucking pregnancy wouldn't have been funny. And I could just imagine Cuckoo going silly afterwards, throwing it all in, not wanting to leave the fucking baby. She was the type; always looking for people to love, for a surrogate family. Those Bristows fucked her up good. They only adopted her as a toy for Yvette, who is the scariest bitch in the world."

"In what way?"

"Possessive. Morbid. Didn't want to let Cuckoo out of her sight in case she died, like the kid she'd been bought to replace. Lady Bristow used to come to all the shows, getting under everyone's feet, till she got too ill. And there was an uncle, who treated Cuckoo like scum until she started pulling in big money. He got a bit more respectful then. They all know the value of a buck, the Bristows."

"They're a wealthy family, aren't they?"

"Alec Bristow didn't leave *that* much, not relatively speaking. Not compared to proper money. Not like *your* old man. How come," said Somé, swerving suddenly off the conversational track, "Jonny Rokeby's son's working as a private dick?"

"Because that's his job," said Strike. "Go on about the Bristows."

Somé did not appear to resent being bossed around; if anything, he seemed to relish it, possibly because it was such an unusual experience.

"I just remember Cuckoo telling me that most of what Alec Bristow left was in shares in his old company, and Albris has gone down the pan in the recession. It's hardly fucking Apple. Cuckoo had outearned the whole fucking lot of them before she was twenty."

"Was that picture," said Strike, indicating the enormous "Fallen Angels" image on the wall behind him, "part of the five-million-pound campaign?"

"Yeah," said Somé. "Those four bags were the start of it. She's holding 'Cashile' there; I gave them all African names, for her. She was fixated on Africa. That whorish real mother she unearthed had told her her father was African, so Cuckoo had gone mad on it; talking about studying there, doing voluntary work...never mind that the old slapper had probably been sleeping with about fifty Yardies. African," said Guy Somé, grinding out his cigarette stub in the glass ashtray, "my Aunt Fanny. The bitch just told Cuckoo what she wanted to hear."

"And you decided to go ahead and use the picture for the campaign, even though Lula had just...?"

"It was meant as a fucking *tribute*." Somé spoke loudly over him. "She'd never looked more beautiful. It was supposed to be a fucking tribute to her, to *us*. She was my muse. If the bastards couldn't understand that, fuck 'em, that's all. The press in this country are lower than scum. Judging everyone by their fucking selves."

"The day before she died, some handbags were sent to Lula..."

"Yeah, they were mine. I sent her one of each of those," said Somé, indicating the picture with the end of a new cigarette, "and I sent Deeby Macc some clothes by the same courier."

"Had he ordered them, or...?"

"Freebies, dear," drawled Somé. "Just good business. Couple of customized hoodies and some accessories. Celebrity endorsements never hurt."

"Did he ever wear the stuff?"

"I don't know," said Somé in a more subdued tone. "I had other things to worry about the next day."

"I've seen YouTube footage of him wearing a hoodie with studs on it, like that," said Strike, pointing at Somé's chest. "Making a fist."

"Yeah, that was one of them. Someone must've sent the stuff on to him. One had a fist, one had a handgun, and some of his lyrics on the backs."

"Did Lula talk to you about Deeby Macc coming to stay in the flat downstairs?"

"Oh yeah. She wasn't *nearly* excited enough. I kept saying to her, babes, if he'd written three tracks about me I'd be waiting behind the front door *naked* when he got in." Somé blew smoke in two long streams from his nostrils, looking sideways at Strike. "I like 'em big and rough," he said. "But Cuckoo didn't. Well, look what she hooked up with. I kept telling her, you're the one making all this fucking song-and-dance about your roots; find yourself a nice black boy and settle down. Deeby would've been fucking perfect; why not?

"Last season's show, I had her walking down the catwalk to Deeby's 'Butterface Girl.' 'Bitch you ain't all that, get a mirror that don' fool ya, Give it up an' tone it down, girl, 'cause you ain't no fuckin' Lula.' Duffield hated it."

Somé smoked for a moment in silence, his eyes on the wall of photographs. Strike asked:

"Where do you live? Around here?" though he knew the answer.

"No, I'm in Charles Street, in Kensington," said Somé. "Moved there last year. It's a long fucking way from Hackney, I can tell you, but it was getting silly, I had to leave. Too much hassle. I grew up in

Hackney," he explained, "back when I was plain old Kevin Owusu. I changed my name when I left home. Like you."

"I was never Rokeby," said Strike, flicking over a page in his note-book. "My parents weren't married."

"We all know that, dear," said Somé, with another flash of malice. "I dressed your old man for a *Rolling Stone* shoot last year: skinny suit and broken bowler. D'you see him much?"

"No," said Strike.

"No, well, you'd make him look fucking old, wouldn't you?" said Somé, with a cackle. He fidgeted in his seat, lit yet another cigarette, clamped it between his lips and squinted at Strike through billows of menthol smoke.

"Why are we talking about me, anyway? Do people usually start telling you their life stories when you get out that notebook?"

"Sometimes."

"Don't you want your tea? I don't blame you. I don't know why I drink this shit. My old dad would have a coronary if he asked for a cup of tea and got this."

"Is your family still in Hackney?"

"I haven't checked," said Somé. "We don't talk. I practice what I preach, see?"

"Why do you think Lula changed her name?"

"Because she hated her fucking family, same as me. She didn't want to be associated with them anymore."

"Why choose the same name as her Uncle Tony, then?"

"He's not famous. It made a good name. Deeby couldn't have written 'Double L U B Mine' if she'd been Lula Bristow, could he?"

"Charles Street isn't too far from Kentigern Gardens, is it?"

"About a twenty-minute walk. I wanted Cuckoo to move in with me when she said she couldn't stand her old place anymore, but she wouldn't; she chose that fucking five-star prison instead, just to get away from the press. They drove her into that place. They bear re-sponsibility."

Strike remembered Deeby Macc: *The motherfuckin' press chased her out that window.*

"She took me to see it. *Mayfair,* full of rich Russians and Arabs and bastards like Freddie Bestigui. I said to her, sweetie, you can't live here; marble everywhere, marble isn't chic in our climate…it's like living in your own *tomb*…"

He faltered, then went on:

"She'd been through this head-fuck for a few months. There'd been a stalker who was hand-delivering letters through her front door at three in the morning; she kept getting woken up by the letter box going. The things he said he wanted to do to her, it scared her. Then she split up with Duffield, and she had the paps round the front of her house all the bloody time. Then she finds out they're hacking all her calls. And *then* she had to go and find that bitch of a mother. It was all getting too much. She wanted to be away from it all, to feel secure. I *told* her to move in with me, but instead she went and bought that fucking mausoleum.

"She took it because it felt like a fortress with the round-the-clock security. She thought she'd be safe from everyone, that nobody would be able to get at her.

"But she hated it from the word go. I knew she would. She was cut off from everything she liked. Cuckoo loved color and noise. She liked being on the street, she liked walking, being free.

"One of the reasons the police said it wasn't murder was the open windows. She'd opened them herself; it was only her prints on the handles. But I know why she opened them. She always opened the windows, even when it was freezing cold, because she couldn't stand the silence. She liked being able to hear London."

Somé's voice had lost all its slyness and sarcasm. He cleared his throat and went on:

"She was trying to connect with something real; we used to talk about it all the time. It was our big thing. That's what made her get involved with bloody Rochelle. It was a case of 'there but for the grace of God.' Cuckoo thought that's what she'd have been, if she hadn't been beautiful; if the Bristows hadn't taken her in as a little plaything for Yvette."

"Tell me about this stalker."

"Mental case. He thought they were married or something. He was given a restraining order and compulsory psychiatric treatment."

"Any idea where he is now?"

"I think he was deported back to Liverpool," said Somé. "But the police checked him out; they told me he was in a secure ward up there the night she died."

"Do you know the Bestiguis?"

"Only what Lula told me, that he was sleazy and she's a walking waxwork. I don't need to know her. I know her type. Rich girls spending their ugly husbands' money. They come to my shows. They want to be my friend. Gimme an honest hooker any day."

"Freddie Bestigui was at the same country-house weekend as Lula, a week before she died."

"Yeah, I heard. He had a hard-on for her," said Somé dismissively. "She knew it, as well; it wasn't exactly a unique experience in her life, you know. He never got further than trying to get in the same lift, though, from what she told me."

"You never spoke to her after their weekend at Dickie Carbury's, did you?"

"No. Did he do something then? You don't suspect Bestigui, do you?"

Somé sat up in his seat, staring.

"Fuck . . . Freddie Bestigui? Well, he's a shit, I know that. This little girl I know . . . well, friend of a friend . . . she was working for his production company, and he tried to fucking rape her. No, I am not exaggerating," said Somé. "Literally. Rape. Got her a bit drunk after work and had her on the floor; some assistant had forgotten his mobile and came back for it, and walked in on them. Bestigui paid them both off. Everyone was telling her to press charges, but she took the money and ran. They say he used to discipline his second wife in some pretty fucking kinky ways; that's why she walked away with three mill; she threatened him with the press. But Cuckoo would never have let Freddie Bes-tigui into her flat at two in the morning. Like I say, she wasn't a stupid girl."

"What do you know about Derrick Wilson?"

"Who's he?"

"The security guard who was on duty the night she died."

"Nothing."

"He's a big guy, with a Jamaican accent."

"This might shock you, but not all the black people in London know each other."

"I wondered whether you'd ever spoken to him, or heard Lula talk about him."

"No, we had more interesting things to talk about than the security guard."

"Does the same apply to her driver, Kieran Kolovas-Jones?"

"Oh, I know who Kolovas-Jones is," said Somé, with a slight smirk. "Striking little poses whenever he thought I might be looking out of the window. He's about five fucking feet too short to model."

"Did Lula ever talk about him?"

"No, why would she?" asked Somé restlessly. "He was her driver."

"He's told me they were quite close. He mentioned that she'd given him a jacket you designed. Worth nine hundred quid."

"Big fucking deal," said Somé, with easy contempt. "My proper stuff goes for upwards of three grand a coat. I slap the logo on shell suits and they sell like crazy, so it'd be silly not to."

"Yeah, I was going to ask you about that," said Strike. "Your—ready-to-wear line, is it?"

Somé looked amused.

"That's right. That's the stuff that isn't made-to-measure, see? You buy it straight off the rack."

"Right. How widely is that stuff sold?"

"It's everywhere. When were you last in a clothes shop?" asked Somé, his wicked bulging eyes roving over Strike's dark blue jacket. "What is that, anyway, your demob suit?"

"When you say 'everywhere'..."

"Smart department stores, boutiques, online," rattled off Somé. "Why?"

"One of two men caught on CCTV running away from Lula's area that night was wearing a jacket with your logo on it."

Somé twitched his head very slightly, a gesture of repudiation and irritation.

"Him and a million other people."

"Didn't you see—?"

"I didn't look at any of that shit," said Somé fiercely. "All the— all the coverage. I didn't want to read about it, I didn't want to think about it. I told them to keep it away from me," he said, gesturing towards the stairs and his staff. "All I knew was that she was dead and Duffield was behaving like someone with something to hide. That's all I knew. That was enough."

"OK. Still on the subject of clothes, in the last picture of Lula, the one where she was walking into the building, she seemed to be wearing a dress and a coat..."

"Yeah, she was wearing Maribelle and Faye," said Somé. "The dress was called Maribelle—"

"Yeah, got it," said Strike. "But when she died, she was wearing something different."

This seemed to surprise Somé.

"Was she?"

"Yeah. In the police pictures of the body—"

But Somé threw up his arm in an involuntary gesture of refutation, of self-protection, then got to his feet, breathing hard, and walked to the photograph wall, where Lula stared out of several pictures, smiling, wistful or serene. When the designer turned to face Strike again, the strange bulging eyes were wet.

"Fucking hell," he said, in a low voice. "Don't talk about her like that. 'The body.' Fucking hell. You're a cold-blooded bastard, aren't you? No fucking wonder old Jonny's not keen on you."

"I wasn't trying to upset you," said Strike calmly. "I only want to know whether you can think of any reason she'd have changed her clothes when she got home. When she fell, she was wearing trousers and a sequined top."

"How the fuck should I know why she changed?" asked Somé, wildly. "Maybe she was cold. Maybe she was—This is fucking ridiculous. How could I know that?"

"I'm only asking," said Strike. "I read somewhere that you'd told the press she died in one of your dresses."

"That wasn't me, I never announced it. Some tabloid bitch rang the office and asked for the name of that dress. One of the seamstresses told her, and they called her my spokesman. Making out I'd tried to get publicity out of it, the cunts. Fucking hell."

"D'you think you could put me in touch with Ciara Porter and Bryony Radford?"

Somé seemed off-balance, confused.

"What? Yeah..."

But he had begun to cry in earnest; not like Bristow, with wild gulps and sobs, but silently, with tears sliding down his smooth dark cheeks and on to his T-shirt. He swallowed and closed his eyes, turned his back on Strike, rested his forehead against the wall and trembled.

Strike waited in silence until Somé had wiped his face several times and turned again towards him. He made no mention of his tears, but walked back to his chair, sat down and lit a cigarette. After two or three deep drags, he said in a practical and unemotional voice:

"If she changed her clothes, it was because she was expecting someone. Cuckoo always dressed the part. She must've been waiting for someone."

"Well that's what I thought," said Strike. "But I'm no expert on women and their clothes."

"No," said Somé, with a ghost of his malicious smile, "you don't look it. You want to speak to Ciara and Bryony?"

"It'd help."

"They're both doing a shoot for me on Wednesday: 1 Arlington Place in Islington. If you come along fivish, they'd be free to talk to you."

"That's good of you, thanks."

"It isn't good of me," said Somé quietly. "I want to know what happened. When are you speaking to Duffield?"

"As soon as I can get hold of him."

"He thinks he's got away with it, the little shit. She must've changed because she knew he was coming, mustn't she? Even though they'd rowed, she knew he'd follow her. But he'll never talk to you."

"He'll talk to me," said Strike easily, as he put away his notebook and checked his watch. "I've taken up a lot of your time. Thanks again."

As Somé led Strike back down the spiral stairs and along the white-walled corridor, some of his swagger returned to him. By the time they shook hands in the cool tiled lobby, no trace of distress remained on show.

"Lose some weight," he told Strike, as a parting shot, "and I'll send you something XXL."

As the warehouse door swung closed behind Strike, he heard Somé call to the tomato-haired girl at the desk: "I know what you're thinking, Trudie. You're imagining him taking you roughly from behind, aren't you? Aren't you, darling? Big rough *soldier boy*," and Trudie's squeal of shocked laughter.

2

CHARLOTTE'S ACCEPTANCE OF STRIKE'S SILENCE was unprecedented. There had been no further calls or texts; she was maintaining the pretense that their last, filthy, volcanic row had changed her irrevocably, stripped away her love and purged her of fury. Strike, however, knew Charlotte as intimately as a germ that had lingered in his blood for fifteen years; knew that her only response to pain was to wound the offender as deeply as possible, no matter what the cost to herself. What would happen if he refused her an audience, and kept refusing? It was the only strategy he had never tried, and all he had left.

Every now and then, when Strike's resistance was low (late at night, alone on his camp bed) the infection would erupt again: regret and longing would spike, and he saw her at close quarters, beautiful, naked, breathing words of love; or weeping quietly, telling him that she knew she was rotten, ruined, impossible, but that he was the best and truest thing she had ever known. Then, the fact that he was a few pressed buttons away from speaking to her seemed too fragile a barricade against temptation, and he sometimes pulled himself back out of his sleeping bag and hopped in the darkness to Robin's abandoned desk, switching on the lamp and poring, even for hours, over the case report. Once or twice he placed early-morning calls to Rochelle Onifade's mobile, but she never answered.

On Thursday morning, Strike returned to the wall outside St. Thomas's, and waited for three hours in the hope of seeing Rochelle again, but she did not turn up. He had Robin call the hospital, but this time they refused to comment on Rochelle's non-attendance, and resisted all attempts at getting an address for her.

On Friday morning, Strike returned from an outing to Starbucks to find Spanner sitting not on the sofa beside Robin's desk, but on the desk itself. He had an unlit roll-up in his mouth, and was leaning over her, apparently being more amusing than Strike had ever found him, because Robin was laughing in the slightly grudging manner of a woman who is entertained, but who wishes, nevertheless, to make it clear that the goal is well defended.

"Morning, Spanner," said Strike, but the faintly repressive quality of his greeting did nothing to moderate either the computer special-ist's ardent body language or his broad smile.

"All right, Fed? Brought your Dell back for you."

"Great. Double decaff latte," Strike told Robin, setting the drink down beside her. "No charge," he added, as she reached for her purse.

She was touchingly averse to charging minor luxuries to petty cash. Robin made no objection in front of their guest, but thanked Strike, and turned again to her work, which involved a small clock-wise swivel of her desk chair, away from the two men.

The flare of a match turned Strike's attention from his own double espresso to his guest.

"This is a non-smoking office, Spanner."

"What? You smoke like a fucking chimney."

"Not in here I don't. Follow me."

Strike led Spanner into his own office and closed the door firmly behind him.

"She's engaged," he said, taking his usual seat.

"Wasting my powder, am I? Ah well. Put in a word for me if the engagement goes down the pan; she's just my type."

"I don't think you're hers."

Spanner grinned knowingly.

"Already queuing, are you?"

"No," said Strike. "I just know her fiancé's a rugby-playing ac-countant. Clean-cut, square-jawed Yorkshireman."

He had formed a surprisingly clear mental image of Matthew, though he had never seen a photograph.

"You never know; she might fancy rebounding on to something a bit edgier," said Spanner, swinging Lula Landry's laptop on to the desk and sitting down opposite Strike. He was wearing a slightly tatty sweatshirt and Jesus sandals on bare feet; it was the warmest day of the year so far. "I've had a good look at this piece of crap. How much technical detail do you want?"

"None; but I need to know that you could explain it clearly in court."

Spanner looked, for the first time, truly intrigued.

"You serious?"

"Very. Would you be able to prove to a defending counsel that you know your stuff?"

" 'Course I could."

"Then just give me the important bits."

Spanner hesitated for a moment, trying to read Strike's expression. Finally he began:

"Password's Agyeman, and it was reset five days before she died."

"Spell it?"

Spanner did so, adding, to Strike's surprise: "It's a surname. Ghanaian. She bookmarked the homepage of SOAS—School of Oriental and African Studies—and it was on there. Look here."

As he spoke, Spanner's nimble fingers were clacking keyboard keys; he had brought up the home page he described, bordered with bright green, with sections on the school, news, staff, students, library and so on.

"When she died, though, it looked like this."

And with another outburst of clicking, he retrieved an almost identical page, featuring, as the rapidly darting cursor soon revealed, a link to the obituary of one Professor J. P. Agyeman, Emeritus Professor of African Politics.

"She saved this version of the page," said Spanner. "And her internet history shows she'd browsed Amazon for his books in the month before she died. She was looking at a lot of books on African history and politics round then."

"Any evidence she applied to SOAS?"

"Not on here."

"Anything else of interest?"

"Well, the only other thing I noticed was that a big photo file was deleted off it on the seventeenth of March."

"How d'you know that?"

"There's software that'll help you recover even stuff people think's gone from the hard drive," said Spanner. "How d'you think they keep catching all those pedos?"

"Did you get it back?"

"Yeah. I've put it on here." He handed Strike a memory stick. "I didn't think you'd want me to put it back on."

"No—so the photographs were...?"

"Nothing fancy. Just deleted. Like I say, your average punter doesn't realize you've got to work a damn sight harder than pressing 'delete' if you really want to hide something."

"Seventeenth of March," said Strike.

"Yeah. St. Patrick's Day."

"Ten weeks after she died."

"Could've been the police," suggested Spanner.

"It wasn't the police," said Strike.

After Spanner had left, he hurried into the outer office and displaced Robin, so that he could view the photographs that had been removed from the laptop. He could feel Robin's anticipation as he explained to her what Spanner had done and opened up the file on the memory stick.

Robin was afraid, for a fraction of a second, as the first photograph bloomed onscreen, that they were about to see something horrible; evidence of criminality or perversion. She had only heard about the concealment of pictures online in the context of dreadful abuse cases. After several minutes, however, Strike voiced her own feelings.

"Just social snaps."

He did not sound as disappointed as Robin felt, and she was a little ashamed of herself; had she wanted to see something awful? Strike scrolled down, through pictures of groups of giggling girls, fellow models, the occasional celebrity. There were several pictures of Lula with Evan Duffield, a few of them clearly taken by one or other of the pair themselves, holding the camera at arm's length, both of them apparently stoned or drunk. Somé made several appearances; Lula looked more formal, more subdued, by his side. There were many of

Ciara Porter and Lula hugging in bars, dancing in clubs and giggling on a sofa in somebody's crowded flat.

"That's Rochelle," said Strike suddenly, pointing to a sullen little face glimpsed under Ciara's armpit in a group shot. Kieran Kolovas-Jones had been roped into this picture; he stood at the end, beaming.

"Do me a favor," said Strike, when he had finished trawling through all two hundred and twelve pictures. "Go through these for me, and try and at least identify the famous people, so we can make a start on finding out who might have wanted the photos off her laptop."

"But there's nothing incriminating here at all," said Robin.

"There must be," said Strike.

He returned to his inner office, where he placed calls to John Bristow (in a meeting, and not to be disturbed; "Please get him to call me as soon as you can"), to Eric Wardle (voicemail: "I've got a question about Lula Landry's laptop") and to Rochelle Onifade (on the off-chance; no answer; no chance of leaving a message: "Voicemail full").

"I'm still having no luck with Mr. Bestigui," Robin told Strike, when he emerged from his inner office to find her performing searches related to an unidentified brunette posing with Lula on a beach. "I phoned again this morning, but he just won't call me back. I've tried everything; I've pretended to be all sorts of people, I've said it's urgent—what's funny?"

"I was just wondering why none of these people who keep interviewing you have offered you a job," said Strike.

"Oh," said Robin, blushing faintly. "They have. All of them. I've accepted the human resources one."

"Oh. Right," said Strike. "You didn't say. Congratulations."

"Sorry, I thought I'd told you," lied Robin.

"So you'll be leaving . . . when?"

"Two weeks."

"Ah. I expect Matthew's pleased, is he?"

"Yes," she said, slightly taken aback, "he is."

It was almost as if Strike knew how little Matthew liked her working for him; but that was impossible; she had been careful not to give the slightest hint of the tensions at home.

The telephone rang, and Robin answered it.

"Cormoran Strike's office?...Yes, who's speaking, please?...It's Derrick Wilson," she told him, passing over the receiver.

"Derrick, hi."

"Mister Bestigui's gone away for a coupla days," said Wilson's voice. "If you wanna come an' look at the building..."

"I'll be there in half an hour," said Strike.

He was on his feet, checking his pockets for wallet and keys, when he became aware of Robin's slight air of dejection, though she was continuing to pore over the unincriminating photographs.

"D'you want to come?"

"Yes!" she said gleefully, seizing her handbag and closing down her computer.

3

THE HEAVY BLACK-PAINTED FRONT door of number 18, Kentigern Gardens, opened on to a marbled lobby. Directly opposite the entrance was a handsome built-in mahogany desk, to the right of which was the staircase, which turned immediately out of sight (marble steps, with a brass and wood handrail); the entrance to the lift, with its burnished gold doors, and a solid dark-wood door set into the white-painted wall. On a white cubic display unit in the corner between this and the front doors was a vast display of deep pink oriental lilies in tall tubular vases, their scent heavy on the warm air. The left-hand wall was mirrored, doubling the apparent size of the space, reflecting the staring Strike and Robin, the lift doors and the modern chandelier hung in cubes of crystal overhead, and lengthening the security desk to a vast stretch of polished wood.

Strike remembered Wardle: "Flats done up with marble and shit like...like a fucking five-star hotel." Beside him, Robin was trying not to look impressed. This, then, was how multimillionaires lived. She and Matthew occupied the lower floor of a semidetached house in Clapham; its sitting room was the same size as that designated for the off-duty guards, which Wilson showed them first. There was just enough room for a table and two chairs; a wall-mounted box contained all the master keys, and another door led into a tiny toilet cubicle.

Wilson was wearing a black uniform that was constabular in design, with its brass buttons, black tie and white shirt.

"Monitors," he pointed out to Strike as they emerged from the back room and paused behind the desk, where a row of four small black-and-white screens was hidden from guests. One showed

footage from the camera over the front door, affording a circum-
scribed view of the street; another displayed a similarly deserted view
of an underground car park; a third the empty back garden of number 18, which comprised lawn, some fancy planting and the high
back wall Strike had hoisted himself up on; and the fourth the interior of the stationary lift. In addition to the monitors, there were
two control panels for the communal alarms and those for the doors
into the pool and car park, and two telephones, one attached to an
outside line, the other connected only to the three flats.

"That," said Wilson, indicating the solid wooden door, "goes to
the gym, the pool an' the car park," and at Strike's request he led
them through it.

The gym was small, but mirrored like the lobby, so that it appeared
twice as big. It had one window, facing the street, and contained a
treadmill, rowing and step machines and a set of weights.

A second mahogany door led to a narrow marble stair, lit by cubic
wall lights, which took them on to a small lower landing, where a
plain painted door led to the underground car park. Wilson opened
it with two keys, a Chubb and a Yale, then flicked a switch. The
floodlit area was almost as long as the street itself, full of millions
of pounds' worth of Ferrari, Audi, Bentley, Jaguar and BMW. At
twenty-foot intervals along the back wall were doors like the one
through which they had just come: inner entrances to each of the
houses of Kentigern Gardens. The electric garage doors leading from
Serf's Way were close by number 18, outlined by silvery daylight.

Robin wondered what the silent men beside her were thinking.
Was Wilson used to the extraordinary lives of the people who lived
here; used to underground car parks and swimming pools and Fer-
raris? And was Strike thinking (as she was) that this long row of
doors represented possibilities she had not once considered: chances
of secret, hidden scurrying between neighbors, and of hiding and
departing in as many ways as there were houses in the street? But
then she noticed the numerous black snouts pointing from regular
spots on the shadowy upper walls, feeding footage back to countless monitors. Was it possible that none of them had been watched
that night?

"OK," said Strike, and Wilson led them back on to the marble staircase, and locked up the car park door behind them.

Down another short flight of stairs, the smell of chlorine became stronger with every step, until Wilson opened a door at the bottom and they were assailed by a wave of warm, damp, chemically laden air.

"This is the door that wasn't locked that night?" Strike asked Wilson, who nodded as he pressed another switch, and light blazed.

They had walked on to the broad marble rim of the pool, which was shielded by a thick plastic cover. The opposite wall was, again, mirrored; Robin saw the three of them standing there, incongruous in full dress against a mural of tropical plants and fluttering butterflies that extended up over the ceiling. The pool was around fifteen meters long, and at the far end was a hexagonal jacuzzi, beyond which were three changing cubicles, fronted by lockable doors.

"No cameras here?" asked Strike, looking around, and Wilson shook his head.

Robin could feel sweat prickling on the back of her neck and under her arms. It was oppressive in the pool area, and she was pleased to climb the stairs ahead of the two men, back to the lobby, which in comparison was pleasant and airy. A petite young blonde had appeared in their absence, wearing a pink overall, jeans and a T-shirt, and carrying a plastic bucket full of cleaning implements.

"Derrick," she said in heavily accented English, when the security guard emerged from downstairs. "I neet key for two."

"This is Lechsinka," said Wilson. "The cleaner."

She favored Robin and Strike with a small, sweet smile. Wilson moved around behind the mahogany desk and handed her a key from beneath it, and Lechsinka then ascended the stairs, her bucket swinging, her tightly bejeaned backside swelling and swaying seductively. Strike, conscious of Robin's sideways glance, withdrew his gaze from it reluctantly.

Strike and Robin followed Wilson upstairs to Flat 1, which he opened up with a master key. The door on to the stairwell, Strike noted, had an old-fashioned peephole.

"Mister Bestigui's place," announced Wilson, stifling the alarm by entering the code on a pad to the right of the door. "Lechsinka's already bin in this morning."

Strike could smell polish and see the track marks of a vacuum cleaner on the white carpet of the hallway, with its brass wall lights and its five immaculate white doors. He noticed the discreet alarm keypad on the right wall, at right angles to a painting in which dreamy goats and peasants floated over a blue-toned village. Tall vases of orchids stood on a black japanned table beneath the Chagall.

"Where's Bestigui?" Strike asked Wilson.

"LA," said the security guard. "Back in two days."

The light, bright sitting room had three tall windows, each of them with a shallow stone balcony beyond; its walls were Wedgwood blue and nearly everything else was white. All was pristine, elegant and beautifully proportioned. Here, too, there was a single superb painting: macabre, surreal, with a spear-bearing man masked as a blackbird, arm in arm with a gray-toned headless female torso.

It was from this room that Tansy Bestigui maintained she had heard a screaming match two floors above. Strike moved up close to the long windows, noting the modern catches, the thickness of the panes, the complete lack of noise from the street, though his ear was barely half an inch from the cold glass. The balcony beyond was narrow, and filled with potted shrubs trimmed into pointed cones.

Strike moved off towards the bedroom. Robin remained in the sitting room, turning slowly where she stood, taking in the chandelier of Venetian glass, the muted rug in shades of pale blue and pink, the enormous plasma TV, the modern glass and iron dining table and silk-cushioned iron chairs; the small silver *objets d'art* on glass side tables and on the white marble mantelpiece. She thought, a little sadly, of the IKEA sofa of which she had, until now, felt so proud; then she remembered Strike's camp bed in the office with a twinge of shame. Catching Wilson's eye, she said, unconsciously echoing Eric Wardle:

"It's a different world, isn't it?"

"Yeah," he said. "You couldn't have kids in here."

"No," said Robin, who had not considered the place from that point of view.

Her employer strode out of the bedroom, evidently absorbed in establishing some point to his own satisfaction, and disappeared into the hall.

Strike was, in fact, proving to himself that the logical route from the Bestiguis' bedroom to their bathroom was through the hall, bypassing the sitting room altogether. Furthermore, it was his belief that the only place in the flat from which Tansy could conceivably have witnessed the fatal fall of Lula Landry—and realized what she was seeing—was from the sitting room. In spite of Eric Wardle's assertion to the contrary, nobody standing in the bathroom could have had more than a partial view of the window past which Landry had fallen: insufficient, at night, to be sure that whatever had fallen was a human, let alone to identify which human it had been.

Strike returned to the bedroom. Now that he was in solitary possession of the marital home, Bestigui was sleeping on the side nearest the door and the hall, judging by the clutter of pills, glasses and books piled on that bedside table. Strike wondered whether this had been the case while he cohabited with his wife.

A large walk-in wardrobe with mirrored doors led off the bedroom. It was full of Italian suits and shirts from Turnbull & Asser. Two shallow subdivided drawers were devoted entirely to cufflinks in gold and platinum. There was a safe behind a false panel at the back of the shoe racks.

"I think that's everything in here," Strike told Wilson, rejoining the other two in the sitting room.

Wilson set the alarm when they left the flat.

"You know all the codes for the different flats?"

"Yeah," said Wilson. "Gotta, in case they go off."

They climbed the stairs to the second floor. The staircase turned so tightly around the lift shaft that it was a succession of blind corners. The door to Flat 2 was identical to that of Flat 1, except that it was standing ajar. They could hear the growl of Lechsinka's vacuum cleaner from inside.

"We got Mister an' Missus Kolchak in here now," said Wilson. "Ukrainian."

The hallway was identical in shape to that of number 1, with many of the same features, including the alarm keypad on the wall at right angles to the front door; but it was tiled instead of carpeted. A large gilt mirror faced the entrance instead of a painting, and two fragile, spindly wooden tables on either side of it bore ornate Tiffany lamps.

"Were Bestigui's roses on something like that?" asked Strike.

"On one that's jus' like 'em, yeah," said Wilson. "It's back in the lounge now."

"And you put it here, in the middle of the hall, with the roses on it?"

"Yeah, Bestigui wanted Macc to see 'em soon as he walked in, but there was plenty of room to walk around 'em, you can see that. No need to knock 'em over. But he was young, the copper," said Wilson tolerantly.

"Where are the panic buttons you told me about?" Strike asked.

"Round here," said Wilson, leading him out of the hall and into the bedroom. "There's one by the bed, and there's another one in the sitting room."

"Have all the flats got these?"

"Yeah."

The relative positions of the bedrooms, sitting room, kitchen and bathroom were identical to those of Flat 1. Many of the finishings were similar, down to the mirrored doors in the walk-in wardrobe, which Strike went to check. While he was opening doors and surveying the thousands of pounds' worth of women's dresses and coats, Lechsinka emerged from the bedroom with a belt, two ties and several polythene-covered dresses, fresh from the dry-cleaner's, over her arm.

"Hi," said Strike.

"Hello," she said, moving to a door behind him and pulling out a tie rack. "Excuse, please."

He stood aside. She was short and very pretty in a pert, girlish way, with a rather flat face, a snub nose and Slavic eyes. She hung up the ties neatly while he watched her.

"I'm a detective," he said. Then he remembered that Eric Wardle had described her English as "crap."

"Like a policeman?" he ventured.

"Ah. Police."

"You were here, weren't you, the day before Lula Landry died?"

It took a few tries to convey exactly what he meant. When she grasped the point, however, she showed no objection to answering questions, as long as she could continue putting the clothes away as she talked.

"I always clean stair first," she said. "Miz Landry is talking very loud at her brudder; he shouting that she gives boyfriend too much moneys, and she very bad with him.

"I clean number two, empty. Is clean already. Quick."

"Were Derrick and the man from the security firm there while you were cleaning?"

"Derrick and . . . ?"

"The repairman? The alarm man?"

"Yes, alarm man and Derrick, yes."

Strike could hear Robin and Wilson talking in the hall, where he had left them.

"Do you set the alarms again after you've cleaned?"

"Put alarm? Yes," she said. "One nine six six, same as door, Derrick tells me."

"He told you the number before he left with the alarm man?"

Again, it took a few tries to get the point across, and when she grasped it, she seemed impatient.

"Yes, I already say this. One nine six six."

"So you set the alarm after you'd finished cleaning in here?"

"Put alarm, yes."

"And the alarm man, what did he look like?"

"Alarm man? Look?" She frowned attractively, her small nose wrinkling, and shrugged. "I not see he's face. But blue—all blue . . ." she added, and with the hand not holding polythened dresses, she made a sweeping gesture down her body.

"Overall?" he suggested, but she met the word with blank incomprehension. "OK, where did you clean after that?"

"Number one," said Lechsinka, returning to her task of hanging up the clothes, moving around him to find the correct rails. "Clean big windows. Miz Bestigui talking on telephone. Angry. Upset. She say she no want to lie no more."

"She didn't want to *lie?*" repeated Strike.

Lechsinka nodded, standing on tiptoes to hang up a floor-length gown.

"You heard her say," he repeated clearly, "on the phone, that she didn't want to lie anymore?"

Lechsinka nodded again, her face blank, innocent.

"Then she see me and she shout 'Go away, go away!' "

"Really?"

Lechsinka nodded and continued to put away clothes.

"Where was Mr. Bestigui?"

"Not there."

"Do you know who she was speaking to? On the phone?"

"No." But then, a little slyly, she said, "Woman."

"A woman? How do you know?"

"Shouting, shouting on telephone. I can hear woman."

"It was a row? An argument? They were yelling at each other? Loud, yeah?"

Strike could hear himself lapsing into the absurd, overdeliberate language of the linguistically challenged Englishman. Lechsinka nodded again as she pulled open drawers in search of the place for the belt, the only item now remaining in her arms. When at last she had coiled it up and put it away, she straightened and walked away from him, into the bedroom. He followed.

While she made the bed and neatened the bedside tables, he established that she had cleaned Lula Landry's flat last that day, after the model had left to visit her mother. She had noticed nothing out of the ordinary, nor had she spotted any blue writing paper, whether written on or blank. Guy Somé's handbags, and the various items for Deeby Macc, had been delivered to the security desk by the time she had finished, and the last thing she had done at work that day had been to take the designer's gifts up to Lula's and Macc's respective flats.

"And you set the alarms again after putting the things in there?"

"I put alarms, yes."

"Lula's?"

"Yes."

"And one nine six six in Flat Two?"

"Yes."

"Can you remember what you put away in Deeby Macc's flat?"

She had to mime some of the items, but she managed to convey that she remembered two tops, a belt, a hat, some gloves and (she made a fiddling mime around her wrists) cufflinks.

After stowing these things in the open shelving area of the walk-in wardrobe, so that Macc could not miss them, she had reset the alarm and gone home.

Strike thanked her very much, and lingered just long enough to admire once more her tightly denimed backside as she straightened the duvet, before rejoining Robin and Wilson in the hall.

As they proceeded up the third flight of stairs, Strike checked Lechsinka's story with Wilson, who agreed that he had instructed the repairman to set the alarm to 1966, like the front door.

"I jus' chose a number that'd be easy for Lechsinka to remember, because of the front door. Macc coulda reset it to somethin' different if he'd wanted."

"Can you remember what the repairman looked like? You said he was new?"

"Really young guy. Hair to here."

Wilson indicated the base of his neck.

"White?"

"Yeah, white. Didn't even look like he was shaving yet."

They had reached the front door of Flat Three, once the home of Lula Landry. Robin felt a frisson of something—fear, excitement—as Wilson opened the third smoothly painted white front door, with its glassy bullet-sized peephole.

The top flat was architecturally different from the other two: smaller and airier. It had been recently decorated throughout in shades of cream and brown. Guy Somé had told Strike that the flat's famous previous inhabitant loved color; but it was now as impersonal as any upmarket hotel room. Strike led the way in silence to the sitting room.

The carpet here was not lush and woolen as in Bestigui's flat, but made of rough sand-colored jute. Strike ran his heel across it; it made no mark or track.

"Was the floor like this when Lula lived here?" he asked Wilson.

"Yeah. She chose it. It was nearly new, so they left it."

Instead of the regularly spaced long windows of the lower flats, each with three separate small balconies, the penthouse flat boasted a single pair of double doors leading on to one wide balcony. Strike unlocked and opened these doors and stepped outside. Robin did not like watching him do it; after a glance at Wilson's impassive face, she turned and stared at the cushions and the black-and-white prints, trying not to think about what had happened here three months previously.

Strike was looking down into the street, and Robin might have been surprised to know that his thoughts were not as clinical or dispassionate as she supposed.

He was visualizing someone who had lost control completely; someone running at Landry as she stood, fine-boned and beautiful, in the outfit she had thrown on to meet a much-anticipated guest; a killer lost in rage, half dragging, half pushing her, and finally, with the brute strength of a highly motivated maniac, throwing her. The seconds it took her to fall through the air towards the concrete, smothered in its deceptively soft covering of snow, must have seemed to last an eternity. She had flailed, trying to find handholds in the merciless empty air; and then, without time to make amends, to explain, to bequeath or to apologize, without any of the luxuries permitted those who are given notice of their impending demise, she had broken on the road.

The dead could only speak through the mouths of those left behind, and through the signs they left scattered behind them. Strike had felt the living woman behind the words she had written to friends; he had heard her voice on a telephone held to his ear; but now, looking down on the last thing she had ever seen in her life, he felt strangely close to her. The truth was coming slowly into focus out of the mass of disconnected detail. What he lacked was proof.

His mobile phone rang as he stood there. John Bristow's name and number were displayed; he took the call.

"Hi, John, thanks for getting back to me."

"No problem. Any news?" asked the lawyer.

"Maybe. I've had an expert look at Lula's laptop, and he found out a file of photographs had been deleted from it after Lula died. Do you know anything about that?"

His words were met by complete silence. The only reason Strike knew that they had not been cut off was that he could hear a small amount of background noise at Bristow's end.

At last the lawyer said, in an altered voice:

"They were taken off *after* Lula died?"

"That's what the expert says."

Strike watched a car roll slowly down the street below, and pause halfway along. A woman got out, swathed in fur.

"I—I'm sorry," Bristow said, sounding thoroughly shaken. "I'm just—just shocked. Perhaps the police removed this file?"

"When did you get the laptop back from them?"

"Oh...sometime in February, I suppose, early February."

"This file was removed on March the seventeenth."

"But—but this just doesn't make sense. Nobody knew the password."

"Well, evidently somebody did. You said the police told your mother what it was."

"My mother certainly wouldn't have removed—"

"I'm not suggesting she did. Is there any chance she could have left the laptop open, and running? Or that she gave somebody else the password?"

He thought that Bristow must be in his office. He could hear faint voices in the background, and, distantly, a woman laughing.

"I suppose that's possible," said Bristow slowly. "But who would have removed photographs? Unless...but God, that's horrible..."

"What is?"

"You don't think one of the nurses could have taken the pictures? To sell to a newspaper? But that's a dreadful thought...a nurse..."

"All the expert knows is that they were deleted; there's no evidence that they were copied and stolen. But as you say—anything's possible."

"But who else—I mean, naturally I hate to think it could be a nurse, but who else *could* it be? The laptop's been at my mother's ever since the police gave it back."

"John, are you aware of every visitor your mother's had in the last three months?"

"I think so. I mean, obviously, I can't be sure..."

"No. Well, there's the difficulty."

"But why—why would anyone do this?"

"I can think of a few reasons. It would be a big help if you could ask your mother about this, though, John. Whether she had the laptop running in mid-March. Whether any of her visitors expressed an interest in it."

"I—I'll try." Bristow sounded very stressed, almost tearful. "She's very, very weak now."

"I'm sorry," said Strike, formally. "I'll be in touch shortly. 'Bye."

He stepped back from the balcony and closed the doors, then turned to Wilson.

"Derrick, can you show me how you searched this place? What order you looked in the rooms that night?"

Wilson thought for a moment, then said:

"I come in here first. Looked around, seen the doors open. Didn't touch 'em. Then," he indicated that they should follow him, "I looked in here..."

Robin, following in the two men's wake, noticed a subtle change in the way that Strike was talking to the security man. He was asking simple, deft questions, focusing on what Wilson had felt, touched, seen and heard at each step of his way through the flat.

Under Strike's guidance, Wilson's body language started to change. He began to enact the way he had held the doorjambs, leaning into rooms, casting a rapid look around. When he crossed to the only bedroom, he did it at a slow-motion run, responding to the spotlight of Strike's undivided attention; he dropped to his knees to demonstrate how he had looked under the bed, and at Strike's prompting remembered that a dress had lain crumpled beneath his legs; he led them, face set with concentration, to the bathroom, and showed them how he had swiveled to check behind the door before sprinting (he almost mimed it, arms moving exaggeratedly as he walked) back to the front door.

"And then," said Strike, opening it and gesturing Wilson through, "you came out..."

"I came out," agreed Wilson, in his bass voice, "an' I jabbed the lift button."

He pretended to do it, and feigned pushing open the doors in his anxiety to see what was inside.

"Nothing—so I started running back down again."

"What could you hear now?" Strike asked, following him; neither of them were paying any attention to Robin, who closed the flat door behind her.

"Very distant—the Bestiguis yelling—and I turn round this corner and—"

Wilson stopped dead on the stair. Strike, who seemed to have anticipated something like this, stopped too; Robin careered straight into him, with a flustered apology that he cut off with a raised hand, as though, she thought, Wilson was in a trance.

"And I slipped," said Wilson. He sounded shocked. "I forgot that. I slipped. Here. Backwards. Sat down hard. There was water. Here. Drops. Here."

He was pointing at the stairs.

"Drops of water," repeated Strike.

"Yeah."

"Not snow."

"No."

"Not wet footprints."

"Drops. Big drops. Here. Mi foot skidded and I slipped. And I just got up and kept running."

"Did you tell the police about the drops of water?"

"No. I forgot. Till now. I forgot."

Something that had bothered Strike all along had at last been made clear. He let out a great satisfied sigh and grinned. The other two stared.

4

THE WEEKEND STRETCHED AHEAD, WARM and empty. Strike sat at his open window again, smoking and watching the hordes of shoppers passing along Denmark Street, the case report open on his lap, the police file on the desk, making a list for himself of points still to be clarified, and sifting the morass of information he had collected.

For a while he contemplated a photograph of the front of number 18 as it had been on the morning after Lula died. There was a small, but to Strike significant, difference between the frontage as it had been then, and as it was now. From time to time he moved to the computer; once to find out the agent who represented Deeby Macc; then to look at the share price for Albris. His notebook lay open beside him at a page full of truncated sentences and questions, all in his dense, spiky handwriting. When his mobile rang, he raised it to his ear without checking who was on the other end.

"Ah, Mr. Strike," said Peter Gillespie's voice. "How nice of you to pick up."

"Oh, hello, Peter," said Strike. "Got you working weekends now, has he?"

"Some of us have no option but to work at weekends. You haven't returned any of my weekday phone calls."

"I've been busy. Working."

"I see. Does that mean we can expect a repayment soon?"

"I expect so."

"You *expect* so?"

"Yeah," said Strike. "I should be in a position to give you something in the next few weeks."

"Mr. Strike, your attitude astounds me. You undertook to repay Mr. Rokeby monthly, and you are now in arrears to the tune of—"

"I can't pay you what I haven't got. If you hold tight, I should be able to give you all of it back. Maybe even in a oner."

"I'm afraid that simply isn't good enough. Unless you bring these repayments up to date—"

"Gillespie," said Strike, his eyes on the bright sky beyond the window, "we both know old Jonny isn't going to sue his one-legged war-hero son for repayment of a loan that wouldn't keep his butler in fucking bath salts. I'll give him back his money, with interest, within the next couple of months, and he can stick it up his arse and set fire to it, if he likes. Tell him that, from me, and now get off my fucking back."

Strike hung up, interested to note that he had not really lost his temper at all, but still felt mildly cheerful.

He worked on, in what he had come to think of as Robin's chair, late into the night. The last thing he did before turning in was to underline, three times, the words "Malmaison Hotel, Oxford" and to circle in heavy ink the name "J. P. Agyeman."

The country was lumbering towards election day. Strike turned in early on Sunday and watched the day's gaffes, counterclaims and promises being tabulated on his portable TV. There was an air of joylessness in every news report he watched. The national debt was so huge that it was difficult to comprehend. Cuts were coming, whoever won; deep, painful cuts; and sometimes, with their weasel words, the party leaders reminded Strike of the surgeons who had told him cautiously that he might experience a degree of discomfort; they who would never personally feel the pain that was about to be inflicted.

On Monday morning Strike set out for a rendezvous in Canning Town, where he was to meet Marlene Higson, Lula Landry's biological mother. The arrangement of this interview had been fraught with difficulty. Bristow's secretary, Alison, had telephoned Robin with Marlene Higson's number, and Strike had called her personally. Though clearly disappointed that the stranger on the phone was not a journalist, she had initially expressed herself willing to meet

Strike. She had then called the office back, twice: firstly to ask Robin whether the detective would pay her expenses to travel into the center of town, to which a negative answer was given; next, in high dudgeon, to cancel the meeting. A second call from Strike had secured a tentative agreement to meet in her local pub; then an irritable voicemail message cancelled once more.

Strike had then telephoned her for a third time, and told her that he believed his investigation to be in its final phase, after which evidence would be laid to the police, resulting, he had no doubt, in a further explosion of publicity. Now that he came to think about it, he said, if she was unable to help, it might be just as well for her to be protected from another deluge of press inquiry. Marlene Higson had immediately clamored for her right to tell everything she knew, and Strike condescended to meet her, as she had already suggested, in the beer garden of the Ordnance Arms on Monday morning.

He took the train out to Canning Town station. It was overlooked by Canary Wharf, whose sleek, futuristic buildings resembled a series of gleaming metal blocks on the horizon; their size, like that of the national debt, impossible to gauge from such a distance. But a few minutes' walk later, he was as far from the shining, suited corporate world as it was possible to be. Crammed up alongside dockside developments where many of those financiers lived in neat designer pods, Canning Town exhaled poverty and deprivation. Strike knew it of old, because it had once been home to the old friend who had given him Brett Fearney's location. Down Barking Road he walked, his back to Canary Wharf, past a building with a sign that advertised "Kills 4 Communities," at which he frowned for a moment before realizing that somebody had swiped the "S."

The Ordnance Arms sat beside the English Pawnbroking Company Ltd. It was a large, low-slung, off-white-painted pub. The interior was no-nonsense and utilitarian, with a selection of wooden clocks on a terracotta-colored wall and a lividly patterned piece of red carpet the only gesture to anything as frivolous as decoration. Otherwise, there were two large pool tables, a long and accessible bar and plenty of empty space for milling drinkers. Just now, at eleven in the morning, it was empty except for one little old man in the corner and a cheery serving girl, who addressed her only customer as "Joey" and gave Strike directions through the back.

The beer garden turned out to be the grimmest of concrete back-yards, containing bins and a solitary wooden table, at which a woman was sitting on a white plastic chair, with her fat legs crossed and her cigarette held at right angles to her cheek. There was barbed wire on top of the high wall, and a plastic bag had caught in it and was rustling in the breeze. Beyond the wall there rose a vast block of flats, yellow-painted and with evidence of squalor bulging over many of the balconies.

"Mrs. Higson?"

"Call me Marlene, love."

She looked him up and down, with a slack smile and a knowing gaze. She was wearing a pink Lycra vest top under a zip-up gray hoodie, and leggings that ended inches above her bare gray-white ankles. There were grubby flip-flops on her feet and many gold rings on her fingers; her yellow hair, with its inches of graying brown root, was pulled back into a dirty toweling scrunchie.

"Can I get you a drink?"

"I'll have a pint of Carling, if you twist my arm."

The way she bent her body towards him, the way she pushed straw-like strands of hair out of her pouchy eyes, even the way she held her cigarette; all were grotesquely coquettish. Perhaps she knew no other way of relating to anything male. Strike found her simultaneously pathetic and repulsive.

"Shock?" said Marlene Higson, after Strike had bought them both beer, and joined her at the table. "You can say that again, when I'd gave 'er up for lost. It near broke my 'eart when she wen', but I fort I was giving 'er a better life. I wouldna 'ad the strenf to do it uvver-wise. Fort I was giving 'er all the fings I never 'ad. I grew up poor, proper poor. We 'ad nothing. Nothing."

She looked away from him, drawing hard on her Rothman's; when her mouth puckered into hard little lines around the cigarette, it looked like a cat's anus.

"And Dez, me boyfriend, see, wasn't too keen—you know, with 'er being colored, it were obvious she weren't 'is. They go darker, see; when she were born, she looked white. But I still never woulda given 'er up if I 'adn't seen a chance for 'er to get a better life, and I fort, she won't miss me, she's too young. I've gave 'er a good start, and mebbe, when she's older, she'll come and find me. And me dream come true," she added, with a ghastly show of pathos. "She come'n' found me.

"I'll tell you somefing reely strange, right," she said, without drawing breath. "A man friend of mine says to me, just a week before I got the call from 'er, 'You know 'oo you look like?' he says. I says, 'Dahn be ser silly,' but he says, 'Straight up. Across the eyes, and the shape of the eyebrows, y'know?' "

She looked hopefully at Strike, who could not bring himself to respond. It seemed impossible that the face of Nefertiti could have sprung from this gray and purple mess.

"You can see it in photos of me when I were younger," she said, with a hint of pique. "Point is, I fort I was giving her a better life, and then they went an' give her to those bastards, pardon my language. If I'd'a known, I'd of kept 'er, and I told 'er that. That made 'er cry. I'd of kept her and never let 'er go.

"Oh yeah. She talked to me. It all poured out. She got on all right wiv the father, with S'Ralec. He sounded all right. The mother's a right mad bitch, though. Oh yeah. Pills. Poppin' pills. Fackin' rich bitches takin' pills f' their fackin' nerves. Lula could talk to me, see. Well, it's a bond, innit. You can' break it, blood.

"She was scared what that bitch'd do, if she found out Lula was lookin' for 'er real mum. She was proper worried about what the cow was gonna do when the press found out about me, but there you are, when yore famous like she was, they find out ev'rythin', don' they? Oh, the lies they tell, though. Some o' the things they said abaht me, I'm still thinkin' o' suin'.

"What was I sayin'? 'Er mother, yeah. I says to Lula, 'Why worry, love, sounds to me like you're better off wivout 'er anyway. Let 'er be pissed off if she don' want us to see each uvver.' But she was a good girl, Lula, an' she kep' visitin' 'er, outta duty.

"Anyway, she 'ad 'er own life, she was free to do what she wanted, weren' she? She 'ad Evan, a man of 'er own. I told 'er I disapproved, mind," said Marlene Higson, with a pantomime of strictness. "Oh yeah. Drugs, I've seen too many go that way. But I 'ave to admit, 'e's a sweet boy underneath. I 'ave to admit that. He di'n't have nothin' to do wiv it. I can tell ya that."

"Met him, did you?"

"No, but she called 'im once while she was with me and I 'eard them on the phone togevver, and they were a lovely couple. No, I got nuthin' bad to say about Evan. 'E 'ad nuthin' to do with it, that's proved. No, I've got nuthin' bad to say about 'im. As long as 'e'd of gone clean, 'e'd of 'ad my blessing. I said to 'er, 'Bring 'im along, see wevver I approve,' but she never. 'E was always busy. 'E's a lovely-lookin' boy, under all that 'air," said Marlene. "You can see it in all 'is photos."

"Did she talk to you about her neighbors?"

"Oh, that Fred Beastigwee? Yeah, she told me all about 'im, offerin' 'er parts hin 'is films. I said to 'er, why not? It might be a larf. Even if she 'adn't liked it, it woulda bin, what, another 'arf mill in the bank?"

Her bloodshot eyes squinted at nothing; she seemed momentarily mesmerized, lost in contemplation of sums so vast and dazzling that they were beyond her ken, like an image of infinity. Merely to speak of them was to taste the power of money, to roll dreams of wealth around her mouth.

"Did you ever hear her talk about Guy Somé?"

"Oh yeah, she liked Gee, 'e was good to 'er. Person'lly, I prefer more classic things. It's not my kinda style."

The shocking-pink Lycra, tight on the rolls of fat spilling over the waistband of her leggings, rippled as she leaned forward to tap her cigarette delicately into the ashtray.

" ' 'E's like a brother to me,' she sez, an' I sez, never mind pretend brothers, why don't we try an' find my boys togevver? But she weren't int'rested."

"Your boys?"

"Me sons, me ovver kids. Yeah, I 'ad two more after 'er: one wiv Dez, an' then later there wuz another one. Social Services took 'em off me, but I sez to 'er, wiv your money we could find 'em, gimme a bit, not much, I dunno, coupla grand, an' I'll try an' get someone to find 'em, keep it quiet from the press, I'll 'andle it, I'll keep you out of it. But she weren' interested," repeated Marlene.

"Do you know where your sons are?"

"They took 'em as babies, I dunno where they are now. I was havin' problems. I ain't gonna lie to ya, I've had a bloody hard life."

And she told him, at length, about her hard life. It was a sordid story littered with violent men, with addiction and ignorance, neglect and poverty, and an animal instinct for survival that jettisoned babies in its wake, for they demanded skills that Marlene had never developed.

"So you don't know where your two sons are now?" Strike repeated, twenty minutes later.

"No, how the fuck could I?" said Marlene, who had talked herself into bitterness. "She weren' int'rested anyway. She already had a white brother, di'n't she? She wuz after black family. That's what she reely wanted."

"Did she ask you about her father?"

"Yeah, an' I told 'er ev'rything I knew. 'E was an African student. Lived upstairs from me, jus' along the road 'ere, Barking Road, wiv two others. There's the bookie's downstairs now. Very good-looking boy. 'Elped me with me shopping a couple of times."

To hear Marlene Higson tell it, the courtship had proceeded with an almost Victorian respectability; she and the African student seemed barely to have progressed past handshakes during the first months of their acquaintance.

"And then, 'cos 'e'd 'elped me all them times, one day I asked 'im in, y'know, jus' as a thank-you, really. I'm not a prejudiced person. Ev'ryone's the same to me. Fancy a cuppa, I sez, that were all. And then," said Marlene, harsh reality clanging down amidst the vague impressions of teacups and doilies, "I finds out I'm expecting."

"Did you tell him?"

"Oh yeah, an' 'e was full of 'ow 'e was gonna 'elp, an' shoulder 'is respons'bilities, an' make sure I wuz all right. An' then it was the college 'olidays. 'E said 'e was coming back," said Marlene, contemptuously. "Then 'e ran a mile. Don't they all? And what was I gonna do, run off to Africa to find 'im?

"It was no skin off my nose, anyway. I wasn't breaking me 'eart; I was seeing Dez by then. 'E didn't mind the baby. I moved in with Dez not long after Joe left."

"Joe?"

"That was his name. Joe."

She said it with conviction, but perhaps, thought Strike, that was because she had repeated the lie so often that the story had become easy, automatic.

"What was his surname?"

"I can' fuckin' remember. You're like her. It was twenny-odd years ago. Mumumba," said Marlene Higson, unabashed. "Or something like that."

"Could it have been Agyeman?"

"No."

"Owusu?"

"I toldya," she said aggressively, "it were Mumumba or something."

"Not Macdonald? Or Wilson?"

"You takin' the piss? Macdonald? Wilson? From Africa?"

Strike concluded that her relationship with the African had never progressed to the exchange of surnames.

"And he was a student, you said? Where was he studying?"

"College," said Marlene.

"Which one, can you remember?"

"I don't bloody know. All right if I cadge a ciggie?" she added, in a slightly more conciliatory tone.

"Yeah, help yourself."

She lit her cigarette with her own plastic lighter, puffed enthusiastically, then said, mellowed by the free tobacco:

"It mighta bin somethin' to do with a museum. Attached, like."

"Attached to a museum?"

"Yeah, 'cause I remember 'im sayin', 'Ay sometimes visit the museum in my free ahrs.' " Her imitation made the African student sound like an upper-class Englishman. She was smirking, as though this choice of recreation was absurd, ludicrous.

"Can you remember which museum it was that he visited?"

"The—the Museum of England or summit," she said; and then, irritably, "You're like her. How the fuck am I s'posedta remember after all this time?"

"And you never saw him again after he went home?"

"Nope," she said. "I wasn't expecting to." She drank lager. "He's probably dead," she said.

"Why do you say that?"

"Africa, innit?" she said. "He coulda bin shot, couldn't 'e? Or starved. Anythin'. Y'know what it's like out there."

Strike did know. He remembered the teeming streets of Nairobi; the aerial view of Angola's rainforest, mist hanging over the treetops, and the sudden breathtaking beauty, as the chopper turned, of a waterfall in the lush green mountainside; and the Masai woman, baby at her breast, sitting on a box while Strike questioned her painstakingly about alleged rape, and Tracey manned the video camera beside him.

"D'you know whether Lula tried to find her father?"

"Yeah, she tried," said Marlene dismissively.

"How?"

"She looked up college records," said Marlene.

"But if you couldn't remember where he went..."

"I dunno, she thought she'd found the place or summit, but she couldn't find 'im, no. Mebbe I wasn' remembrin' his name right, I dunno. She used to go on an' fuckin' on; what did 'e look like, where was 'e studyin'. I said to 'er, he was tall an' skinny an' you wanna be grateful you got my ears, not 'is, 'cause there wouldna bin no fuckin' modelin' career if you'd got them fucking elephant lugs."

"Did Lula ever talk to you about her friends?"

"Oh, yeah. There was that little black bitch, Raquelle, or whatever she called 'erself. Leechin' all she could outta Lula. Oh, she did herself all right. Fuckin' clothes an' jew'lry an' I-dunno-what-the-fuck else. I sez to Lula once, 'I wouldn' mind a new coat.' But I wasn' pushy, see. That Raquelle din' mind askin'."

She sniffed, and drained her glass.

"Did you ever meet Rochelle?"

"That was 'er name, was it? Yeah, once. She come along in a fuckin' car with a driver to pick Lula up from seein' me. Like Lady Muck out the back window, sneerin' at me. She'll be missin' all of that now, I 'spect. In it for all she could get.

"An' there was that Ciara Porter," Marlene plowed on, with, if possible, even greater spite, "sleepin' with Lula's boyfriend the night she fuckin' died. Nasty fuckin' bitch."

"Do you know Ciara Porter?"

"I seen it in the fuckin' papers. 'E wen' off to 'er place, di'n't 'e, Evan? After he rowed with Lula. Went to Ciara. Fuckin' bitch."

It became clear, as Marlene talked on, that Lula had kept her natural mother firmly segregated from her friends, and that, with the exception of a brief glimpse of Rochelle, Marlene's opinions and deductions about Lula's social set were based entirely on the press reports she had greedily consumed.

Strike fetched more drinks, and listened to Marlene describe the horror and shock she had experienced on hearing (from the neighbor who had run in with the news, early in the morning of the 8th) that her daughter had fallen to her death from her balcony. Careful questioning revealed that Lula had not seen Marlene for two months before she died. Strike then listened to a diatribe about the treatment she had received from Lula's adoptive family, following the model's death.

"They di'n't want me around, 'specially that fuckin' uncle. 'Ave ya met 'im, 'ave ya? Fuckin' Tony Landry? I contacted 'im abou' the funeral an' all I got was threats. Oh yeah. Fuckin' threats. I said to 'im, 'I'm 'er mother. I gotta right to be there.' An' he tole me I wasn't 'er mother, that mad bitch was 'er mother, *Lady* Bristow. Funny, I says, 'cause I remember pushing 'er outta *my* fanny. Sorry for my crudity, but there you are. An' he said I was causing distress, talkin' to the press. They come an' found *me,*" she told Strike furiously, and she jabbed her finger at the block of flats overlooking them. "Press come an' foun' *me.* 'Course I tole my side o' the fuckin' story. 'Course I did.

"Well, I didn't wanna scene, not at a funeral, I didn't wanna ruin things, but I wasn't gonna be kept away. I went an' sat in the back. I seen fuckin' Rochelle there, givin' me looks like I wuz dirt. But nobody stopped me in the end.

"They got what they wanted, that fuckin' family. I di'n' get nothin'. Nothin'. Tha's not what Lula woulda wanted, I know that for a fact. She woulda wanted me to 'ave something. Not," said Marlene, with an assumption of dignity, "that I cared abou' the money. It weren' about the money for me. Nuthin' was gonna replace my daughter, not ten, not twenny mill.

"Mind you, she'd of bin livid if she'd known I didn't get nuthin'," she went on. "All that money goin' begging; people can't believe it when I tell 'em that I got nuthin'. Struggling to make the rent, and me own daughter lef' millions. But there you are. That's how the rich stay rich, ain't it? They didn' need it, but they didn' mind a bit more. I dunno how that Landry sleeps at night, but that's 'is business."

"Did Lula ever tell you she was going to leave you anything? Did she mention having made a will?"

Marlene seemed suddenly alert to a whiff of hope.

"Oh yeah, she said she'd look aft'r me, yeah. Yeah, she tole me she'd see me all right. D'you think I shoulda tole someone that? Mentioned it, like?"

"I don't think it would have made any difference, unless she made a will and left you something in it," said Strike.

Her face fell back into its sullen expression.

"They prob'ly fuckin' destroyed it, them bastards. They coulda done. That's the sort of people they are. I wouldn't put nuthin' past that uncle."

5

"I'm so sorry he hasn't got back to you," Robin told the caller, seven miles away in the office. "Mr. Strike's incredibly busy at the moment. Let me take your name and number, and I'll make sure he phones you this afternoon."

"Oh, there's no need for that," said the woman. She had a pleasant, cultivated voice with a faint suspicion of hoarseness, as though her laugh would be sexy and bold. "I don't really need to speak to him. Could you just give him a message for me? I wanted to warn him, that's all. God, this is . . . it's a bit embarrassing; it isn't the way I'd have chosen . . . Well, anyway. Could you please just tell him that Charlotte Campbell called, and that I'm engaged to Jago Ross? I didn't want him to hear about it from anyone else, or read about it. Jago's parents have gone and put it in the bloody *Times*. Mortifying."

"Oh. All right," said Robin, her mind suddenly paralyzed like her pen.

"Thanks very much—Robin, did you say? Thanks. 'Bye."

Charlotte rang off first. Robin replaced the receiver in slow motion, feeling acutely anxious. She did not want to deliver this news. She might be only the messenger, but she would feel as though she were delivering an assault on Strike's determination to keep his private life under wraps, on his firm avoidance of the subject of the boxes of possessions, the camp bed, the detritus of his evening meals in the bins every morning.

Robin pondered her options. She could forget to relay the message, and simply tell him to call Charlotte and get her to do her own dirty work (as Robin put it to herself). What, though, if Strike refused to call, and somebody else told him about the engagement? Robin had no means of knowing whether Strike and his ex (girlfriend? fiancée? wife?) had legions of mutual friends. If she and Matthew ever split up, if he became engaged to another woman (it gave her a twisting feeling in her chest to even think of it), all her closest friends and family would feel involved, and would undoubtedly stampede to tell her; she would, she supposed, prefer to be forewarned in as low-key and private a way as possible.

When she heard Strike ascending the stair nearly an hour later, apparently talking on his mobile and in good spirits, Robin experienced a sharp stab of panic to the stomach as though she were about to sit an exam. When he pushed open the glass door, and she saw that he was not holding a mobile at all, but rapping under his breath, she felt even worse.

"Fuck yo' meds and fuck Johari," muttered Strike, who was holding a boxed electric fan in his arms. "Afternoon."

"Hello."

"Thought we could use this. It's stuffy in here."

"Yes, that would be good."

"Just heard Deeby Macc playing in the shop," Strike informed her, setting down the fan in a corner and peeling off his jacket. 'Something something and Ferrari, Fuck yo' meds and fuck Johari.' Wonder who Johari was. Some rapper he was having a feud with, d'you think?"

"No," said Robin, wishing that he was not so cheerful. "It's a psychological term. The Johari window. It's all to do with how well we know ourselves, and how well other people know us."

Strike paused in the act of hanging up his jacket and stared at her.

"You didn't get that out of *Heat* magazine."

"No. I was doing psychology at university. I dropped out."

She felt, obscurely, that it might somehow even the playing field to tell him about one of her own personal failures, before delivering the bad news.

"You dropped out of university?" He seemed uncharacteristically interested. "That's a coincidence. I did, too. So why 'fuck Johari'?"

"Deeby Macc had therapy in prison. He became interested and

did a lot of reading on psychology. I got that bit out of the papers," she added.

"You're a mine of useful information."

She experienced another elevator-drop in the pit of her stomach.

"There was a call, when you were out. From a Charlotte Campbell."

He looked up quickly, frowning.

"She asked me to give you a message, which was," Robin's gaze slid sideways, to hover momentarily on Strike's ear, "that she's engaged to Jago Ross."

Her eyes were drawn, irresistibly, back to his face, and she felt a horrible chill.

One of the earliest and most vivid memories of Robin's childhood was of the day that the family dog had been put down. She herself had been too young to understand what her father was saying; she took the continuing existence of Bruno, her oldest brother's beloved Labrador, for granted. Confused by her parents' solemnity, she had turned to Stephen for a clue as to how to react, and all security had crumbled, for she had seen, for the first time in her short life, happiness and comfort drain out of his small and merry face, and his lips whiten as his mouth fell open. She had heard oblivion howling in the silence that preceded his awful scream of anguish, and then she had cried, inconsolably, not for Bruno, but for the terrifying grief of her brother.

Strike did not speak immediately. Then he said, with palpable difficulty:

"Right. Thanks."

He walked into the inner office, and closed the door.

Robin sat back down at her desk, feeling like an executioner. She could not settle to anything. She considered knocking on the door again, and offering a cup of tea, but decided against. For five minutes she restlessly reorganized the items on her desk, glancing regularly at the closed inner door, until it opened again, and she jumped, and pretended to be busy at the keyboard.

"Robin, I'm just going to nip out," he said.

"OK."

"If I'm not back at five, you can lock up."

"Yes, of course."

"See you tomorrow."

He took down his jacket, and left with a purposeful tread that did not deceive her.

The roadworks were spreading like a lesion; every day there was an extension of the mayhem, and of the temporary structures to protect pedestrians and enable them to pick their way through the devastation. Strike noticed none of it. He walked automatically over trembling wooden boards to the Tottenham, the place he associated with escape and refuge.

Like the Ordnance Arms, it was empty but for one other drinker; an old man just inside the door. Strike bought a pint of Doom Bar and sat down on one of the low red leather seats against the wall, almost beneath the sentimental Victorian maid who scattered rosebuds, sweet and silly and simple. He drank as though his beer was medicine, without pleasure, intent on the result.

Jago Ross. She must have been in touch with him, seeing him, while they were still living together. Even Charlotte, with all her mesmeric power over men, her astonishing sure-handed skill, could not have moved from reacquaintance to engagement in three weeks. She had been meeting Ross on the sly, while swearing undying love to Strike.

This put a very different light on the bombshell she had dropped on him a month before the end, and the refusal to show him proof, and the shifting dates, and the sudden conclusion of it all.

Jago Ross had been married once already. He had kids; Charlotte had heard on the grapevine that he was drinking hard. She had laughed with Strike about her lucky escape of so many years before; she had expressed pity for his wife.

Strike bought a second pint, and then a third. He wanted to drown the impulses, crackling like electrical charges, to go and find her, to bellow, to rampage, to break Jago Ross's jaw.

He had not eaten at the Ordnance Arms, nor since, and it had been a long time since he had consumed so much alcohol in one sitting. It took him barely an hour of steady, solitary, determined beer consumption to become properly drunk.

Initially, when the slim, pale figure appeared at his table, he told it thickly that it had the wrong man and the wrong table.

"No I haven't," said Robin firmly. "I'm just going to get myself a drink too, all right?"

She left him staring hazily at her handbag, which she had placed on the stool. It was comfortingly familiar, brown, a little shabby. She usually hung it up on a coat peg in the office. He gave it a friendly smile, and drank to it.

Up at the bar, the barman, who was young and timid-looking, said to Robin: "I think he's had enough."

"That's hardly my fault," she retorted.

She had looked for Strike in the Intrepid Fox, which was nearest to the office, in Molly Moggs, the Spice of Life and the Cambridge. The Tottenham had been the last pub she was planning to try.

"Whassamatter?" Strike asked her, when she sat down.

"Nothing's the matter," said Robin, sipping her half-lager. "I just wanted to make sure you're OK."

"Yez'm fine," said Strike, and then, with an effort at clarity, "I yam fine."

"Good."

"Jus' celebratin' my fiancée zengagement," he said, raising his eleventh pint in an unsteady toast. "She shou' never've left'm. Never," he said, loudly and clearly, "have. Left. The Hon'ble. Jago Ross. Who is'n outstanding *cunt.*"

He virtually shouted the last word. There were more people in the pub than when Strike had arrived, and most of them seemed to have heard him. They had been casting him wary looks even before he shouted. The scale of him, with his drooping eyelids and his bellicose expression, had ensured a small no-go zone around him; people skirted his table on the way to the bathrooms as though it was three times the size.

"Shall we take a walk?" Robin suggested. "Get something to eat?"

"D'you know what?" he said, leaning forwards with his elbows on the table, almost knocking over his pint. "D'you know what, Robin?"

"What?" she said, holding his beer steady. She was suddenly possessed of a strong desire to giggle. Many of their fellow drinkers were watching them.

"Y're a very nice girl," said Strike. "Y'are. Y're a very nice p'son. I've noticed," he said, nodding solemnly. "Yes. 'Ve noticed that."

"Thank you," she said, smiling, trying not to laugh.

He sat back in his seat, closed his eyes and said:

"Sorry. 'M'pissed."

"Yes."

"Don' do it much these days."

"No."

"Haven' eat'n anything."

"Shall we go and get something to eat, then?"

"Yeah, we c'do," he said, with his eyes still shut. "She tol' me she was pregnant."

"Oh," said Robin, sadly.

"Yeah. Tol' me. An' then sh'said it was gone. Can't've been mine. Nev' added up."

Robin said nothing. She did not want him to remember that she had heard this. He opened his eyes.

"She left 'im for me, an' now she's left 'im...no, she's lef' me fr'im..."

"I'm sorry."

"...lef' me fr'im. Don't be sorry. Y're a nice person."

He pulled cigarettes out of his pocket, and inserted one between his lips.

"You can't smoke in here," she reminded him gently, but the barman, who seemed to have been waiting for a cue, came hurrying over towards them now, looking tense.

"You need to go outside to do that," he told Strike loudly.

Strike peered up at the boy, bleary-eyed, surprised.

"It's all right," Robin told the barman, gathering up her handbag. "Come on, Cormoran."

He stood, massive, ungainly, swaying, unfolding himself out of the cramped space behind the table and glaring at the barman, whom Robin could not blame for taking a step backwards.

"There'z no need," Strike told him, "t'shout. No need. Fuckin' rude."

"OK, Cormoran, let's go," said Robin, standing back to give him space to pass.

"Juz a moment, Robin," said Strike, one large hand held aloft. "Juz a moment."

"Oh God," said Robin quietly.

" 'V' you ever done any boxing?" Strike asked the barman, who looked terrified.

"Cormoran, let's go."

"I wuzza boxer. 'Narmy, mate."

Over at the bar, some wisecracker murmured, "I could've been a contender."

"Let's go, Cormoran," said Robin. She took his arm, and to her great relief and surprise he came along meekly. It reminded her of leading the enormous Clydesdale her uncle had kept on his farm.

Out in the fresh air Strike leaned back against one of the Tottenham's windows and tried, fruitlessly, to light his cigarette; Robin had to work the lighter for him in the end.

"What you need is food," she told him, as he smoked with his eyes closed, listing slightly so that she was afraid he would fall over. "Sober you up."

"I don' wanna sober up," Strike muttered. He overbalanced and only saved himself from falling with several rapid sidesteps.

"Come on," she said, and she guided him across the wooden bridge spanning the gulf in the road, where the clattering machines and builders had at last fallen silent and departed for the night.

"Robin, didjer know I wuzza boxer?"

"No, I didn't know that," she said.

She had meant to take him back to the office and give him food there, but he came to a halt at the kebab shop at the end of Denmark Street and had lurched through the door before she could stop him. Sitting outside on the pavement at the only table, they ate kebabs, and he told her about his boxing career in the army, digressing occasionally to remind her what a nice person she was. She managed to persuade him to keep his voice down. The full effect of all the alcohol he had consumed was still making itself felt, and food seemed to be doing little to help. When he went off to the bathroom, he took such a long time that she began to worry that he had passed out.

Checking her watch, she saw that it was now ten past seven. She called Matthew, and told him she was dealing with an urgent situation at the office. He did not sound pleased.

Strike wound his way back on to the street, bouncing off the door frame as he emerged. He planted himself firmly against the window and tried to light another cigarette.

"R'bin," he said, giving up and gazing down at her. "R'bin, d'you know wadda *kairos* mo . . ." He hiccoughed. "Mo . . . moment is?"

"A *kairos* moment?" she repeated, hoping against hope it was not something sexual, something that she would not be able to forget afterwards, especially as the kebab shop owner was listening in and smirking behind them. "No, I don't. Shall we go back to the office?"

"You don't know whadditis?" he asked, peering at her.

"No."

" 'SGreek," he told her. "*Kairos. Kairos* moment. An' it means," and from somewhere in his soused brain he dredged up words of surprising clarity, "the telling moment. The special moment. The supreme moment."

Oh please, thought Robin, *please don't tell me we're having one.*

"An' d'you know what ours was, R'bin, mine an' Charlotte's?" he said, staring into the middle distance, his unlit cigarette hanging from his hand. "It was when she walk'd into the ward—I was in hosp'tal f'long time an' I hadn' seen her f'two years—no warning— an' I saw her in the door an' ev'ryone turned an' saw her too, an' she walked down the ward an' she never said a word an'," he paused to draw breath, and hiccoughed again, "an' she kissed me aft' two years, an' we were back together. Nobody talkin'. Fuckin' beautiful. Mos' beaut'ful woman I've 'ver seen. Bes' moment of the whole fuckin'— 'fmy whole fuckin' life, prob'bly. I'm sorry, R'bin," he added, "f'r sayin' 'fuckin'.' Sorry 'bout that."

Robin felt equally inclined to laughter and tears, though she did not know why she should feel so sad.

"Shall I light that cigarette for you?"

"Y're a great person, Robin, y'know that?"

Near the turning into Denmark Street he stopped dead, still swaying like a tree in the wind, and told her loudly that Charlotte did not love Jago Ross; it was all a game, a game to hurt him, Strike, as badly as she could.

Outside the black door to the office he halted again, holding up both hands to stop her following him upstairs.

"Y' gotta go home now, R'bin."

"Let me just make sure you get upstairs OK."

"No. No. 'M fine now. An' I might chunder. 'M legless. An'," said Strike, "you don' get that fuckin' tired old fuckin' joke. Or do you? Know most of it now. Did I tell you?"

"I don't know what you mean."

"Ne'r mind, R'bin. You go home now. I gotta be sick."

"Are you sure . . . ?"

" 'M sorry I kep' sayin' fuck—swearin'. Y're a nice pers'n, R'bin. G'bye now."

She looked back at him when she reached Charing Cross Road. He was walking with the awful, clumsy deliberation of the very drunk towards the dingy entrance to Denmark Place, there, no doubt, to vomit in the dark alleyway, before staggering upstairs to his camp bed and kettle.

6

THERE WAS NO CLEAR MOMENT of moving from sleep to consciousness. At first he was lying facedown in a dreamscape of broken metal, rubble and screams, bloodied and unable to speak; then he was lying on his stomach, doused in sweat, his face pressed into the camp bed, his head a throbbing ball of pain and his open mouth dry and rank. The sun pouring in at the unblinded windows scoured his retinas even with his eyelids closed: raw red, with capillaries spread like fine black nets over tiny, taunting, popping lights.

He was fully clothed, his prosthesis still attached, lying on top of his sleeping bag as though he had fallen there. Stabbing memories, like glass shards through his temple: persuading the barman that another pint was a good idea. Robin, across the table, smiling at him. Could he really have eaten a kebab in the state he was in? At some point he remembered wrestling his fly, desperate to piss but unable to extract the end of shirt caught in his zip. He slid a hand underneath himself—even this slight movement made him want to groan or vomit—and found, to his vague relief, that the zip was closed.

Slowly, like a man balancing some fragile package on his shoulders, Strike moved himself into a sitting position and squinted around the brightly lit room with no idea what time it could be, or indeed what day it was.

The door between inner and outer offices was closed, and he could not hear any movement on the other side. Perhaps his temp had left for good. Then he saw a white oblong lying on the floor, just inside the door, pushed under the gap at the bottom. Strike moved gingerly on to his hands and knees, and retrieved what he soon saw was a note from Robin.

Dear Cormoran (he supposed there was no going back to "Mr. Strike" now),

I read your list of points to investigate further at the front of the file. I thought I might be able to follow up the first two (Agyeman and the Malmaison Hotel). I will be on my mobile if you would rather I came back to the office.

I have set an alarm just outside your door for 2 p.m., so that you have enough time to get ready for your 5 p.m. appointment at 1 Arlington Place, to interview Ciara Porter and Bryony Radford.

There is water, paracetamol and Alka-Seltzer on the desk outside.

Robin

PS Please don't be embarrassed about last night. You didn't say or do anything you should regret.

He sat quite still on his camp bed for five minutes, holding the note, wondering whether he was about to throw up, but enjoying the warm sunshine on his back.

Four paracetamol and a glass of Alka-Seltzer, which almost decided the vomiting question for him, were followed by fifteen minutes in the dingy toilet, with results offensive to both nose and ear; but he was sustained throughout by a feeling of profound gratitude for Robin's absence. Back in the outer office, he drank two more bottles of water and turned off the alarm, which had set his throbbing brains rattling in his skull. After some deliberation, he chose a set of clean clothes, took shower gel, deodorant, razor, shaving cream and towel out of the kitbag, pulled a pair of swimming trunks out of the bottom of one of the cardboard boxes on the landing, extracted the pair of gray metal crutches from another, then limped down the metal stair with a sports bag over his shoulder and the crutches in his other hand.

He bought himself a family-sized bar of Dairy Milk on the way to Malet Street. Bernie Coleman, an acquaintance in the Army Medical Corps, had once explained to Strike how the majority of the symptoms associated with a crashing hangover were due to dehydration and hypoglycemia, which were the inevitable results of prolonged vomiting. Strike munched his way through the chocolate, crutches jammed under his arm and every step jarring his head, which still felt as though it was being compressed by tight wires.

But the laughing god of drunkenness had not yet forsaken him. Agreeably detached from reality and from his fellow human beings, he walked down the steps to the ULU pool with an unfeigned sense of entitlement, and as usual nobody challenged him, not even the only other occupant of the changing room, who, after one glance of arrested interest at the prosthesis Strike was unstrapping, kept his eyes politely averted. His false leg stuffed into a locker along with yesterday's clothes, and leaving the door open due to lack of change, Strike moved towards the shower on crutches, his belly spilling over the top of his trunks.

He noted, as he soaped himself, that the chocolate and paracetamol were beginning to take the edge off his nausea and pain. Now, for the first time, he walked out to the large pool. There were only two students in here, both in the fast lane and wearing goggles, oblivious to everything but their own prowess. Strike proceeded to the far side, set the crutches down carefully beside the steps and slid into the slow lane.

He was more unfit than he had ever been in his life. Ungainly and lopsided, he kept swimming into the side of the pool, but the cool, clean water was soothing to body and spirit. Panting, he completed a single length and rested there, his thick arms spread along the side of the pool, sharing the responsibility for his heavy body with the caressing water and gazing up at the high white ceiling.

Little waves, outrunners sent by the young athletes on the other side of the pool, tickled his chest. The terrible pain in his head was receding into the distance; a fiery red light viewed through mist. The chlorine was sharp and clinical in his nostrils, but it no longer made him want to be sick. Deliberately, like a man ripping off a bandage on a congealing wound. Strike turned his attention to the thing he had attempted to drown in alcohol.

Jago Ross; in every respect the antithesis of Strike: handsome in the manner of an Aryan prince, possessor of a trust fund, born to fulfill a preordained place in his family and the world; a man with all the confidence twelve generations of well-documented lineage can give. He had quit a succession of high-flying jobs, developed a persistent drinking problem, and was vicious in the manner of an overbred, badly disciplined animal.

Charlotte and Ross belonged to that tight, interconnected network of public-schooled blue bloods who all knew each other's families, connected through generations of interbreeding and old-school ties. While the water lapped his thickly hairy chest, Strike seemed to see himself, Charlotte and Ross at a great distance, from the wrong end of a telescope, so that the arc of their story became clear: it mirrored Charlotte's restless day-to-day behavior, that craving for heightened emotion that expressed itself most typically in destructiveness. She had secured Jago Ross as a prize when eighteen, the most extreme example she could find of his type and the very epitome of eligibility, as her parents had seen it. Perhaps that had been too easy, and certainly too expected, because she had then dumped him for Strike, who, for all his brains, was anathema to Charlotte's family; an uncategorizable mongrel. What was left, after all these years, to a woman who craved emotional storms, but to leave Strike again and again, until at last the only way to leave with real éclat was to move full circle, back to the place where he had found her?

Strike allowed his aching body to float in the water. The racing students were still thrashing their way up and down the fast lane.

Strike knew Charlotte. She was waiting for him to rescue her. It was the final, cruelest test.

He did not swim back down the pool, but hopped sideways through the water, using his arms to grip the long side of the pool as he had done during physiotherapy in the hospital.

The second shower was more pleasurable than the first; he made the water as hot as he could stand, lathered himself all over, then turned the dial to cold to rinse himself.

The prosthesis reattached, he shaved over a sink with a towel tied around his waist, then dressed with unusual care. He had never worn the most expensive suit and shirt that he owned. They had been gifts from Charlotte on his last birthday: raiment suitable for her fiancé; he remembered her beaming at him as he stared at his unfamiliarly well-styled self in a full-length mirror. The suit and shirt had hung in their carry case ever since, because he and Charlotte had not gone out much after last November; because his birthday had been the last truly happy day they had spent together. Soon afterwards, the relationship had begun to stagger back into the old familiar grievances, into the same mire in which it had foundered before, but which, this time, they had sworn to avoid.

He might have incinerated the suit. Instead, in a spirit of defiance, he chose to wear it, to strip it of its associations and render it mere pieces of cloth. The tailoring of the jacket made him look slimmer and fitter. He left the white shirt open at the throat.

Strike had had a reputation, in the army, for being able to bounce back from excessive alcohol consumption with unusual speed. The man staring at him out of the small mirror was pale, with purple shadows under his eyes, yet in the sharp Italian suit he looked better than he had done in weeks. His black eye had vanished at last, and his scratches had healed.

A cautiously light meal, copious amounts of water, another evacuatory trip to the restaurant bathroom, more painkillers; then, at five o'clock, a prompt arrival at number 1, Arlington Place.

The door was answered, after his second knock, by a cross-looking woman in black-framed glasses and a short gray bob. She let him in with an appearance of reluctance, then walked briskly away across a stone-floored hall which incorporated a magnificent staircase with a wrought-iron banister, calling "Guy! Somebody Strike?"

There were rooms on both sides of the hall. To the left, a small knot of people, all of whom seemed to be dressed in black, were staring in the direction of some powerful light source that Strike could not see, but which illuminated their rapt faces.

Somé appeared, striding through this door into the hall. He too was wearing glasses, which made him look older; his jeans were baggy and ripped and his white T-shirt was emblazoned with an eye that appeared to be weeping glittering blood, which on closer examination proved to be red sequins.

"You'll have to wait," he said curtly. "Bryony's busy and Ciara's going to be hours. You can park yourself in there if you want," he pointed towards the right-hand room, where the edge of a tray-laden table was visible, "or you can stand around and watch like these useless fuckers," he went on, suddenly raising his voice and glaring at the huddle of elegant young men and women who were staring towards the light source. They dispersed at once, without protest, some of them crossing the hall into the room opposite.

"Better suit, by the way," Somé added, with a flash of his old archness. He marched back into the room from which he had come.

Strike followed the designer, and took up the space vacated by the roughly dispatched onlookers. The room was long and almost bare, but its ornate cornices, pale blank walls and curtainless windows gave it an atmosphere of mournful grandeur. A further group of people, including a long-haired male photographer bent over his camera, stood between Strike and the scene at the far end of the room, which was dazzlingly illuminated by a series of arc lights and light screens. Here was an artful arrangement of tattered old chairs, one on its side, and three models. They were a breed apart, with faces and bodies in rare proportions that fell precisely between the categories of strange and impressive. Fine-boned and recklessly slim, they had been chosen, Strike assumed, for the dramatic contrast in their coloring and features. Sitting like Christine Keeler on a back-to-front chair, long legs splayed in spray-on white leggings, but apparently naked from the waist up, was a black girl as dark-skinned as Somé himself, with an Afro and slanting, seductive eyes. Standing over her in a white vest decorated in chains, which just covered her pubis, was a Eurasian beauty with flat black hair cut into an asymmetric fringe. To one side, leaning alone and sideways on the back of another chair, was Ciara Porter; alabaster fair, with long baby-blonde hair, wearing a white semitransparent jumpsuit through which her pale, pointed nipples were clearly visible.

The makeup artist, almost as tall and thin as the models, was bending over the black girl, pressing a pad into the sides of her nose. The three models waited silently in position, still as portraits, all three faces blank and empty, waiting to be called to attention. The other people in the room (the photographer appeared to have two assistants; Somé, now biting his fingernails on the sidelines, was accompanied by the cross-looking woman in glasses) all spoke in low mutters, as though frightened of disturbing some delicate equilibrium.

At last the makeup artist joined Somé, who talked inaudibly and rapidly to her, gesticulating; she stepped back into the bright light and, without speaking to the model, ruffled and rearranged Ciara Porter's long mane of hair; Ciara showed no sign that she knew she was being touched, but waited in patient silence. Bryony retreated into the shadows once more, and asked Somé something; he responded with a shrug and gave her some inaudible instruction that had her look around until her eyes rested on Strike.

They met at the foot of the magnificent staircase.

"Hi," she whispered. "Let's go through here."

She led him across the hall into the opposite room, which was slightly smaller than the first, and dominated by the large table covered with buffet-style food. Several long, wheeled clothing racks, jammed with sequined, ruffled and feathered creations arranged according to color, stood in front of a marble fireplace. The displaced onlookers, all of them in their twenties, were gathered in here; talking quietly, picking in desultory fashion at the half-empty platters of mozzarella and Parma ham and talking into, or playing with, their phones. Several of them subjected Strike to appraising looks as he followed Bryony into a small back room which had been turned into a makeshift makeup station.

Two tables with big portable mirrors stood in front of the large single window, which looked out on to a spruce garden. The black plastic boxes standing around reminded Strike of those his Uncle Ted had taken fly-fishing, except that Bryony's drawers were crammed with colored powders and paints; tubes and brushes lay lined up on towels spread across the table tops.

"Hi," she said, in a normal voice. "*God.* Talk about cutting the tension with a knife, eh? Guy's always a perfectionist, but this is his first proper shoot since Lula died, so he's, you know, *seriously* uptight."

She had dark, choppy hair; her skin was sallow, her features, though large, were attractive. She was wearing tight jeans on long, slightly bandy legs, a black vest, several fine gold chains around her neck, rings on her fingers and thumbs, and also what looked like black leather ballet shoes. This kind of footwear always had a slightly anaphrodisiac effect on Strike, because it reminded him of the fold-up slippers his Aunt Joan used to carry in her handbag, and therefore of bunions and corns.

Strike began to explain what he wanted from her, but she cut him off.

"Guy's told me everything. Want a ciggie? We can smoke in here if we open this."

So saying, she wrenched open the door that led directly on to a paved area of the garden.

She made a small space on one of the cluttered makeup tables and perched herself on it; Strike took one of the vacated chairs and drew out his notebook.

"OK, fire away," she said, and then, without giving him time to speak, "I've been thinking about that afternoon nonstop ever since, actually. So, so sad."

"Did you know Lula well?" asked Strike.

"Yeah, pretty well. I'd done her makeup for a couple of shoots, made her up for the Rainforest Benefit. When I told her I can thread eyebrows..."

"You can what?"

"Thread eyebrows. It's like plucking, but with threads?"

Strike could not imagine how this worked.

"Right..."

"...she asked me to do them for her at home. The paps were all over her, *all* the time, even if she was going to the salon. It was insane. So I helped her out."

She had a habit of tossing back her head to flick her overlong fringe out of her eyes, and a slightly breathy manner. Now she threw her hair over to one side, raked it with her fingers and peered at him through her fringe.

"I got there about three. She and Ciara were all excited about

Deeby Macc arriving. Girlie gossip, you know. I'd *never* have guessed what was coming. *Never*."

"Lula was excited, was she?"

"Oh God, yeah, what d'you think? How would you feel if someone had written songs about... Well," she said, with a breathy little laugh, "maybe it's a girl thing. He's *so* charismatic. Ciara and I were having a laugh about it while I did Lula's eyebrows. Then Ciara asked me to do her nails. I ended up making them both up, as well, so I was there for, must've been three hours. Yeah, I left about six."

"So you'd describe Lula's mood as excited, would you?"

"Yeah. Well, you know, she was a bit distracted; she kept checking her phone; it was lying in her lap while I was doing her eyebrows. I knew what that meant: Evan was messing her around again."

"Did she say that?"

"No, but I knew she was really pissed off at him. Why do you think she said that to Ciara about her brother? About leaving him everything?"

This seemed a stretch to Strike.

"Did you hear her say that too?"

"What? No, but I heard *about* it. I mean, afterwards. Ciara told us all. I think I was in the loo when she actually said it. Anyway, I totally believe it. Totally."

"Why's that?"

She looked confused.

"Well—she really loved her brother, didn't she? God, that was always obvious. He was probably the only person she could really rely on. Months before, around the time she and Evan split up the first time, I was making her up for the Stella show, and she was telling everyone her brother was really pissing her off, going on and on about what a freeloader Evan was. And you know, Evan was jacking her around again, that last afternoon, so she was thinking that James—is it James?—had had him right all along. She always knew he had her interests at heart, even if he was a bit bossy sometimes. This is a really, really exploitative business, you know. Everyone's got an agenda."

"Who do you think had an agenda for Lula?"

"Oh my God, *everyone*," said Bryony, making a wide sweeping gesture with her cigarette-holding hand, which encompassed all of the inhabited rooms outside. "She was the *hottest* model out there, *everyone* wanted a piece of her. I mean, Guy—" But Bryony broke off. "Well, Guy's a businessman, but he did *adore* her; he wanted her to go and live with him after that stalker business. He's still not right about her dying. I heard he tried to contact her through some spiritualist. Margo Leiter told me. He's still devastated, he can barely hear her name without crying. *Anyway*," said Bryony, "that's all I know. I never dreamed that afternoon would be the last time I saw her. I mean, *my God*."

"Did she talk about Duffield at all, while you were—er—threading her eyebrows?"

"No," said Bryony, "but she wouldn't, would she, if he was really hacking her off?"

"So as far as you can remember, she mainly spoke about Deeby Macc?"

"Well . . . it was more Ciara and me talking about him."

"But you think she was excited to meet him?"

"God, yeah, of course."

"Tell me, did you see a blue piece of paper with Lula's handwriting on it when you were in the flat?"

Bryony shook her hair over her face again, and combed it with her fingers.

"What? No. No, I didn't see anything like that. Why, what was it?"

"I don't know," said Strike. "That's what I'd like to find out."

"No, I didn't see it. Blue, did you say? No."

"Did you see any paper at all with her writing on it?"

"No, I can't remember any papers. No." She shook her hair out of her face. "I mean, something like that could've been lying around, but I wouldn't have necessarily noticed it."

The room was dingy. Perhaps he only imagined that she had changed color, but he had not invented the way she twisted her right foot up on to her knee and examined the sole of the leather ballet slipper for something that was not there.

"Lula's driver, Kieran Kolovas-Jones . . ."

"Oh, that really, really cute guy?" said Bryony. "We used to tease her about Kieran; he had such a gigantic crush on her. I think Ciara uses him now sometimes." Bryony gave a meaningful little giggle. "She's got a *bit* of a rep as a good-time girl, Ciara. I mean, you can't help liking her, but..."

"Kolovas-Jones says that Lula was writing something on blue paper in the back of his car, when she left her mother's that day..."

"Have you talked to Lula's mother yet? She's a bit weird."

"...and I'd like to find out what it was."

Bryony flicked her cigarette stub out of the open door and shifted restlessly on the desk.

"It could have been anything." He waited for the inevitable suggestion, and was not disappointed. "A shopping list or something."

"Yeah, it could've been; but if, for the sake of argument, it was a suicide note..."

"But it wasn't—I mean, that's silly—how could it've been? Who'd write a suicide note that far in advance, and then get their face done and go out dancing? That doesn't make any sense at all!"

"It doesn't seem likely, I agree, but it would be good to find out what it was."

"Maybe it had nothing to do with her dying. Why couldn't it have been a letter to Evan or something, telling him how hacked off she was?"

"She doesn't seem to have become hacked off with him until later that day. Anyway, why would she write a letter, when she had his telephone number and was going to see him that night?"

"I don't know," said Bryony restlessly. "I'm just saying, it could've been something that doesn't make any difference."

"And you're quite sure you didn't see it?"

"Yes, I'm quite sure," she said, her color definitely heightened. "I was there to do a job, not go snooping around her stuff. Is that everything, then?"

"Yeah, I think that's all I've got to ask about that afternoon," said Strike, "but you might be able to help me with something else. Do you know Tansy Bestigui?"

"No," said Bryony. "Only her sister, Ursula. She's hired me a couple of times for big parties. She's awful."

"In what way?"

"Just one of those spoiled rich women—well," said Bryony, with a twist to her mouth, "she isn't *nearly* as rich as she'd like to be. Both those Chillingham sisters went for old men with bags of money; wealth-seeking missiles, the pair of them. Ursula thought she'd hit the jackpot when she married Cyprian May, but he hasn't got *nearly* enough for her. She's knocking forty now; the opportunities aren't there the way they used to be. I suppose that's why she hasn't been able to trade up."

Then, evidently feeling that her tone needed some explanation, she continued:

"I'm sorry, but she accused me of listening to her bloody voice-mail messages." The makeup artist folded her arms across her chest, glaring at Strike. "I mean, *please.* She chucked me her mobile and told me to call her a cab, without so much as a bloody please or thank you. I'm dyslexic. I hit the wrong button and the next thing I know, she's screaming her bloody head off at me."

"Why do you think she was so upset?"

"Because I heard a man she wasn't married to telling her he was lying in a hotel room fantasizing about going down on her, I expect," said Bryony, coolly.

"So she might be trading up after all?" asked Strike.

"*That's* not up," said Bryony; but then she added hastily, "I mean, pretty tacky message. Anyway, listen, I've got to get back out there, or Guy will be going ballistic."

He let her go. After she had left, he made two more pages of notes. Bryony Radford had shown herself a highly unreliable witness, suggestible and mendacious, but she had told him much more than she knew.

THE SHOOT LASTED FOR ANOTHER three hours. Strike waited in the garden, smoking and consuming more bottled water, while dusk fell. From time to time he wandered back into the building to check on progress, which seemed immensely slow. Occasionally he glimpsed or heard Somé, whose temper seemed frayed, barking instructions at the photographer or one of the black-clad minions who flitted between clothes racks. Finally, at nearly nine o'clock, after Strike had consumed a few slices of the pizza that had been ordered by the morose and exhausted stylist's assistant, Ciara Porter descended the stairs where she had been posing with her two colleagues, and joined Strike in the makeup room, which Bryony was busy stripping bare.

Ciara was still wearing the stiff silver minidress in which she had posed for the last pictures. Attenuated and angular, with milk-white skin, hair almost as fair, and pale blue eyes set very wide apart, she stretched out her endless legs, in platform shoes that were tied with long silver threads up her calves, and lit a Marlboro Light.

"God, I can't *believe* you're Rokers' son!" she said breathlessly, her chrysoberyl eyes and full lips both wide. "Just *beyond* weird! I know him; he invited Looly and me to the Greatest Hits launch last year! And I know your brothers, Al and Eddie! They *told* me they had a big brother in the army! God. *Mad.* Is that you done, Bryony?" Ciara added pointedly.

The makeup artist seemed to be making a laborious business of gathering up the tools of her trade. Now she sped up perceptibly, while Ciara smoked and watched her in silence.

"Yep, that's me," said Bryony brightly at last, hoisting a heavy box over her shoulder and picking up more cases in each hand. "See you, Ciara. Goodbye," she added to Strike, and left.

"She is *so* bloody nosy, and *such* a gossip," Ciara told Strike. She threw back her long white hair, rearranged her coltish legs and asked: "D'you see a lot of Al and Eddie?"

"No," said Strike.

"And your *mum*," she said, unfazed, blowing smoke out of the corner of her mouth. "I mean, she's just, like, a *legend*. You know how Baz Carmichael did a whole collection two seasons back called 'Supergroupie,' and it was like, Bebe Buell and your mum were the *whole* inspiration? Maxi skirts and buttonless shirts and boots?"

"I didn't," said Strike.

"Oh, it was, like—you know that great quote about Ossie Clark dresses, how men liked them because they could just, like, open them up really easily and fuck the girls? That's, like, your mum's whole *era.*"

She shook her hair out of her eyes again and gazed at him, not with the chilling and offensive appraisal of Tansy Bestigui, but in what seemed to be frank and open wonder. It was difficult for him to decide whether she was sincere, or performing her own character; her beauty got in the way, like a thick cobweb through which it was difficult to see her clearly.

"So, if you don't mind, I'd like to ask you about Lula."

"God, yeah. Yeah. No, I really want to help. When I heard someone was investigating it, I was, like, well, *good. At last.*"

"Really?"

"God, yeah. The whole thing was *so* fucking shocking. I just couldn't believe it. She's still on my phone, look at this."

She rummaged in an enormous handbag, finally retrieving a white iPhone. Scrolling down the contact list, she leaned into him, showing him the name "Looly." Her perfume was sweet and peppery.

"I keep expecting her to *call* me," said Ciara, momentarily subdued, slipping the phone back into her bag. "I can't delete her; I keep *going* to do it, and then just, like, *bottling* it, you know?"

She raised herself restlessly, twisted one of the long legs underneath her, sat back down and smoked in silence for a few seconds.

"You were with her most of her last day, weren't you?" Strike asked.

"*Don't* fucking remind me," said Ciara, closing her eyes. "I've only been over it, like, a *million* times. Trying to get my head around how you can go from, like, completely bloody happy to *dead* in, like, *hours.*"

"She was completely happy?"

"God, happier than I'd *ever* seen her, that last week. We got back from a job in Antigua for *Vogue,* and she and Evan got back together and they had the commitment ceremony; it was all *fantastic* for her, she was on cloud *nine.*"

"You were at this commitment ceremony?"

"Oh yeah," said Ciara, dropping her cigarette end into a can of Coke, where it was extinguished with a small hiss. "God, it was *beyond* romantic. Evan just, like, *sprang* it on her at Dickie Carbury's house. You know Dickie Carbury, the restaurateur? He's got this *fabulous* place in the Cotswolds, and we were all there for the weekend, and Evan had bought them both matching bangles from Fergus Keane, *gorgeous,* oxidized silver. He *forced* us all down to the lake after dinner in the freezing cold and the snow, and then he recited this *poem* he'd written to her, and put the bangle on her wrist. Looly was laughing her head off, but then she just, like, recited a poem she knew back to him. Walt Whitman. It was," said Ciara, with an air of sudden seriousness, "honestly, like, *so* impressive, just to have the perfect poem to say, just like *that.* People think models are dumb, you know." She threw her hair back again and offered Strike a cigarette before taking another herself. "I get *so bored* of telling people I've got a deferred place to read English at Cambridge."

"Have you?" asked Strike, unable to suppress the surprise in his voice.

"Yeah," she said, blowing out smoke prettily, "but, you know, the modeling's going so well, I'm going to give it another year. It's opening doors, you know?"

"So this commitment ceremony was when—a week before Lula died?"

"Yeah," said Ciara, "the Saturday before."

"And it was just an exchange of poems and bangles. No vows, no officiant?"

"No, it wasn't *legally binding* or anything, it was just, like, this lovely, this perfect *moment*. Well, except for Freddie Bestigui, he was being a bit of a pain. But at least," Ciara drew hard on her cigarette, "his bloody wife wasn't there."

"Tansy?"

"Tansy Chillingham, yeah. She's a bitch. It's *so* not a surprise they're divorcing; they led, like, *totally* separate lives, you never saw them out together.

"To tell you the truth, Freddie wasn't *too* bad that weekend, seeing what a nasty rep he's got. He was just a bore, the way he kept trying to suck up to Looly, but he wasn't *awful* like they say he can be. I heard a story about this, like, *totally* naive girl he promised a bit part in a film... Well, I don't know whether it was true." Ciara squinted for a moment at the end of her cigarette. "She never reported it, any-way."

"You said Freddie was being a pain; in what way?"

"Oh God, he kept, like, *cornering* Looly and going on about how great she'd be on screen, and like, what a *great* bloke her dad was."

"Sir Alec?"

"Yeah, Sir Alec, of course. Oh my God," said Ciara, wide-eyed, "if he'd known her *real* father, Looly would've, like, flipped out *completely!* That would have been, like, the dream of her life! No, he just said he'd known Sir Alec years and years ago, and they came from, like, the same East End *manor* or something, so he should be consid-ered, like, her godfather or something. I think he was trying to be funny, but *not*. Anyway, *everyone* could tell he was just trying to work out how to get her into a film. He was a jerk about the commitment ceremony; he kept shouting 'I'll give away the bride.' He was pissed; he drank like crazy all through dinner. Dickie had to shut him up. Then after the ceremony, we all had champagne back at the house and Freddie had, like, another two bottles on top of everything he'd already put away. He kept yelling at Looly that she'd make such a great actress, but she didn't care. She just ignored him. She was cud-dled up with Evan on the sofa, just, like..."

And suddenly, tears were sparkling in Ciara's kohled eyes, and she squashed them out of sight with the flat palms of her pretty white hands.

"...*crazy* in love. She was so fucking happy, I'd never seen her happier."

"You met Freddie Bestigui again, didn't you, on the evening before Lula died? Didn't the two of you pass him in the lobby, on your way out?"

"Yeah," said Ciara, still dabbing at her eyes. "How did you know that?"

"Wilson, the security guard. He thought Bestigui said something to Lula that she didn't like."

"Yeah. He's right. I'd forgotten about that. Freddie said something about Deeby Macc, about Looly being excited about him coming, how he really wanted to get them on film together. I can't remember exactly what it was, but he made it sound dirty, you know?"

"Did Lula know that Bestigui and her adoptive father had been friends?"

"She told me it was the first she'd ever heard of it. She always stayed out of Freddie's way at the flats. She didn't like Tansy."

"Why not?"

"Oh, Looly wasn't interested in that whole, like, whose husband's got the biggest fucking *yacht* crap, she didn't want to get into their crowd. She was *so* much better than that. *So* not like the Chillingham girls."

"OK," said Strike, "can you talk me through the afternoon and evening you were with her?"

Ciara dropped her second fag end into the Coke can, with another little spitting fizz, and immediately lit another.

"Yeah. OK, let me think. Well, I met her at her place in the afternoon. Bryony came over to do her eyebrows and ended up giving us both manicures. We just had, like, a girlie afternoon together."

"How did she seem?"

"She was..." Ciara hesitated. "Well, she wasn't *quite* as happy as she'd been that week. But not suicidal, I mean, *no way.*"

"Her driver, Kieran, thought she seemed strange when she left her mother's house in Chelsea."

"Oh God, yeah, well why wouldn't she be? Her mum had *cancer,* didn't she?"

"Did Lula discuss her mother, when she saw you?"

"No, not really. I mean, she said she'd just been sitting with her, because she was a bit, you know, pulled down after her op, but nobody thought then that Lady Bristow was going to *die.* The op was supposed to *cure* her, wasn't it?"

"Did Lula mention any other reason that she was feeling less happy than she had been?"

"No," said Ciara, slowly shaking her head, the white-blonde hair tumbling around her face. She raked it back again and took a deep drag on her cigarette. "She *did* seem a bit down, a bit distracted, but I just put it down to having seen her mum. They had a weird relationship. Lady Bristow was, like, *really* overprotective and possessive. Looly found it, you know, a bit claustrophobic."

"Did you notice Lula telephoning anyone while she was with you?"

"No," said Ciara, after a thoughtful pause. "I remember her *checking* her phone a lot, but she didn't speak to anyone, as far as I can remember. If she was phoning anyone, she was doing it on the quiet. She was in and out of the room a bit. I don't know."

"Bryony thought she seemed excited about Deeby Macc."

"Oh, for God's sake," said Ciara impatiently. "It was everyone else who was excited about Deeby Macc—Guy and Bryony and—well, even I was, a bit," she said, with endearing honesty. "But Looly wasn't that fussed. She was in love with Evan. You can't believe everything Bryony says."

"Did Lula have a piece of paper with her, that you can remember? A bit of blue paper, which she'd written on?"

"No," said Ciara again. "Why? What was it?"

"I don't know yet," said Strike, and Ciara looked suddenly thunderstruck.

"God—you're not telling me she left a *note*? Oh my *God.* How fucking mad would that be? But—no! That would mean she'd have, like, already decided she was going to do it."

324 • R<small>OBERT</small> G<small>ALBRAITH</small>

"Maybe it was something else," said Strike. "You mentioned at the inquest that Lula expressed an intention to leave everything to her brother, didn't you?"

"Yeah, that's right," said Ciara earnestly, nodding. "Yeah, what happened was, Guy had sent Looly these *fabby* handbags from the new range. I *knew* he wouldn't have sent me any, even though *I* was in the advert too. Anyway, I unwrapped the white one, Cashile, you know, and it was just, like, *beautiful*; he does these detachable silk linings and he'd had it custom-printed for her with this amazing African print. So I said, 'Looly, will you leave me this one?' just as a joke. And she said, like, *really* seriously, 'I'm leaving everything to my brother, but I'm sure he'd let you have anything you want.'"

Strike was watching and listening for any sign that she was lying or exaggerating, but the words came easily and, to all appearances, frankly.

"That was a strange thing to say, wasn't it?" he asked.

"Yeah, I s'pose," said Ciara, shaking the hair back off her face again. "But Looly was like that; she could go a bit dark and *dramatic* sometimes. Guy used to say, 'Less of the cuckoo, Cuckoo.' Anyway," Ciara sighed, "she didn't take the hint about the Cashile bag. I was hoping she'd just give it to me; I mean, she had *four*."

"Would you say you were close to Lula?"

"Oh God, yeah, *super*-close, she told me *everything*."

"A couple of people have mentioned that she didn't trust too easily. That she was scared of confidences turning up in the press. I've been told that she tested people to see whether she could trust them."

"Oh yeah, she did get a bit, like, *paranoid* after her real mum started selling stories about her. She actually asked me," said Ciara, with an airy wave of her cigarette, "whether I'd told anyone she was back with Evan. I mean, *come on*. There was *no way* she was going to keep that quiet. *Everyone* was talking about it. I said to her, 'Looly, the only thing worse than being talked about is not being talked about.' That's Oscar Wilde," she added, kindly. "But Looly didn't like that side of being famous."

"Guy Somé thinks that Lula wouldn't have got back with Duffield if he hadn't been out of the country."

Ciara glanced towards the door, and dropped her voice.

"Guy *would* say that. He was just, like, *super*-protective of Looly. He adored her; he really loved her. He thought Evan was bad for her, but *honestly*, he doesn't know the real Evan. Evan's, like, *totally* fucked up, but he's a good person. He went to see Lady Bristow not long ago, and I said to him, '*Why*, Evan, what on *earth* did you put yourself through that for?' Because, you know, her family hated him. And d'you know what he said? 'I just wanna speak to somebody who cares as much as I do that she's gone.' I mean, how sad is that?"

Strike cleared his throat.

"The press have *totally* got it in for Evan, it's just *so* unfair, he can't do anything right."

"Duffield came to your place, didn't he, the night she died?"

"God, yeah, and there you are!" said Ciara indignantly. "They made out we were, like, *shagging* or something! He had no money, and his driver had disappeared, so he just, like, *hiked* across London so he could crash at mine. He slept on the sofa. So we were together when we heard the news."

She raised her cigarette to her full mouth and drew deeply on it, her eyes on the floor.

"It was terrible. You can't imagine. Terrible. Evan was...oh my God. And then," she said, in a voice barely louder than a whisper, "they were all saying it was *him*. After Tansy Chillingham said she'd heard a row. The press just went crazy. It was awful."

She looked up at Strike, holding her hair off her face. The harsh overhead light merely illuminated her perfect bone structure.

"You haven't met Evan, have you?"

"No."

"D'you want to? You could come with me now. He said he was going along to Uzi tonight."

"That'd be great."

"Fabby. Hang on."

She jumped up and called through the open door:

"Guy, sweetie, can I wear this tonight? Go on. To Uzi?"

Somé entered the small room. He looked exhausted behind his glasses.

"All right. Make sure you're photographed. Wreck it and I'll sue your skinny white arse."

"I'm not going to wreck it. I'm taking Cormoran to meet Evan."

She stuffed her cigarettes away into her enormous bag, which appeared to hold her day clothes too, and hoisted it over her shoulder. In her heels, she was within an inch of the detective's height. Somé looked up at Strike, his eyes narrowed.

"Make sure you give the little shit a hard time."

"Guy!" said Ciara, pouting. "Don't be horrible."

"And watch yourself, Master Rokeby," Somé added, with his usual edge of spite. "Ciara's a terrible slut, aren't you, dear? And she's like me. She likes them big."

"*Guy!*" said Ciara, in mock horror. "Come on, Cormoran. I've got a driver outside."

8

STRIKE, FOREWARNED, WAS NOWHERE NEAR as surprised to see Kieran Kolovas-Jones as the driver was to see him. Kolovas-Jones was holding open the left-hand passenger door, faintly lit by the car's interior light, but Strike spotted his momentary change of expression when he laid eyes on Ciara's companion.

"Evening," said Strike, moving around the car to open his own door and get in beside Ciara.

"Kieran, you've met Cormoran, haven't you?" said Ciara, buckling herself in. Her dress had ridden up to the very top of her long legs. Strike could not be absolutely certain that she was wearing anything beneath it. She had certainly been braless in the white jumpsuit.

"Hi, Kieran," said Strike.

The driver nodded at Strike in the rearview mirror, but did not speak. He had assumed a strictly professional demeanor that Strike doubted was habitual in the absence of detectives.

The car pulled away from the curb. Ciara started rummaging again in her bag; she removed a perfume spray and squirted herself liberally in a wide circle around her face and shoulders; then dabbed lip gloss over her lips, talking all the while.

"What am I going to need? Money. Cormoran, could you be a total darling and keep this in your pocket? I'm not going to take this massive thing in." She handed him a crumpled wad of twenties. "You're a sweetheart. Oh, and I'll need my phone. Have you got a pocket for my phone? *God*, this bag's a mess."

She dropped it on the car floor.

"When you said that it would have been the dream of Lula's life to find her real father..."

"Oh God, it *would* have been. She used to talk about that *all the time*. She got really excited when that bitch—her birth mother—told her he was African. Guy always said that was bullshit, but he hated the woman."

"He met Marlene Higson, did he?"

"Oh no, he just hated the whole, like, *idea* of her. He could see how excited Looly got, and he just wanted to *protect* her from being disappointed."

So much protection, Strike thought, as the car turned a corner in the dark. Had Lula been that fragile? The back of Kolovas-Jones's head was rigid, correct; his eyes flickering more often than was necessary to rest upon Strike's face.

"And then Looly thought she had a lead on him—her real father—but that went completely cold on her. Dead end. Yeah, it was so sad. She really thought she'd found him and then it all just fell through her fingers."

"What lead was this?"

"It was something about where the college was. Something her mother said. Looly thought she'd found the place it must have been, and she went to look at the records, or something, with this funny friend of hers called . . ."

"Rochelle?" suggested Strike. The Mercedes was now purring up Oxford Street.

"Yeah, Rochelle, that's right. Looly met her in rehab or something, poor little thing. Looly was, like, *unbelievably* sweet to her. Used to take her shopping and stuff. Anyway, they never found him, or it was the wrong place, or something. I can't remember."

"Was she looking for a man called Agyeman?"

"I don't think she ever told me the name."

"Or Owusu?"

Ciara turned her beautiful light eyes upon him in astonishment.

"That's *Guy's* real name!"

"I know."

"Oh my God," Ciara giggled. "*Guy's* dad never went to college. He was a *bus driver*. He used to beat Guy up for sketching dresses all the time. That's why Guy changed his name."

The car was slowing down. The long queue, four people wide, stretching along the block, led to a discreet entrance that might have been to a private house. A gaggle of dark figures was gathered around a white-pillared doorway.

"Paps," said Kolovas-Jones, speaking for the first time. "Careful how you get out of the car, Ciara."

He slid out of the driver's seat and walked around to the left-hand back door; but the paparazzi were already running; ominous, darkly clad men, raising their long-nosed cameras as they closed in.

Ciara and Strike emerged into flashes like gunfire; Strike's retinas were in sudden, dazzling whiteout; he ducked his head, his hand closed instinctively around Ciara Porter's slender upper arm, and he steered her ahead of him through the black oblong that represented sanctuary, as the doors opened magically to admit them. The queuing hordes were shouting, protesting at their easy entry, yelping with excitement; and then the flashes stopped, and they were inside, where there was an industrial roar of noises, and a loud insistent bass line.

"*Wow*, you've got a great sense of direction," said Ciara. "I usually, like, ricochet off the bouncers and they have to push me in."

Streaks and blazes of purple and yellow light were still burned across Strike's field of vision. He dropped her arm. She was so pale that she looked almost luminous in the gloom. Then they were jostled further inside the club by the entry of another dozen people behind them.

"C'mon," said Ciara, and she slipped a soft, long-fingered hand inside his and tugged him along behind her.

Faces turned as they walked through the packed crowd, both of them taller by far than the majority of clubbers. Strike could see what looked like long glass fish tanks set into the walls, containing what seemed to be great floating blobs of wax, reminding him of his mother's old lava lamps. There were long black leather banquettes along the walls, and, further in, nearer the dance floor, booths. It was hard to tell how big the club was, because of judiciously placed mirrors; at one point, Strike caught a glimpse of himself, head-on, looking like a sharply dressed heavy behind the silvery sylph that was Ciara. The music pounded through every part of him, vibrating through his head and body; the crowd on the dance floor was so dense that it seemed miraculous that they were managing even to stamp and sway.

They had reached a padded doorway, guarded by a bald bouncer who grinned at Ciara, revealing two gold teeth, and pushed open the concealed entrance.

They entered a quieter, though hardly less crowded bar area that was evidently reserved for the famous and their friends. Strike noticed a miniskirted television presenter, a soap actor, a comedian primarily famous for his sexual appetite; and then, in a distant corner, Evan Duffield.

He was wearing a skull-patterned scarf wound around his neck and skintight black jeans, sitting at the join of two black leather banquettes with arms stretched at right angles along the backs of the benches on either side, where his companions, mostly women, were crammed. His dark shoulder-length hair had been dyed blonde; he was pallid and bony-faced, and the smudges around his bright turquoise eyes were dark purple.

The group containing Duffield was emanating an almost magnetic force over the room. Strike saw it in the sneaking sidelong glances other occupants were shooting them; in the respectful space left around them, a wider orbit than anybody else had been granted. Duffield and his cohorts' apparent unselfconsciousness was, Strike recognized, nothing but expert artifice; they had, all of them, the hyper-alertness of the prey animal combined with the casual arrogance of predators. In the inverted food chain of fame, it was the big beasts who were stalked and hunted; they were receiving their due.

Duffield was talking to a sexy brunette. Her lips were parted as she listened, almost ludicrously immersed in him. As Ciara and Strike drew nearer, Strike saw Duffield glance away from the brunette for a fraction of a second, making, Strike thought, a lightning-fast recce of the bar, taking the measure of the room's attention, and of other possibilities it might offer.

"Ciara!" he yelled hoarsely.

The brunette looked deflated as Duffield jumped nimbly to his feet; thin and yet well muscled, he slid out from behind the table to embrace Ciara, who was eight inches taller than he in her platform shoes; she dropped Strike's hand to return the hug. The whole bar seemed, for a few shining moments, to be watching; then they remembered themselves, and returned to their chat and their cocktails.

"Evan, this is Cormoran Strike," said Ciara. She moved her mouth close to Duffield's ear and Strike saw rather than heard her say, "He's Jonny Rokeby's son!"

"All right, mate?" asked Duffield, holding out a hand, which Strike shook.

Like other inveterate womanizers Strike had encountered, Duffield's voice and mannerisms were slightly camp. Perhaps such men became feminized by prolonged immersion in women's company, or perhaps it was a way of disarming their quarry. Duffield indicated with a flutter of the hand that the others should move along the bench to make room for Ciara; the brunette looked crestfallen. Strike was left to find himself a low stool, drag it alongside the table and ask Ciara what she wanted to drink.

"Oooh, get me a Boozy-Uzi," she said, "and use my money, sweetie."

Her cocktail smelled strongly of Pernod. Strike bought himself water, and returned to the table. Ciara and Duffield were now almost nose to nose, talking; but when Strike set down the drinks, Duffield looked around.

"So what d'you do, Cormoran? Music biz?"

"No," said Strike. "I'm a detective."

"No shit," said Duffield. "Who'm I supposed to have killed this time?"

The group around him permitted themselves wry, or nervous, smiles, but Ciara said:

"Don't joke, Evan."

"I'm not joking, Ciara. You'll notice when I am, because it'll be fucking funny."

The brunette giggled.

"I said I'm *not* joking," snapped Duffield.

The brunette looked as though she had been slapped. The rest of the group seemed imperceptibly to withdraw, even in the cramped space; they began their own conversation, temporarily excluding Ciara, Strike and Duffield.

"Evan, not nice," said Ciara, but her reproach seemed to caress rather than sting, and Strike noticed that the glance she threw the brunette held no pity.

Duffield drummed his fingers on the edge of the table.

"So, what kind of a detective are you, Cormoran?"

"A private one."

"Evan, darling, Cormoran's been hired by Looly's brother..."

But Duffield had apparently spotted someone or something of interest up at the bar, for he leapt to his feet and disappeared into the crowd there.

"He's always a bit ADHD," said Ciara apologetically. "Plus, he's still really, really fucked up about Looly. He *is*," she insisted, half cross, half amused, as Strike raised his eyebrows and looked pointedly in the direction of the voluptuous brunette, who was now cradling an empty mojito glass and looking morose. "You've got something on your smart jacket," Ciara added, and she leaned forwards to brush off what Strike thought were pizza crumbs. He caught a strong whiff of her sweet, spicy perfume. The silver material of her dress was so stiff that it gaped, like armor, away from her body, affording him an unhampered view of small white breasts and pointed shell-pink nipples.

"What's that perfume you're wearing?"

She thrust a wrist under his nose.

"It's Guy's new one," she said. "It's called Éprise—it's French for 'smitten,' you know?"

"Yeah," he said.

Duffield had returned, holding another drink, cleaving his way back through the crowd, whose faces revolved after him, tugged by his aura. His legs in their tight jeans were like black pipe cleaners, and with his darkly smudged eyes he looked like a Pierrot gone bad.

"Evan, babes," said Ciara, when Duffield had reseated himself, "Cormoran's investigating—"

"He heard you the first time," Strike interrupted her. "There's no need."

He thought that the actor had heard that, too. Duffield drank his drink quickly, and tossed a few comments into the group beside them. Ciara sipped her cocktail, then nudged Duffield.

"How's the film going, sweetie?"

"Great. Well. Suicidal drug dealer. It's not a stretch, y'know."

Everyone smiled, except Duffield himself. He drummed his fingers on the table, his legs jerking in time.

"Bored now," he announced.

He was squinting towards the door, and the group was watching him, openly yearning, Strike thought, to be scooped up and taken along.

Duffield looked from Ciara to Strike.

"Wanna come back to mine?"

"Fabby," squeaked Ciara, and with a feline glance of triumph at the brunette, she downed her drink in one.

Just outside the VIP area, two drunk girls ran at Duffield; one of them pulled up her top and begged him to sign her breasts.

"Don't be dirty, love," said Duffield, pushing past her. "You gotta car, Cici?" he yelled over his shoulder, as he plowed his way through the crowds, ignoring shouts and pointing fingers.

"Yes, sweetie," she shouted. "I'll call him. Cormoran, darling, have you got my phone?"

Strike wondered what the paparazzi outside would make of Ciara and Duffield leaving the club together. She was shouting into her iPhone. They reached the entrance; Ciara said, "Wait—he's going to text when he's right outside."

Both she and Duffield looked slightly nervy; watchful, self-aware, like competitors waiting to enter a stadium. Then Ciara's phone gave a little buzz.

"OK, he's there," she said.

Strike stood back to let her and Duffield out first, then walked rapidly to the front passenger seat as Duffield ran around the back of the car in the blinding popping lights, to screams from the queue, and threw himself into the backseat with Ciara, whom Kolovas-Jones had helped inside. Strike slammed the front passenger door, forcing the two men who had leaned in to take shot after shot of Duffield and Ciara to jump backwards out of the way.

Kolovas-Jones seemed to take an unconscionable amount of time to return to the car; Strike felt as though the Mercedes' interior was a test tube, simultaneously enclosed and exposed as more and more flashes fired. Lenses were pressed to the windows and windscreen; unfriendly faces floated in the darkness, and black figures darted back and forth in front of the stationary car. Beyond the explosions of light, the shadowy crowd-queue surged, curious and excited.

"Put your foot down, for fuck's sake!" Strike growled at Kolovas-Jones, who revved the engine. The paparazzi blocking the road moved backwards, still taking pictures.

"Bye-bye, you cunts," said Evan Duffield from the backseat as the car pulled away from the curb.

But the photographers ran alongside the vehicle, flashes erupting on either side; and Strike's whole body was bathed in sweat: he was suddenly back on a yellow dirt road in the juddering Viking, with a sound like firecrackers popping in the Afghanistan air; he had glimpsed a youth running away from the road ahead, dragging a small boy. Without conscious thought he had bellowed *"Brake!"* lunged forwards and seized Anstis, a new father of two days' standing, who was sitting right behind the driver; the last thing he remembered was Anstis's shouted protest, and the low metallic boom of him hitting the back doors, before the Viking disintegrated with an ear-splitting bang, and the world became a hazy blur of pain and terror.

The Mercedes had rounded the corner on to an almost deserted road; Strike realized that he had been holding himself so tensely that his remaining calf muscles were sore. In the wing mirror he could see two motorbikes, each being ridden pillion, following them. Princess Diana and the Parisian underpass; the ambulance bearing Lula Landry's body, with cameras held high to the darkened glass as it passed; both careered through his thoughts as the car sped through the dark streets.

Duffield lit a cigarette. Out of the corner of his eye, Strike saw Kolovas-Jones scowl at his passenger in the rearview mirror, though he made no protest. After a moment or two, Ciara began whispering to Duffield. Strike thought he heard his own name.

Five minutes later, they turned another corner and saw, ahead of them, another small crowd of black-clad photographers, who began flashing and running towards the car the moment it appeared. The motorbikes were pulling up right behind them; Strike saw the four men running to catch the moment when the car doors opened. Adrenaline erupted: Strike imagined himself exploding out of the car, punching, sending expensive cameras crashing on to concrete as their holders crumpled. And as if he had read Strike's mind, Duffield said, with his hand poised on the door handle:

"Knock their fucking lights out, Cormoran, you're built for it."

The open doors, the night air and more maddening flashes; bull-like, Strike walked fast with his big head bowed, his eyes on Ciara's tottering heels, refusing to be blinded. Up three steps they ran, Strike at the rear; and it was he who slammed the front door of the building in the faces of the photographers.

Strike felt himself momentarily allied with the other two by the experience of being hunted. The tiny, dimly lit lobby felt safe and friendly. The paparazzi were still yelling to each other on the other side of the door, and their terse shouts recalled soldiers recceing a building. Duffield was fiddling at an inner door, trying a succession of keys in the lock.

"I've only been here a couple of weeks," he explained, finally opening it with a barging shoulder. Once over the threshold, he wriggled out of his tight jacket, threw it on to the floor by the door and then led the way, his narrow hips swinging in only slightly less exaggerated fashion than Guy Somé's, down a short corridor into a sitting room, where he switched on lamps.

The spare, elegant gray and black decor had been overlaid by clutter and stank of cigarette smoke, cannabis and alcohol fumes. Strike was reminded vividly of his childhood.

"Need a slash," announced Duffield, and called over his shoulder as he disappeared, with a directive jab of the thumb, "Drinks are in the kitchen, Cici."

She threw a smile at Strike, then left through the door Duffield had indicated.

Strike glanced around the room, which looked as though it had been left, by parents of impeccable taste, in the care of a teenager.

Every surface was covered in debris, much of it in the form of scribbled notes. Three guitars stood propped against the walls. A cluttered glass coffee table was surrounded by black-and-white seats, angled towards an enormous plasma TV. Bits of debris had overflowed from the coffee table on to the black fur rug below. Beyond the long windows, with their gauzy gray curtains, Strike could make out the shapes of the photographers still prowling beneath the street light.

Duffield had returned, tugging up his fly. On finding himself alone with Strike, he gave a nervous giggle.

"Make yourself at home, big fella. Hey, I know your old man, actually."

"Yeah?" said Strike, sitting down in one of the squashy ponyskin cube-shaped armchairs.

"Yeah. Met him a couple of times," said Duffield. "Cool dude."

He picked up a guitar, began to pick out a twiddling tune on it, thought better of it and put the instrument back against the wall.

Ciara returned, carrying a bottle of wine and three glasses.

"Couldn't you get a cleaner, dearie?" she asked Duffield reprovingly.

"They give up," said Duffield. He vaulted over the back of a chair and landed with his legs sprawled over the side. "No fucking stamina."

Strike pushed aside the mess on the coffee table so that Ciara could set down the bottle and glasses.

"I thought you'd moved in with Mo Innes," she said, pouring out wine.

"Yeah, that didn't work out," said Duffield, raking through the detritus on the table for cigarettes. "Ol' Freddie's rented me this place just for a month, while I'm going out to Pinewood. He wants to keep me away from me old *haunts.*"

His grubby fingers passed over a string of what seemed to be rosary beads; numerous empty cigarette packets with bits of card torn out of them; three lighters, one of them an engraved Zippo; Rizla papers; tangled leads unattached to appliances; a pack of cards; a sordid stained handkerchief; sundry crumpled pieces of grubby paper; a music magazine featuring a picture of Duffield in moody black and white on the cover; opened and unopened mail; a pair of crumpled black leather gloves; a quantity of loose change and, in a clean china ashtray on the edge of the debris, a single cufflink in the form of a tiny silver gun. At last he unearthed a soft packet of Gitanes from under the sofa; lit up, blew a long jet of smoke at the ceiling, then addressed Ciara, who had placed herself on the sofa at right angles to the two men, sipping her wine.

"They'll say we're fucking each other, again, Ci," he said, pointing out of the window at the prowling shadows of the waiting photographers.

"And what'll they say Cormoran's here for?" asked Ciara, with a sidelong glance at Strike. "A threesome?"

"Security," said Duffield, appraising Strike through narrowed eyes. "He looks like a boxer. Or a cage fighter. Don't you want a proper drink, Cormoran?"

"No, thanks," said Strike.

"What's that, AA or being on duty?"

"Duty."

Duffield raised his eyebrows and sniggered. He seemed nervous, shooting Strike darting looks, drumming his fingers on the glass table. When Ciara asked him whether he had visited Lady Bristow again, he seemed relieved to be offered a subject.

"Fuck, no. Once was enough. It was fucking horrible. Poor bitch. On her fucking deathbed."

"It was *beyond* nice of you to go, though, Evan."

Strike knew that she was trying to show Duffield off in his best light.

"Do you know Lula's mother well?" he asked Duffield.

"No. I only met her once before Lu died. She didn't approve of me. None of Lu's family approved of me. I dunno," he fidgeted, "I just wanted to talk to someone who really gives a shit that she's dead."

"Evan!" Ciara pouted. "*I* care she's dead, excuse me!"

"Yeah, well..."

With one of his oddly feminine, fluid movements, Duffield curled up in the chair so that he was almost fetal, and sucked hard on his cigarette. On a table behind his head, illuminated by a cone of lamplight, was a large, stagey photograph of him with Lula Landry, clearly taken from a fashion shoot. They were mock-wrestling against a backdrop of fake trees; she was wearing a floor-length red dress, and he was in a slim black suit, with a hairy wolf's mask pushed up on top of his forehead.

"I wonder what *my* mum would say if I carked it? My parents've got an injunction out against me," Duffield informed Strike. "Well, it was mainly my fucking father. Because I nicked their telly a couple of years ago. D'you know what?" he added, craning his neck to look at Ciara, "I've been clean five weeks, two days."

"That's so fabulous, baby! That's fantastic!"

"Yeah," he said. He swiveled upright again. "Aren't you gonna ask me any questions?" he demanded of Strike. "I thought you were investigating Lu's *murder?*"

The bravado was undermined by the tremor in his fingers. His knees began bouncing up and down, just like John Bristow's.

"D'you think it was murder?" Strike asked.

"No." Duffield dragged on his cigarette. "Yeah. Maybe. I dunno. Murder makes more sense than fucking suicide, anyway. Because she wouldn'ta gone without leaving me a note. I keep waiting for a note to turn up, y'know, and then I'll know it's real. It don't feel real. I can't even remember the funeral. I was out of my fucking head. I took so much stuff I couldn't fucking walk. I think, if I could just remember the funeral, it'd be easier to get my head round."

He jammed his cigarette between his lips and began drumming with his fingers on the edge of the glass table. After a while, apparently discomforted by Strike's silent observation, he demanded:

"Ask me something, then. Who's hired you, anyway?"

"Lula's brother John."

Duffield stopped drumming.

"That money-grabbing, poker-arsed wanker?"

"Money-grabbing?"

"He was fucking *obsessed* with how she spent her fucking money, like it was any of his fucking business. Rich people always think everyone else is a fucking freeloader, have you noticed that? Her whole frigging family thought I was gold-digging, and after a bit," he raised a finger to his temple and made a boring motion, "it went in, it planted doubts, y'know?"

He snatched one of the Zippos from the table and began flicking at it, trying to make it ignite. Strike watched tiny blue sparks erupt and die as Duffield talked.

"I expect he thought she'd be better off with some rich fucking accountant, like him."

"He's a lawyer."

"Whatever. What's the difference, it's all about helping rich people keep their mitts on as much money as they can, innit? He's got his fucking trust fund from Daddy, what skin is it off his nose what his sister did with her own money?"

"What was it that he objected to her buying, specifically?"

"Shit for me. The whole fucking family was the same; they didn't mind if she chucked it their way, keep it in the fucking family, that was OK. Lu knew they were a mercenary load of fuckers, but, like I say, it still left its fucking mark. Planted ideas in her head."

He threw the dead Zippo back on to the table, drew his knees up to his chest and glared at Strike with his disconcerting turquoise eyes.

"So he still thinks I did it, does he? Your client?"

"No, I don't think he does," said Strike.

"He's changed his narrow fuckwitted mind, then, because I heard he was going round telling everyone it was me, before they ruled it as suicide. Only, I've got a cast-iron fucking alibi, so fuck him. Fuck. Them. All."

Restless and nervy, he got to his feet, added wine to his almost untouched glass, then lit another cigarette.

"What can you tell me about the day Lula died?" Strike asked.

"The night, you mean."

"The day leading up to it might be quite important too. There are a few things I'd like to clear up."

"Yeah? Go on, then."

Duffield dropped back down into the chair, and pulled his knees up to his chest again.

"Lula called you repeatedly between around midday and six in the evening, but you didn't answer your phone."

"No," said Duffield. He began picking, childishly, at a small hole in the knee of his jeans. "Well, I was busy. I was working. On a song. Didn't want to stem the flow. The old inspiration."

"So you didn't know she was calling you?"

"Well, yeah. I saw her number coming up." He rubbed his nose, stretched his legs out on to the glass table, folded his arms and said, "I felt like teaching her a little lesson. Let her wonder what I was up to."

"Why did you think she needed a lesson?"

"That fucking rapper. I wanted her to move in with me while he was staying in her building. 'Don't be silly, don't you trust me?' " His imitation of Lula's voice and expression was disingenuously girlish. "I said to her, 'Don't *you* be fucking silly. Show me I got nothing to worry about, and come and stay with me.' But she wouldn't. So then I thought, two can play at that fucking game, darling. Let's see how you like it. So I got Ellie Carreira over to my place, and we did a bit of writing together, and then I brought Ellie along to Uzi with me. Lu couldn't fucking complain. Just business. Just songwriting. Just friends, like her and that rapper-gangster."

"I didn't think she'd ever met Deeby Macc."

"She hadn't, but he'd made his intentions pretty fucking public, hadn't he? Have you heard that song he wrote? She was creaming her panties over it."

" 'Bitch you ain't all that...' " Ciara began to quote obligingly, but a filthy look from Duffield silenced her.

"Did she leave you voicemail messages?"

"Yeah, a couple. 'Evan, will you call me, please. It's urgent. I don't want to say it on the phone.' It was always fucking urgent when she wanted to find out what I was up to. She knew I was pissed off. She was worried I might've called Ellie. She had a real hang-up about Ellie, because she knew we'd fucked."

"She said it was urgent, and that she didn't want to say it on the phone?"

"Yeah, but that was just to try and make me call. One of her little games. She could be fucking jealous, Lu. And pretty fucking manipulative."

"Can you think why she'd be calling her uncle repeatedly that day as well?"

"What uncle?"

"His name's Tony Landry; he's another lawyer."

"*Him?* She wouldn't be calling *him,* she fucking hated him worse than her brother."

"She called him, repeatedly, over the same period that she was calling you. Leaving more or less the same message."

Duffield raked his unshaven chin with dirty nails, staring at Strike.

"I dunno what that was about. Her mum, maybe. Old Lady B going into hospital or something."

"You don't think something might have happened that morning which she thought was either relevant to or of interest to both you and her uncle?"

"There isn't any subject that could interest me and her fucking uncle at the same time," said Duffield. "I've met him. Share prices and shit are all he'd be interested in."

"Maybe it was something about her, something personal?"

"If it was, she wouldn't call that fucker. They didn't like each other."

"What makes you say that?"

"She felt about him like I feel about my fucking father. Neither of them thought we were worth shit."

"Did she talk to you about that?"

"Oh, yeah. He thought her mental problems were just attention-seeking, bad behavior. Put on. Burden on her mother. He got a bit smarmier when she started making money, but she didn't forget."

"And she didn't tell you why she'd been calling you, once she got to Uzi?"

"Nope," said Duffield. He lit another cigarette. "She was fucked off from the moment she arrived, because Ellie was there. Didn't like that at all. In a right fucking mood, wasn't she?"

For the first time he appealed to Ciara, who nodded sadly.

"She didn't really talk to me," said Duffield. "She was mostly talking to you, wasn't she?"

"Yes," said Ciara. "And she didn't tell me there was anything, like, *upsetting* her or anything."

"A couple of people have told me her phone was hacked . . ." began Strike; Duffield talked over him.

"Oh yeah, they were listening in on our messages for fucking weeks. They knew everywhere we were meeting and everything. Fucking bastards. We changed our phone numbers when we found out what was going on and we were fucking careful what messages we left after that."

"So you wouldn't be surprised, if Lula had had something important or upsetting to tell you, that she didn't want to be explicit over the phone?"

"Yeah, but if it was that fucking important, she woulda told me at the club."

"But she didn't?"

"No, like I say, she never spoke to me all night." A muscle was jumping in Duffield's chiseled jaw. "She kept checking the time on her fucking phone. I knew what she was doing; trying to wind me up. Showing me she couldn't wait to get home and meet fucking Deeby Macc. She waited until Ellie went off to the bog; then got up, came over to tell me she was leaving, and said I could have my bangle back; the one I gave her when we had our commitment ceremony. She chucked it down on the table in front of me, with everyone fucking gawping. So I picked it up and said, 'Anyone fancy this, it's going spare?' and she fucked off."

He did not speak as though Lula had died three months previously, but as though it had all happened the day before, and there was still a possibility of reconciliation.

"You tried to restrain her, though, right?" asked Strike.

Duffield's eyes narrowed.

"Restrain her?"

"You grabbed her arms, according to witnesses."

"Did I? I can't remember."

"But she pulled free, and you stayed behind, is that right?"

"I waited ten minutes, because I wasn't gonna give her the satisfaction of chasing her in front of all those people, and then I left the club and got my driver to take me to Kentigern Gardens."

"Wearing the wolf mask," said Strike.

"Yeah, to stop those fucking scumbags," he nodded towards the window, "selling pictures of me looking wasted or pissed off. They hate it when you cover your face. Depriving them of making their fucking parasitic living. One of them tried to pull Wolfie off me, but I held on. I got in the car and gave 'em a few pictures of the Wolf giving them the finger, out the back window. Got to the corner of Kentigern Gardens and there were more paps everywhere. I knew she must've got in already."

"Did you know the key code?"

"Nineteen sixty-six, yeah. But I knew she'd've told security not to let me up. I wasn't gonna walk in in front of all of them and then get chucked out on me arse five minutes later. I tried to phone her from the car, but she wouldn't pick up. I thought she'd probably gone downstairs to welcome Deeby fucking Macc to London. So I went off to see a man about pain relief."

He ground out his cigarette on a loose playing card on the edge of the table and began hunting for more tobacco. Strike, who wanted to oil the flow of conversation, offered him one of his own.

"Oh, cheers. Cheers. Yeah. Well, I got the driver to drop me off and I went to visit my friend, who has since given the police a full statement *to that effect,* as Uncle Tony might say. Then I wandered around a bit, and there's camera footage in that station to prove that, and then about, I dunno...threeish? Fourish?"

"Half past four," said Ciara.

"Yeah, I went to crash at Ciara's."

Duffield sucked on the cigarette, watching the tip burn, then, exhaling, said cheerfully:

"So my arse is covered, is it not?"

Strike did not find his satisfaction likable.

"And when did you find out that Lula was dead?"

Duffield drew his legs up to his chest again.

"Ciara woke me up and told me. I couldn't—I was fucking— yeah, well. Fucking hell."

He put his arms over the top of his head and stared at the ceiling.

"I couldn't fucking...I couldn't believe it. Couldn't fucking believe it."

And as Strike watched, he thought he saw realization wash over Duffield that the girl of whom he spoke so flippantly, and who he had, by his own account, provoked, taunted and loved, was really and definitely never coming back; that she had been smashed into pulp on snow-covered asphalt, and that she and their relationship were now beyond the possibility of repair. For a moment, staring at the blank white ceiling, Duffield's face became grotesque as he appeared to grin from ear to ear; it was a grimace of pain, of the exertion necessary to beat back tears. His arms slipped down, and he buried his face in them, his forehead on his knees.

"Oh, *sweetie,*" said Ciara, putting her wine down on the table with a clunk, and reaching forward to place a hand on his bony knee.

"This has fucked me up proper," said Duffield thickly from behind his arms. "This has fucked me up good. I wanted to marry her. I fucking loved her, I did. Fuck, I don't wanna talk about it anymore."

He jumped up and left the room, sniffing ostentatiously and wiping his nose on his sleeve.

"Didn't I *tell* you?" Ciara whispered to Strike. "He's a *mess.*"

"Oh, I don't know. He seems to have cleaned up his act. Off heroin for a month."

"I *know,* and I don't want him to fall off the wagon."

"This is a lot gentler than he would have had from the police. This is polite."

"You've got an awful look on your face, though. Really, like, *stern* and as if you don't believe a word he's saying."

"D'you think he's going to come back?"

"Yes, of course he is. *Please* be a bit nicer..."

She sat quickly back in her seat as Duffield walked back in; he was grim-faced and his camp strut was very slightly subdued. He flung himself into the chair he had previously occupied and said to Strike:

"I'm out of fags. Can I have another one of yours?"

Reluctantly, because he was down to three, Strike handed it across, lit it for him, then said:

"All right to keep talking?"

"About Lula? You can talk, if you want. I dunno what else I can tell you. I ain't got any more information."

"Why did you split up? The first time, I mean; I'm clear on why she ditched you in Uzi."

Out of the corner of his eye, he saw Ciara make an indignant little gesture; apparently this did not qualify as "nicer."

"What the fuck's that got to do with anything?"

"It's all relevant," said Strike. "It all gives a picture of what was going on in her life. It all helps explain why she might've killed herself."

"I thought you were looking for a murderer?"

"I'm looking for the truth. So why *did* you break up, the first time?"

"Fuck, how's this fucking important?" exploded Duffield. His temper, as Strike had expected, was violent and short-fused. "What, are you trying to make out it's my fault she fucking jumped off a balcony? How can us splitting up the first time have anything to do with it, knucklehead? That was two fucking months before she died. Fuck, I could call meself a detective and ask a lot of fuckass questions. Bet it pays all right, dunnit, if you can find some fuckwit rich client?"

"Evan, don't," said Ciara, distressed. "You said you wanted to help..."

"Yeah, I wanna help, but how's this fucking fair?"

"No problem, if you don't want to answer," said Strike. "You're under no obligation here."

"I ain't got nothing to hide, it's just fucking personal stuff, innit? We split up," he shouted, "because of drugs, and her family and her friends putting down poison about me, and because she didn't trust nobody because of the fucking press, all right? Because of all the *pressure.*"

And Duffield made his hands into trembling claws and pressed them, like earphones, over his ears, making a compressing movement.

"Pressure, fucking *pressure,* that's why we split up."

"You were taking a lot of drugs at the time, were you?"

"Yeah."

"And Lula didn't like it?"

"Well, people round her were telling her she didn't like it, you know?"

"Like who?"

"Like her family, like fucking Guy Somé. That little pansy *twat*."

"When you say that she didn't trust anybody because of the press, what do you mean by that?"

"Fuck, innit obvious? Don't you know all this, from your old man?"

"I know jack shit about my father," said Strike coolly.

"Well, they were tapping her fucking *phone,* man, and that gives you a weird fucking *feeling;* haven't you got any imagination? She started getting paranoid about people selling stuff on her. Trying to work out what she'd said on the phone, and what she hadn't, and who mighta given stuff to the papers and that. It fucked with her head."

"Was she accusing *you* of selling stories?"

"No," snapped Duffield, and then, just as vehemently, "Yeah, sometimes. *How did they know we were coming here, how did they know I said that to you, yadda yadda yadda* . . . I said to her, it's all part and fucking parcel of fame, innit, but she thought she could have her cake and eat it."

"But you didn't ever sell stories about her to the press?"

He heard Ciara's hissing intake of breath.

"No I fucking didn't," said Duffield quietly, holding Strike's gaze without blinking. "No I fucking did not. All right?"

"And you split up for how long?"

"Two months, give or take."

"But you got back together, what, a week before she died?"

"Yeah. At Mo Innes's party."

"And you had this commitment ceremony forty-eight hours later? At Carbury's house in the Cotswolds?"

"Yeah."

"And who knew that was going to happen?"

"It was a spontaneous thing. I bought the bangles and we just did it. It was beautiful, man."

"It really was," echoed Ciara sadly.

"So, for the press to have found out so quickly, someone who was there must have told them?"

"Yeah, I s'pose so."

"Because your phones weren't being tapped then, were they? You'd changed your numbers."

"I don't fucking know if they were being tapped. Ask the shits at the rags who do it."

"Did she talk to you at all about trying to trace her father?"

"He was dead . . . what, you mean the real one? Yeah, she was interested, but it was no go, wannit? Her mother didn't know who he was."

"She never told you whether she'd managed to find out anything about him?"

"She tried, but she didn't get anywhere, so she decided that she was gonna to do a course in African studies. That was gonna be Daddy, the whole fucking continent of Africa. Fucking Somé was behind that, shit-stirring as usual."

"In what way?"

"Anything that took her away from me was good. Anything that bracketed them together. He was one possessive bastard where she was concerned. He was in love with her. I know he's a poof," Duffield added impatiently, as Ciara began to protest, "but he's not the first one I've known who's gone funny over a girlfriend. He'll fuck anything, man-wise, but he didn't want to let her out of his sight. He threw hissy fits if she didn't see him, he didn't like her working for anyone else.

"He hates my fucking guts. Right back atcha, you little shit. Egging Lu on with Deeby Macc. He'd've got a real kick out of her fucking him. Doing me over. Hearing all the fucking details. Getting her to introduce him, get his fucking clothes photographed on a gangster. He's no fucking fool, Somé. He used her for his business all the time. Tried to get her cheap and for free, and she was dumb enough to let him."

"Did Somé give you these?" asked Strike, pointing at the black leather gloves on the coffee table. He had recognized the tiny gold GS logo on the cuff.

"You what?"

Duffield leaned over and hooked one of the gloves on to an index finger; he dangled it in front of his eyes, examining it.

"Fuck, you're right. They're going in the bin, then," and he threw the glove into a corner; it hit the abandoned guitar, which let out a hollow, echoing chord. "I kept them from that shoot," said Duffield, pointing at the black-and-white magazine cover. "Somé wouldn't give me the steam off his piss. Have you got another fag?"

"I'm all out," lied Strike. "Are you going to tell me why you invited me home, Evan?"

There was a long silence. Duffield glared at Strike, who intuited that the actor knew he was lying about having no cigarettes. Ciara was gazing at him too, her lips slightly parted, the epitome of beautiful bewilderment.

"What makes you think I've got anything to tell you?" sneered Duffield.

"I don't think you asked me back here for the pleasure of my company."

"I dunno," said Duffield, with a distinct overtone of malice. "Maybe I hoped you were a laugh, like your old man?"

"Evan," snapped Ciara.

"OK, if you haven't got anything to tell me . . ." said Strike, and he pushed himself up out of the armchair. To his slight surprise, and Duffield's evident displeasure, Ciara set her empty wineglass down and began to unfold her long legs, preparatory to standing.

"All right," said Duffield sharply. "There's one thing."

Strike sank back into his chair. Ciara thrust one of her own cigarettes at Duffield, who took it with muttered thanks, then she too sat down, watching Strike.

"Go on," said the latter, while Duffield fiddled with his lighter.

"All right. I dunno whether it matters," said the actor. "But I don't want you to say where you got the information."

"I can't guarantee that," said Strike.

Duffield scowled, his knees jumping up and down, smoking with his eyes on the floor. Out of the corner of his eye, Strike saw Ciara open her mouth to speak, and forestalled her, one hand in the air.

"Well," said Duffield, "two days ago I was having lunch with Freddie Bestigui. He left his BlackBerry on the table when he went up to the bar." Duffield puffed and jiggled. "I don't wanna be fired," he said, glaring at Strike. "I need this fucking job."

"Go on," said Strike.

"He got an email. I saw Lula's name. I read it."

"OK."

"It was from his wife. It said something like, 'I know we're supposed to be talking through lawyers, but unless you can do better than £1.5 million, I will tell everyone exactly where I was when Lula Landry died, and exactly how I got there, because I'm sick of taking shit for you. This is not an empty threat. I'm starting to think I should tell the police anyway.' Or something like that," said Duffield.

Dimly, through the curtained window, came the sound of a couple of the paparazzi outside laughing together.

"That's very useful information," Strike told Duffield. "Thank you."

"I don't want Bestigui to know it was me who told you."

"I don't think your name'll need to come into it," said Strike, standing up again. "Thanks for the water."

"Hang on, sweetie, I'm coming," said Ciara, her phone pressed to her ear. "Kieran? We're coming out now, Cormoran and me. Right now. Bye-bye, Evan darling."

She bent over and kissed him on both cheeks, while Duffield, halfway out of his chair, looked disconcerted.

"You can crash here if you—"

"No, sweetie, I've got a job tomorrow afternoon; need my beauty sleep," she said.

More flashes blinded Strike as he stepped outside; but the paparazzi seemed confused this time. As he helped Ciara down the steps, and followed her into the back of the car, one of them shouted at Strike: "Who the fuck are you?"

Strike slammed the door, grinning. Kolovas-Jones was back in the driver's seat; they were pulling away from the curb, and this time they were not pursued.

After a block or so of silence, Kolovas-Jones looked in the rear-view mirror and asked Ciara:

"Home?"

"I suppose so. Kieran, will you turn on the radio? I fancy a bit of music," she said. "Louder than that, sweetie. Oh, I love this."

"Telephone" by Lady Gaga filled the car.

She turned to Strike as the orange glow of street lights swept across her extraordinary face. Her breath smelled of alcohol, her skin of that sweet, peppery perfume.

"Don't you want to ask me anything else?"

"You know what?" said Strike. "I do. Why would you have a detachable lining in a handbag?"

She stared at him for several seconds, then let out a great giggle, slumping sideways into his shoulder, nudging him. Lithe and slight, she continued to rest against him as she said:

"You *are* funny."

"But why would you?"

"Well, it just makes the bag more, like, individual; you can customize them, you see; you can buy a couple of linings and swap them over; you can pull them out and use them as scarves; they're beautiful. Silk with gorgeous patterns. The zip edging is very rock-and-roll."

"Interesting," said Strike, as her upper leg moved to rest lightly along his own, and she gave a second, deep-throated giggle.

Call all you want, but there's no one home, sang Lady Gaga.

The music masked their conversation, but Kolovas-Jones's eyes were moving with unnecessary regularity from road ahead to rear-view mirror. After another minute, Ciara said:

"Guy's right, I do like them big. You're very *butch*. And, like, *stern*. It's sexy."

A block later she whispered:

"Where do you live?" while rubbing her silky cheek against his, like a cat.

"I sleep on a camp bed in my office."

She giggled again. She was definitely a little drunk.

"Are you serious?"

"Yeah."

"We'll go to mine, then, shall we?"

Her tongue was cool and sweet and tasted of Pernod.

"Have you slept with my father?" he managed to say, between the pressings of her full lips on to his.

"No... *God*, no..." A little giggle. "He dyes his hair... it's, like, *purple* close up... I used to call him the rocking prune..."

And then, ten minutes later, a lucid voice in his mind urging him not to let desire lead on to humiliation, he surfaced for air to mutter:

"I've only got one leg."

"Don't be silly..."

"I'm not being silly... it got blown off in Afghanistan."

"Poor baby..." she whispered. "I'll rub it better."

"Yeah—that's not my leg... It's helping, though..."

9

ROBIN RAN UP THE CLANGING metal stairs in the same low heels that she had worn the previous day. Twenty-four hours ago, unable to dislodge the word "gumshoe" from her mind, she had selected her frumpiest footwear for a day's walking; today, excited by what she had achieved in the old black shoes, they had taken on the glamour of Cinderella's glass slippers. Hardly able to wait to tell Strike everything she had found out, she had almost run to Denmark Street through the sunlit rubble. She was confident that any lingering awkwardness after Strike's drunken escapades of two nights previously would be utterly eclipsed by their mutual excitement about her dazzling solo discoveries of the previous day.

But when she reached the second landing, she pulled up short. For the third time, the glass door was locked, and the office beyond it unlit and silent.

She let herself in and made a swift survey of the evidence. The door to the inner office stood open. Strike's camp bed was folded neatly away. There was no sign of an evening meal in the bin. The computer monitor was dark, the kettle cold. Robin was forced to conclude that Strike had not (as she phrased it to herself) spent the night at home.

She hung up her coat, then took from her handbag a small note-book, turned on the computer and, after a few minutes' hopeful but fruitless wait, began to type up a precis of what she had found out the day before. She had barely slept for the excitement of telling Strike everything in person. Typing it all out was a bitter anticlimax. Where was he?

As her fingers flew over the keyboard, an answer she did not much like presented itself for her consideration. Devastated as he had been at the news of his ex's engagement, was it not likely that he had gone to beg her not to marry this other man? Hadn't he shouted to the whole of Charing Cross Road that Charlotte did not love Jago Ross? Perhaps, after all, it was true; perhaps Charlotte had thrown herself into Strike's arms, and they were now reconciled, lying asleep, entwined, in the house or flat from which he had been ejected four weeks ago. Robin remembered Lucy's oblique inquiries and insinuations about Charlotte, and suspected that any such reunion would not bode well for her job security. *Not that it matters,* she reminded herself, typing furiously, and with uncharacteristic inaccuracy. *You're leaving in a week's time.* The reflection made her feel even more agitated.

Alternatively, of course, Strike had gone to Charlotte and she had turned him away. In that case, the matter of his current whereabouts became a matter of more pressing, less personal concern. What if he had gone out, unchecked and unprotected, hell-bent on intoxication again? Robin's busy fingers slowed and stopped, mid-sentence. She swiveled on her computer chair to look at the silent office telephone.

She might well be the only person who knew that Cormoran Strike was not where he was supposed to be. Perhaps she ought to call him on his mobile? And if he did not pick up? How many hours ought she to let elapse before contacting the police? The idea of ringing Matthew at his office and asking his advice came to her, only to be swatted away.

She and Matthew had rowed when Robin arrived home, very late, after walking a drunken Strike back to the office from the Tottenham. Matthew had told her yet again that she was naive, impressionable and a sucker for a hard-luck story; that Strike was after a secretary on the cheap, and using emotional blackmail to achieve his ends; that there was probably no Charlotte at all, that it was all an extravagant ploy to engage Robin's sympathy and services. Then Robin had lost her temper, and told Matthew that if anybody was blackmailing her it was he, with his constant harping on the money she ought to be bringing in, and his insinuation that she was not pulling her weight. Hadn't he noticed that she was enjoying working for

Strike; hadn't it crossed his insensitive, obtuse *accountant's* mind that she might be dreading the tedious bloody job in human resources? Matthew had been aghast, and then (though reserving the right to deplore Strike's behavior) apologetic; but Robin, usually conciliatory and amiable, had remained aloof and angry. The truce effected the following morning had prickled with antagonism, mainly Robin's.

Now, in the silence, watching the telephone, some of her anger at Matthew spilled over on to Strike. Where was he? What was he doing? Why was he acting up to Matthew's accusations of irresponsibility? She was here, holding the fort, and he was presumably off chasing his ex-fiancée, and never mind their business...

...*his* business...

Footsteps on the stairwell: Robin thought she recognized the very slight unevenness in Strike's tread. She waited, glaring towards the stairs, until she was sure that the footfalls were proceeding beyond the first landing; then she turned her chair resolutely back to face the monitor and began pounding at the keys again, while her heart raced.

"Morning."

"Hi."

She accorded Strike a fleeting glance while continuing to type. He looked tired, unshaven and unnaturally well dressed. She was instantly confirmed in her view that he had attempted a reconciliation with Charlotte; by the looks of it, successfully. The next two sentences were pockmarked with typos.

"How're things?" asked Strike, noting Robin's clench-jawed profile, her cold demeanor.

"Fine," said Robin.

She now intended to lay her perfectly typed report in front of him, and then, with icy calm, discuss the arrangements for her departure. She might suggest that he hire another temp this week, so that she could instruct her replacement in the day-to-day management of the office before she left.

Strike, whose run of appalling luck had been broken in fabulous style just a few hours previously, and who was feeling as close to buoyant as he had been for many months, had been looking forward to seeing his secretary. He had no intention of regaling her with an account of his night's activities (or at least, not those that had done so much to restore his battered ego), for he was instinctively close-lipped about such matters, and he was hoping to shore up as much as remained of the boundaries that had been splintered by his copious consumption of Doom Bar. He had, however, been planning an eloquent speech of apology for his excesses of two nights before, an avowal of gratitude, and an exposition of all the interesting conclusions he had drawn from yesterday's interviews.

"Fancy a cup of tea?"

"No thanks."

He looked at his watch.

"I'm only eleven minutes late."

"It's up to you when you arrive. I mean," she attempted to backtrack, for her tone had been too obviously hostile, "it's none of my business what you—when you get here."

From having mentally rehearsed a number of soothing and magnanimous responses to Strike's imagined apologies for his drunken behavior of forty-eight hours previously, she now felt that his attitude was distastefully free of shame or remorse.

Strike busied himself with kettle and cups, and a few minutes later set down a mug of steaming tea beside her.

"I said I didn't—"

"Could you leave that important document for a minute while I say something to you?"

She saved the report with several thumps of the keys and turned to face him, her arms folded across her chest. Strike sat down on the old sofa.

"I wanted to say sorry about the night before last."

"There's no need," she said, in a small, tight voice.

"Yeah, there is. I can't remember much of what I did. I hope I wasn't obnoxious."

"You weren't."

"You probably got the gist. My ex-fiancée's just got engaged to an old boyfriend. It took her three weeks after we split to get another ring on her finger. That's just a figure of speech; I never actually bought her a ring; I never had the money."

Robin gathered, from his tone, that there had been no reconciliation; but in that case, where had he spent the night? She unfolded her arms and unthinkingly picked up her tea.

"It wasn't your responsibility to come and find me like that, but you probably stopped me collapsing in a gutter or punching someone, so thanks very much."

"No problem," said Robin.

"And thanks for the Alka-Seltzer," said Strike.

"Did it help?" asked Robin, stiffly.

"I nearly puked all over this," said Strike, dealing the sagging sofa a gentle punch with his fist, "but once it kicked in, it helped a lot."

Robin laughed, and Strike remembered, for the first time, the note she had pushed under the door while he slept, and the excuse she had given for her tactful absence.

"Right, well, I've been looking forward to hearing how you got on yesterday," he lied. "Don't keep me in suspense."

Robin expanded like a water blossom.

"I was just typing it up . . ."

"Let's have it verbally, and you can put it into the file later," said Strike, with the mental reservation that it would be easy to remove if useless.

"OK," said Robin, both excited and nervous. "Well, like I said in my note, I saw that you wanted to look into Professor Agyeman, and the Malmaison Hotel in Oxford."

Strike nodded, grateful for the reminder, because he had not been able to remember the details of the note, read once in the depths of his blinding hangover.

"So," said Robin, a little breathlessly, "first of all I went along to Russell Square, to SOAS; the School of Oriental and African Studies. That's what your notes meant, isn't it?" she added. "I checked a map: it's walking distance from the British Museum. Isn't that what all those scribbles meant?"

Strike nodded again.

"Well, I went in there and pretended I was writing a dissertation on African politics, and I wanted some information on Professor Agyeman. I ended up speaking to this really helpful secretary in the politics department, who'd actually worked for him, and she gave me loads of information on him, including a bibliography and a brief biography. He studied at SOAS as an undergraduate."

"He did?"

"Yes," said Robin. "And I got a picture."

From inside the notebook she pulled out a photocopy, and passed it across to Strike.

He saw a black man with a long, high-cheekboned face; close-cropped graying hair and beard and gold-rimmed glasses supported by overlarge ears. He stared at it for several long moments, and when at last he spoke, he said:

"Christ."

Robin waited, elated.

"*Christ,*" said Strike again. "When did he die?"

"Five years ago. The secretary got upset talking about it. She said he was so clever, and the nicest, kindest man. A committed Christian."

"Any family?"

"Yes. He left a widow and a son."

"A son," repeated Strike.

"Yes," said Robin. "He's in the army."

"In the army," said Strike, her deep and doleful echo. "Don't tell me."

"He's in Afghanistan."

Strike got up and started pacing up and down, the picture of Professor Josiah Agyeman in his hand.

"Didn't get a regiment, did you? Not that it matters. I can find out," he said.

"I did ask," said Robin, consulting her notes, "but I don't really understand—is there a regiment called the Sappers or some—"

"Royal Engineers," said Strike. "I can check up on all that."

He stopped beside Robin's desk, and stared again at the face of Professor Josiah Agyeman.

"He was from Ghana originally," she said. "But the family lived in Clerkenwell until he died."

Strike handed her back the picture.

"Don't lose that. You've done bloody well, Robin."

"That's not all," she said, flushed, excited and trying to keep from smiling. "I took the train out to Oxford in the afternoon, to the Malmaison. Do you know, they've made a hotel out of an old prison?"

"Really?" said Strike, sinking back on to the sofa.

"Yes. It's quite nice, actually. Well, anyway, I thought I'd pretend to be Alison and check whether Tony Landry had left something there or something..."

Strike sipped his tea, thinking that it was highly implausible that a secretary would be dispatched in person for such an inquiry three months after the event.

"Anyway, that was a mistake."

"Really?" he said, his tone carefully neutral.

"Yes, because Alison actually did go to the Malmaison on the seventh, to try and find Tony Landry. It was incredibly embarrassing, because one of the girls on reception had been there that day, and she remembered her."

Strike lowered his mug.

"Now that," he said, "is very interesting indeed."

"I know," said Robin excitedly. "So then I had to think really fast."

"Did you tell them your name was Annabel?"

"No," she said, on a half-laugh. "I said, well, OK then, I'll tell the truth, I'm his girlfriend. And I cried a bit."

"You cried?"

"It wasn't actually that hard," said Robin, with an air of surprise. "I got right into character. I said I thought he was having an affair."

"*Not* with Alison? If they've seen her, they wouldn't believe that..."

"No, but I said I didn't think he'd really been at the hotel at all... Anyway, I made a bit of a scene and the girl who'd spoken to Alison took me aside and tried to calm me down; she said they couldn't give out information about people without a good reason, they had a policy, blah blah... you know. But just to stop me crying, in the end she told me that he had checked in on the evening of the sixth, and checked out on the morning of the eighth. He made a fuss about being given the wrong newspaper while he was checking out, that's why she remembered. So he was *definitely* there. I even asked her a bit, you know, hysterically, how she knew it was him, and she described him to a T. I know what he looks like," she added, before Strike could ask. "I checked before I left; his picture's on the Landry, May, Patterson website."

"You're brilliant," said Strike, "and this is all bloody fishy. What did she tell you about Alison?"

"That she arrived and asked to see him, but he wasn't there. They confirmed that he was staying with them, though. And then she left."

"Very odd. She should have known he was at the conference; why didn't she go there first?"

"I don't know."

"Did this helpful hotel employee say she'd seen him at any times other than check-in and check-out?"

"No," said Robin. "But we know he went to the conference, don't we? I checked that, remember?"

"We know he signed in, and probably picked up a name tag. And then he drove back to Chelsea to see his sister, Lady Bristow. Why?"

"Well . . . she was ill."

"Was she? She'd just had an operation that was supposed to cure her."

"A hysterectomy," said Robin. "I don't imagine you'd feel wonderful after that."

"So we've got a man who doesn't like his sister very much—I've had that from his own lips—who believes she's just had a life-saving operation and knows she's got two of her children in attendance. Why the urgency to see her?"

"Well," said Robin, with less certainty, "I suppose . . . she'd just got out of hospital . . ."

"Which he presumably knew was going to happen before he drove off to Oxford. So why not stay in town, visit her if he felt that strongly about it, and then head out to the afternoon session of the conference? Why drive fifty-odd miles, stay overnight in this plush prison, go to the conference, sign in and then double back to town?"

"Maybe he got a call saying she was feeling bad, something like that? Maybe John Bristow rang him and asked him to come?"

"Bristow's never mentioned asking his uncle to drop in. I'd say they were on bad terms at the time. They're both shifty about that visit of Landry's. Neither of them likes talking about it."

Strike stood up and began to walk up and down, limping slightly, barely noticing the pain in his leg.

"No," he said, "Bristow asking his sister, who by all accounts was the apple of his mother's eye, to drop by—that makes sense. Asking his mother's brother, who was out of town and by no means her biggest fan, to make a massive detour to see her . . . that doesn't smell right. And now we find out that Alison went looking for Landry at his hotel in Oxford. It was a workday. Was she checking up on him on her own account, or did someone send her?"

The telephone rang. Robin picked up the receiver. To Strike's surprise, she immediately affected a very stilted Australian accent.

"Oy'm sorry, shiz not here . . . Naoh . . . Naoh . . . I dunnaoh where she iz . . . Naoh . . . My nem's Annabel . . ."

Strike laughed quietly. Robin threw him a look of mock anguish. After nearly a minute of strangled Australian, she hung up.

"Temporary Solutions," she said.

"I'm getting through a lot of Annabels. That one sounded more South African than Australian."

"Now I want to hear what happened to you yesterday," said Robin, unable to conceal her impatience any longer. "Did you meet Bryony Radford and Ciara Porter?"

Strike told her everything that had happened, omitting only the aftermath of his excursion to Evan Duffield's flat. He placed particular emphasis on Bryony Radford's insistence that it was dyslexia that had caused her to listen to Ursula May's voicemail messages; on Ciara Porter's continuing assertion that Lula had told her she would leave everything to her brother; on Evan Duffield's annoyance that Lula had kept checking the time while she was in Uzi; and on the threatening email that Tansy Bestigui had sent her estranged husband.

"So where *was* Tansy?" asked Robin, who had listened to every word of Strike's story with gratifying attention. "If we can just find out . . ."

"Oh, I'm pretty sure I know where she was," said Strike. "It's getting her to admit it, when it might blow her chances of a multimillion-pound settlement from Freddie, that's going to be the difficult bit. You'll be able to work it out too, if you just look through the police photographs again."

"But..."

"Have a look at the pictures of the front of the building on the morning Lula died, and then think about how it was when we saw it. It'll be good for your detective training."

Robin experienced a great surge of excitement and happiness, immediately tempered by a cold pang of regret, because she would soon be leaving for human resources.

"I need to change," said Strike, standing up. "Please will you try Freddie Bestigui again for me?"

He disappeared into the inner room, closed the door behind him and swapped his lucky suit (as he thought he might henceforth call it) for an old and comfortable shirt, and a roomier pair of trousers. When he passed Robin's desk on the way to the bathroom, she was on the telephone, wearing that expression of disinterested attentiveness that betokens a person on hold. Strike cleaned his teeth in the cracked basin, reflecting on how much easier life with Robin would be, now that he had tacitly admitted that he lived in the office, and returned to find her off the telephone and looking exasperated.

"I don't think they're even bothering to take my messages now," she told Strike. "They say he's out at Pinewood Studios and can't be disturbed."

"Ah well, at least we know he's back in the country," said Strike.

He took the interim report out of the filing cabinet, sank back down on the sofa and began to add his notes of yesterday's conversations, in silence. Robin watched out of the corner of her eye, fascinated by the meticulousness with which Strike tabulated his findings, making a precise record of how, where and from whom he had gained each piece of information.

"I suppose," she asked, after a long stretch of silence, during which she had divided her time between covert observation of Strike at work, and examination of a photograph of the front of number 18,

Kentigern Gardens on Google Earth, "you have to be very careful, in case you forget anything?"

"It's not only that," said Strike, still writing, and not looking up. "You don't want to give defending counsel any footholds."

He spoke so calmly, so reasonably that Robin considered the implication of his words for several moments, in case she could have misunderstood.

"You mean . . . in general?" she said at last. "On principle?"

"No," said Strike, continuing his report. "I mean that I specifically do not want to allow the defending counsel in the trial of the person who killed Lula Landry to get off because he was able to show that I can't keep records properly, thereby calling into question my reliability as a witness."

Strike was showing off again, and he knew it; but he could not help himself. He was, as he put it to himself, on a roll. Some might have questioned the taste of finding amusement in the midst of a murder inquiry, but he had found humor in darker places.

"Couldn't nip out for some sandwiches, Robin, could you?" he added, just so that he could glance up at her satisfyingly astonished expression.

He finished his notes during her absence, and was just about to call an old colleague in Germany when Robin burst back in, holding two packs of sandwiches and a newspaper.

"Your picture's on the front of the *Standard,*" she panted.

"What?"

It was a photograph of Ciara following Duffield into his flat. Ciara looked stunning; for half a second Strike was transported back to half past two that morning, when she had lain, white and naked, beneath him, that long silky hair spread on the pillow like a mermaid's as she whispered and moaned.

Strike refocused: he was half cropped out of the picture; one arm raised to keep the paparazzi at bay.

"That's all right," he told Robin with a shrug, handing her back the paper. "They think I was the minder."

"It says," said Robin, turning to the inside page, "that she left Duffield's with her security guard at two."

"There you go, then."

Robin stared at him. His account of the night had terminated with himself, Duffield and Ciara at Duffield's flat. She had been so interested in the various pieces of evidence he had laid out before her, she had forgotten to wonder where he had slept. She had assumed that he had left the model and the actor together.

He had arrived at the office still wearing the clothes in the photograph.

She turned away, reading the story on page two. The clear implication of the piece was that Ciara and Duffield had enjoyed an amorous encounter while the supposed minder waited in the hall.

"Is she stunning-looking in person?" asked Robin with an unconvincing casualness as she folded the *Standard*.

"Yeah, she is," said Strike, and he wondered whether it was his imagination that the three syllables sounded like a boast. "D'you want cheese and pickle, or egg mayonnaise?"

Robin made her selection at random and returned to her desk chair to eat. Her new hypothesis about Strike's overnight whereabouts had eclipsed even her excitement over the progress of the case. It was going to be difficult to reconcile her view of him as a blighted romantic with the fact that he had just (it seemed incredible, and yet she had heard his pathetic attempt to conceal his pride) slept with a supermodel.

The telephone rang again. Strike, whose mouth was full of bread and cheese, raised a hand to forestall Robin, swallowed, and answered it himself.

"Cormoran Strike."

"Strike, it's Wardle."

"Hi, Wardle; how's it going?"

"Not so good, actually. We've just fished a body out of the Thames with your card on it. Wondered what you could tell us about it."

10

IT WAS THE FIRST TAXI that Strike had felt justified in taking since the day he had moved his belongings out of Charlotte's flat. He watched the charges mount with detachment, as the cab rolled towards Wapping. The taxi driver was determined to tell him why Gordon Brown was a fucking disgrace. Strike sat in silence for the entire trip.

This would not be the first morgue Strike had visited, and far from the first corpse he had viewed. He had become almost immune to the despoliation of gunshot wounds; bodies ripped, torn and shattered, innards revealed like the contents of a butcher's shop, shining and bloody. Strike had never been squeamish; even the most mutilated corpses, cold and white in their freezer drawers, became sanitized and standardized to a man with his job. It was the bodies he had seen in the raw, unprocessed and unprotected by officialdom and procedure, that rose again and crawled through his dreams. His mother in the funeral parlor, in her favorite floor-length bell-sleeved dress, gaunt yet young, with no needle marks on view. Sergeant Gary Topley lying in the blood-spattered dust of that Afghanistan road, his face unscathed, but with no body below the upper ribs. As Strike had lain in the hot dirt, he had tried not to look at Gary's empty face, afraid to glance down and see how much of his own body was missing... but he had slid so swiftly into the maw of oblivion that he did not find out until he woke up in the field hospital...

An Impressionist print hung on the bare brick walls of the small anteroom to the morgue. Strike fixed his gaze on it, wondering where he had seen it before, and finally remembering that it hung over the mantelpiece at Lucy and Greg's.

"Mr. Strike?" said the gray-haired mortician, peering around the inner door, in white coat and latex gloves. "Come on in."

They were almost always cheerful, pleasant men, these curators of corpses. Strike followed the mortician into the chilly glare of the large, windowless inner room, with its great steel freezer doors all along the right-hand wall. The gently sloping tiled floor ran down to a central drain; the lights were dazzling. Every noise echoed off the hard and shiny surfaces, so that it sounded as though a small group of men was marching into the room.

A metal trolley stood ready in front of one of the freezer doors, and beside it were the two CID officers, Wardle and Carver. The former greeted Strike with a nod and a muttered greeting; the latter, paunchy and mottle-faced, with suit shoulders covered in dandruff, merely grunted.

The mortician wrenched down the thick metal arm on the freezer door. The tops of three anonymous heads were revealed, stacked one above the other, each draped in a white sheet worn limp and fine through repeated washings. The mortician checked the tag pinned to the cloth covering the central head; it bore no name, only the previous day's scribbled date. He slid the body out smoothly on its long-runnered tray and deposited it efficiently on to the waiting trolley. Strike noticed Carver's jaw working as he stepped back, giving the mortician room to wheel the trolley clear of the freezer door. With a clunk and a slam, the remaining corpses vanished from view.

"We won't bother with a viewing room, seeing as we're the only ones here," said the mortician briskly. "Light's best in the middle," he added, positioning the trolley just beside the drain, and pulling back the sheet.

The body of Rochelle Onifade was revealed, bloated and distended, her face forever wiped of suspicion, replaced by a kind of empty wonder. Strike had known, from Wardle's brief description on the telephone, whom he would see when the sheet was revealed, but the awful vulnerability of the dead struck him anew as he looked down on the body, far smaller than it had been when she had sat opposite him, consuming fries and concealing information.

Strike told them her name, spelling it so that both the mortician and Wardle could transcribe it accurately on to clipboard and note-book respectively; he also gave the only address he had ever known for her: St. Elmo's Hostel for the Homeless, in Hammersmith.

"Who found her?"

"River police hooked her out late last night," said Carver, speaking for the first time. His voice, with its south London accent, held a def-inite undertone of animosity. "Bodies usually take about three weeks to rise to the surface, eh?" he added, directing the comment, more statement than question, at the mortician, who gave a tiny, cautious cough.

"That's the accepted average, but I wouldn't be surprised if it turns out to be less in this case. There are certain indications . . ."

"Yeah, well, we'll get all that from the pathologist," said Carver, dismissively.

"It can't have been three weeks," said Strike, and the mortician gave him a tiny smile of solidarity.

"Why not?" demanded Carver.

"Because I bought her a burger and chips two weeks ago yester-day."

"Ah," said the mortician, nodding at Strike across the body. "I was going to say that a lot of carbohydrates taken prior to death can affect the body's buoyancy. There's a degree of bloating . . ."

"That's when you gave her your card, is it?" Wardle asked Strike.

"Yeah. I'm surprised it was still legible."

"It was stuck in with her Oyster card, in a plastic cover inside her back jeans pocket. The plastic protected it."

"What was she wearing?"

"Big pink fake-fur coat. Like a skinned Muppet. Jeans and train-ers."

"That's what she was wearing when I bought her the burger."

"In that case, the contents of the stomach should give an accurate—" began the mortician.

"D'you know if she's got any next of kin?" Carver demanded of Strike.

"There's an aunt in Kilburn. I don't know her name."

Slivers of glistening eyeball showed through Rochelle's almost closed lids; they had the characteristic brightness of the drowned. There were traces of bloody foam in the creases around her nostrils.

"How are her hands?" Strike asked the mortician, because Rochelle was uncovered only to the chest.

"Never mind her hands," snapped Carver. "We're done here, thanks," he told the mortician loudly, his voice reverberating around the room; and then, to Strike: "We want a word with you. Car's outside."

He was helping police with their inquiries. Strike remembered hearing the phrase on the news when he had been a small boy, obsessed by every aspect of police work. His mother had always blamed this strange early preoccupation on her brother, Ted, ex-Red Cap and fount of (to Strike) thrilling stories of travel, mystery and adventure. *Helping police with their inquiries:* as a five-year-old, Strike had imagined a noble and disinterested citizen volunteering to give up his time and energy to assist the police, who issued him with magnifying glass and truncheon and allowed him to operate under a cloak of glamorous anonymity.

This was the reality: a small interrogation room, with a cup of machine-made coffee given to him by Wardle, whose attitude towards Strike was devoid of the animosity that crackled from Carver's every open pore, but free of every trace of former friendliness. Strike suspected that Wardle's superior did not know the full extent of their previous interactions.

A small black tray on the scratched desk held seventeen pence in change, a single Yale key and a plastic-covered bus pass; Strike's card was discolored and crinkled but still legible.

"What about her bag?" Strike asked Carver, who was sitting across the desk, while Wardle leaned up against the filing cabinet in the corner. "Gray. Cheap and plastic-looking. That hasn't turned up, has it?"

"She probably left it in her squat, or wherever the fuck she lived," said Carver. "Suicides don't usually pack a bag to jump."

"I don't think she jumped," said Strike.

"Oh don't you, now?"

"I wanted to see her hands. She hated water over her face, she told me so. When people have struggled in the water, the position of their hands—"

"Well, it's nice to get your expert opinion," said Carver, with sledgehammer irony. "I know who you are, Mr. Strike."

He leaned back in his chair, placing his hands behind his head, revealing dried patches of sweat on the underarms of his shirt. The sharp, sour, oniony smell of BO wafted across the desk.

"He's ex-SIB," threw in Wardle, from beside the filing cabinet.

"I know that," barked Carver, raising wiry eyebrows flecked with scurf. "I've heard from Anstis all about the fucking leg and the life-saving medal. Quite the colorful CV."

Carver removed his hands from behind his head, leaned forwards and laced his fingers together on the desk instead. His corned-beef complexion and the purple bags under his hard eyes were not flattered by the strip lighting.

"I know who your old man is and all."

Strike scratched his unshaven chin, waiting.

"Like to be as rich and famous as Daddy, would you? Is that what all this is about?"

Carver had the bright blue, bloodshot eyes that Strike had always (since meeting a major in the Paras with just such eyes, who was subsequently cashiered for serious bodily harm) associated with a choleric, violent nature.

"Rochelle didn't jump. Nor did Lula Landry."

"Bollocks," shouted Carver. "You're speaking to the two men who *proved* Landry jumped. We went through every bit of fucking evidence with a fine-toothed fucking comb. I know what you're up to. You're milking that poor sod Bristow for all you can get. Why are you fucking smiling at me?"

"I'm thinking what a tit you're going to look when this interview gets reported in the press."

"Don't you dare fucking threaten me with the press, dickhead."

Carver's blunt, wide face was clenched; his glaring blue eyes vivid in the purple-red face.

"You're in a heap of trouble here, pal, and a famous dad, a peg leg and a good war aren't going to get you out of it. How do we know you didn't scare the poor bitch into fucking jumping? Mentally ill, wasn't she? How do we know you didn't make her think she'd done something wrong? You were the last person to see her alive, pal. I wouldn't like to be sitting where you are now."

"Rochelle crossed Grantley Road and walked away from me, as alive as you are. You'll find someone who saw her after she left me. Nobody's going to forget that coat."

Wardle pushed himself off the filing cabinets, dragged a hard plastic chair over to the desk and sat down.

"Let's have it, then," he told Strike. "Your theory."

"She was blackmailing Lula Landry's killer."

"Piss off," snapped Carver, and Wardle snorted in slightly stagey amusement.

"The day before she died," said Strike, "Landry met Rochelle for fifteen minutes in that shop. She dragged Rochelle straight into a changing cubicle, where she made a telephone call begging somebody to meet her at her flat in the early hours of the following morning. That call was overheard by an assistant at the shop; she was in the next cubicle; they're separated by a curtain. Girl called Mel, red hair and tattoos."

"People will spout any amount of shit when there's a celebrity involved," said Carver.

"If Landry phoned anyone from that cubicle," said Wardle, "it was Duffield, or her uncle. Her phone records show they were the only people she called, all afternoon."

"Why did she want Rochelle there when she made the call?" asked Strike. "Why drag her friend into the cubicle with her?"

"Women do that stuff," said Carver. "They piss in herds, too."

"Use your fucking intelligence: she was making the call on Rochelle's phone," said Strike, exasperated. "She'd tested everyone she knew to try and see who was talking to the press about her. Rochelle was the only one who kept her mouth shut. She established that the girl was trustworthy, bought her a mobile, registered it in Rochelle's name but took care of all the charges. She'd had her own phone hacked, hadn't she? She was getting paranoid about people listening in and reporting on her, so she bought a Nokia and registered it to somebody else, to give herself a totally secure means of communication when she wanted it.

"I grant you, that doesn't necessarily rule out her uncle, or Duffield, because calling them on the alternative number might have been a signal they'd organized between them. Alternatively, she was using Rochelle's number to speak to somebody else; someone she didn't want the press to know about. I've got Rochelle's mobile number. Find out what network she was with and you'll be able to check all this. The unit itself is a crystal-covered pink Nokia, but you won't find that."

"Yeah, because it's at the bottom of the Thames," said Wardle.

"Course it isn't," said Strike. "The killer's got it. He'll have got it off her before he threw her into the river."

"Fuck off!" jeered Carver, and Wardle, who had seemed interested against his better judgment, shook his head.

"Why did Landry want Rochelle there when she made the call?" Strike repeated. "Why not make it from the car? Why, when Rochelle was homeless, and virtually destitute, did she never sell her story on Landry? They'd have given her a great wad for it. Why didn't she cash in, once Landry was dead, and couldn't be hurt?"

"Decency?" suggested Wardle.

"Yeah, that's one possibility," said Strike. "The other's that she was making enough by blackmailing the killer."

"*Boll-ocks,*" moaned Carver.

"Yeah? That Muppet coat she was pulled up wearing cost one and a half grand."

A tiny pause.

"Landry probably gave it to her," said Wardle.

"If she did, she managed to buy her something that wasn't in the shops back in January."

"Landry was a model, she had inside contacts—fuck this shit," snapped Carver, as though he had irritated himself.

"Why," said Strike, leaning forwards on his arms into the miasma of body odor that surrounded Carver, "did Lula Landry make a detour to that shop for fifteen minutes?"

"She was in a hurry."

"Why go at all?"

"She didn't want to let the girl down."

"She got Rochelle to come right across town—this penniless, homeless girl, the girl she usually gave a lift home afterwards, in her chauffeur-driven car—dragged her into a cubicle, and then walked out fifteen minutes later, leaving her to make her own way home."

"She was a spoiled bitch."

"If she was, why turn up at all? Because it was worth it, for some purpose of her own. And if she wasn't a spoiled bitch, she must have been in some kind of emotional state that made her act out of character. There's a living witness to the fact that Lula begged somebody, over the phone, to come and see her, at her flat, sometime after one in the morning. There's also that piece of blue paper she had before she went into Vashti, and which nobody's admitting to having seen since. What did she do with it? Why was she writing in the back of the car, before she saw Rochelle?"

"It could've been—" said Wardle.

"It wasn't a fucking shopping list," groaned Strike, thumping the desk, "and nobody writes a suicide note eight hours in advance, and then goes dancing. She was writing a bloody *will*, don't you get it? She took it into Vashti to get Rochelle to witness it, and I think she tricked a pushy Aussie shop assistant into signing it as well—"

"Bollocks!" said Carver, yet again, but Strike ignored him, addressing Wardle.

" . . . which fits with her telling Ciara Porter that she was going to leave everything to her brother, doesn't it? She'd just made it legal. It was on her mind."

"Why suddenly make a will?"

Strike hesitated and sat back. Carver leered at him.

"Imagination run out?"

Strike let out his breath in a long sigh. An uncomfortable night of alcohol-sodden unconsciousness; last night's pleasurable excesses; half a cheese and pickle sandwich in twelve hours: he felt hollowed-out, exhausted.

"If I had hard evidence, I'd have brought it to you."

"The odds of people close to a suicide killing themselves go right up, did you know that? This Raquelle was a depressive. She has a bad day, remembers the way out her mate took, and does a copycat jump.

Which leads us right back to *you*, pal, persecuting people and pushing them..."

"...over the edge, yeah," said Strike. "People keep saying that. Very poor fucking taste, in the circumstances. What about Tansy Bestigui's evidence?"

"How many times, Strike? We proved she couldn't have heard it," Wardle said. "We proved it beyond doubt."

"No you didn't," said Strike—finally, when he least expected it, losing his temper. "You based your whole case on one almighty fuckup. If you'd taken Tansy Bestigui seriously, if you'd broken her down and got her to tell you the whole fucking truth, Rochelle Onifade would still be alive."

Pulsating with rage, Carver kept Strike there for another hour. His last act of contempt was to tell Wardle to make sure he saw "Rokeby Junior" firmly off the premises.

Wardle walked Strike to the front door, not speaking.

"I need you to do something," said Strike, halting at the exit, beyond which they could see the darkening sky.

"You've had enough from me already, mate," said Wardle, with a wry smile. "I'm gonna be dealing with that," he jerked his thumb over his shoulder, towards Carver and his temper, "for days because of you. I told you it was suicide."

"Wardle, unless someone brings the fucker in, there are two more people in danger of being knocked off."

"Strike..."

"What if I bring you proof that Tansy Bestigui wasn't in her flat at all when Lula fell? That she was somewhere she could have heard everything?"

Wardle looked up towards the ceiling, and closed his eyes momentarily.

"If you've got proof..."

"I haven't, but I will have in the next couple of days."

Two men walked past them, talking, laughing. Wardle shook his head, looking exasperated, and yet he did not turn away.

"If you want something from the police, call Anstis. He's the one who owes you."

"Anstis can't do this for me. I need you to call Deeby Macc."

"What the fuck?"

"You heard me. He's not going to take my calls, is he? But he'll speak to you; you've got the authority, and it sounds as though he liked you."

"You're telling me Deeby Macc knows where Tansy Bestigui was when Lula Landry died?"

"No, of course he bloody doesn't, he was in Barrack. I want to know what clothes he got sent on from Kentigern Gardens to Claridge's. Specifically, what stuff he got from Guy Somé."

Strike did not pronounce the name *Ghee* for Wardle.

"You want...why?"

"Because one of the runners on that CCTV footage was wearing one of Deeby's sweatshirts."

Wardle's expression, arrested for a moment, relapsed into exasperation.

"You see that stuff everywhere," he said after a moment or two. "That GS stuff. Shell suits. Trackies."

"This was a customized hoodie, there was only one of them in the world. Call Deeby, and ask him what he got from Somé. That's all I need. Whose side d'you want to be on if it turns out I'm right, Wardle?"

"Don't threaten me, Strike..."

"I'm not threatening you. I'm thinking about a multiple murderer who's walking around out there planning the next one—but if it's the papers you're worried about, I don't think they're going to go too easy on anyone who clung to the suicide theory once another body surfaced. Call Deeby Macc, Wardle, before someone else gets killed."

11

"No," said Strike forcefully, on the telephone that evening. "This is getting dangerous. Surveillance doesn't fall within the scope of secretarial duties."

"Nor did visiting the Malmaison Hotel in Oxford, or SOAS," Robin pointed out, "but you were happy enough that I did both of them."

"You're not following anyone, Robin. I doubt Matthew would be very happy about it, either."

It was funny, Robin thought, sitting in her dressing gown on her bed, with the phone pressed to her ear, how Strike had retained the name of her fiancé, without ever having met him. In her experience, men did not usually bother to log that kind of information. Matthew frequently forgot people's names, even that of his newborn niece; but she supposed that Strike must have been trained to recall such details.

"I don't need Matthew's permission," she said. "Anyway, it wouldn't be dangerous; you don't think *Ursula May*'s killed anyone..."

(There was an inaudible "*do* you?" at the end of the sentence.)

"No, but I don't want anyone to hear I'm taking an interest in her movements. It might make the killer nervous, and I don't want anyone else thrown from a height."

Robin could hear her own heart thumping through the thin material of her dressing gown. She knew that he would not tell her who he thought the killer was; she was even a little frightened of knowing, notwithstanding the fact that she could think of nothing else.

It was she who had called Strike. Hours had passed since she had received a text saying that he had been compelled to go with the police to Scotland Yard, and asking her to lock up the office behind her at five. Robin had been worried.

"Call him, then, if it's going to keep you awake," Matthew had said; not quite snapping, not quite indicating that he was, without knowing any of the details, firmly on the side of the police.

"Listen, I want you to do something for me," said Strike. "Call John Bristow first thing tomorrow and tell him about Rochelle."

"All right," said Robin, with her eyes on the large stuffed elephant Matthew had given her on their first Valentine's Day together, eight years previously. The present-giver himself was watching *Newsnight* in the sitting room. "What are you going to be doing?"

"I'm going to be on my way to Pinewood Studios for a few words with Freddie Bestigui."

"How?" said Robin. "They won't let you near him."

"Yeah, they will," said Strike.

After Robin had hung up, Strike sat motionless for a while in his dark office. The thought of the semi-digested McDonald's meal lying inside Rochelle's bloated corpse had not prevented him consuming two Big Macs, a large box of fries and a McFlurry on the way back from Scotland Yard. Gassy noises from his stomach were now mingling with the muffled thuds of the bass from the 12 Bar Café, which Strike barely noticed these days; the sound might have been his own pulse.

Ciara Porter's messy, girlish flat, her wide, groaning mouth, the long white legs wrapped tightly around his back, belonged to a life lived long ago. All his thoughts, now, were for squat and graceless Rochelle Onifade. He remembered her talking fast into her phone, not five minutes after she had left him, dressed in exactly the same clothes she had been wearing when they pulled her out of the river.

He was sure he knew what had happened. Rochelle had called the killer to say that she had just lunched with a private detective; a meeting had been arranged over her glittering pink phone; that night, after a meal or a drink, they had sauntered through the dark towards the river. He thought of Hammersmith Bridge, sage green and gold, in the area where she claimed to have a new flat: a famous suicide spot, with its low sides, and the fast-flowing Thames below. She could not swim. Nighttime: two lovers play-fighting, a car sweeps by, a scream and a splash. Would anyone have seen?

Not if the killer had iron-clad nerves and a liberal dash of luck; and this was a murderer who had already demonstrated plenty of the former, and an unnerving, reckless reliance on the latter. Defending counsel would undoubtedly argue diminished responsibility, because of the vainglorious overreaching that made Strike's quarry unique in his experience; and perhaps, he thought, there was some pathology there, some categorizable madness, but he was not much interested in the psychology. Like John Bristow, he wanted justice.

In the darkness of his office, his thoughts veered suddenly and un-helpfully back in time, to the most personal death of all; the one that Lucy assumed, quite wrongly, haunted Strike's every investigation, colored every case; the killing that had fractured his and Lucy's lives into two epochs, so that everything in their memory was cleaved clearly into that which had happened before their mother died, and that which had happened afterwards. Lucy thought he had run away to join the RMP because of Leda's death; that he had been driven to it by his unsatisfied belief in his stepfather's guilt; that every corpse he saw in the course of his professional life must recall their mother to his mind; that every killer he met must seem to be an echo of their stepfather; that he was driven to investigate other deaths in an eternal act of personal exculpation.

But Strike had aspired to this career long before the last needle had entered Leda's body; long before he had understood that his mother (and every other human) was mortal, and that killings were more than puzzles to be solved. It was Lucy who never forgot, who lived in a swarm of memories like coffin flies; who projected on to any and all unnatural deaths the conflicting emotions aroused in her by their mother's untimely demise.

Tonight, however, he found himself doing the very thing that Lucy was sure must be habitual: he was remembering Leda and con-necting her to this case. *Leda Strike, supergroupie.* It was how they always captioned her in the most famous photograph of all, and the only one that featured his parents together. There she was, in black and white, with her heart-shaped face, her shining dark hair and her marmoset eyes; and there, separated from each other by an art dealer, an aristocratic playboy (one since dead by his own hand, the other of AIDS) and Carla Astolfi, his father's second wife, was Jonny Rokeby himself, androgynous and wild: hair nearly as long as Leda's. Martini glasses and cigarettes, smoke curling out of the model's mouth, but his mother more stylish than any of them.

Everyone but Strike had seemed to view Leda's death as the deplorable but unsurprising result of a life lived perilously, beyond societal norms. Even those who had known her best and longest were satisfied that she herself had administered the overdose they found in her body. His mother, by almost unanimous consent, had walked too close to the unsavory edges of life, and it was only to be expected that she would one day topple out of sight and fall to her death, stiff and cold, on a filthy-sheeted bed.

Why she had done it, nobody could quite explain, not even Uncle Ted (silent and shattered, leaning against the kitchen sink) or Aunt Joan (red-eyed but angry at her little kitchen table, with her arms around nineteen-year-old Lucy, who was sobbing into Joan's shoulder). An overdose had simply seemed consistent with the trend of Leda's life; with the squats and the musicians and the wild parties; with the squalor of her final relationship and home; with the constant presence of drugs in her vicinity; with her reckless quest for thrills and highs. Strike alone had asked whether anyone had known his mother had taken to shooting up; he alone had seen a distinction between her predilection for cannabis and a sudden liking for heroin; he alone had unanswered questions and saw suspicious circumstances. But he had been a student of twenty, and nobody had listened.

After the trial and the conviction, Strike had packed up and left everything behind: the short-lived burst of press, Aunt Joan's desperate disappointment at the end of his Oxford career, Charlotte, bereft and incensed by his disappearance and already sleeping with someone new, Lucy's screams and scenes. With the sole support of Uncle Ted, he had vanished into the army, and refound there the life he had been taught by Leda: constant uprootings, self-reliance and the endless appeal of the new.

Tonight, though, he could not help seeing his mother as a spiritual sister to the beautiful, needy and depressive girl who had broken apart on a frozen road, and to the plain, homeless outsider now lying in the chilly morgue. Leda, Lula and Rochelle had not been women like Lucy, or his Aunt Joan; they had not taken every reasonable precaution against violence or chance; they had not tethered themselves to life with mortgages and voluntary work, safe husbands and clean-faced dependants: their deaths, therefore, were not classed as "tragic," in the same way as those of staid and respectable housewives.

How easy it was to capitalize on a person's own bent for self-destruction; how simple to nudge them into non-being, then to stand back and shrug and agree that it had been the inevitable result of a chaotic, catastrophic life.

Nearly all the physical evidence of Lula's murder had long since been wiped away, trodden underfoot or covered by thickly falling snow; the most persuasive clue Strike had was, after all, that grainy black-and-white footage of two men running away from the scene: a piece of evidence given a cursory check and tossed aside by the police, who were convinced that nobody could have entered the building, that Landry had committed suicide, and that the film showed nothing more than a pair of larcenous loiterers with intent.

Strike roused himself and looked at his watch. It was half past ten, but he was sure the man to whom he wished to speak would be awake. He flicked on his desk lamp, took up his mobile and dialed, this time, a number in Germany.

"Oggy," bellowed the tinny voice on the other end of the phone. "How the fuck are you?"

"Need a favor, mate."

And Strike asked Lieutenant Graham Hardacre to give him all the information he could find on one Agyeman of the Royal Engineers, Christian name and rank unknown, but with particular reference to the dates of his tours of duty in Afghanistan.

12

IT WAS ONLY THE SECOND car he had driven since his leg had been blown off. He had tried driving Charlotte's Lexus, but today, trying not to feel in any way emasculated, he had hired an automatic Honda Civic.

The journey to Iver Heath took under an hour. Entrance into Pinewood Studios was effected by a combination of fast talk, intimidation and the flashing of genuine, though outdated, official documentation; the security guard, initially impassive, was rocked by Strike's air of easy confidence, by the words "Special Investigation Branch," by the pass bearing his photograph.

"Have you got an appointment?" he asked Strike, feet above him in the box beside the electric barrier, his hand covering the telephone receiver.

"No."

"What's it about?"

"Mr. Evan Duffield," said Strike, and he saw the security guard scowl as he turned away and muttered into the receiver.

After a minute or so, Strike was given directions and waved through. He followed a gently winding road around the outskirts of the studio building, reflecting again on the convenient uses to which some people's reputations for chaos and self-destruction could be put.

He parked a few rows behind a chauffeured Mercedes occupying a space with a sign in it reading: PRODUCER FREDDIE BESTIGUI, made his unhurried exit from the car while Bestigui's driver watched him in the rearview mirror, and proceeded through a glass door that led to a nondescript, institutional set of stairs. A young man was jogging down them, looking like a slightly tidier version of Spanner.

"Where can I find Mr. Freddie Bestigui?" Strike asked him.

"Second floor, first office on the right."

He was as ugly as his pictures, bull-necked and pockmarked, sitting behind a desk on the far side of a glass partition wall, scowling at his computer monitor. The outer office was busy and cluttered, full of attractive young women at desks; film posters were tacked to pillars and photographs of pets were pinned up beside filming schedules. The pretty girl nearest the door, who was wearing a switchboard microphone in front of her mouth, looked up at Strike and said:

"Hello, can I help you?"

"I'm here to see Mr. Bestigui. Not to worry, I'll see myself in."

He was inside Bestigui's office before she could respond.

Bestigui looked up, his eyes tiny between pouches of flesh, black moles sprinkled over the swarthy skin.

"Who are you?"

He was already pushing himself up, thick-fingered hands clutching the edge of his desk.

"I'm Cormoran Strike. I'm a private detective, I've been hired..."

"*Elena!*" Bestigui knocked his coffee over; it was spreading across the polished wood, into all his papers. "Get the fuck out! Out! OUT!"

"...by Lula Landry's brother, John Bristow—"

"*ELENA!*"

The pretty, thin girl wearing the headset ran inside and stood fluttering beside Strike, terrified.

"Call security, you dozy little bitch!"

She ran outside. Bestigui, who was five feet six inches at the most, had pushed his way out from behind his desk now; as unafraid of the enormous Strike as a pit bull whose yard has been invaded by a Rottweiler. Elena had left the door open; the inhabitants of the outer office were staring in, frightened, mesmerized.

"I've been trying to get hold of you for a few weeks, Mr. Bestigui..."

"You are in a shitload of trouble, my friend," said Bestigui, advancing with a set jaw, his thick shoulders braced.

"...to talk about the night Lula Landry died."

Two men in white shirts and carrying walkie-talkies were running along the glass wall to Strike's right; young, fit, tense-looking.

"Get him out of here!" Bestigui roared, pointing at Strike, as the two guards bounced off each other in the doorway, then forced their way inside.

"Specifically," said Strike, "about the whereabouts of your wife, Tansy, when Lula fell..."

"Get him out of here and call the fucking police! How did he get in here?"

"...because I've been shown some photographs that make sense of your wife's testimony. Get your hands off me," Strike added to the younger of the guards now tugging his upper arm, "or I'll knock you through that window."

The security guard did not let go, but looked towards Bestigui for instructions.

The producer's bright dark eyes were fixed intently on Strike. He clenched and relaxed his thug's hands. After several long seconds he said:

"You're full of shit."

But he did not instruct the waiting guards to drag Strike from his room.

"The photographer was standing on the pavement opposite your house in the early hours of the eighth of January. The guy who took the pictures doesn't realize what he's got. If you don't want to discuss it, fine; police or press, I don't care. It'll come to the same thing in the end."

Strike took a few steps towards the door; the guards, each of whom was still holding him by the arm, were caught by surprise, and momentarily forced into the absurd position of holding him back.

"Get out," Bestigui said abruptly to his minions. "I'll let you know if I need you. Close the door behind you."

They left. When the door had closed, Bestigui said:

"All right, whatever your fucking name is, you can have five minutes."

Strike sat down, uninvited, in one of the black leather chairs facing Bestigui's desk, while the producer returned to his seat behind it, subjecting Strike to a hard, cold glare that was quite unlike the one

Strike had received from Bestigui's estranged wife; this was the intense scrutiny of a professional gambler. Bestigui reached for a packet of cigarillos, pulled a black glass ashtray towards himself and lit up with a gold lighter.

"All right, let's hear what these alleged photographs show," he said, squinting through clouds of pungent smoke, the picture of a film mafioso.

"The silhouette," said Strike, "of a woman crouching on the balcony outside your sitting-room windows. She looks naked, but as you and I know, she was in her underwear."

Bestigui puffed hard for a few seconds, then removed the cigarillo and said:

"Bullshit. You couldn't see that from the street. Solid stone bottom of the balcony; from that angle you wouldn't see anything. You're taking a punt."

"The lights were on in your sitting room. You can see her outline through the gaps in the stone. There was room then, of course, because the shrubs weren't there, were they? People can't resist fiddling with the scene afterwards, even when they've got away with it," Strike added, conversationally. "You were trying to pretend that there was never any room for anyone to squat on that balcony, weren't you? But you can't go back and Photoshop reality. Your wife was perfectly positioned to hear what happened up on the third-floor balcony just before Lula Landry died.

"Here's what I think happened," Strike went on, while Bestigui continued to squint through the smoke rising from his cigarillo. "You and your wife had a row while she was undressing for bed. Perhaps you found her stash in the bathroom, or you interrupted her doing a couple of lines. So you decided an appropriate punishment would be to shut her outside on the sub-zero balcony.

"People might ask how a street full of paps didn't notice a part-naked woman being shoved out on a balcony over their heads, but the snow was falling very thickly, and they'll have been stamping their feet trying to keep the circulation going, and their attention was focused on the ends of the street, while they were waiting for Lula and Deeby Macc. And Tansy didn't make any noise, did she? She ducked down and hid; she didn't want to show herself, half naked, in front of thirty photographers. You might even have shoved her out there at the same time that Lula's car came round the corner. Nobody would have been looking at your windows if Lula Landry had just appeared in a skimpy little dress."

"You're full of shit," said Bestigui. "You haven't got any photographs."

"I never said I had them. I said I'd been shown them."

Bestigui took the cigarillo from his lips, changed his mind about talking, and replaced it. Strike allowed several moments to elapse, but when it became clear that Bestigui was not going to avail himself of the opportunity to speak, he continued:

"Tansy must've started hammering on the window immediately after Landry fell past her. You weren't expecting your wife to start screaming and banging on the glass, were you? Understandably averse to anyone witnessing your bit of domestic abuse, you opened up. She ran straight past you, screaming her head off, out of the flat, and downstairs to Derrick Wilson.

"At which point you looked down over the balustrade and saw Lula Landry lying dead in the street below."

Bestigui puffed smoke slowly, without taking his eyes off Strike's face.

"What you did next might seem quite incriminating to a jury. You didn't dial 999. You didn't run after your half-frozen, hysterical wife. You didn't even—which the jury might find more understandable— run and flush away the coke you knew was lying in open view in the bathroom.

"No, what you did next, before following your wife or calling the police, was to wipe that window clean. There'd be no prints to show that Tansy had placed her hands on the outside of the glass, would there? Your priority was to make sure that nobody could prove you had shoved your wife out on to a balcony in a temperature of minus ten. What with your unsavory reputation for assault and abuse, and the possibility of a lawsuit from a young employee in the air, you weren't going to hand the press or a prosecutor any additional evidence, were you?

"Once you'd satisfied yourself that you'd removed any trace of her prints from the glass, you ran downstairs and compelled her to return to your flat. In the short time available to you before the police arrived, you bullied her into agreeing not to admit where she'd been when the body fell. I don't know what you promised her, or threatened her with; but whatever it was, it worked.

"You still didn't feel completely safe, though, because she was so shocked and distressed you thought she might blurt out the whole story. So you tried to distract the police by ranting about the flowers that had been knocked over in Deeby Macc's flat, hoping Tansy would pull herself together and stick to the deal.

"Well she has, hasn't she? God knows how much it's cost you, but she's let herself be dragged through the dirt in the press; she's put up with being called a coke-addled fantasist; she's stuck to her cock-and-bull story about hearing Landry and the murderer argue, through two floors, and soundproofed glass.

"Once she realizes there's photographic proof of where she was, though," said Strike, "I think she'll be glad to come clean. Your wife might think she loves money more than anything in the world, but her conscience is troubling her. I'm confident she'll crack pretty fast."

Bestigui had smoked his cigarillo down to its last few millimeters. Slowly he ground it out in the black glass ashtray. Long seconds passed, and the noise in the outside office filtered through the glass wall beside them: voices, the ringing of a telephone.

Bestigui stood up and lowered Roman blinds of canvas down over the glass partition, so that none of the nervy girls in the office beyond could see in. He sat back down and ran thick fingers thoughtfully over the crumpled terrain of his lower face, glancing at Strike and away again, towards the blank cream canvas he had created. Strike could almost see options occurring to the producer, as though he was riffling a deck of cards.

"The curtains were drawn," Bestigui said finally. "There wasn't enough light coming out of the windows to make out a woman hiding on the balcony. Tansy's not going to change her story."

"I wouldn't bet on that," said Strike, stretching out his legs; the prosthesis was still uncomfortable. "When I put it to her that the legal term for what the pair of you have done is 'conspiring to prevent the course of justice,' and that a belated show of conscience might keep her out of the nick; when I add in the public sympathy she's bound to get as the victim of domestic abuse, and the amount of money she's likely to be offered for exclusive rights to her story; when she realizes she's going to get her say in court, and that she'll be believed, and that she'll be able to bring about the conviction of the man she heard murdering her neighbor—Mr. Bestigui, I don't think even you've got enough money to keep her quiet."

The coarse skin around Bestigui's mouth flickered. He picked up his packet of cigarillos but did not extract one. There was a long silence during which he turned the packet between his fingers, round and round.

At last he said:

"I'm admitting nothing. Get out."

Strike did not move.

"I know you're keen to phone your lawyer," he said, "but I think you're overlooking the silver lining here."

"I've had enough of you. I said, get out."

"However unpleasant it's going to be, having to admit to what happened that night, it's still preferable to becoming the prime suspect in a murder case. It's going to be about the lesser of evils from here on in. If you cough to what really happened, you're putting yourself in the clear for the actual murder."

He had Bestigui's attention now.

"You couldn't have done it," said Strike, "because if you'd been the one who threw Landry off the balcony two floors above, you wouldn't have been able to let Tansy back inside within seconds of the body falling. I think you shut your wife outside, headed off into the bedroom, got into bed, got comfy—the police said the bed looked disarranged and slept in—and kept an eye on the clock. I don't think you wanted to fall asleep. If you'd left her too long on that balcony, you'd have been up for manslaughter. No wonder Wilson said she was shaking like a whippet. Probably in the early stages of hypothermia."

Another silence, except for Bestigui's fat fingers drumming lightly on the edge of the desk. Strike took out his notebook.

"Are you ready to answer a few questions now?"

"Fuck you!"

The producer was suddenly consumed by the rage he had so far suppressed, his jaw jutting and his shoulders hunched, level with his ears. Strike could imagine him looking thus as he bore down on his emaciated, coked-up wife, hands outstretched.

"You're in the shit here," said Strike calmly, "but it's entirely up to you how deep you sink. You can deny everything, battle it out with your wife in the court and the papers, end up in jail for perjury and obstructing the police. Or you can start cooperating, right now, and earn Lula's family's gratitude and good will. That'd go a long way to demonstrating remorse, and it'll help when it comes to pleas for clemency. If your information helps catch Lula's killer, I can't see you getting much worse than a reprimand from the bench. It's going to be the police who'll get the real going-over from the public and the press."

Bestigui was breathing noisily, but seemed to be pondering Strike's words. At last he snarled:

"There wasn't any fucking killer. Wilson never found anyone up there. Landry jumped," he said, with a small, dismissive jerk of his head. "She was a fucked-up little druggie, like my fucking wife."

"There was a killer," said Strike simply, "and you helped him get away with it."

Something in Strike's expression stifled Bestigui's clear urge to jeer. His eyes were slits of onyx as he mulled over what Strike had said.

"I've heard you were keen to put Lula in a film?"

Bestigui seemed disconcerted by the change of subject.

"It was just an idea," he muttered. "She was a flake but she was fucking gorgeous."

"You fancied getting her and Deeby Macc into a film together?"

"License to print money, those two together."

"What about this film you've been thinking of making since she died—what do they call it, a biopic? I hear Tony Landry wasn't happy about it?"

To Strike's surprise, a satyr's grin impressed itself on Bestigui's pouchy face.

"Who told you that?"

"Isn't it true?"

For the first time, Bestigui seemed to feel he had the upper hand in the conversation.

"No, it's not true. Anthony Landry has given me a pretty broad hint that once Lady Bristow's dead, he'll be happy to talk about it."

"He wasn't angry, then, when he called you to talk about it?"

"As long as it's tastefully handled, yadda yadda..."

"D'you know Tony Landry well?"

"I know of him."

"In what context?"

Bestigui scratched his chin, smiling to himself.

"He's your wife's divorce lawyer, of course."

"For now he is," said Bestigui.

"You think she's going to sack him?"

"She might have to," said Bestigui, and the smile became a self-satisfied leer. "Conflict of interest. We'll see."

Strike glanced down at his notebook, considering, with the gifted poker player's dispassionate calculation of the odds, how much risk there was in pushing this line of questioning to the limit, on no proof.

"Do I take it," he said, looking back up, "that you've told Landry you know he's sleeping with his business partner's wife?"

One moment's stunned surprise, and then Bestigui laughed out loud, a boorish, aggressive blast of glee.

"Know that, do you?"

"How did *you* find out?"

"I hired one of your lot. I thought Tansy was doing the dirty, but it turned out she was giving alibis to her bloody sister, while Ursula was having it away with Tony Landry. It'll be a shitload of fun to watch the Mays divorcing. High-powered lawyers on both sides. Old family firm broken up. Cyprian May's not as limp as he looks. He represented my second wife. I'm going to have a fucking blast watching that one play out. Watching the lawyers screw each other for a change."

"That's a nice bit of leverage you've got with your wife's divorce lawyer, then?"

Bestigui smiled nastily through the smoke.

"Neither of them know I know yet. I've been waiting for a good moment to tell them."

But Bestigui seemed to remember, suddenly, that Tansy might now be in possession of an even more powerful weapon in their divorce battle, and the smile faded from his crumpled face, leaving it bitter.

"One last thing," said Strike. "The night that Lula died: after you'd followed your wife down into the lobby, and brought her back upstairs, did you hear anything outside the flat?"

"I thought your whole fucking point is that you can't hear anything inside my flat with the windows closed?" snapped Bestigui.

"I'm not talking about outside in the street; I'm talking about outside your front door. Tansy might've been making too much noise to hear anything, but I'm wondering whether, when the pair of you were in your own hall—perhaps you stayed there, trying to calm her down, once you'd got her inside?—you heard any movement on the other side of the door? Or was Tansy screaming too much?"

"She was making a fuck of a lot of noise," said Bestigui. "I didn't hear anything."

"Nothing at all?"

"Nothing suspicious. Just Wilson, running past the door."

"Wilson."

"Yeah."

"When was this?"

"When you're talking about. When we'd got back inside our flat."

"Immediately after you'd shut the door?"

"Yeah."

"But Wilson had already run upstairs while you were still in the lobby, hadn't he?"

"Yeah."

The crevices in Bestigui's forehead and around his mouth deepened.

"So when you got to your flat on the first floor, Wilson must've been out of sight and earshot already?"

"Yeah . . ."

"But you heard footsteps on the stairs, immediately after closing your front door?"

Bestigui did not answer. Strike could see him putting it all together in his own mind for the very first time.

"I heard...yeah...footsteps. Running past. On the stairs."

"Yes," said Strike. "And could you make out whether there was one set, or two?"

Bestigui frowned, his eyes unfocused, looking beyond the detective into the treacherous past. "There was...one. So I thought it was Wilson. But it couldn't...Wilson was still up on the third floor, searching her flat...because I heard him coming down again, afterwards...after I'd called the police, I heard him go running past the door...

"I forgot that," said Bestigui, and for a fraction of a second he seemed almost vulnerable. "I forgot. There was a lot going on. Tansy screaming."

"And, of course, you were thinking about your own skin," said Strike briskly, inserting notepad and pen back in his pocket and hoisting himself out of the leather chair. "Well, I won't keep you; you'll be wanting to call your lawyer. You've been very helpful. I expect we'll see each other again in court."

13

ERIC WARDLE CALLED STRIKE THE following day.

"I phoned Deeby," he said curtly.

"And?" said Strike, motioning to Robin to pass him pen and paper. They had been sitting together at her desk, enjoying tea and biscuits while discussing the latest death threat from Brian Mathers, in which he promised, not for the first time, to slit open Strike's guts and piss on his entrails.

"He got sent a customized hoodie by Somé. Handgun in studs on the front and a couple of lines of Deeby's own lyrics on the back."

"Just the one?"

"Yeah."

"What else?" asked Strike.

"He remembers a belt, a beanie hat and a pair of cufflinks."

"No gloves?"

Wardle paused, perhaps checking his notes.

"No, he didn't mention gloves."

"Well, that clears that up," said Strike.

Wardle said nothing at all. Strike waited for the policeman to either hang up or impart more information.

"The inquest is on Thursday," said Wardle abruptly. "On Rochelle Onifade."

"Right," said Strike.

"You don't sound that interested."

"I'm not."

"I thought you were sure it was murder?"

"I am, but the inquest won't prove that one way or the other. Any idea when her funeral's going to be?"

"No," said Wardle irritably. "What does that matter?"

"I thought I might go."

"What for?"

"She had an aunt, remember?" said Strike.

Wardle rang off in what Strike suspected was disgust.

Bristow called Strike later that morning with the time and place of Rochelle's funeral.

"Alison managed to find out all the details," he told the detective on the telephone. "She's super-efficient."

"Clearly," said Strike.

"I'm going to come. To represent Lula. I ought to have helped Rochelle."

"I think it was always going to end this way, John. Are you bringing Alison?"

"She says she wants to come," said Bristow, though he sounded less than enamored of the idea.

"I'll see you there, then. I'm hoping to speak to Rochelle's aunt, if she turns up."

When Strike told Robin that Bristow's girlfriend had discovered the time and place of the funeral, she appeared put out. She herself had been trying to find out the details at Strike's request, and seemed to feel that Alison had put one over on her.

"I didn't realize you were this competitive," said Strike, amused. "Not to worry. Maybe she had some kind of head start on you."

"Like what?"

But Strike was looking at her speculatively.

"What?" repeated Robin, a little defensively.

"I want you to come with me to the funeral."

"Oh," said Robin. "OK. Why?"

She expected Strike to reply that it would look more natural for them to turn up as a couple, just as it had seemed more natural for him to visit Vashti with a woman in tow. Instead he said:

"There's something I want you to do for me there."

Once he had explained, clearly and concisely, what it was that he wanted her to do, Robin looked utterly bewildered.

"But why?"

"I can't say."

"Why not?"

"I'd rather not say that, either."

Robin no longer saw Strike through Matthew's eyes; no longer wondered whether he was faking, or showing off, or pretending to be cleverer than he was. She did him the credit, now, of discounting the possibility that he was being deliberately mysterious. All the same, she repeated, as though she must have heard him wrongly:

"Brian Mathers."

"Yeah."

"The Death Threat Man."

"Yeah."

"But," said Robin, "what on earth can he have to do with Lula Landry's death?"

"Nothing," said Strike, honestly enough. "Yet."

The north London crematorium where Rochelle's funeral was held three days later was chilly, anonymous and depressing. Everything was smoothly nondenominational; from the dark-wood pews and blank walls, carefully devoid of any religious device; to the abstract stained-glass window, a mosaic of little jewel-bright squares. Sitting on hard wood, while a whiny-voiced minister called Rochelle "Roselle" and the fine rain speckled the gaudy patchwork window above him, Strike understood the appeal of gilded cherubs and plaster saints, of gargoyles and Old Testament angels, of gem-set golden crucifixes; anything that might give an aura of majesty and grandeur, a firm promise of an afterlife, or retrospective worth to a life like Rochelle's. The dead girl had had her glimpse of earthly paradise: littered with designer goods, and celebrities to sneer at, and handsome drivers to joke with, and the yearning for it had brought her to this: seven mourners, and a minister who did not know her name.

There was a tawdry impersonality about the whole affair; a feeling of faint embarrassment; a painful avoidance of the facts of Rochelle's life. Nobody seemed to feel that they had the right to sit in the front row. Even the obese black woman wearing thick-lensed glasses and a knitted hat, who Strike assumed was Rochelle's aunt, had chosen to sit three benches from the front of the crematorium, keeping her distance from the cheap coffin. The balding worker whom Strike had met at the homeless hostel had come, in an open shirt and a leather jacket; behind him was a fresh-faced, neatly suited young Asian man who Strike thought might turn out to be the psychiatrist who had run Rochelle's outpatient group.

Strike, in his old navy suit, and Robin, in the black skirt and jacket she wore to interviews, sat at the very back. Across the aisle were Bristow, miserable and pale, and Alison, whose damp double-breasted black raincoat glistened a little in the cold light.

Cheap red curtains opened, the coffin slid out of sight, and the drowned girl was consumed by fire. The silent mourners exchanged pained, awkward smiles at the back of the crematorium; hovering, trying not to add unseemly haste of departure to the other inadequacies of the service. Rochelle's aunt, who projected an aura of eccentricity that bordered on instability, introduced herself as Winifred, then announced loudly, with an accusatory undertone:

"Dere's sandwiches in the pub. I thought dere would be more people."

She led the way outside, as if brooking no opposition, up the street to the Red Lion, the six other mourners following in her wake, heads bowed slightly against the rain.

The promised sandwiches sat, dry and unappetizing, on a metal foil tray covered in cling film, on a small table in the corner of the dingy pub. At some point on the walk to the Red Lion Aunt Winifred had realized who John Bristow was, and she now took overpowering possession of him, pinning him up against the bar, gabbling at him without pause. Bristow responded whenever she allowed him to get a word in edgewise, but the looks he cast towards Strike, who was talking to Rochelle's psychiatrist, became more frequent and desperate as the minutes passed.

The psychiatrist parried all Strike's attempts to engage him in conversation about the outpatients' group he had run, finally countering a question about disclosures Rochelle might have made with a polite but firm reminder about patient confidentiality.

"Were you surprised that she killed herself?"

"No, not really. She was a very troubled girl, you know, and Lula Landry's death was a great shock to her."

Shortly afterwards he issued a general farewell and left.

Robin, who had been trying to make conversation with a mono-syllabic Alison at a small table beside the window, gave up and headed for the Ladies.

Strike ambled across the small lounge and sat down in Robin's abandoned seat. Alison threw him an unfriendly look, then resumed her contemplation of Bristow, who was still being harangued by Rochelle's aunt. Alison had not unbuttoned her rain-flecked coat. A small glass of what looked like port stood on the table in front of her, and a slightly scornful smile played around her mouth, as though she found her surroundings ramshackle and inadequate. Strike was still trying to think of a good opener when she said unexpectedly:

"John was supposed to be at a meeting with Conway Oates's executors this morning. He's left Tony to meet them on his own. Tony's absolutely furious."

Her tone implied that Strike was in some way responsible for this, and that he deserved to know what trouble he had caused. She took a sip of port. Her hair hung limply to her shoulders and her big hands dwarfed the glass. In spite of a plainness that would have made wallflowers of other women, she radiated a great sense of self-importance.

"You don't think it was a nice gesture for John to come to the funeral?" asked Strike.

Alison gave a scathing little "huh," a token laugh.

"It's not as though he *knew* this girl."

"Why did *you* come along, then?"

"Tony wanted me to."

Strike noted the pleasurable self-consciousness with which she pronounced her boss's name.

"Why?"

"To keep an eye on John."

"Tony thinks John needs watching, does he?"

She did not answer.

"They share you, John and Tony, don't they?"

"What?" she said sharply.

He was glad to have discomposed her.

"They share your services? As a secretary?"

"Oh—oh, no. I work for Tony and Cyprian; I'm the senior partners' secretary."

"Ah. I wonder why I thought you were John's too?"

"I work on a completely different level," said Alison. "John uses the typing pool. I have nothing to do with him at work."

"Yet romance blossomed across secretarial rank and floors?"

She met his facetiousness with more disdainful silence. She seemed to see Strike as intrinsically offensive, somebody undeserving of manners, beyond the pale.

The hostel worker stood alone in a corner, helping himself to sandwiches, palpably killing time until he could decently leave. Robin emerged from the Ladies, and was instantly suborned by Bristow, who seemed eager for assistance in coping with Aunt Winifred.

"So, how long have you and John been together?" asked Strike.

"A few months."

"You got together before Lula died, did you?"

"He asked me out not long afterwards," she said.

"He must have been in a pretty bad way, was he?"

"He was a complete mess."

She did not sound sympathetic, but slightly contemptuous.

"Had he been flirting for a while?"

He expected her to refuse to answer; but he was wrong. Though she tried to pretend otherwise, there was unmistakable self-satisfaction and pride in her answer.

"He came upstairs to see Tony. Tony was busy, so John came to wait in my office. He started talking about his sister, and he got emotional. I gave him tissues, and he ended up asking me out to dinner."

In spite of what seemed to be lukewarm feelings for Bristow, he thought that she was proud of his overtures; they were a kind of trophy. Strike wondered whether Alison had ever, before desperate John Bristow came along, been asked out to dinner. It had been the collision of two people with an unhealthy need: *I gave him tissues, and he asked me out to dinner.*

The hostel worker was buttoning up his jacket. Catching Strike's eye, he gave a farewell wave, and departed without speaking to anyone.

"So how does the big boss feel about his secretary dating his nephew?"

"It's not up to Tony what I do in my private life," she said.

"True enough," said Strike. "Anyway, he can't talk about mixing business with pleasure, can he? Sleeping with Cyprian May's wife as he is."

Momentarily fooled by his casual tone, Alison opened her mouth to respond; then the meaning of his words hit her, and her self-assurance shattered.

"That's not true!" she said fiercely, her face burning. "Who said that to you? It's a lie. It's a *complete* lie. It's not true. It isn't."

He heard a terrified child behind the woman's protest.

"Really? Why did Cyprian May send you to Oxford to find Tony on the seventh of January then?"

"That—it was only—he'd forgotten to get Tony to sign some documents, that's all."

"And he didn't use a fax machine or a courier because...?"

"They were sensitive documents."

"Alison," said Strike, enjoying her agitation, "we both know that's balls. Cyprian thought Tony had sloped off somewhere with Ursula for the day, didn't he?"

"He didn't! He hadn't!"

Up at the bar, Aunt Winifred was waving her arms, windmill-like, at Bristow and Robin, who were wearing frozen smiles.

"You found him in Oxford, did you?"

"No, because—"

"What time did you get there?"

"About eleven, but he'd—"

"Cyprian must've sent you out the moment you got to work, did he?"

"The documents were urgent."

"But you didn't find Tony at his hotel or in the conference center?"

"I missed him," she said, in furious desperation, "because he'd gone back to London to visit Lady Bristow."

"Ah," said Strike. "Right. Bit odd that he didn't let you or Cyprian know that he was going back to London, isn't it?"

"No," she said, with a valiant attempt at regaining her vanished superiority. "He was contactable. He was still on his mobile. It didn't matter."

"Did you call his mobile?"

She did not answer.

"Did you call it, and not get an answer?"

She sipped her port in simmering silence.

"In fairness, it would break the mood, taking a call from your secretary while you're on the job."

He thought that she would find this offensive, and was not disappointed.

"You're disgusting. You're really disgusting," she said thickly, her cheeks a dull dark red with the prudishness she tried to disguise under a show of superiority.

"Do you live alone?" he asked her.

"What's that got to do with anything?" she asked, completely off-balance now.

"Just wondered. So you don't see anything odd in Tony booking into an Oxford hotel for the night, driving back to London the following morning, then returning to Oxford again, in time to check out of his hotel the next day?"

"He went back to Oxford so that he could attend the conference in the afternoon," she said doggedly.

"Oh, really? Did you hang around and meet him there?"

"He was there," she said evasively.

"You've got proof, have you?"

She said nothing.

"Tell me," said Strike, "would you rather think that Tony was in bed with Ursula May all day, or having some kind of confrontation with his niece?"

Over at the bar, Aunt Winifred was straightening her knitted hat and retying her belt. She seemed to be preparing to leave.

For several seconds Alison fought herself, and then, with an air of unleashing something long suppressed, she said in a ferocious whisper:

"They aren't having an affair. I *know* they aren't. It wouldn't happen. Ursula only cares about money; it's all that matters to her, and Tony's got less than Cyprian. Ursula wouldn't want Tony. She wouldn't."

"Oh, you never know. Physical passion might have overpowered her mercenary tendencies," said Strike, watching Alison closely. "It can happen. It's hard for another man to judge, but he's not bad-looking, Tony, is he?"

He saw the rawness of her pain, her fury, and her voice was choked as she said:

"Tony's right—you're taking advantage—in it for all you can get—John's gone funny—Lula *jumped*. She *jumped*. She was always unbalanced. John's like his mother, he's hysterical, he imagines things. Lula took drugs, she was one of those sort of people, out of control, always causing trouble and trying to get attention. Spoiled. Throwing money around. She could have anything she liked, anyone she wanted, but nothing was enough for her."

"I didn't realize you knew her."

"I—Tony's told me about her."

"He really didn't like her, did he?"

"He just saw her for what she was. She was no good. Some women," she said, her chest heaving beneath the shapeless raincoat, "aren't."

A chill breeze cut through the musty air of the lounge as the door swung shut behind Rochelle's aunt. Bristow and Robin kept smiling weakly until the door had closed completely, then exchanged looks of relief.

The barman had disappeared. Only four of them were left in the little lounge now. Strike became aware, for the first time, of the eighties ballad playing in the background: Jennifer Rush, "The Power of Love." Bristow and Robin approached their table.

"I thought you wanted to speak to Rochelle's aunt?" asked Bristow, looking aggrieved, as though he had been through an ordeal for nothing.

"Not enough to chase after her," replied Strike cheerfully. "You can fill me in."

Strike could tell, by the expressions on Robin's and Bristow's faces, that both thought this attitude strangely lackadaisical. Alison was fumbling for something in her bag, her own face hidden.

The rain had stopped, the pavements were slippery and the sky was gloomy, threatening a fresh downpour. The two women walked ahead in silence, while Bristow earnestly related to Strike all that he could remember of Aunt Winifred's conversation. Strike, however, was not listening. He was watching the backs of the two women, both in black—almost, to the careless observer, alike, interchangeable. He remembered the sculptures on either side of the Queen's Gate; not identical at all, in spite of the assumptions made by lazy eyes; one male, one female, the same species, yes, but profoundly different.

When he saw Robin and Alison come to a halt beside a BMW he assumed must be Bristow's, he too slowed up, and cut across Bristow's rambling recital of Rochelle's stormy relations with her family.

"John, I need to check something with you."

"Fire away."

"You say you heard your uncle come into your mother's flat on the morning before Lula died?"

"Yep, that's right."

"Are you absolutely sure that the man you heard was Tony?"

"Yes, of course."

"You didn't see him, though?"

"I . . ." Bristow's rabbity face was suddenly puzzled. ". . . no, I—I don't think I actually saw him. But I heard him let himself in. I heard his voice from the hall."

"You don't think that, perhaps, because you were expecting Tony, you assumed it *was* Tony?"

Another pause.

Then, in a changed voice:

"Are you saying Tony wasn't there?"

"I just want to know how certain you are that he was."

"Well . . . until this moment, I was completely certain. Nobody else has got a key to my mother's flat. It couldn't have been anyone *except* Tony."

"So you heard someone let themselves into the flat. You heard a male voice. Was he talking to your mother, or to Lula?"

"Er . . ." Bristow's large front teeth were much in evidence as he pondered the question. "I heard him come in. I think I heard him speaking to Lula . . ."

"And you heard him leave?"

"Yes. I heard him walk down the hall. I heard the door close."

"When Lula said goodbye to you, did she make any mention of Tony having just been there?"

More silence. Bristow raised a hand to his mouth, thinking.

"I—she hugged me, that's all I . . . Yes, I think she said she'd spoken to Tony. Or did she? Did I assume she'd spoken to him, because I thought . . . ? But if it wasn't my uncle, who was it?"

Strike waited. Bristow stared at the pavement, thinking.

"But it must have been him. Lula must have seen whoever it was, and not thought their presence remarkable, and who else could that have been, except Tony? Who else would have had a key?"

"How many keys are there?"

"Four. Three spares."

"That's a lot."

"Well, Lula and Tony and I all had one. Mum liked us all to be able to let ourselves in and out, especially while she's been ill."

"And all these keys are present and accounted for, are they?"

"Yes—well, I think so. I assume Lula's came back to my mother with all her other things. Tony's still got his, I've got mine, and my mother's . . . I expect it's somewhere in the flat."

"So you aren't aware of any key that's been lost?"

"No."

"And none of you has ever lent your key to anyone?"

"My God, why would we do that?"

"I keep remembering how that file of photographs was removed from Lula's laptop while it was in your mother's flat. If there's another key floating around . . ."

"There can't be," said Bristow. "This is ... I ... why are you saying Tony wasn't there? He must have been. He says he saw me through the door."

"You went into the office on the way back from Lula's, right?"

"Yes."

"To get files?"

"Yes. I just ran in and grabbed them. I was quick."

"So you were back at your mother's house ... ?"

"It can't have been later than ten."

"And the man who came in, when did he arrive?"

"Maybe ... maybe half an hour afterwards? I can't honestly re-member. I wasn't watching the clock. But why would Tony say he was there if he wasn't?"

"Well, if he knew you'd been working at home, he could easily say that he came in, and didn't want to disturb you, and just walked down the hall to speak to your mother. She, presumably, confirmed his presence to the police?"

"I suppose so. Yes, I think so."

"But you're not sure?"

"I don't think we've ever discussed it. Mum was groggy and in pain; she slept a lot that day. And then the next morning we had the news about Lula ..."

"But you've never thought it was strange that Tony didn't come into the study and speak to you?"

"It wasn't strange at all," said Bristow. "He was in a foul temper about the Conway Oates business. I'd have been more surprised if he had been chatty."

"John, I don't want to alarm you, but I think that both you and your mother could be in danger."

Bristow's little bleat of nervous laughter sounded thin and uncon-vincing. Strike could see Alison standing fifty yards away, her arms folded, ignoring Robin, watching the two men.

"You—you can't be serious?" said Bristow.

"I'm very serious."

"But ... does ... Cormoran, are you saying you know who killed Lula?"

"Yeah, I think I do—but I still need to speak to your mother before we wrap this up."

Bristow looked as though he wished he could drink the contents of Strike's mind. His myopic eyes scanned every inch of Strike's face, his expression half afraid, half imploring.

"I must be there," he said. "She's very weak."

"Of course. How about tomorrow morning?"

"Tony will be livid if I take off any more time during work hours."

Strike waited.

"All right," said Bristow. "All right. Ten thirty tomorrow."

14

THE FOLLOWING MORNING WAS FRESH and bright. Strike took the underground to genteel and leafy Chelsea. This was a part of London that he barely knew, for Leda had never, even in her most spendthrift phases, managed to secure a toehold in the vicinity of the Royal Chelsea Hospital, pale and gracious in the spring sun.

Franklin Row was an attractive street of more red brick; here were plane trees, and a great grassy space bordered with railings, in which a throng of primary school children were playing games in pale blue Aertex tops and navy blue shorts, watched by tracksuited teachers. Their happy cries punctuated the sedate quiet otherwise disturbed only by birdsong; no cars passed as Strike strolled down the pavement towards the house of Lady Yvette Bristow, his hands in his pockets.

The wall beside the partly glass door, set at the top of four white stone steps, bore an old-fashioned Bakelite panel of doorbells. Strike checked to see that Lady Yvette Bristow's name was clearly marked beside Flat E, then retreated to the pavement and stood waiting in the gentle warmth of the day, looking up and down the street.

Ten thirty arrived, but John Bristow did not. The square remained deserted, but for the twenty small children running between hoops and colored cones beyond the railings.

At ten forty-five, Strike's mobile vibrated in his pocket. The text was from Robin:

Alison has just called to say that JB is unavoidably detained. He does not want you to speak to his mother without him present.

Strike immediately texted Bristow:

How long are you likely to be detained? Any chance of doing this later today?

He had barely sent the message when the phone began to ring.

"Yeah, hello?" said Strike.

"Oggy?" came Graham Hardacre's tinny voice, all the way from Germany. "I've got the stuff on Agyeman."

"Your timing's uncanny." Strike pulled out his notebook. "Go on."

"He's Lieutenant Jonah Francis Agyeman, Royal Engineers. Aged twenty-one, unmarried, last tour of duty started eleventh of January. He's back in June. Next of kin, a mother. No siblings, no kids."

Strike scribbled it all down in his notebook, with the mobile phone held between jaw and shoulder.

"I owe you one, Hardy," he said, putting the notebook away. "Haven't got a picture, have you?"

"I could email you one."

Strike gave Hardacre the office email address, and, after routine inquiries about each other's lives, and mutual expressions of goodwill, terminated the call.

It was five to eleven. Strike waited, phone in hand, in the peaceful, leafy square, while the gamboling children played with their hoops and their beanbags, and a tiny silver plane drew a thick white line across the periwinkle sky. At last, with a small chirrup clearly audible in the quiet street, Bristow's texted reply arrived:

No chance today. I've been forced to go out to Rye. Maybe tomorrow?

Strike sighed.

"Sorry, John," he muttered, and he climbed the steps and rang Lady Bristow's doorbell.

The entrance hall, quiet, spacious and sunny, nevertheless had a faintly depressing air of communality that a bucket-shaped vase of dried flowers and a dull green carpet and pale yellow walls, probably chosen for their inoffensiveness, could not dissipate. As at Kentigern Gardens, there was a lift, this one with wooden doors. Strike chose to walk upstairs. The building had a faint shabbiness that in no way diminished its quiet aura of wealth.

The door of the top flat was opened by the smiling West Indian Macmillan nurse who had buzzed him through the front door.

"You're not Mister Bristow," she said brightly.

"No, I'm Cormoran Strike. John's on his way."

She let him in. Lady Bristow's hallway was pleasantly cluttered, papered in faded red and covered in watercolors in old gilt frames; an umbrella stand was full of walking sticks, and coats hung on a row of pegs. Strike glanced right, and saw a sliver of the study at the end of the corridor: a heavy wooden desk and a swivel chair with its back to the door.

"Will you wait in the sitting room while I check whether Lady Bristow is ready to see you?"

"Yeah, of course."

He walked through the door she indicated into a charming room with primrose walls, lined with bookcases bearing photographs. An old-fashioned dial telephone sat on an end table beside a comfortable chintz-covered sofa. Strike checked that the nurse was out of sight before slipping the receiver off the hook and repositioning it, unobtrusively skewed on its rests.

Close by the bay window on a *bonheur du jour* stood a large photograph, framed in silver, showing the wedding of Sir and Lady Alec Bristow. The groom looked much older than his wife, a rotund, beaming, bearded man; the bride was thin, blonde and pretty in an insipid way. Ostensibly admiring the photograph, Strike stood with his back to the door, and slid open a little drawer in the delicate cherrywood desk. Inside was a supply of fine pale blue writing paper and matching envelopes. He slid the drawer shut again.

"Mister Strike? You can come through."

Back through the red-papered hall, a short passage, and into a large bedroom, where the dominant colors were duck-egg blue and white, and everywhere gave an impression of elegance and taste. Two doors on the left, both ajar, led to a small en-suite bathroom, and what seemed to be a large walk-in wardrobe. The furniture was delicate and Frenchified; the props of serious illness—the drip on its metal stand, the bedpan lying clean and shiny on a chest of drawers, with an array of medications—were glaring impostors.

The dying woman wore a thick ivory-colored bed jacket and reclined, dwarfed by her carved wooden bed, on many white pillows. No trace of Lady Bristow's youthful prettiness remained. The raw bones of the skeleton were clearly delineated now, beneath fine skin that was shiny and flaking. Her eyes were sunken, filmy and dim, and her wispy hair, fine as a baby's, was gray against large expanses of pink scalp. Her emaciated arms lay limp on top of the covers, a catheter protruded. Her death was an almost palpable presence in the room, as though it stood waiting patiently, politely, behind the curtains.

A faint smell of lime blossom pervaded the atmosphere, but did not entirely eclipse that of disinfectant and bodily decay; smells that recalled, to Strike, the hospital where he had lain helpless for months. A second large bay window had been raised a few inches, so that the warm fresh air and the distant cries of the sports-playing children could enter the room. The view was of the topmost branches of the leafy sunlit plane trees.

"Are you the detective?"

Her voice was thin and cracked, her words slightly slurred. Strike, who had wondered whether Bristow had told her the truth about his profession, was glad that she knew.

"Yes, I'm Cormoran Strike."

"Where's John?"

"He's been held up at the office."

"Again," she murmured, and then: "Tony works him very hard. It isn't fair." She peered at him, blurrily, and indicated a small painted chair with one slightly raised finger. "Do sit down."

There were chalky white lines around her faded irises. As he sat, Strike noticed two more silver-framed photographs standing on the bedside table. With something akin to an electric shock, he found himself looking into the eyes of ten-year-old Charlie Bristow, chubby-faced, with his slightly mullety haircut: frozen forever in the eighties, his school shirt with its long pointed collar, and the huge knot in his tie. He looked just as he had when he had waved goodbye to his best friend, Cormoran Strike, expecting to meet each other again after Easter.

Beside Charlie's photograph was a smaller one, of an exquisite little girl with long black ringlets and big brown eyes, in a navy blue school uniform: Lula Landry, aged no more than six.

"Mary," said Lady Bristow, without raising her voice, and the nurse bustled over. "Could you get Mr. Strike...coffee? Tea?" she asked him, and he was transported back two and a half decades, to Charlie Bristow's sunlit garden, and the gracious blonde mother, and the iced lemonade.

"A coffee would be great, thank you very much."

"I do apologize for not making it myself," said Lady Bristow, as the nurse departed, with heavy footfalls, "but as you can see, I am entirely dependent, now, on the kindness of strangers. Like poor Blanche Dubois."

She closed her eyes for a moment, as though to concentrate better on some internal pain. He wondered how heavily medicated she was. Beneath the gracious manner, he divined the faintest whiff of something bitter in her words, much as the lime blossom failed to cover the smell of decay, and he wondered at it, considering that Bristow spent most of his time dancing attendance on her.

"Why isn't John here?" asked Lady Bristow again, with her eyes still shut.

"He's been held up at the office," repeated Strike.

"Oh, yes. Yes, you said."

"Lady Bristow, I'd like to ask you a few questions, and I apologize in advance if they seem over-personal, or distressing."

"When you have been through what I have," she said quietly, "nothing much can hurt you anymore. Do call me Yvette."

"Thank you. Do you mind if I take notes?"

"No, not at all," she said, and she watched him take out his pen and notebook with a dim show of interest.

"I'd like to start, if you don't mind, with how Lula came into your family. Did you know anything about her background when you adopted her?"

She looked the very picture of helplessness and passivity lying there with her limp arms on the covers.

"No," she said. "I didn't know anything. Alec might have known, but if he did, he never told me."

"What makes you think your husband knew something?"

"Alec always went into things as deeply as he could," she said, with a faint, reminiscent smile. "He was a very successful businessman, you know."

"But he never told you anything about Lula's first family?"

"Oh no, he wouldn't have done that." She seemed to find this a strange suggestion. "I wanted her to be mine, just mine, you see. Alec would have wanted to protect me, if he knew anything. I could not have borne the idea that somebody out there might come and claim her one day. I had already lost Charlie, and I wanted a daughter so badly; the idea of losing her, too..."

The nurse returned bearing a tray with two cups on it and a plate of chocolate bourbons.

"One coffee," she said cheerfully, placing it beside Strike on the nearer of the bedside tables, "and one camomile tea."

She bustled out again. Lady Bristow closed her eyes. Strike took a gulp of black coffee and said:

"Lula went looking for her biological parents in the year before she died, didn't she?"

"That's right," said Lady Bristow, with her eyes still closed. "I had just been diagnosed with cancer."

There was a pause, in which Strike put down his coffee cup with a soft chink, and the distant cheers of the small children in the square outside floated through the open window.

"John and Tony were very, very angry with her," said Lady Bristow. "They didn't think she ought to have started trying to find her biological mother, when I was so very ill. The tumor was already advanced when they found it. I had to go straight on to chemotherapy. John was very good; he drove me back and forth to the hospital, and came to stay with me during the worst bits, and even Tony rallied round, but all Lula seemed to care about..." She sighed, and opened her faded eyes, seeking Strike's face. "Tony always said that she was very spoiled. I daresay it was my fault. I had lost Charlie, you see; I couldn't do enough for her."

"Do you know how much Lula managed to find out about her birth family?"

"No, I don't, I'm afraid. I think she knew how much it upset me. She didn't tell me a great deal. I know that she found the mother, of course, because there was all the dreadful publicity. She was exactly what Tony had predicted. She hadn't ever wanted Lula. An awful, awful woman," whispered Lady Bristow. "But Lula kept seeing her. I was having chemotherapy all through that time. I lost my hair . . ."

Her voice trailed away. Strike felt, as perhaps she meant him to, like a brute as he pressed on:

"What about her biological father? Did she ever tell you she'd found out anything about him?"

"No," said Lady Bristow weakly. "I didn't ask. I had the impression that she had given up on the whole business once she found that horrible mother. I didn't want to discuss it, any of it. It was too distressing. I think she realized that."

"She didn't mention her biological father the last time you saw her?" Strike pressed on.

"Oh no," she said, in her soft voice. "No. That was not a very long visit, you know. She told me, the moment she arrived, I remember, that she could not stay long. She had to meet her friend Ciara Porter."

Her sense of ill-usage wafted gently towards him like the smell of the bedridden she exuded: a little fusty, a little overripe. Something about her recalled Rochelle; although they were as different as two women could be, both gave off the resentment of those who feel shortchanged and neglected.

"Can you remember what you and Lula talked about that day?"

"Well, I had been given so many painkillers, you understand. I had had a very serious operation. I can't remember every detail."

"But you remember Lula coming to see you?" asked Strike.

"Oh yes," she said. "She woke me up, I had been sleeping."

"Can you remember what you talked about?"

"My operation, of course," she said, with just a touch of asperity. "And then, a little bit, about her big brother."

"Her big...?"

"Charlie," said Lady Bristow, pitifully. "I told her about the day he died. I had never really talked to her about it before. The worst, the very worst day of my life."

Strike could imagine her, prostrate and a little groggy, but no less resentful for all that, holding her unwilling daughter there at her side by talking about her pain, and her dead son.

"How could I have known that that would be the last time I would ever see her?" breathed Lady Bristow. "I didn't realize that I was about to lose a second child."

Her bloodshot eyes filled. She blinked, and two fat tears fell down on to her hollow cheeks.

"Could you please look in that drawer," she whispered, pointing a withered finger at the bedside table, "and get me out my pills?"

Strike slid it open and saw many white boxes inside, of varying types and with various labels upon them.

"Which...?"

"It doesn't matter. They're all the same," she said.

He took one out; it was clearly labeled Valium. She had enough in there to overdose ten times.

"If you could pop a couple out for me?" she said. "I'll take them with some tea, if it's cool enough."

He handed her her pills and the cup; her hands trembled; he had to support the saucer and he thought, inappropriately, of a priest offering communion.

"Thank you," she murmured, relaxing back on to her pillows as he replaced her tea on the table, and fixing him with her plaintive eyes. "Didn't John tell me you knew Charlie?"

"Yes, I did," said Strike. "I've never forgotten him."

"No, of course not. He was a most lovable child. Everyone always said so. The sweetest boy, the very sweetest I have ever known. I miss him every single day."

Outside the window, the children shrieked, and the plane trees rustled, and Strike thought of how the room would have looked on a winter morning months ago, when the trees must have been bare-limbed, when Lula Landry had sat where he was sitting, with her beautiful eyes perhaps fixed on the picture of dead Charlie while her groggy mother told the horrible story.

"I had never really talked to Lula about it before. The boys had gone out on their bikes. We heard John screaming, and then Tony shouting, shouting..."

Strike's pen had not made contact with paper yet. He watched the dying woman's face as she talked.

"Alec wouldn't let me look, wouldn't let me anywhere near the quarry. When he told me what had happened, I fainted. I thought I would die. I wanted to die. I could not understand how God could have let it happen.

"But since then, I've come to think that perhaps I have deserved all of it," said Lady Bristow distantly, her eyes fixed on the ceiling. "I've wondered whether I'm being punished. Because I loved them too much. I spoiled them. I couldn't say no. Charlie, John and Lula. I think it must be punishment, because otherwise it would be too unspeakably cruel, wouldn't it? To make me go through it again, and again, and again."

Strike had no answer to give. She invited pity, but he found he could not pity her even as much as, perhaps, she deserved. She lay dying, wrapped in invisible robes of martyrdom, presenting her helplessness and passivity to him like adornments, and his dominant feeling was distaste.

"I wanted Lula so much," said Lady Bristow, "but I don't think she ever... She was a darling little thing. So beautiful. I would have done anything for that girl. But she didn't love me the way Charlie and John loved me. Maybe it was too late. Maybe we got her too late.

"John was jealous when she first came to us. He had been devastated about Charlie... but they ended up being very close friends. Very close."

A tiny frown crumpled the paper-fine skin of her forehead.

"So Tony was quite wrong."

"What was he wrong about?" asked Strike quietly.

Her fingers twitched upon the covers. She swallowed.

"Tony didn't think we should have adopted Lula."

"Why not?" asked Strike.

"Tony never liked any of my children," said Yvette Bristow. "My brother is a very hard man. Very cold. He said dreadful things after Charlie died. Alec hit him. It wasn't true. It wasn't true—what Tony said."

Her milky gaze slid to Strike's face, and he thought he glimpsed the woman she must have been when she still had her looks: a little clingy, a little childish, prettily dependent, an ultra-feminine creature, protected and petted by Sir Alec, who strove to satisfy her every whim and wish.

"What did Tony say?"

"Horrible things about John and Charlie. Awful things. I don't," she said weakly, "want to repeat them. And then he phoned Alec, when he heard that we were adopting a little girl, and told him we ought not to do it. Alec was furious," she whispered. "He forbade Tony our house."

"Did you tell Lula about all this when she visited that day?" asked Strike. "About Tony, and the things he said after Charlie died; and when you adopted her?"

She seemed to sense a reproach.

"I can't remember exactly what I said to her. I had just had a very serious operation. I was a little drowsy from all the drugs. I can't remember precisely what I said now . . ."

And then, with an abrupt change of subject:

"That boy reminded me of Charlie. Lula's boyfriend. The very handsome boy. What is his name?"

"Evan Duffield?"

"That's right. He came to see me a little while ago, you know. Quite recently. I don't know exactly . . . I lose track of time. They give me so many drugs now. But he came to see me. It was so sweet of him. He wanted to talk about Lula."

Strike remembered Bristow's assertion that his mother had not known who Duffield was, and he wondered whether Lady Bristow had played this little game with her son; making herself out to be more confused than she really was, to stimulate his protective instincts.

"Charlie would have been handsome like that, if he'd lived. He might have been a singer, or an actor. He loved performing, do you remember? I felt very sorry for that boy Evan. He cried here, with me. He told me that he thought she was meeting another man."

"What other man was that?"

"The singer," said Lady Bristow vaguely. "The singer who'd written songs about her. When you are young, and beautiful, you can be very cruel. I felt very sorry for him. He told me he felt guilty. I told him he had nothing to feel guilty about."

"Why did he say he felt guilty?"

"For not following her into her apartment. For not being there, to stop her dying."

"If we could just go back for a moment, Yvette, to the day before Lula's death?"

She looked reproachful.

"I'm afraid I can't remember anything else. I've told you everything I remember. I was just out of hospital. I was not myself. They'd given me so many drugs, for the pain."

"I understand that. I just wanted to know whether you remember your brother, Tony, visiting you that day?"

There was a pause, and Strike saw something harden in the weak face.

"No, I don't remember Tony coming," said Lady Bristow at last. "I know he says he was here, but I don't remember him coming. Maybe I was asleep."

"He claims to have been here when Lula was visiting," said Strike.

Lady Bristow gave the smallest shrug of her fragile shoulders.

"Maybe he was here," she said, "but I don't remember it." And then, her voice rising, "My brother's being much nicer to me now he knows that I'm dying. He visits a lot now. Always putting down poison about John, of course. He's always done that. But John has always been very good to me. He has done things for me while I've been ill . . . things no son should have to do. It would have been more appropriate for Lula . . . but she was a spoiled girl. I loved her, but she could be selfish. Very selfish."

"So on that last day, the last time you saw Lula—" said Strike, returning doggedly to the main point, but Lady Bristow cut across him.

"After she left, I was very upset," she said. "Very upset indeed. Talking about Charlie always does that to me. She could see how distressed I was, but she still left to meet her friend. I had to take pills, and I slept. No, I never saw Tony; I didn't see anyone else. He might say he was here, but I don't remember anything until John woke me up with a supper tray. John was cross. He told me off."

"Why was that?"

"He thinks I take too many pills," said Lady Bristow, like a little girl. "I know he wants the best for me, poor John, but he doesn't realize...he couldn't...I've had so much pain in my life. He sat with me for a long time that night. We talked about Charlie. We talked into the early hours of the morning. And while we were talking," she said, dropping her voice to a whisper, "at the very time we were talking, Lula fell...she fell off the balcony.

"So it was John who had to break the news to me, the next morning. The police had arrived on the doorstep, at the crack of dawn. He came into the bedroom to tell me and..."

She swallowed, and shook her head, limp, barely alive.

"That's why the cancer came back, I know it. People can only bear so much pain."

Her voice was becoming more slurred. He wondered how much Valium she had already taken, as she closed her eyes drowsily.

"Yvette, would it be all right if I used your bathroom?" he asked.

She assented with a sleepy nod.

Strike got up, and moved quickly, and surprisingly quietly for a man of his bulk, into the walk-in wardrobe.

The space was lined with mahogany doors that reached to the ceiling. Strike opened one of the doors and glanced inside, at overstuffed railings of dresses and coats, with a shelf of bags and hats above, breathing in the musty smell of old shoes and fabric which, in spite of the evident costliness of the contents, evoked an old charity shop. Silently he opened and closed door after door, until, on the fourth attempt, he saw a cluster of clearly brand-new handbags, each of a different color, that had been squeezed on to the high shelf.

He took down the blue one, shop-new and shiny. Here was the GS logo, and the silk lining that was zipped into the bag. He ran his fingers around it, into every corner, then replaced it deftly on the shelf.

He selected the white bag next: the lining was patterned with a stylized African print. Again he ran his fingers all around the interior. Then he unzipped the lining.

It came out, just as Ciara had described, like a metal-edged scarf, exposing the rough interior of the white leather. Nothing was visible inside until he looked more closely, and then he saw the line of pale blue running down the side of the stiff rectangular cloth-covered board holding the base of the bag in shape. He lifted up the board and saw, beneath it, a folded piece of pale blue paper, scribbled all over in an untidy hand.

Strike replaced the bag swiftly on the shelf with the lining bundled inside, and took from an inside pocket of his jacket a clear plastic bag, into which he inserted the pale blue paper, shaken open but unread. He closed the mahogany door and continued to open others. Behind the penultimate door was a safe, operated by a digital keypad.

Strike took a second plastic bag from inside his jacket, slid it over his hand and began to press keys, but before he had completed his trial, he heard movement outside. Hastily thrusting the crumpled bag back into a pocket, he closed the wardrobe door as quietly as possible and walked back into the bedroom, to find the Macmillan nurse bending over Yvette Bristow. She looked around when she heard him.

"Wrong door," said Strike. "I thought it was the bathroom."

He went into the small en-suite, and here, with the door closed, before flushing the toilet and turning on the taps for the nurse's benefit, he read the last will and testament of Lula Landry, scribbled on her mother's writing paper and witnessed by two women. First came the childlike signature of Rochelle Onifade and her address: St. Elmo's Hostel, Hammersmith. Below was the unfamiliar name of Mia Thompson, who had given as her contact address a house in Adelaide. A deep fold just above Mia Thompson's signature told Strike that she had almost certainly not seen what she was signing. The fact that she had given Lula contact details in Australia suggested that she had known her days at Vashti, and in London, were numbered, knowledge that had perhaps emboldened her to burst into Lula Landry's changing room and ask for assistance with a new career.

Yvette Bristow was still lying with her eyes closed when he returned to the bedroom.

"She's asleep," said the nurse, gently. "She does this a lot."

"Yes," said Strike, the blood pounding in his ears. "Please tell her I said goodbye, when she wakes up. I'm going to have to leave now."

They walked together down the comfortable passageway.

"Lady Bristow seems very ill," Strike commented.

"Oh yes, she is," said the nurse. "She could die any time now. She's very poorly."

"I think I might have left my . . ." said Strike vaguely, wandering left into the yellow sitting room he had first visited, leaning over the sofa to block the nurse's view and carefully replacing the telephone receiver he had taken off the hook.

"Yes, here it is," he said, pretending to palm something small and put it in his pocket. "Well, thanks very much for the coffee."

With his hand on the door, he turned to look at her.

"Her Valium addiction's as bad as ever, then?" he said.

Unsuspicious, trusting, the nurse smiled a tolerant smile.

"Yes, it is, but it can't hurt her now. Mind you," she said, "I'd give those doctors a piece of my mind. She's had three of them giving her prescriptions for years, from the labels on the boxes."

"Very unprofessional," said Strike. "Thanks again for the coffee. Goodbye."

He jogged down the stairs, his mobile already out of his pocket, so exhilarated that he did not concentrate on where he was going, so that he took a corner on the stair and let out a bellow of pain as the prosthetic foot slipped on the edge; his knee twisted and he fell, hard and heavy, down six stairs, landing in a heap at the bottom with an excruciating, fiery pain in both the joint and the end of his stump, as though it was freshly severed, as though the scar tissue was still healing.

"Fuck. *Fuck!*"

"Are you all right?" shouted the Macmillan nurse, gazing down at him over the banisters, her face comically inverted.

"I'm fine—fine!" he shouted back. "Slipped! Don't worry! *Fuck, fuck, fuck,*" he moaned under his breath, as he pulled himself back to his feet on the newel post, scared to put his full weight on the prosthesis.

He limped downstairs, leaning on the banisters as much as possible; half hopped across the lobby floor and hung on the heavy front door as he maneuvered himself out on to the front steps.

The sporting children were receding in a distant crocodile, pale and navy blue, winding their way back to their school and lunch. Strike stood leaning against warm brick, cursing himself fluently and wondering what damage he had done. The pain was excruciating, and the skin that had already been irritated felt as though it had been torn; it burned beneath the gel pad that was supposed to protect it, and the idea of walking all the way to the underground was miserably unappealing.

He sat down on the top step and phoned a taxi, after which he made a further series of calls, firstly to Robin, then to Wardle, then to the offices of Landry, May, Patterson.

The black cab swung around the corner. For the very first time, it occurred to Strike how like miniature hearses they were, these stately black vehicles, as he hoisted himself upright and limped, in escalating pain, down to the pavement.

Part Five

Felix qui potuit rerum cognoscere causas.

Lucky is he who has been able to understand the
causes of things

Virgil, *Georgics,* Book 2

1

"I'D HAVE THOUGHT," SAID ERIC Wardle slowly, looking down at the will in its plastic pocket, "you'd have wanted to show this to your client first."

"I would, but he's in Rye," said Strike, "and this is urgent. I've told you, I'm trying to prevent two more murders. We're dealing with a maniac here, Wardle."

He was sweating with pain. Even as he sat here, in the sunlit window of the Feathers, urging the policeman to action, Strike was wondering whether he might have dislocated his knee or fractured the small amount of tibia left to him in the fall down Yvette Bristow's stairwell. He had not wanted to start fiddling with his leg in the taxi, which was now waiting for him at the curb outside. The meter was eating steadily away at the advance Bristow had paid him, of which he would never receive another installment, for today would see an arrest, if only Wardle would rouse himself.

"I grant you, this might show motive..."

"Might?" repeated Strike. "Might? Ten million might constitute a motive? For fuck's—"

"...but I need evidence that'll stand up in court, and you haven't brought me any of that."

"I've just told you where you can find it! Have I been wrong yet? I told you it was a fucking will, and there," Strike jabbed the plastic sleeve, "it fucking is. Get a warrant!"

Wardle rubbed the side of his handsome face as though he had toothache, frowning at the will.

"Jesus Christ," said Strike, "how many more times? Tansy Bestigui was on the balcony, she heard Landry say 'I've already done it'..."

"You put yourself on very thin ice there, mate," said Wardle. "Defense makes mincemeat of lying to suspects. When Bestigui finds out there aren't any photos, he's going to deny everything."

"Let him. She won't. She's ripe to tell anyway. But if you're too much of a pussy to do anything about this, Wardle," said Strike, who could feel cold sweat on his back and a fiery pain in what remained of his right leg, "and anyone else who was close to Landry turns up dead, I'm gonna go straight to the fucking press. I'll tell them I gave you every bit of information I had, and that you had every fucking chance to bring this killer in. I'll make up my fee in selling the rights to my story, and you can pass that message on to Carver for me.

"Here," he said, pushing across the table a piece of torn paper, on which he had scribbled several six-figure numbers. "Try them first. Now get a fucking warrant."

He pushed the will across the table to Wardle and slid off the high bar stool. The walk from the pub to the taxi was agony. The more pressure he put on his right leg, the more excruciating the pain became.

Robin had been calling Strike every ten minutes since one o'clock, but he had not picked up. She rang again as he was climbing, with enormous difficulty, up the metal stairs towards the office, heaving himself up with the use of his arms. She heard his ringtone echoing up the stairwell, and hurried out on to the top landing.

"There you are! I've been calling and calling, there's been loads... What's the matter, are you all right?"

"I'm fine," he lied.

"No you're... What's happened to you?"

She hastened down the stairs towards him. He was white, and sweaty, and looked, in Robin's opinion, as though he might be sick.

"Have you been drinking?"

"No I haven't been bloody drinking!" he snapped. "I've—sorry, Robin. In a bit of pain here. I just need to sit down."

"What's happened? Let me..."

"I've got it. No problem. I can manage."

Slowly he pulled himself to the top landing and limped very heavily to the old sofa. When he dropped his weight into it, Robin thought she heard something deep in the structure crack, and noted, *We'll need a new one,* and then, *But I'm leaving.*

"What happened?" she asked.

"I fell down some stairs," said Strike, panting a little, still wearing his coat. "Like a complete tit."

"What stairs? What happened?"

From the depths of his agony he grinned at her expression, which was part horrified, part excited.

"I wasn't wrestling anyone, Robin. I just slipped."

"Oh, I see. You're a bit—you look a bit pale. You don't think you could have done something serious, do you? I could get a cab—maybe you should see a doctor."

"No need for that. Have we still got any of those painkillers lying around?"

She brought him water and paracetamol. He took them, then stretched out his legs, flinched and asked:

"What's been going on here? Did Graham Hardacre send you a picture?"

"Yes," she said, hurrying to her computer monitor. "Here."

With a shunt of her mouse and a click, the picture of Lieutenant Jonah Agyeman filled the monitor.

In silence, they contemplated the face of a young man whose irrefutable handsomeness was not diminished by the overlarge ears he had inherited from his father. The scarlet, black and gold uniform suited him. His grin was slightly lopsided, his cheekbones high, his jaw square and his skin dark with an undertone of red, like freshly brewed tea. He conveyed the careless charm that Lula Landry had had too; the indefinable quality that made the viewer linger over her image.

"He looks like her," said Robin in a hushed voice.

"Yeah, he does. Anything else been going on?"

Robin seemed to snap back to attention.

"Oh God, yes…John Bristow called half an hour ago, to say he couldn't get hold of you, and Tony Landry's called three times."

"I thought he might. What did he say?"

"He was absolutely—well, the first time, he asked to speak to you, and when I said you weren't here, he hung up before I could give him your mobile number. The second time, he told me you had to call him straightaway, but slammed down the phone before I could tell him you still weren't back. But the third time, he was just—well—he was incredibly angry. Screaming at me."

"He'd better not have been offensive," said Strike, scowling.

"He wasn't really. Well, not to me—it was all about you."

"What did he say?"

"He didn't make a lot of sense, but he called John Bristow a 'stupid prick,' and then he was bawling something about Alison walking out, which he seemed to think had something to do with you, because he was yelling about suing you, and defamation, and all kinds of things."

"Alison's left her job?"

"Yes."

"Did he say where she—no, of course he didn't, why would he know?" he finished, more to himself than to Robin.

He looked down at his wrist. His cheap watch seemed to have hit something when he had fallen downstairs, because it had stopped at a quarter to one.

"What's the time?"

"Ten to five."

"Already?"

"Yes. Do you need anything? I can hang around a bit."

"No, I want you out of here."

His tone was such that instead of going to fetch her coat and hand-bag, Robin remained exactly where she was.

"What are you expecting to happen?"

Strike was busy fiddling with his leg, just below the knee.

"Nothing. You've just worked a lot of overtime lately. I'll bet Matthew will be glad to see you back early for once."

There was no adjusting the prosthesis through his trouser leg.

"Please, Robin, go," he said, looking up.

She hesitated, then went to fetch her trench coat and bag.

"Thanks," he said. "See you tomorrow."

She left. He waited for the sound of her footsteps on the stairs before rolling up his trouser leg, but heard nothing. The glass door opened, and she reappeared.

"You're expecting someone to come," she said, clutching the edge of the door. "Aren't you?"

"Maybe," said Strike, "but it doesn't matter."

He mustered a smile at her tight, anxious expression.

"Don't worry about me." When her expression did not change, he added: "I boxed a bit, in the army, you know."

Robin half laughed.

"Yes, you mentioned that."

"Did I?"

"Repeatedly. That night you . . . you know."

"Oh. Right. Well, it's true."

"But who are you . . . ?"

"Matthew wouldn't thank me for telling you. Go home, Robin, I'll see you tomorrow."

And this time, albeit reluctantly, she left. He waited until he heard the door on to Denmark Street bang shut, then rolled up his trouser leg, detached the prosthesis and examined his swollen knee, and the end of his leg, which was inflamed and bruised. He wondered exactly what he had done to himself, but there was no time to take the problem to an expert tonight.

He half wished, now, that he had asked Robin to fetch him something to eat before she left. Clumsily, hopping from spot to spot, holding on to the desk, the top of the filing cabinet and the arm of the sofa to balance, he managed to make himself a cup of tea. He drank it sitting in Robin's chair, and ate half a packet of digestives, spending most of the time in contemplation of the face of Jonah Agyeman. The paracetamol had barely touched the pain in his leg.

When he had finished all the biscuits, he checked his mobile. There were many missed calls from Robin, and two from John Bristow.

Of the three people who Strike thought might present themselves at his office this evening, it was Bristow he hoped would make it there first. If the police wanted concrete evidence of murder, his client alone (though he might not realize it) could provide it. If either

Tony Landry or Alison Cresswell turned up at his offices, *I'll just have to* . . . then Strike snorted a little in his empty office, because the expression that had occurred to him was "think on my feet."

But six o'clock came, and then half past, and nobody rang the bell. Strike rubbed more cream into the end of his leg, and reattached the prosthesis, which was agony. He limped through into the inner office, emitting grunts of pain, slumped down in his chair and, giving up, took the false leg off again and slid down, to lay his head on his arms, intending to do no more than rest his tired eyes.

2

FOOTSTEPS ON THE METAL STAIRS. Strike sat bolt upright, not knowing whether he had been asleep five minutes or fifty. Somebody rapped on the glass door.

"Come in, it's open!" he shouted, and checked that the unattached prosthesis was covered by his trouser leg.

To Strike's immense relief, it was John Bristow who entered the room, blinking through his thick-lensed glasses and looking agitated.

"Hi, John. Come and sit down."

But Bristow strode towards him, blotchy-faced, as full of rage as he had been the day that Strike had refused to take the case, and gripped the back of the offered chair instead.

"I told you," he said, the color waxing and waning in his thin face as he pointed a bony finger at Strike, "I told you *quite clearly* that I didn't want you to see my mother without me present!"

"I know you did, John, but—"

"She's *unbelievably* upset. I don't know what you said to her, but I've had her crying and sobbing down the phone to me this afternoon!"

"I'm sorry to hear that; she didn't seem to mind my questions when—"

"She's in a dreadful state!" shouted Bristow, his buck teeth glinting. "How *dared* you go and see her without me? How *dared* you?"

"Because, John, as I told you after Rochelle's funeral, I think we're dealing with a murderer who might kill again," said Strike. "The situation's dangerous, and I want an end to it."

"*You* want an end to it? How do you think *I* feel?" shouted Bristow, and his voice cracked and became a falsetto. "Do you have any idea of how much damage you've done? My mother's devastated, and now my girlfriend seems to have vanished into thin air, which Tony is blaming on you! What have you done to Alison? Where is she?"

"I don't know. Have you tried calling her?"

"She's not picking up. What the hell's been going on? I've been on a wild goose chase all day, and I come back——"

"Wild goose chase?" repeated Strike, surreptitiously shifting his leg to keep the prosthesis upright.

Bristow threw himself into the seat opposite, breathing hard and squinting at Strike in the bright evening sun streaming in through the window behind him.

"Somebody," he said furiously, "called my secretary up this morning, purporting to be a very important client of ours in Rye, who was requesting an urgent meeting. I traveled all the way there to find that he's out of the country, and nobody had called me at all. Would you mind," he added, raising a hand to shield his eyes, "pulling down that blind? I can't see a thing."

Strike tugged the cord, and the blind fell with a clatter, casting them both into a cool, faintly striped gloom.

"That's a very strange story," said Strike. "It's almost as though somebody wanted to lure you away from town."

Bristow did not reply. He was glaring at Strike, his chest heaving.

"I've had enough," he said abruptly. "I'm terminating this investigation. You can keep all the money I've given you. I've got to think of my mother."

Strike slid his mobile out of his pocket, pressed a couple of buttons and laid it on his lap.

"Don't you even want to know what I found today in your mother's wardrobe?"

"You went—*you went inside my mother's wardrobe?*"

"Yeah. I wanted to have a look inside those brand-new handbags Lula got, the day she died."

Bristow began to stutter:

"You—you..."

"The bags have got detachable linings. Bizarre idea, isn't it? Hidden under the lining of the white bag was a will, handwritten by Lula on your mother's blue notepaper, and witnessed by Rochelle Oni-fade. I've given it to the police."

Bristow's mouth fell open. For several seconds he seemed unable to speak. Finally he whispered:

"But...what did it say?"

"That she was leaving everything, her entire estate, to her brother, Lieutenant Jonah Agyeman of the Royal Engineers."

"Jonah...who?"

"Go and look on the computer monitor outside. You'll find a picture there."

Bristow got up and moved like a sleepwalker towards the computer in the next room. Strike watched the screen illuminate as Bristow shifted the mouse. Agyeman's handsome face shone out of the monitor, with his sardonic smile, pristine in his dress uniform.

"Oh my God," said Bristow.

He returned to Strike and lowered himself back into the chair, gaping at the detective.

"I—I can't believe it."

"That's the man who was on the CCTV footage," said Strike, "running away from the scene the night that Lula died. He was staying in Clerkenwell with his widowed mother while he was on leave. That's why he was hotfooting it along Theobalds Road twenty minutes later. He was heading home."

Bristow drew breath in a loud gasp.

"They all said I was deluded," he almost shouted. "But I wasn't bloody deluded at all!"

"No, John, you weren't deluded," said Strike. "Not deluded. More like bat-shit insane."

Through the shaded window came the sounds of London, alive at all hours, rumbling and growling, part man, part machine. There was no noise inside the room but Bristow's ragged breathing.

"Excuse me?" he said, ludicrously polite. "What did you call me?"

Strike smiled.

"I said you're bat-shit insane. You killed your sister, got away with it, and then asked me to reinvestigate her death."

"You—you cannot be serious."

"Oh yeah, I can. It's been obvious to me from the start that the person who benefits most from Lula's death is you, John. Ten million quid, once your mother gives up the ghost. Not to be sniffed at, is it? Especially as I don't think you've got much more than your salary, however much you bang on about your trust fund. Albris shares are hardly worth the paper they're written on these days, are they?"

Bristow gaped at him for several long moments; then, sitting up a little straighter, he glanced at the camp bed propped in the corner.

"Coming from a virtual down-and-out who sleeps in his office, I find that a laughable assertion." Bristow's voice was calm and derisory, but his breathing was abnormally fast.

"I know you've got much more money than I have," said Strike. "But, as you rightly point out, that's not saying much. And I will say for myself that I haven't yet stooped to embezzling from clients. How much of Conway Oates's money did you steal before Tony realized what you were up to?"

"Oh, I'm an embezzler too, am I?" said Bristow, with an artificial laugh.

"Yeah, I think so," said Strike. "Not that it matters to me. I don't care whether you killed Lula because you needed to replace the money you'd nicked, or because you wanted her millions, or because you hated her guts. The jury will want to know, though. They're always suckers for motive."

Bristow's knee had begun jiggling up and down again.

"You're unhinged," he said, with another forced laugh. "You've found a will in which she leaves everything not to me, but to *that man.*" He pointed towards the outer room, where he had viewed Jonah's picture. "You tell me that it was that same man who was walking towards Lula's flat, on camera, the night she fell to her death, and who was seen sprinting back past the camera ten minutes later. And yet you accuse me. *Me.*"

"John, you knew before you ever came to see me that it was Jonah on that CCTV footage. Rochelle told you. She was there in Vashti when Lula called Jonah and arranged to meet him that night, and she witnessed a will leaving him everything. She came to you, told you everything and started blackmailing you. She wanted money for a flat and some expensive clothes, and in return she promised to keep her mouth shut about the fact that you weren't Lula's heir.

"Rochelle didn't realize you were the killer. She thought Jonah pushed Lula out of the window. And she was bitter enough, after seeing a will in which she didn't feature, and being dumped in that shop on the last day of Lula's life, not to care about the killer walking free as long as she got the money."

"This is utter rubbish. You're out of your mind."

"You put every obstacle you could in the way of me finding Rochelle," Strike went on, as though he had not heard Bristow. "You pretended you didn't know her name, or where she lived; you acted incredulous that I thought she might be useful to the inquiry and you took photos off Lula's laptop so that I couldn't see what she looked like. True, she could have pointed me directly to the man you were trying to frame for murder, but on the other hand, she knew that there was a will that would deprive you of your inheritance, and your number one objective was to keep that will quiet while you tried to find and destroy it. Bit of a joke, really, it being in your mother's wardrobe all along.

"But even if you'd destroyed it, John, what then? For all you knew, Jonah himself knew that he was Lula's heir. And there was another witness to the fact that there was a will, though you didn't know it: Bryony Radford, the makeup artist."

Strike saw Bristow's tongue flick around his mouth, moistening his lips. He could feel the lawyer's fear.

"Bryony doesn't want to admit that she went snooping through Lula's things, but she saw that will at Lula's place, before Lula had time to hide it. Bryony's dyslexic, though. She thought 'Jonah' said 'John.' She tied that in with Ciara saying that Lula was leaving her brother everything, and concluded that she needn't tell anybody what she'd read on the sly, because you were getting the money anyway. You've had the luck of the devil at times, John.

"But I can see how—to a twisted mind like yours—the best solution to your predicament was to fit Jonah up for murder. If he was doing life, it wouldn't matter whether or not the will ever surfaced—

or whether he, or anyone else, knew about it—because the money would come to you in any case."

"Ridiculous," said Bristow breathlessly. "You ought to give up detecting and try fantasy writing, Strike. You haven't got a shred of proof for anything you're saying—"

"Yes I have." Strike cut across him, and Bristow stopped talking immediately, his pallor visible through the gloom. "The CCTV footage."

"That footage shows Jonah Agyeman running from the scene of the killing, as you've just acknowledged!"

"There was another man caught on camera."

"So he had an accomplice—a lookout."

"I wonder what defending counsel will say is wrong with you, John?" asked Strike softly. "Narcissism? Some kind of God complex? You think you're completely untouchable, don't you, a genius who makes the rest of us look like chimps? The second man running from the scene wasn't Jonah's accomplice, or his lookout, or a car thief. He wasn't even black. He was a white man in black gloves. He was you."

"No," said Bristow. The one word throbbed with panic; but then, with an almost visible effort, he hitched a contemptuous smile back on to his face. "How can it be me? I was in Chelsea with my mother. She told you so. Tony saw me there. I was in Chelsea."

"Your mother is a Valium-addicted invalid who was asleep most of that day. You didn't get back to Chelsea until after you'd killed Lula. I think you went into your mother's room in the small hours, reset her clock and then woke her up, pretending it was dinnertime. You think you're a criminal genius, John, but that's been done a million times before, though rarely with such an easy mark. Your mother hardly knows what day it is, the amount of opiates she's got in her system."

"I was in Chelsea all day," repeated Bristow, his knee jiggling up and down. "All day, except for when I nipped into the office for files."

"You took a hoodie and gloves out of the flat beneath Lula's. You're wearing them in the CCTV footage," said Strike, ignoring the interruption, "and that was a big mistake. That hoodie was unique.

There was only one of them in the world; it had been customized for Deeby Macc by Guy Somé. It could only have come out of the flat beneath Lula's, so we know that's where you'd been."

"You have absolutely no proof," said Bristow. "I am waiting for proof."

"Of course you are," said Strike, simply. "An innocent man wouldn't be sitting here listening to me. He'd have stormed out by now. But don't worry. I've got proof."

"You can't have," said Bristow hoarsely.

"Motive, means and opportunity, John. You had the lot.

"Let's start at the beginning. You don't deny that you went to Lula's first thing in the morning..."

"No, of course not."

"...because people saw you there. But I don't think Lula ever gave you the contract with Somé that you used to get upstairs to see her. I think you'd swiped that at some point previously. Wilson waved you up, and minutes later you were having a shouting match with Lula on her doorstep. You couldn't pretend that didn't happen, because the cleaner overheard it. Fortunately for you, Lechsinka's English is so bad that she confirmed your version of the row: that you were furious that Lula had reunited with her freeloading druggie boyfriend.

"But I think that row was really about Lula's refusal to give you money. All her sharper friends have told me you had quite the reputation for coveting her fortune, but you must have been particularly desperate for a handout that day, to force your way in and start shouting like that. Had Tony noticed a lack of funds in Conway Oates's account? Did you need to replace it urgently?"

"Baseless speculation," said Bristow, his knee still jerking up and down.

"We'll see whether it's baseless or not once we get to court," said Strike.

"I've never denied that Lula and I argued."

"After she refused to hand over a check, and slammed the door in your face, you went back down the stairs, and there was the door to Flat Two standing open. Wilson and the alarm repairman were busy looking at the keypad, and Lechsinka was somewhere in there by then—maybe vacuuming, because that would have helped mask the noise of you creeping into the hall behind the two men.

"It wasn't that much of a risk, really. If they'd turned and seen you, you could have pretended you'd come in to thank Wilson for letting you up. You crossed the hall while they were busy with the alarm fuse box, and you hid somewhere in that big flat. There's loads of space. Empty cupboards. Under the bed."

Bristow was shaking his head in silent denial. Strike continued in the same matter-of-fact tone:

"You must have heard Wilson telling Lechsinka to set the alarm to 1966. Finally, Lechsinka, Wilson and the Securibell guy left, and you had sole possession of the flat. Unfortunately for you, however, Lula had now left the building, so you couldn't go back upstairs and try and bully her into coughing up."

"Total fantasy," said the lawyer. "I never set foot in Flat Two in my life. I left Lula's and went in to the office to pick up files—"

"From Alison, isn't that what you said, the first time we went through your movements that day?" asked Strike.

Patches of pink blossomed again up Bristow's stringy neck. After a small hesitation, he cleared his throat and said:

"I don't remember whether—I just know that I was very quick; I wanted to get back to my mother."

"What effect do you think it's going to have in court, John, when Alison takes the stand and tells the jury how you asked her to lie for you? You played the devastated bereaved brother in front of her, and then asked her out to dinner, and the poor bitch was so delighted to have a chance to look like a desirable female in front of Tony that she agreed. A couple of dates later, you persuaded her to say she saw you at the office on the morning before Lula died. She thought you were just overanxious and paranoid, didn't she? She believed that you already had a cast-iron alibi from her adored Tony, later in the day. She didn't think it mattered if she told a little white lie to calm you down.

"But Alison wasn't there that day, John, to give you any files. Cyprian sent her off to Oxford the moment she got to work, to look for Tony. You became a bit nervous, after Rochelle's funeral, when you realized I knew all about that, didn't you?"

"Alison isn't very bright," said Bristow slowly, his hands washing themselves in dumb show, and his knee jiggling up and down. "She must have confused the days. She clearly misunderstood me. I never asked her to say she saw me at the office. It's her word against mine. Maybe she's trying to revenge herself on me, because we've split up."

Strike laughed.

"Oh, you're definitely dumped, John. After my assistant rang you this morning to lure you to Rye——"

"Your assistant?"

"Yeah, of course; I didn't want you around while I searched your mother's flat, did I? Alison helped us out with the name of the client. I rang her, you see, and told her everything, including the fact that I've got proof that Tony's sleeping with Ursula May, and that you're about to be arrested for murder. That seemed to convince her that she ought to look for a new boyfriend and a new job. I hope she's gone to her mother's place in Sussex—that's what I told her to do. You've been keeping Alison close because you thought she was your fail-safe alibi, and because she's a conduit to knowing what Tony, whom you fear, is thinking. But lately, I've been getting worried that she might outlive her usefulness to you, and fall off something high."

Bristow tried for another scathing laugh, but the sound was artificial and hollow.

"So it turns out that nobody saw you nip into your office for files that morning," continued Strike. "You were still hiding out in the middle flat at number eighteen, Kentigern Gardens."

"I wasn't there. I was in Chelsea, at my mother's," said Bristow.

"I don't think you were planning to murder Lula at that point," Strike continued regardless. "You probably just had some idea of waylaying her again when she came back. Nobody was expecting you at the office that day, because you were supposed to be working from home, to keep your sick mother company. There was a full fridge and you knew how to get in and out without setting off the alarm. You had a clear view of the street, so if Deeby Macc and entourage were to appear, you had plenty of time to get out of there, and walk downstairs with some cock-and-bull story about having been waiting for your sister at her place. The only remote risk was the possibility of deliveries into the flat; but that massive vase of roses arrived without anyone noticing you hiding in there, didn't it?

"I expect the idea of the murder started to germinate then, all those hours you were alone, in all that luxury. Did you start to imagine how wonderful it would be if Lula, who you were sure was intestate, died? You must've known your sick mother would be a much softer touch, especially once you were her only remaining child. And that in itself must have felt great, John, didn't it? The idea of being the only child, at long last? And never losing out again to a better-looking, more lovable sibling?"

Even in the thickening gloom, he could see Bristow's jutting teeth, and the intense stare of the weak eyes.

"No matter how much you've fawned over your mother, and played the devoted son, you've never come first with her, have you? She always loved Charlie most, didn't she? Everyone did, even Uncle Tony. And the moment Charlie had gone, when you might have expected to be the center of attention at last, what happens? Lula arrives, and everyone starts worrying about Lula, looking after Lula, adoring Lula. Your mother hasn't even got a picture of you by her deathbed. Just Charlie and Lula. Just the two she loved."

"Fuck you," snarled Bristow. "Fuck you, Strike. What do you know about anything, with your whore of a mother? What was it she died of, the clap?"

"Nice," said Strike, appreciatively. "I was going to ask you whether you looked into my personal life when you were trying to find some patsy to manipulate. I bet you thought I'd be particularly sympathetic to poor bereaved John Bristow, didn't you, what with my own mother having died young, in suspicious circumstances? You thought you'd be able to play me like a fucking violin...

"But never mind, John. If your defense team can't find a personality disorder for you, I expect they'll argue that your upbringing's to blame. Unloved. Neglected. Overshadowed. Always felt hard done by, haven't you? I noticed it the first day I met you, when you burst into those moving tears at the memory of Lula being carried up the drive into your home, into your life. Your parents hadn't even taken you with them to get her, had they? They left you at home like a pet dog, the son who wasn't enough for them once Charlie had died; the son who was about to come a poor second all over again."

"I don't have to listen to this," whispered Bristow.

"You're free to leave," said Strike, watching the place where he could no longer make out eyes in the deepening shadows behind Bristow's glasses. "Why not leave?"

But the lawyer merely sat there, one knee still jiggling up and down, his hands sliding over each other, waiting to hear Strike's proof.

"Was it easier the second time?" the detective asked quietly. "Was it easier killing Lula than killing Charlie?"

He saw the pale teeth, bared as Bristow opened his mouth, but no sound came out.

"Tony knows you did it, doesn't he? All that bullshit about the hard, cruel things he said after Charlie died. Tony was there; he saw you cycling away from the place where you'd pushed Charlie over. Did you dare him to ride close to the edge? I knew Charlie: he couldn't resist a dare. Tony saw Charlie dead at the bottom of that quarry, and he told your parents that he thought you'd done it, didn't he? That's why your father hit him. That's why your mother fainted. That's why Tony was thrown out of the house after Charlie died: not because Tony said that your mother had raised delinquents, but because he told her she was raising a psychopath."

"This is—No," croaked Bristow. "No!"

"But Tony couldn't face a family scandal. He kept quiet. Panicked a bit when he heard they were adopting a little girl, though, didn't he? He called them and tried to stop it happening. He was right to be worried, wasn't he? I think you've always been a bit scared of Tony. What a fucking irony that he backed himself into a corner where he had to give you an alibi for Lula's murder."

Bristow said nothing at all. He was breathing very fast.

"Tony needed to pretend he was somewhere, anywhere, other than shacked up in a hotel with Cyprian May's wife that day, so he said he doubled back to London to go and visit his sick sister. Then he realized that both you and Lula were supposed to have been there at the same time.

"His niece was dead, so she couldn't contradict him; but he had no choice but to pretend he saw you through the study door, and didn't talk to you. And you backed him up. Both of you, lying through your teeth, wondering what the other one was up to, but too scared to question each other. I think Tony kept telling himself he'd wait until your mother died before he confronted you. Perhaps that's how he kept his conscience quiet. But he's still been worried enough to ask Alison to keep an eye on you. And meanwhile, you've been feeding me that bullshit about Lula hugging you, and the touching reconciliation before she returned home."

"I was there," said Bristow, in a rasping whisper. "I was in my mother's flat. If Tony wasn't there, that's his affair. You can't prove I wasn't."

"I'm not in the business of proving negatives, John. All I'm saying is, you've now lost every alibi except your Valium-addled mother.

"But for the sake of argument, let's assume that while Lula's visiting your groggy mother, and Tony's off fucking Ursula in a hotel somewhere, you're still hiding out in Flat Two, and starting to think out a much more daring solution to your cash-flow problem. You wait. At some point you put on the black leather gloves that have been left in the wardrobe for Deeby, as a precaution against fingerprints. That looks fishy. Almost as though you're starting to contemplate violence.

"Finally, in the early afternoon, Lula comes back home, but unfortunately for you—as you no doubt saw through the peephole of the flat—she's with friends.

"And now," said Strike, his voice hardening, "I think the case against you starts to become serious. A defense of manslaughter—it was an accident, we tussled a bit and she fell over the balcony—might have held water if you hadn't stayed downstairs all that time, while you knew she had visitors. A man with nothing worse on his mind than bullying his sister into giving him a large check might, just might, wait until she was alone again; but you'd already tried that and it hadn't worked. So why not go up there when she was, perhaps, in a better mood, and have a go with the restraining presence of her friends in the next room? Maybe she'd have given you something just to get rid of you?"

Strike could almost feel the waves of fear and hatred emanating from the figure fading into the shadows across the desk.

"But instead," he said, "you waited. You waited all that evening, having watched her leave the building. You must have been pretty tightly wound by then. You'd had time to formulate a rough plan. You'd been watching the street; you knew exactly who was in the building, and who wasn't; you'd worked out that there might just be a means of getting clean away, without anyone being the wiser. And let's not forget—you'd killed before. That makes a difference."

Bristow made a sharp movement, little more than a jerk; Strike tensed, but Bristow remained stationary, and Strike was acutely aware of the unattached prosthesis merely resting against his leg.

"You were watching out of the window and you saw Lula come home alone, but the paparazzi were still out there. You must have despaired at that point, did you?

"But then, miraculously, as though the universe really did want nothing more than to help John Bristow get what he wanted, they all left. I'm pretty sure that Lula's regular driver tipped them off. He's a man who's keen to forge good contacts with the press.

"So now the street's empty. The moment has arrived. You pulled on Deeby's hoodie. Big mistake. But you must admit, with all the lucky breaks you got that night, something had to go wrong.

"And then—and I'm going to give you full marks for this, because it puzzled me for a long time—you took a few of those white roses out of their vase, didn't you? You wiped the ends dry—not quite as thoroughly as you should have done, but pretty well—and you carried them out of Flat Two, leaving the door ajar again, and climbed the stairs to your sister's flat.

"You didn't notice that you'd left a few little drops of water from the roses, by the way. Wilson slipped on them, later.

"You got up to Lula's flat, and you knocked. When she looked through the peephole, what did she see? White roses. She'd been standing on her balcony, with the windows wide open, watching and waiting for her long-lost brother to come down the street, but somehow he seems to have got in without her seeing him! In her excitement, she throws open the door—and you're in."

Bristow was completely still. Even his knee had stopped jiggling.

"And you killed her, just the same way you killed Charlie, just the same way you later killed Rochelle: you pushed her, hard and fast—maybe you lifted her—but she was caught by surprise, wasn't she, just like the others?

"You were yelling at her for not giving you money, for depriving you, just as you've always been deprived, haven't you, John, of your portion of parental love.

"She yelled at you that you wouldn't get a penny, even if you killed her. As you fought, and you forced her across her sitting room towards that balcony and the drop, she told you she had another brother, a real brother, and that he was on his way, and that she'd made a will in his favor.

" 'It's too late, I've already done it!' she screamed. And you called her a lying fucking bitch, and you threw her down into the street to her death."

Bristow was barely breathing.

"I think you must have dropped the roses at her front door. You ran back out, picked them up, sprinted down the stairs and back into Flat Two, where you rammed them back into their vase. Fuck me, you were lucky. That vase got smashed accidentally by a copper, and those roses were the one clue to show that someone had been in that flat; you can't have replaced them the way the florist had arranged them, not when you knew you had minutes to get clear of that building.

"The next bit took nerve. I doubt you expected anyone to raise the alarm straight away, but Tansy Bestigui had been on the balcony below you. You heard her screaming, and realized you had even less time to get out of there than you'd been counting on. Wilson ran out to the street to check Lula, and then, waiting at the door, staring through the peephole, you saw him run upstairs to the top floor.

"You reset the alarm, let yourself out of the flat and edge down the stairwell. The Bestiguis are bellowing at each other in their own flat. You run downstairs—heard by Freddie Bestigui, though he had other preoccupations at the time—the lobby's empty—you run through it and out on to the street, where it's snowing thick and fast.

"And you ran, didn't you; hoodie up, face covered, gloved hands pumping. And at the end of the street, you saw another man running, running for his life, away from the corner where he'd just seen his sister fall to her death. You didn't know each other. I don't think you had a thought to spare for who he was, not then. You ran as fast as you could, in Deeby Macc's borrowed clothes, past the CCTV camera that caught you both on film, and off down Halliwell Street, where your luck caught up with you again, and there were no more cameras.

"I expect you chucked the hoodie and the gloves in a bin and grabbed a taxi, did you? The police never bothered looking for a suited white man who was out and about that night. You went home to your mother's, you made food for her, you changed the time on her clock and you woke her up. She's still convinced that the two of you were talking about Charlie—nice touch, John—at the precise moment that Lula plunged to her death.

"You got away with it, John. You could have afforded to keep paying Rochelle for life. With your luck, Jonah Agyeman might even have died in Afghanistan; you've been getting your hopes up every time you've seen a picture of a black soldier in the paper, haven't you? But you didn't want to trust to luck. You're a twisted, arrogant fucker, and you thought you could arrange things better."

There was a long silence.

"No proof," said Bristow, at last. It was so dark in the office now that he was barely more than a silhouette to Strike. "No proof at all."

"I'm afraid you're wrong there," said Strike. "The police should have got a warrant by now."

"For what?" asked Bristow, and he finally felt confident enough to laugh. "To search the bins of London for a hoodie that you say was thrown away three months ago?"

"No, to look in your mother's safe, of course."

Strike was wondering whether he could raise the blind quickly enough. He was a long way from a light switch, and the office was very dark, but he did not want to take his eyes off Bristow's shadowy figure. He was sure that this triple murderer would not have come unprepared.

"I've given them a few combinations to try," Strike went on. "If they don't work, I suppose they'll have to call in an expert to open it. But if I were a betting man, I'd put my money on 030483."

A rustle, the blur of a pale hand, and Bristow lunged. The knife point grazed Strike's chest as he slammed Bristow sideways; the lawyer slid off the desk, rolled over and attacked again, and this time Strike fell over backwards in his chair, with Bristow on top of him, trapped between the wall and the desk.

Strike had one of Bristow's wrists, but he couldn't see where the knife was: all was darkness, and he threw a punch that hit Bristow hard under the chin, knocking his head back and sending his glasses flying; Strike punched again, and Bristow hit the wall; Strike tried to sit up, with Bristow's lower body pinning his agonizing half-leg to the ground, and the knife struck him hard in the upper arm: he felt it pierce the flesh, and the flow of warm blood, and the white-hot stinging pain.

He saw Bristow raise his arm in dim silhouette against the faint window; forcing himself up against the lawyer's weight, he deflected the second knife blow, and with an almighty effort managed to throw the lawyer off, and the prosthesis slid out of his trouser leg as he tried to pin Bristow down, with his hot blood spattering over everything, and no knowledge of where the knife was now.

The desk was knocked over by Strike's wrestling weight, and then, as he knelt with his good knee on Bristow's thin chest, groping with his good hand to find the knife, light split his retinas in two, and a woman was screaming.

Dazzled, Strike glimpsed the knife rising to his stomach; he seized the prosthetic leg beside him and brought it down like a club on Bristow's face, once, twice—

"Stop! Cormoran, STOP! YOU'RE GOING TO KILL HIM!"

Strike rolled off Bristow, who was no longer moving, dropped the prosthetic leg and lay on his back, clutching his bleeding arm beside the overturned desk.

"I thought," he panted, unable to see Robin, "I told you to go home?"

But she was already on the telephone.

"Police and ambulance!"

"And get a taxi," Strike croaked from the floor, his throat dry from so much talking. "I'm not traveling to hospital with this piece of shit."

He stretched out an arm and retrieved the mobile that lay several feet away. The face was smashed, but it was still recording.

Epilogue

Nihil est ab omni
  Parte beatum.

Nothing is an unmixed blessing.

Horace, *Odes,* Book 2

Ten Days Later

THE BRITISH ARMY REQUIRES OF its soldiers a subjugation of individual needs and ties that is almost incomprehensible to the civilian mind. It recognizes virtually no claims higher than its own; and the unpredictable crises of human life—births and deaths, weddings, divorces and illness—generally cause no more deviation to the military's plans than pebbles pinging on the underbelly of a tank. Nevertheless, there are exceptional circumstances, and it was due to one such circumstance that Lieutenant Jonah Agyeman's second tour of duty in Afghanistan was cut short.

His presence in Britain was urgently required by the Metropolitan Police, and while the army does not generally rate the claims of the Met higher than its own, in this case it was prepared to be helpful. The circumstances surrounding the death of Agyeman's sister were garnering international attention, and a media storm around a hitherto obscure Sapper was deemed unhelpful both to the individual and the army he served. And so Jonah was put on a plane back to Britain, where the army did its impressive best to shield him from the ravenous press.

It was assumed by considerable numbers of the news-reading public that Lieutenant Agyeman would be delighted, firstly to be home from combat, and secondly to have returned to the prospect of wealth beyond his wildest imaginings.

Mia Thompson had already been tracked by the press to her parents' house in Adelaide, where she had confirmed in a blaze of publicity that she had had no idea what she was signing that day in the changing room. The will, in consequence, was invalid. Nevertheless, it seemed certain that Lula's last wishes would be honored by her family. The dying Yvette Bristow was of the same opinion as the news-reading public: if anyone was to inherit a fortune it ought to be the young soldier, not the uncle who was now known to have concealed crucial evidence in his niece's murder and to be a philanderer to boot. Jonah, in short, would shortly be in possession of the ten million pounds for which his sister had been murdered.

However much the public might assume this prospect to gladden the young Sapper's heart, the soldier whom Cormoran Strike met in the Tottenham pub one lunchtime, ten days after the arrest of his sister's killer, was almost truculent, and seemed still to be in a state of shock.

The two men had, for different periods of time, lived the same life, and risked the same death. It was a bond that no civilian could understand, and for half an hour they talked about nothing but the army.

"You were a Suit, yeah?" Agyeman said. "Trust a Suit to fuck up my whole life."

Strike smiled. He saw no ingratitude in Agyeman, even though the stitches in his arm pulled painfully every time he raised his pint.

"My mother wants me to come out," said the soldier. "She keeps saying, that'll be one good thing to come out of this mess."

It was the first, oblique reference to the reason they were here, and that Jonah was not where he belonged, with his regiment, in the life he had chosen.

Then, quite suddenly, he began to talk, as though he had been waiting for Strike for months.

"She never knew my dad had another kid. He never told her. He was never even sure that Marlene woman was telling the truth about being pregnant. Right before he died, when he knew he had days left, he told me. 'Don't upset your mother,' he said. 'I'm telling you this because I'm dying, and I don't know whether you've got a half-brother or sister out there.' He said the mother had been white, and that she'd disappeared. She might have aborted it. Fuck me. If you'd known my dad. Never missed a Sunday at church. Took communion on his deathbed. I'd never expected anything like that, never.

"I was never even going to say anything to her about Dad and this woman. But then, out of the blue, I get this phone call. Thank Christ I was there, on leave. Only, Lula," he said her name tentatively, as though he was not sure whether he had the right to it, "said she'd've hung up if it'd been my mum. She said she didn't want to hurt anyone. She sounded all right."

"I think she was," said Strike.

"Yeah... but fuck me, it was weird. Would you believe it if some supermodel called you up and told you she was your sister?"

Strike thought of his own bizarre family history.

"Probably," he said.

"Yeah, well, I suppose. Why would she lie? That's what I thought, anyway. So I gave her my mobile number and we talked a few times, when she could hook up with her friend Rochelle. She had it all figured out, so the press wouldn't find out. Suited me. I didn't want my mother upset."

Agyeman had pulled out a packet of Lambert and Butler cigarettes and was turning the box nervously in his fingers. They would have been bought cheap, Strike thought, with a small pang of remembrance, at the NAAFI.

"So she phones me up the day before it—it happened," Jonah continued, "and she was begging me to come over. I'd already told her I couldn't meet her that leave. Man, the situation was doing my head in. My sister the supermodel. Mum was worried about me leaving for Helmand. I couldn't spring it on her, that Dad had had another kid. Not then. So I told Lula I couldn't see her.

"She begged me to meet her before I left. She sounded upset. I said maybe I could get out later, you know, after Mum was in bed. I'd tell her I was going out for a quick drink with a mate or something. She told me to come really late, like at half one.

"So," said Jonah, scratching the back of his neck uncomfortably, "I went. I was on the corner of her road... and I saw it happen."

He wiped his hand across his mouth.

"I ran. I just ran. I didn't know what the hell to think. I didn't want to be there, I didn't want to have to explain anything to anyone. I knew she'd had mental problems, and I remembered how upset she'd been on the phone, and I thought, did she lure me here to see her jump?

"I couldn't sleep. I was glad to leave, to tell you the truth. To get away from all the fucking news coverage."

The pub buzzed around them, crowded with lunchtime customers.

"I think the reason she wanted to meet you so badly was because of what her mother had just told her," Strike said. "Lady Bristow had taken a lot of Valium. I'm guessing she wanted to make the girl feel too bad to leave her, so she told Lula what Tony had said about John all those years before: that he pushed his younger brother Charlie into that quarry, and killed him.

"That's why Lula was in such a state when she left her mother's flat, and that's why she kept trying to call her uncle and find out whether there was any truth in the story. And I think she was desperate to see you, because she wanted someone, anyone, she could love and trust. Her mother was difficult and dying, she hated her uncle, and she'd just been told her adoptive brother was a killer. She must have been desperate. And I think she was scared. The day before she died, Bristow had tried to force her to give him money. She must have been wondering what he'd do next."

The pub clattered and rang with talk and clinking glasses, but Jonah's voice sounded clearly over all of it.

"I'm glad you broke the bastard's jaw."

"And his nose," said Strike cheerfully. "It's lucky he'd stuck a knife in me, or I might not have got off with 'reasonable force.' "

"He came armed," said Jonah thoughtfully.

" 'Course he did," said Strike. "I'd had my secretary tip him off, at Rochelle's funeral, that I was getting death threats from a nutter who wanted to slit me open. That planted the seed in his head. He thought, if it came to it, he'd try and pass off my death as the work of poor old Brian Mathers. Then, presumably, he'd have gone home, doctored his mother's clock and tried to pull the same trick all over again. He's not sane. Which isn't to say he's not a clever fucker."

There seemed little more to say. As they left the pub, Agyeman, who had bought the drinks with nervous insistence, made what might have been a tentative offer of money to Strike, whose impecunious existence had padded out much of the media coverage. Strike cut the offer short, but he was not offended. He could see that the young Sapper was struggling to deal with the idea of his enormous new wealth; that he was buckling under the responsibility of it, the demands it made, the appeals it attracted, the decisions it entailed; that he was much more overawed than glad. There was also, of course, the horrible and ever-present knowledge of how his millions had come to him. Strike guessed that Jonah Agyeman's thoughts were flitting wildly between his comrades back in Afghanistan, visions of sports cars and of his half-sister lying dead in the snow. Who was more conscious than the soldier of capricious fortune, of the random roll of the dice?

"He won't get off, will he?" asked Agyeman suddenly, as they were about to part.

"No, of course not," said Strike. "The papers haven't got it yet, but the police found Rochelle's mobile phone in his mother's safe. He didn't dare get rid of it. He'd reset the code of the safe so that no one could get in but him: 030483. Easter Sunday, nineteen eighty-three: the day he killed my mate Charlie."

It was Robin's last day. Strike had invited her to come with him to meet Jonah Agyeman, whom she had done so much to find, but she had refused. Strike had the feeling that she was deliberately withdrawing from the case, from the work, from him. He had an appointment at the Amputee Center at Queen Mary's Hospital that afternoon; she would be gone by the time he returned from Roehampton. Matthew was taking her to Yorkshire for the weekend.

As Strike limped back to the office through the continuing chaos of the building work, he wondered whether he would ever see his temporary secretary again after today, and doubted it. Not so very long ago, the impermanence of their arrangement had been the only thing that reconciled him to her presence, but now he knew that he would miss her. She had come with him in the taxi to the hospital, and wrapped her trench coat around his bleeding arm.

The explosion of publicity around Bristow's arrest had done Strike's business no harm at all. He might even genuinely need a secretary before long; and indeed, as he made his way painfully up the stairs to his office, he heard Robin's voice on the telephone.

"...an appointment for Tuesday, I'm afraid, because Mr. Strike's busy all day Monday...Yes...absolutely...I'll put you down for eleven o'clock, then. Yes. Thank you. Goodbye."

She swung around on her swivel chair as Strike entered.

"What was Jonah like?" she demanded.

"Nice guy," said Strike, lowering himself into the collapsed sofa. "Situation's doing his head in. But the alternative was Bristow winding up with ten mill, so he'll have to cope."

"Three prospective clients phoned while you were out," she said, "but I'm a bit worried about that last one. He could be another journalist. He was much more interested in discussing you than his own problem."

There had been quite a few such calls. The press had seized with glee upon a story that had angles aplenty, and everything they loved best. Strike himself had featured heavily in the coverage. The photograph they had used most, and he was glad of it, was ten years old and had been taken while he was still a Red Cap; but they had also dug out the picture of the rock star, his wife and the supergroupie.

There had been plenty written about police incompetence; Carver had been snapped hurrying down the street, his jacket flying, the sweat patches just visible on his shirt; but Wardle, handsome Wardle, who had helped Strike bring Bristow in, had so far been treated with indulgence, especially by female journalists. Mostly, however, the news media had feasted all over again on the corpse of Lula Landry; every version of the story sparkling with pictures of the dead model's flawless face, and her lithe and sculpted body.

Robin was talking; Strike had not been listening, his attention diverted by the throbbing in his arm and leg.

"...a note of all the files and your diary. Because you'll need someone, now, you know; you're not going to be able to take care of all this on your own."

"No," he agreed, struggling to his feet; he had intended to do this later, at the moment of her departure, but now was as good a moment as any, and it made an excuse to leave the sofa, which was extremely uncomfortable. "Listen, Robin, I haven't ever said a proper thank-you..."

"Yes you have," she said hurriedly. "In the cab on the way to the hospital—and anyway, there's no need. I've enjoyed it. I've loved it, actually."

He was hobbling away into the inner office, and did not hear the catch in her voice. The present was hidden at the bottom of his kit-bag. It was very badly wrapped.

"Here," he said. "This is for you. I couldn't have done it without you."

"Oh," said Robin, on a strangled note, and Strike was both touched and faintly alarmed to see tears spill down her cheeks. "You didn't have to..."

"Open it at home," he said, but too late; the package was literally coming apart in her hands. Something slithered, poison-green, out of the split in the paper, on to the desk in front of her. She gasped.

"You...oh my God, Cormoran..."

She held up the dress she had tried on, and loved, in Vashti, and stared at him over the top of it, pink-faced, her eyes sparkling.

"You can't afford this!"

"Yeah, I can," he said, leaning back against the partition wall, because it was marginally more comfortable than sitting on the sofa. "Work's rolling in now. You've been incredible. Your new place is lucky to get you."

She was frantically mopping her eyes with the sleeves of her shirt. A sob and some incomprehensible words escaped her. She reached blindly for the tissues that she had bought from petty cash, in anticipation of more clients like Mrs. Hook, blew her nose, wiped her eyes and said, with the green dress lying limp and forgotten across her lap:

"I don't want to go!"

"I can't afford you, Robin," he said flatly.

It was not that he had not thought about it; the night before, he had lain awake on the camp bed, running calculations through his mind, trying to come up with an offer that might not seem insulting beside the salary offered by the media consultancy. It was not possible. He could no longer defer payment on the largest of his loans; he was facing an increase in rent and he needed to find somewhere to live other than his office. While his short-term prospects were immeasurably improved, the outlook remained uncertain.

"I wouldn't expect you to match what they'd give me," Robin said thickly.

"I couldn't come close," said Strike.

(But she knew the state of Strike's finances almost as well as he did and had already guessed at the most she could expect. The previous evening, when Matthew had found her in tears at the prospect of leaving, she had told him her estimate of Strike's best offer.

"But he hasn't offered you anything at all," Matthew had said. "Has he?"

"No, but if he did..."

"Well, it would be up to you," Matthew had said stiffly. "It'd be your choice. You'd have to decide."

She knew that Matthew did not want her to stay. He had sat for hours in Casualty while they stitched Strike up, waiting to take Robin home. He had told her, rather formally, that she had done very well, showing such initiative, but he had been distant and faintly disapproving ever since, especially when their friends clamored for the inside details on everything that had appeared in the press.

But surely Matthew would like Strike, if only he met him? And Matthew himself had said that it was up to her what she did...)

Robin drew herself up a little, blew her nose again and told Strike, with calmness slightly undermined by a small hiccough, the figure for which she would be happy to stay.

It took Strike a few seconds to respond. He could just afford to pay what she had suggested; it was within five hundred pounds of what he himself had calculated that he could manage. She was, whichever way you looked at it, an asset that it would be impossible to replace at the price. There was only one tiny fly in the ointment...

"I could manage that," he said. "Yeah. I could pay you that."

The telephone rang. Beaming at him, she answered it, and the delight in her voice was such that it sounded as though she had been eagerly anticipating the call for days.

"Oh, hullo, Mr. Gillespie! How are you? Mr. Strike's just sent you a check, I put it in the post myself this morning...All the arrears, yes, and a little bit more...Oh no, Mr. Strike's adamant he wants to pay off the loan...Well, that's very kind of Mr. Rokeby, but Mr. Strike would rather pay. He's hopeful he'll be able to clear the full amount within the next few months..."

An hour later, as Strike sat on a hard plastic chair at the Amputee Center, his injured leg stretched in front of him, he reflected that if he had known that Robin was going to stay, he would not have bought her the green dress. The gift would not, he was sure, find favor with Matthew, especially once he had seen her in it, and heard that she had previously modeled it for Strike.

With a sigh, he reached for a copy of *Private Eye* lying on the table beside him. When the consultant first called him, Strike did not respond; he was immersed in the page headed "LandryBalls," crammed with examples of journalistic excess relating to the case that he and Robin had solved. So many columnists had mentioned Cain and Abel that the magazine had run a special feature.

"Mr. Strick?" shouted the consultant, for the second time. "Mr. Cameron Strick?"

He looked up, grinning.

"Strike," he said clearly. "My name's Cormoran Strike."

"Oh, I do apologize...this way..."

As Strike limped after the doctor, a phrase floated up out of his subconscious, a phrase he had read long before he had seen his first dead body, or marveled at a waterfall in an African mountainside, or watched the face of a killer collapsing as he realized he was caught.

I am become a name.

"On to the table, please, and take off the prosthesis."

Where had it come from, that phrase? Strike lay back on the table and frowned up at the ceiling, ignoring the consultant now bending over the remainder of his leg, muttering as he stared and gently prodded.

It took minutes to dredge up the lines Strike had learned so long ago.

I cannot rest from travel: I will drink
Life to the lees; all times I have enjoy'd
Greatly, have suffer'd greatly, both with those
That loved me, and alone; on shore and when
Thro' scudding drifts the rainy Hyades
Vext the dim sea: I am become a name . . .

ABOUT THE AUTHOR

Robert Galbraith is a pseudonym for J.K. Rowling, author of the Harry Potter series and *The Casual Vacancy*. The Cormoran Strike series continues with the novels *The Silkworm* and *Career or Evil*.

ABOUT *THE SILKWORM*

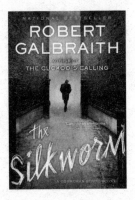

This second novel in the highly acclaimed series featuring Cormoran Strike and his determined young assistant, Robin Ellacott, is a compulsively readable crime novel with twists at every turn.

Following is an excerpt from the novel's opening pages.

1

QUESTION
What dost thou feed on?
ANSWER
Broken sleep.

Thomas Dekker, *The Noble Spanish Soldier*

"SOMEONE BLOODY FAMOUS," SAID THE hoarse voice on the end of the line, "better've died, Strike."

The large unshaven man tramping through the darkness of pre-dawn, with his telephone clamped to his ear, grinned.

"It's in that ballpark."

"It's six o'clock in the fucking morning!"

"It's half past, but if you want what I've got, you'll need to come and get it," said Cormoran Strike. "I'm not far away from your place. There's a—"

"How d'you know where I live?" demanded the voice.

"You told me," said Strike, stifling a yawn. "You're selling your flat."

"Oh," said the other, mollified. "Good memory."

"There's a twenty-four-hour caff—"

"Fuck that. Come into the office later—"

"Culpepper, I've got another client this morning, he pays better than you do and I've been up all night. You need this now if you're going to use it."

A groan. Strike could hear the rustling of sheets.

"It had better be shit-hot."

"Smithfield Café on Long Lane," said Strike and rang off.

The slight unevenness in his gait became more pronounced as he walked down the slope towards Smithfield Market, monolithic in the winter darkness, a vast rectangular Victorian temple to meat, where from four every weekday morning animal flesh was unloaded, as it had been for centuries past, cut, parceled and sold to butchers and restaurants across London. Strike could hear voices through the gloom, shouted instructions and the growl and beep of reversing lorries unloading the carcasses. As he entered Long Lane, he became merely one among many heavily muffled men moving purposefully about their Monday-morning business.

A huddle of couriers in fluorescent jackets cupped mugs of tea in their gloved hands beneath a stone griffin standing sentinel on the corner of the market building. Across the road, glowing like an open fireplace against the surrounding darkness, was the Smithfield Café, open twenty-four hours a day, a cupboard-sized cache of warmth and greasy food.

The café had no bathroom, but an arrangement with the bookies a few doors along. Ladbrokes would not open for another three hours, so Strike made a detour down a side alley and in a dark doorway relieved himself of a bladder bulging with weak coffee drunk in the course of a night's work. Exhausted and hungry, he turned at last, with the pleasure that only a man who has pushed himself past his physical limits can ever experience, into the fat-laden atmosphere of frying eggs and bacon.

Two men in fleeces and waterproofs had just vacated a table. Strike maneuvered his bulk into the small space and sank, with a grunt of satisfaction, onto the hard wood and steel chair. Almost before he asked, the Italian owner placed tea in front of him in a tall white mug, which came with triangles of white buttered bread. Within five minutes a full English breakfast lay before him on a large oval plate.

Strike blended well with the strong men banging their way in and out of the café. He was large and dark, with dense, short, curly hair that had receded a little from the high, domed forehead that topped a boxer's broad nose and thick, surly brows. His jaw was grimy with stubble and bruise-colored shadows enlarged his dark eyes. He ate gazing dreamily at the market building opposite. The nearest arched entrance, numbered two, was taking substance as the darkness thinned: a stern stone face, ancient and bearded, stared back at him from over the doorway. Had there ever been a god of carcasses?

He had just started on his sausages when Dominic Culpepper arrived. The journalist was almost as tall as Strike but thin, with a choirboy's complexion. A strange asymmetry, as though somebody had given his face a counterclockwise twist, stopped him being girlishly handsome.

"This better be good," Culpepper said as he sat down, pulled off his gloves and glanced almost suspiciously around the café.

"Want some food?" asked Strike through a mouthful of sausage.

"No," said Culpepper.

"Rather wait till you can get a croissant?" asked Strike, grinning.

"Fuck off, Strike."

It was almost pathetically easy to wind up the ex–public schoolboy, who ordered tea with an air of defiance, calling the indifferent waiter (as Strike noted with amusement) "mate."

"Well?" demanded Culpepper, with the hot mug in his long pale hands.

Strike fished in his overcoat pocket, brought out an envelope and slid it across the table. Culpepper pulled out the contents and began to read.

"Fucking hell," he said quietly, after a while. He shuffled feverishly through the bits of paper, some of which were covered in Strike's own writing. "Where the hell did you get this?"

Strike, whose mouth was full of sausage, jabbed a finger at one of the bits of paper, on which an office address was scribbled.

"His very fucked-off PA," he said, when he had finally swallowed. "He's been shagging her, as well as the two you know about. She's only just realized she's not going to be the next Lady Parker."

"How the hell did you find *that* out?" asked Culpepper, staring up at Strike over the papers trembling in his excited hands.

"Detective work," said Strike thickly, through another bit of sausage. "Didn't your lot used to do this, before you started outsourcing to the likes of me? But she's got to think about her future employment prospects, Culpepper, so she doesn't want to appear in the story, all right?"

Culpepper snorted.

"She should've thought about that before she nicked—"

With a deft movement, Strike tweaked the papers out of the journalist's fingers.

"She didn't nick them. He got her to print this lot off for him this afternoon. The only thing she's done wrong is show it to me. But if you're going to splash her private life all over the papers, Culpepper, I'll take 'em back."

"Piss off," said Culpepper, making a grab for the evidence of wholesale tax evasion clutched in Strike's hairy hand. "All right, we'll leave her out of it. But he'll know where we got it. He's not a complete tit."

"What's he going to do, drag her into court where she can spill the beans about every other dodgy thing she's witnessed over the last five years?"

"Yeah, all right," sighed Culpepper after a moment's reflection. "Give 'em back. I'll leave her out of the story, but I'll need to speak to her, won't I? Check she's kosher."

"*Those* are kosher. You don't need to speak to her," said Strike firmly.

The shaking, besotted, bitterly betrayed woman whom he had just left would not be safe left alone with Culpepper. In her savage desire for retribution against a man who had promised her marriage and children she would damage herself and her prospects beyond repair. It had not taken Strike long to gain her trust. She was nearly forty-two; she had thought that she was going to have Lord Parker's children; now a kind of bloodlust had her in its grip. Strike had sat with her for several hours, listening to the story of her infatuation, watching her pace her sitting room in tears, rock backwards and forwards on her sofa, knuckles to her forehead. Finally she had agreed to this: a betrayal that represented the funeral of all her hopes.

"You're going to leave her out of it," said Strike, holding the papers firmly in a fist that was nearly twice the size of Culpepper's. "Right? This is still a fucking massive story without her."

After a moment's hesitation and with a grimace, Culpepper caved in. "Yeah, all right. Give me them."

The journalist shoved the statements into an inside pocket and gulped his tea, and his momentary disgruntlement at Strike seemed to fade in the glorious prospect of dismantling the reputation of a British peer.

"Lord Parker of Pennywell," he said happily under his breath, "you are well and truly screwed, mate."

"I take it your proprietor'll get this?" Strike asked, as the bill landed between them.

"Yeah, yeah ..."

Culpepper threw a ten-pound note down onto the table and the two men left the café together. Strike lit up a cigarette as soon as the door had swung closed behind them.

"How did you get her to talk?" Culpepper asked as they set off together through the cold, past the motorbikes and lorries still arriving at and departing the market.

"I listened," said Strike.

Culpepper shot him a sideways glance.

"All the other private dicks I use spend their time hacking phone messages."

"Illegal," said Strike, blowing smoke into the thinning darkness.

"So how—?"

"You protect your sources and I'll protect mine."

They walked fifty yards in silence, Strike's limp more marked with every step.

"This is going to be massive. Massive," said Culpepper gleefully. "That hypocritical old shit's been bleating on about corporate greed and he's had twenty mill stashed in the Cayman Islands ... "

"Glad to give satisfaction," said Strike. "I'll email you my invoice."

Culpepper threw him another sideways look.

"See Tom Jones's son in the paper last week?" he asked.

"Tom Jones?"

"Welsh singer," said Culpepper.

"Oh, him," said Strike, without enthusiasm. "I knew a Tom Jones in the army."

"Did you see the story?"

"No."

"Nice long interview he gave. He says he's never met his father, never had a word from him. I bet he got more than your bill is going to be."

"You haven't seen my invoice yet," said Strike.

"Just saying. One nice little interview and you could take a few nights off from interviewing secretaries."

"You're going to have to stop suggesting this," said Strike, "or I'm going to have to stop working for you, Culpepper."

"Course," said Culpepper, "I could run the story anyway. Rock star's estranged son is a war hero, never knew his father, working as a private—"

"Instructing people to hack phones is illegal as well, I've heard."

At the top of Long Lane they slowed and turned to face each other. Culpepper's laugh was uneasy.

"I'll wait for your invoice, then."

"Suits me."

They set off in different directions, Strike heading towards the Tube station.

"Strike!" Culpepper's voice echoed through the darkness behind him. "Did you fuck her?"

"Looking forward to reading it, Culpepper," Strike shouted wearily, without turning his head.

He limped into the shadowy entrance of the station and was lost to Culpepper's sight.

2

How long must we fight? for I cannot stay,
Nor will not stay! I have business.

Francis Beaumont and Philip Massinger,
The Little French Lawyer

THE TUBE WAS FILLING UP already. Monday-morning faces: sagging, gaunt, braced, resigned. Strike found a seat opposite a puffy-eyed young blonde whose head kept sinking sideways into sleep. Again and again she jerked herself back upright, scanning the blurred signs of the stations frantically in case she had missed her stop.

The train rattled and clattered, speeding Strike back towards the meager two and a half rooms under a poorly insulated roof that he called home. In the depths of his tiredness, surrounded by these blank, sheep-like visages, he found himself pondering the accidents that had brought all of them into being. Every birth was, viewed properly, mere chance. With a hundred million sperm swimming blindly through the darkness, the odds against a person becoming themselves were staggering. How many of this Tube-full had been planned, he wondered, light-headed with tiredness. And how many, like him, were accidents?

There had been a little girl in his primary school class who had a port-wine stain across her face and Strike had always felt a secret kinship with her, because both of them had carried something indelibly different with them since birth, something that was not their fault. They couldn't see it, but everybody else could, and had the bad manners to keep mentioning it. The occasional fascination of total strangers, which at five years old he had thought had something to do with his own uniqueness, he eventually realized was because they saw him as no more than a famous singer's zygote, the incidental evidence of a celebrity's unfaithful fumble. Strike had only met his biological father twice. It had taken a DNA test to make Jonny Rokeby accept paternity.

Dominic Culpepper was a walking distillation of the prurience and presumptions that Strike met on the very rare occasions these days that anybody connected the surly-looking ex-soldier with the aging rock star. Their thoughts leapt at once to trust funds and handsome handouts, to private flights and VIP lounges, to a multi-millionaire's largesse on tap. Agog at the modesty of Strike's existence and the punishing hours he worked, they asked themselves: what must Strike have done to alienate his father? Was he faking penury to wheedle more money out of Rokeby? What had he done with the millions his mother had surely squeezed out of her rich paramour?

And at such times, Strike would think nostalgically of the army, of the anonymity of a career in which your background and your parentage counted for almost nothing beside your ability to do the job. Back in the Special Investigation Branch, the most personal question he had faced on introduction was a request to repeat the odd pair of names with which his extravagantly unconventional mother had saddled him.

Traffic was already rolling busily along Charing Cross Road by the time Strike emerged from the Tube. The November dawn was breaking now, gray and halfhearted, full of lingering shadows. He turned into Denmark Street feeling drained and sore, looking forward to the short sleep he might be able to squeeze in before his next client arrived at nine thirty. With a wave at the girl in the guitar shop, with whom he often took cigarette breaks on the street, Strike let himself in through the black outer door beside the 12 Bar Café and began to climb the metal staircase that curled around the broken birdcage lift inside. Up past the graphic designer on the first floor, past his own office with its engraved glass door on the second; up to the third and smallest landing where his home now lay.

The previous occupant, manager of the bar downstairs, had moved on to more salubrious quarters and Strike, who had been sleeping in his office for a few months, had leapt at the chance to rent the place, grateful for such an easy solution to the problem of his homelessness. The space under the eaves was small by any standards, and especially for a man of six foot three. He scarcely had room to turn around in the shower; kitchen and living room were uneasily combined and the bedroom was almost entirely filled by the double bed. Some of Strike's possessions remained boxed up on the landing, in spite of the landlord's injunction against this.

His small windows looked out across rooftops, with Denmark Street far below. The constant throb of the bass from the bar below was muffled to the point that Strike's own music often obliterated it.

Strike's innate orderliness was manifest throughout: the bed was made, the crockery clean, everything in its place. He needed a shave and shower, but that could wait; after hanging up his overcoat, he set his alarm for nine twenty and stretched out on the bed fully clothed.

He fell asleep within seconds and within a few more—or so it seemed—he was awake again. Somebody was knocking on his door.

"I'm sorry, Cormoran, I'm really sorry—"

His assistant, a tall young woman with long strawberry-blond hair, looked apologetic as he opened the door, but at the sight of him her expression became appalled.

"Are you all right?"

"Wuzassleep. Been 'wake all night—two nights."

"I'm really sorry," Robin repeated, "but it's nine forty and William Baker's here and getting—"

"Shit," mumbled Strike. "Can't've set the alarm right—gimme five min—"

"That's not all," said Robin. "There's a woman here. She hasn't got an appointment. I've told her you haven't got room for another client, but she's refusing to leave."

Strike yawned, rubbing his eyes.

"Five minutes. Make them tea or something."

Six minutes later, in a clean shirt, smelling of toothpaste and deodorant but still unshaven, Strike entered the outer office where Robin was sitting at her computer.

"Well, better late than never," said William Baker with a rigid smile. "Lucky you've got such a good-looking secretary, or I might have got bored and left."

Strike saw Robin flush angrily as she turned away, ostensibly organizing the post. There had been something inherently offensive in the way that Baker had said "secretary." Immaculate in his pinstriped suit, the company director was employing Strike to investigate two of his fellow board members.

"Morning, William," said Strike.

"No apology?" murmured Baker, his eyes on the ceiling.

"Hello, who are you?" Strike asked, ignoring him and addressing instead the slight, middle-aged woman in an old brown overcoat who was perched on the sofa.

"Leonora Quine," she replied, in what sounded, to Strike's practiced ear, like a West Country accent.

"I've got a very busy morning ahead, Strike," said Baker.

He walked without invitation into the inner office. When Strike did not follow, he lost a little of his suavity.

"I doubt you got away with shoddy time-keeping in the army, Mr. Strike. Come along, please."

Strike did not seem to hear him.

"What exactly is it you were wanting me to do for you, Mrs. Quine?" he asked the shabby woman on the sofa.

"Well, it's my husband—"

"Mr. Strike, I've got an appointment in just over an hour," said William Baker, more loudly.

"—your secretary said you didn't have no appointments but I said I'd wait."

"Strike!" barked William Baker, calling his dog to heel.

"Robin," snarled the exhausted Strike, losing his temper at last. "Make up Mr. Baker's bill and give him the file; it's up to date."

"What?" said William Baker, thrown. He reemerged into the outer office.

"He's sacking you," said Leonora Quine with satisfaction.

"You haven't finished the job," Baker told Strike. "You said there was more—"

"Someone else can finish the job for you. Someone who doesn't mind tossers as clients."

The atmosphere in the office seemed to become petrified. Wooden-faced, Robin retrieved Baker's file from the outer cabinet and handed it to Strike.

"How *dare*—"

"There's a lot of good stuff in that file that'll stand up in court," said Strike, handing it to the director. "Well worth the money."

"You haven't finished—"

"He's finished with *you*," interjected Leonora Quine.

"Will you shut up, you stupid wom—" William Baker began, then took a sudden step backwards as Strike took a half-step forwards. Nobody said anything. The ex-serviceman seemed suddenly to be filling twice as much space as he had just seconds before.

"Take a seat in my office, Mrs. Quine," said Strike quietly.

She did as she was told.

"You think she'll be able to afford you?" sneered a retreating William Baker, his hand now on the door handle.

"My fees are negotiable," said Strike, "if I like the client."

He followed Leonora Quine into his office and closed the door behind him with a snap.

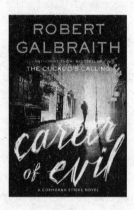